The Waterway Girls

Milly Adams

arrow books

1 3 5 7 9 10 8 6 4 2

Arrow Books
20 Vauxhall Bridge Road
London SW1V 2SA

Arrow Books is part of the Penguin Random House
group of companies whose addresses can be found at
global.penguinrandomhouse.com.

Copyright © Milly Adams 2017

First published in Great Britain by Arrow Books in 2017

www.penguin.co.uk

A CIP catalogue record for this book
is available from the British Library.

ISBN 9781784756918

Typeset in 11.5/14.5 pt Palatino by
Jouve (UK), Milton Keynes
Printed and bound in Great Britain by Clays Ltd, St Ives Plc

The Waterway Girls

Milly Adams lives in Buckinghamshire with her husband, dog and cat. Her children live nearby. Her grandchildren are fun, and lead her astray. She insists that it is that way round.

Milly Adams is also the author of *Above Us The Sky*, *Sisters at War* and *At Long Last Love*. This is Milly's first novel featuring her waterway girls.

Why YOU love Milly Adams

'A really superb book which I just could not put down . . . the characters are so real, the dialogue so natural, and the details so interesting. More books please Milly!'

'I have just finished reading this wonderful book . . . I felt like I was living through everything with all the characters. A great read.'

'Such an engrossing, moving novel with much amusing dialogue. I learned a lot.'

'Milly Adams is an exciting new author, with a wonderful knack of bringing characters to life vividly and bringing the story off the page and into the imagination. *Above Us The Sky* is a brilliantly researched, and hugely enjoyable novel.'

'A really superb book. Great characters. I loved, and lived it.'

'Read *At Long Last Love* non-stop today; I couldn't put it down . . . A fabulous, satisfying read, full of heart, passion and wisdom.'

'Milly Adams sweeps you straight into the story and keeps you turning the pages . . . I was totally captivated.'

To lovely Wynne and Ilva.

And let's not forget that 2017 is the 75th anniversary of the launch of the Ministry of War Transport's Women's Training Scheme, in which robust women were to be trained to work cargo-carrying narrowboats on the inland waterways – I raise a glass to them all.

Map of the London to Birmingham Grand Union Canal

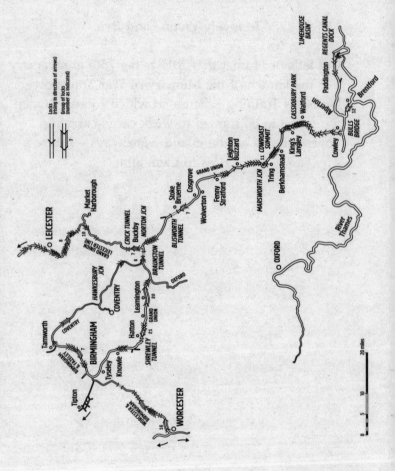

Locks
(rise in direction of arrows)

Group of locks
(number as indicated)

LEICESTER
Market Harborough
CRICK TUNNEL
Buckby
NORTON JCN
GRAND UNION LEICESTER LINE
Stoke Bruerne
Cosgrove
BLISWORTH TUNNEL
Wolverton
Fenny Stratford
BRAUNSTON TUNNEL
Leighton Buzzard
GRAND UNION
COWROAST SUMMIT
HAWKESBURY JCN
MARSWORTH JCN
Tring
Berkhamsted
King's Langley
OXFORD
CASSIOBURY PARK
Watford
Cowley
BULLS BRIDGE
Alperton
Paddington
REGENTS CANAL DOCK
'LIMEHOUSE BASIN'
Brentford
River Thames

Tamworth
COVENTRY
COVENTRY
OXFORD
Leamington
GRAND UNION
SHREWLEY TUNNEL
Hatton
BIRMINGHAM
Tyseley
Knowle
BIRMINGHAM & WARLEY
Tipton
WORCESTER & BIRMINGHAM
WORCESTER

20 miles
0   5   10   20

Broaden your waterways vocabulary . . .

Basin – a partly enclosed area of water at the end of or alongside a canal, housing wharves and moorings

Bilges – the bottom of the boat

Butty – engineless boat towed by the motorboat

Canal frontage – land abutting the canal

Counter – deck

Cut – canal

Fender – a bumper put over the side of a vessel to protect it from colliding with other vessels, objects or structures

Gunwale – inner ledge around boat

Hold – where the cargo is carried; both motors and butties have holds

Lock – the main means of raising or lowering a boat between changes in water levels on a canal

Long pound – a long length of impounded water between two locks

Moor – to secure a boat against the bank

Motorboat – the narrowboat with an engine

Port – left

Prow or fore-end – front

Short pound – a short length of impounded water between two locks

Slide hatch – sliding 'lid' above cabin doors to keep out the rain

Snubber – long strong rope for towing a butty along a long pound

Starboard – right

Stern – rear

Straps – mooring and lashing ropes

Tiller – the handle attached to the rudder; steers the boat

Wharf – structure built for cargo loading or discharge

Windlass – L-shaped handle for operating lock paddles

Bull's Bridge, Southall, is the location of Grand Union Canal Carrying Company's (GUCCC) depot

Limehouse Basin, also known as Regent's Canal Dock

Grand Union Canal **Paddington Arm** runs into Regent's Canal leading to Limehouse/Regent's Canal Dock

Tyseley Wharf, Birmingham

Chapter 1

Monday 25 October 1943 – London

Polly Holmes stood on the train shivering. She was on the way to Southall, west London where she could, at last, do something useful. Even better was the fact that it would be on the canal, which was not the same as sailing, but at least it was something. She had run from her Ministry of War Transport interview in Mayfair, to her medical, to the bus and then the station and each time the heavens had opened. Finally her ancient mackintosh could cope no more and she was soaked through to her knickers. Of course, if she had remembered her umbrella she would have been able to sit down on the train, but it seemed unfair to drip where others might sit.

Her mind played with this rhyme rather than think of her destination, one that the Ministry official, Mr Thompson, had arranged as the final part of the interview. It was this meeting that would decide whether she was to be accepted on the Boatwomen Training Scheme for cargo-carrying canal boats. She thought Will would approve. No, not Will.

She swayed as the train pulled into a station. Rain still dripped from her hem on to her legs. She glanced down at the pool of water in which she was standing. Worse, her felt hat had blown away so her hair hung like rats' tails, having escaped the hairgrips which pinned it up.

Some passengers disembarked, and others came on board. A businessman gestured her before him to the remaining seat, his black umbrella hooked over his arm. 'I'm fine standing,' she said with a smile that didn't reach her eyes.

He nodded, sat, and dragged out a newspaper from his briefcase. She wasn't fine and wasn't sure she ever really would be again. Her twin brother, Will, had been killed six months before in Montgomery's North Africa campaign, aged nineteen. She was surprised to have been able to put that thought together, the first time she had done so since she had heard the news. Perhaps it was because today could be the start of something else, a going forward.

It was a 'going forward' that she had mentioned to her parents two weeks ago, as she showed them the advertisement the Ministry of War Transport had placed in the newspaper, one which explained that they were to operate a war work scheme with the co-operation of the Grand Union Canal Carrying Company. It appeared that young women would be trained to replace narrowboat men who had already signed up, and, what's more, as Mr Thompson had said today, 'There will be no other men allowed to leave the canal. We need every means of transport we can get. We're running a war, not a village fete.'

Fear had been her parents' reaction. 'I will be safe,' she had said. 'Safe. So trust me, one of your children will live.'

They had agreed to her applying, and to her giving provisional notice from her secretarial job at the solicitors' office in her home town of Woking, Surrey. Her dad had said, 'It will be good for you to move on. I know you loved sailing with Will. It won't be the same, but you will be on the water. You always said it made you feel in a different world.'

Mr Thompson at the Ministry had barely given her time to sit down on the hardback chair on the other side of his desk before he had talked, and talked, steepling his fingers against his lower lip, explaining the world she would enter, emphasising the relentless travelling in narrowboats along the canal, or cut, as the boaters called it. 'Narrowboats, you hear,' he said. 'Barges are bigger, and can't squeeze along all the canals.'

He continued, telling her of the long hours in appalling weather conditions, the loading of freight at Limehouse Basin, which some chose to call Regent's Canal Docks, in east London. He explained the staircase of locks that would need to be traversed along the route to Birmingham as their narrowboat, the one with the Bolinder motor, towed their engine-less narrowboat butty. 'They're both the same size and will be heavily loaded. On arrival there will be the unloading of freight which could be wood, steel, whatever, and the loading of coal at Coventry on your return trip.'

The rain had beaten on his window. A spider plant with babies hanging off perched on top of a grey metal filing cabinet. His brown leather briefcase was propped up behind that, with his initials stamped into the leather: P.O.T. Polly had wondered what the P and O stood for, and if his nickname was Pot.

He'd continued, staring over her head, his fingers now beating against his lower lip. 'Of course, the actual unloading will be done by others, but you will be expected to prepare the boats, and generally do as is bid.' Finally he lowered his hands, then picked up a pencil which had a rubber on the end. He had looked at her, and made a note as she nodded.

Do as she was bid? she thought as the train rumbled on. It's almost what Will had said when they went to sea for the first time in their little sailing boat, *Sunspot*, when they were sixteen. 'Do as you are bid, girl, just for once, or you'll have us over.' She'd had some pluck then. It had gone missing, along with him.

The train was fetid and warm from so many bodies, but her shivering increased and it was nerves. Was Mr Thompson going to take her on the scheme? What he had said was, 'If you still want to help the war effort in this way, it's as well you go

4

and meet a trainer today and see what it really entails, as there is no time to waste. You must decide if you think it will suit and, importantly, we need to know whether Miss Burrows feels you have what it takes.'

He had straightened the sheet of inked blotting paper on his desk, and muttered, 'We can't have time-wasters. We have a war to win. Idle Women might be the nickname given to the canal girls because of the Inland Waterways badge they are awarded after training, but trust me, they are anything but.'

He had stood, the interview at an end. She had asked if she was in the running. 'All in good time,' he had said and sent her for the medical. The doctor had said the same after she had coughed, breathed in then out, and her feet had been checked for arches.

The train was slowing, sliding into the station. Polly peered through the window: Southall at last. The bus and train journey had taken over an hour with its wartime stops and starts. She disembarked and found the exit, shivering even more as the chill of October collided with her nervousness.

Outside the station the clouds were looming, though the rain had stopped. She heard the distant rumble of thunder as she gripped her handbag and tried to get her bearings. Behind her the sandbags at the entrance to the station stank of dogs' pee, but so did all the sandbags in poor bombed London.

Polly checked her watch: 1.15. She should be

meeting Miss Burrows at 1.30 at the Grand Union Canal Carrying Company depot situated a little over half a mile away on the canal at Bull's Bridge. She was going to be late. She looked both ways – was it left or right? What had Thompson said? But her mind was blank as the panic rose.

A man approached, on his way into the station. She called, 'Please, I need to head for the Grand Union—'

He interrupted. 'Go left, head south and straight across the crossroads. Just keep going.' He hurried on.

'Thanks so much.' She started running along the pavement. As she reached the Green she grew more confident, at last remembering Mr Thompson's instructions. Still racing along, she skirted the puddles and running gutters, looking for the 1930s cinema Mr Thompson had mentioned, and which seemed unscathed; she didn't stop to see what was playing but ran on, panting. Her sodden raincoat slapped the back of her legs, wiping away the remnants of her gravy-browning seams. Somewhere a bird sang. For a moment she stopped, lifted her head. Yes, birds still sang even though the world was turning upside down.

Polly passed women queuing at a butcher's shop, but the chalked blackboard, declaring what produce was on offer, had been washed by the rain. Was it a tiny rationed bit of bacon or perhaps ... well, who knew?

She was panting as she ran on past more shops, then a church with its typed service details pinned on the noticeboard. The details had been rendered indecipherable by the rain, as indecipherable as the blackboard, or the doctor's face as he conducted her medical.

The rain began again and it drove into her face as she ran past the war memorial, but no ... She looked away without altering her stride. A woman was hurrying past on the other side of the road, her head down, umbrella up. Sensible soul, Polly thought. How her mum would approve. Now she slowed and almost stopped, longing to be home on familiar ground, not here on this pavement with the red letterbox, the lamp posts, one bent as though it had been hit by a car. At a pub with sandbags at the door a woman wearing a headscarf was cleaning the inside of the windows and smiled at her.

Polly took heart, and pounded on hard and fast, forcing herself on until she reached a crossroads. On the other side she ran through a residential area with its schools; a Methodist chapel too, or so she thought, but didn't have time to double-check. It was 1.32. Already she was late, so she roared on but now she had a stitch, and as she trotted past allotments she was forced to slow, and then stop. She bent over and drew in ragged breaths, then out. In then out. To her left was a hawthorn hedge which lined the allotments, and behind it stood a greenhouse missing most of its glass.

She checked her watch: 1.35. She stretched and started trotting again, this time passing a scarecrow in the middle of rows of cabbages, its straw stuffing being sucked from a ripped sleeve by the wind.

She slipped on some mud, recovered, searching for evidence of the canal and the depot through the driving rain, and yes there were buildings ahead which must be the Grand Union Canal Carrying Company depot. She slowed to a walk, catching her breath, recalling her mum's parting words. 'Remember your manners before your elders and betters.' These had been followed by her dad's. 'Whatever else you do, don't be late.'

Polly sighed, pulled her muffler straight, tucked her handbag over her arm then walked on, with some sort of decorum she hoped, and reached the gate to the depot. She asked the guard huddling in his hut, 'Would you direct me to Enquiries, please?'

'Who may you be, Miss?'

'Oh, Miss Polly Holmes to see Miss Burrows.'

'Got any paperwork?'

She dug in her handbag for the letter from the Ministry and handed it to him in his hut, since he clearly had no intention of exposing himself to the elements, even though the rain was easing. He read it, and then checked on a clipboard, running his finger down a list. He reached the bottom, and shook his head. Polly wanted to snatch it from him and check for herself, but instead she asked him to give it another go.

He did, and this time his finger stopped midway. 'There you are, hiding between Graham and Ingles, you little rascal. Go straight ahead, and on the right there's a big Enquiries sign on that block of offices. They'll be glad to see you, they like drowned rats.'

Polly smiled politely. He winked. She hurried into the yard, almost reeling from its noise and bustle, weaving between men in overalls who must have been heading towards or from the workshops, large and small, which stood around a huge yard. She smelt stew, and to the left she saw a long building from which came the clattering of dishes. Ah, a canteen. Some men came out, and shut the door behind them. The tannoy leapt to life, blasting the yard with tinny music.

Ahead there were no buildings, just a hard-standing frontage to the canal which she glimpsed through the scurrying men. To the left she could see a dry dock where repairs to the narrowboats would be carried out. The canal, though, was much wider than she had expected and for a moment it looked so like the lake frontage of the sailing club, where they had accessed the water or pulled up the boats, that she relaxed. 'Yes,' she murmured aloud. 'Yes, I sort of know this world.' A worker in overalls brushed past her. 'You lost, love?'

She looked at him. 'No, but thank you. I know exactly where I am.'

She headed towards the door below the Enquiries

sign, weaving her way through the boiler-suited men who were almost running as the rain intensified, though it hadn't made them put their cigarettes out. She felt they would have barged over her if she hadn't leapt out of their way, so invisible did she seem to them.

She pulled open the door but the wind snatched it from her, slamming it back against the outside brick wall. She reached over and dragged it shut behind her. All went quiet. A young man was standing behind a counter to the rear of the office, an 'Enquiries' sign on his left.

'Name?' He didn't even look up.

'Miss Polly Holmes,' she said, but her nervousness had returned and it came out louder than she had meant it to. On the wall the clock said 1.40. 'I'm late,' she added. 'I should have been here at 1.30. It's at least a mile walk, surely, though I was told half a mile.'

Behind her, the door opened. The draught slapped her raincoat against her legs, and her hair lifted, dripped, and fell to her shoulders. She turned to see a woman of about thirty in overalls several sizes too big, with hair that was as wet as Polly's but still shone a deep red, and had somehow stayed pinned up. Her face was drawn and tired, but a certain energy seemed to shine from her eyes. She also wore a grubby blue seaman's sweater.

'Honestly, Alf, you need to fix a chain on this door or you'll have it snatched off its hinges. Bloody sodding thing.' She spoke quickly, just as she moved. She reached the counter and tapped out a tattoo.

Alf shrugged. 'Miss Polly Holmes for you, Bet. Another lamb to the slaughter, or is that a duck? She looks wet enough to have webbed feet, but give her 'ell anyway. She's late. Lost her tit for tat, too, it seems.'

Bet laughed, a great booming sound, as Polly remembered her lost hat and winced. What on earth must she look like? Miss Burrows was beckoning to her. 'Polly my dear, let me rescue you from Alf, who any minute now will be snatched up by the powers that be and given a gun, heaven help us all. Makes you feel the war will be won in a click of the fingers, doesn't it? Or not. I am Bet, Elisabeth Burrows, and I'll be your trainer. That is if you prove satisfactory to me, the team and the life, and what's more, we to *you*. But that'll be known all in good time, I suppose.'

Polly echoed before she could stop herself. 'All in good time.'

Bet laughed. 'Ah, yes of course, you've spent time at the Ministry and with Potty Thompson. Come along, let's take you to the canal and my narrowboats and leave Alf to his hive of industry.' She battled with the door again, and gestured Polly out before her into the yard where men still bustled and music still played over the tannoy. Somewhere a man shouted, 'Shift your arses, for pity's sake, you gormless lumps of lard.'

Together they hurried towards the canal frontage, and as they passed an idling lorry it backfired. Polly jumped. The driver jerked forward, driving into and out of a water-filled pothole just beside them. Bet and Polly leapt back as the wave of muddy water threatened to drench their legs. Bet yelled, 'Watch what you're doing, Henry.' He hooted, and yelled through the open window, 'Can't stop, won't get the old tart started again. Got to pick up some gear.'

A couple of blokes in overalls crossed their path and saluted Bet. One said, 'Your *Marigold*'s out of dry dock, I 'eard, Bet, so you'll be off to Limehouse to pick up a load. That your replacement boater?'

'Maybe,' she said. Polly hung on that word. Maybe. A woman left an office huddled under an umbrella which was promptly blown inside out. Polly heard 'Bugger and blast'. The woman waved at Bet, tucked the wrecked umbrella under her arm, but didn't stop as she ran to the canteen.

Bet gripped Polly's arm and hurried her towards the canal. 'This is the canal frontage, Polly.'

'We had a similar one at our sailing club, but smaller.'

'Ah, so do you understand about the dry dock too, where repair work is done?'

Polly nodded. Together they stood for a moment gazing at the canal, then Polly studied the three narrowboats moored further along to her left, some twenty yards away. To the right of where she and Miss Burrows stood were many more narrowboats, packed closely together like sardines in a tin, smoke curling from their cabin chimneys, their painted sides bright beneath the grey of the sky. They were moored stern first against the kerb, stretching their great length out across half the cut. Top planks rested on stands along the length of the empty holds. People moved around on the craft, some men ran along the planks, and women in long skirts and any old jackets or cardigans were heading along the concrete strip towards the two of them, carrying string bags. On their way to the shops, presumably. No umbrellas for them either.

Miss Burrows said, 'That's the lay-by where we all moor up at the kerb and await orders.'

Polly tried to brush her hair out of her face, but the wind and rain only swept it back again. The water ran down her face and neck.

Miss Burrows said, 'We're landsmen, or bankers, to these boaters, until we prove ourselves. It takes time but can be done, if we're committed to the job.' There was a warning in her voice.

Polly looked again at the narrowboats nudging and tugging at their moorings, and at the width of the cut. It was time for another question because her dad had said she should ask things in an interview. Across on the other bank were trees and sheds, and beyond, through the gaps, a grey sky. No questions there.

'So, this is Bull's Bridge, on the Grand Union Canal,' Polly murmured at last, but that wasn't a question. The water lapped and slapped at the frontage in front of them. It was then Polly realised that the rain had almost ceased. The wind, though, was whipping up the surface of the canal into a hissing fury. Come on, ask something.

Polly said, 'Let me get this straight. The boats come in from the Birmingham direction, moor up here and then set off again for Limehouse Basin once they have orders. They need the space to manoeuvre, so that's why it's so wide? Then they come back to Bull's Bridge and turn right to head up the northern Grand Union Canal past Cowley.'

'Yes, exactly right, Polly,' Bet murmured. 'The canals are transport arteries, which are doing their bit to deliver vital supplies, with the help of people like us. If we're heading to Limehouse we use the Grand Union Canal up to Paddington, where it becomes the Regent's Canal. The Regent's Canal then runs to Limehouse Basin, or some call it the Regent's Canal Dock, but either way, it's where the canal meets the Thames. Don't worry about those details. You'll know the route after just one trip, it's only a long strip of water, after all, and it's hard to go wrong.'

Polly smiled, her brain trying to keep up. 'Much easier than trying to find my way to Southall from Mayfair, anyway.'

Bet laughed that great booming laugh, and smiled. 'Let's go and see my babies, shall we? Look to your left, past those three narrowboats waiting for repairs, and in front of the largest fitting shed you'll see *Marigold* moored. Her engine is now running perfectly, and beside her there's the motorless butty *Horizon*. Can you see them?' Her voice was urgent and as proud and fond as any mother's, Polly thought as she stepped back and sighted the two boats double parked, lying parallel to one another, and lashed together.

'The blokes working in the sheds are worth their weight in gold; they keep us running.'

Bet set off, then stopped, turned, and looked hard at Polly. 'You *have* been told they're not barges, haven't you?'

Polly nodded. 'Yes, Miss Burrows.'

'Good. Well, just remember that you never call a narrowboat a barge to a boater, and never call a boater a bargee either. It sets them off something chronic. Barges are much bigger, and operate in wider waterways. And you must call me Bet. Miss Burrows makes me feel old but, at thirty, I probably am to you.'

Polly hurried after Bet who had set off again towards the fitting sheds, the wind still powering off the water. Polly called, 'And the cut is the canal, isn't it? Or so Mr Thompson said.' Bet shouted over her shoulder, 'Quite right again, Polly. I suppose it's called that because it was cut through the country-side, but who knows.'

Polly smiled to herself. Perhaps she was doing well?

They reached Bet's boats. 'This is *Marigold*, the motorboat moored alongside the frontage, and *Horizon*, the butty, lashed the other side of her, both at your service.'

Bet leapt on to *Marigold*'s small rear deck which the cabin opened on to. 'Chop-chop, don't hang about, leg it over to *Horizon*'s cabin. The range is beating out heat in the cabin so it'll be snug on board.'

Polly stared at the narrowboats, which must have been seventy feet long. The motorboat deck on which Bet still stood was small. The cabin too – though it had what she thought must be the engine house attached to the back of it, and then another small cabin, or lean-to, attached to that. The rest of the boat was merely a massive hold for carrying the cargo, along which there were top planks similar to those she had seen on the 'sardines' at the lay-by. Around the sides of the hold and cabin was a narrow gunwale. She knew exactly what a gunwale was, from her sailing days: no more nor less than a strip of decking about four inches wide along which you could inch, or walk, depending on your courage.

Would she be expected to inch her way along that to do something to the engine, or to get to the hold? And then it would be along the top planks?˙ She swallowed.

Bet was already stepping from the motorboat on to *Horizon*, the butty. Polly scrambled after her, handbag over her arm, her smart straight skirt an encumbrance but she made it. Here too there was an empty hold behind the cabin. The rain had begun again, and was beating hard, the wind too, but she was beyond worrying.

Bet Burrows waited at *Horizon*'s door, grinning. 'Well done, you made it without a fuss, and I like the fact that you've not been unduly bothered about the wet.'

She slid back what looked like a small horizontal lid above the cabin's double doors. These doors Bet now opened; they led to a couple of steps down into the cabin. 'Duck as you go down, there's not much headroom,' she said. 'The slide hatch I've just shoved back helps access.' She grinned. 'Come into my parlour said the spider to the fly.'

'I'll drip all over the furniture and floor,' Polly protested as *Horizon* rocked slightly in the wake of a butty and motor heading east towards Limehouse. An elderly man in a hat and shabby jacket stood at the tiller of the pat-pattering motorboat; a woman, with a heavy cardigan pulled tight, at the tiller of the butty.

Bet followed Polly's gaze, and explained, 'They're riding high like us because they've discharged their load somewhere. They'll be heading into the lay-by to reverse to the kerb and moor up to await more orders. Come on, you're getting wet and so is the cabin while you gawp, so shake a leg.' Bet coughed, and somehow it caught, and continued, racking her body for at least a minute.

Polly wondered if she should pat Bet's back, but just as she lifted her hand Bet straightened, and smiled, coughed a few more times, then stopped. 'So sorry. My chest's been a total pain since pneumonia a couple of years ago. Come on, hop to it.'

Polly stepped down two steps into the warmth, but at five foot four she was able to stand upright with a couple of inches to spare in a cabin, the tiny size of which completely took her by surprise, though it shouldn't have. She'd seen it from the outside, after all, but . . . Yes, on their sailing boat there had been an apology for a cabin but it was a small day sailing craft, whereas this was for cooking and all sorts.

To her left against the cabin wall was a small range, the flue pipe of which ran up and out through the roof. The space between the range and the door was taken up by shelves with things like washing powder. On the other side of the range was a cupboard, its front painted with large colourful blooms and a castle, on a black background. Cupboards and shelves filled every available space, and where there weren't shelves there were horse brasses and pierced plates hanging on the walls.

On the right was a narrow side bench, with a porthole above, against which the rain drove. Ahead of her, a young woman of about her own age sat on a bench at the rear of the cabin, leafing through a newspaper. Surely the cabin length was only about nine feet? The width no more than about six, perhaps seven feet? The young woman looked up; her hair was blonde and pinned into loops, with a tortoise-shell slide on the right-hand side. Crikey, thought Polly, that must have cost a bob or two. The young woman wore lipstick and was impossibly elegant, even in overalls.

'Oh God, you're dripping,' the young woman said. 'There's a cloth on that hook to wipe up the floor.' She nodded towards the side of the tiny range.

Bet said quietly, 'Verity Clement, this poor girl, Polly Holmes, is soaked through, and it is not her task but ours to— Ah, I see you realise that.' Verity was reaching for the cloth. 'Good girl.' Bet sounded relieved.

Bet waved Polly towards the side bench immedi-ately to the right of the steps, saying, as Verity swished the cloth around with her foot, then wrung it out over the bowl at the side of the range, 'Sit yourself down, Polly, but before you do, let's have your mac. No mopping up puddles until you're taken on, or not.'

Polly dropped her handbag on the side bench and shrugged out of her mackintosh. Bet threw it to Verity, who had returned to reading *The Times*. The mackintosh collapsed her newspaper and Verity yelped. Bet said, 'Sorry about that, but do come on, Verity, all hands to the pump. You really should know the drill by now. Hang up the mackintosh, please. Tea is ready, I hope?'

'Indeed, boss. The teapot is on the range rest.'

Polly sat while Verity Clement hung her mackintosh on a hook to the right of the range, within arm's reach, but what wasn't? How could people manage in this tiny kitchen? What were the bedrooms like, and the bathroom? And where were they?

Bet reached up, closed the sliding hatch and the cabin doors: the room seemed even smaller, but suddenly quiet, though Polly could still hear the rain. The floor was wooden and a hurricane lamp hung on the wall, but there was also an electric light hanging from the ceiling, and this is what illuminated the cabin.

Verity resumed her seat, then pulled down the front of the hinged cupboard to form a small table in front of her, on which she rested her newspaper. She reached down a tin of biscuits from the cupboard, which was packed with groceries, and placed it on the table. She resumed reading, then said, without looking up from her paper, 'Polly Holmes, you can see that the cupboard flap is our table, which, trust me, we can all reach from wherever we are. The light is powered by the battery. We have two batteries, and charge one off the engine while the other is doing its stuff. The hurricane lamp is used frequently to save the battery.' She turned the page of *The Times*.

Polly didn't know if she should answer, but nodded, then said, 'I see, thank you.'

Bet stood by the pristine blackleaded range. Her seaman's sweater was steaming and would bounce the rain back, keeping the wearer almost dry. Will had one. Polly shut out the thought.

The brass towel bar gleamed, the grate was heaped with burning coal. An enamel kettle hissed on the top of the range and a pot of tea waited on the side. A crocheted curtain was hooked to the left of Verity's bench. Polly was thinking hard, because the cabin reminded her of something, and then it came. It was like the playhouse a neighbour had constructed for his children, with a pretend stove, and cups.

Bet poured tea into three enamel mugs and handed them out. Polly clutched hers, warming her hands. Her hair and clothes were steaming as they had done on the train, only more so, but the bench was wooden so that was all right. A pool was forming at her feet again, and at the feet of Bet, who sat down beside her. Verity continued reading.

Polly sipped her tea. She was desperate for the loo, and reached forward, putting her mug on the side of the range. 'May I use your toilet?' she said.

Verity snorted into her mug. 'Should have thought of that at the yard. Oh dear, she has much to learn and our naughty boss didn't tell her.'

Bet ignored Verity and said, 'I'm sorry, I should have mentioned the plumbing, Polly. Verity is right, there is no toilet, instead there's a bucket that's kept in the lean-to at the back-end of each cabin. We usually call it just the back-end. We empty the bucket where we can, either borrowing a pub's lavatory, or the cut. You might have noticed the water can and

21

dipper on the roof of both boats. We use the dipper to gather water to wash our clothes or whatever. There are taps along the way for drinking water, which we collect in the water can. If you ever fall into the cut, keep your mouth shut.'

'I see,' said Polly faintly, crossing her legs, trying not to listen to the sound of the rain on the roof. It would be best not to mention any of this to her mother.

Verity looked up, grinning, then ducked back down to her newspaper. Polly sipped her tea. 'And the bedrooms?' she asked.

Verity shook her newspaper, threw back her head and laughed, but it was Bet who spoke. 'Right, let me explain, starting with basics. This is my butty cabin, Polly. It's bigger than the motor's cabin because there is no gunwale; that takes about eight inches off the motorboat cabin width. A gunwale is—'

Polly interrupted, 'Yes, I know from my sailing days.'

'Ah, of course, you said. Well, since the trainees bunk up in the smaller motor cabin it must seem unfair. However, as trainer I have to live on the boats for the duration of the war, except for occasional leave, so I choose the butty cabin as my permanent home. On the other hand, you, as trainees, will move on to boats of your own as and when you receive your Inland Waterways badges. When you get your own pair of narrowboats, you can have your chance at the butty cabin then, but remember, there will be three of you, so willingness to share will be the order of the day.'

Polly stared around the cabin, not really understanding. How on earth could this serve anything like even a quarter of anyone's requirements, whether it was a paltry eight inches bigger or not – and where were the beds?

Bet continued, as if reading her mind. 'The older children would normally sleep in the butty cabin, utilising the side-bed on which you are sitting. Then there is the unfolding double cross-bed where Verity is planted, which I always keep down because I'm not going to mess about at the end of the day making it up. See the door behind it?'

Polly nodded.

'It leads to the back-end or lean-to, where the bucket and brooms, things like that are kept. I nip over the roof of the cabin and hoik 'em out through the outside door. I also take my bucket comfort breaks in there. The babies and toddlers would sleep with the parents in the motorboat cabin, the parents using the cross-bed, the children the side-bed and perhaps the floor too. Soon you'll see that the life of a boater is so busy that the cabin is barely used, except for sleeping, or perhaps a bit of sitting when eating. Beneath the beds are cupboards which hold the bedding. You must bring your own if you join us. Have you got all that?'

Polly nodded, not a bit sure she had. Bet was off

again. 'Sometimes we strap up the boats abreast just as we are now, and travel in parallel on a wide stretch, or instead we tow the butty on a narrower stretch. But there's time to learn all of that on the job.' Bet leaned towards her. 'I believe Mr Thompson at the Ministry gave you a vague brief in the interview?'

Polly nodded. 'Yes, he did.'

She felt she was drowning in information and as one piece entered her head, another piece dropped out.

'So, the jam on all of this is that you girls are entitled to two days' leave after a couple of trips. Once you're trained it'll be a week's unpaid leave after three weeks' work.'

Polly asked, 'How long does a return trip take?'

Verity spoke. 'Five to six glorious days, each way, darling. Longer if there's a hold-up. We rise at five-thirty or thereabouts. Ghastly bum ache, quite frankly.'

Polly couldn't help hearing her mother saying, 'Language, if you please.'

Bet was saying, 'Now, Polly, let's talk about training. I take trainees on two trips, and you learn on the job. If all goes well you will be transferred to a different boat and butty, as I've just said. Verity has done one trip and still has much to learn, but then so does every trainee. Remember, there's no shame in admitting it's not your cup of tea. Best we know sooner rather than later.'

Bet sounded thoughtful, and Verity flushed as she banged her cup of tea down on the table and shook out the newspaper before burying her head in it again.

Polly spoke into the silence. 'So, it's obviously not just gliding along through lovely scenery?'

'Absolutely not,' Verity piped up. She turned another page. 'I most certainly wouldn't say that.'

Polly sat while Bet told her of the filth of the coal cargo they picked up from Coventry coalfields, the pain of blistered hands as they sheeted up tarpaulins, or in other words covered the loads, before securing the tarpaulins with ropes. 'But I'm not going into the detail of ropes and knots until decisions are made.'

Mercilessly, and barely taking a breath as though she didn't want to waste her time, or Polly's, she talked of the bitter cold. 'You will steer, hour after hour, the wind chafing your face and lips. In the summer the sun's glare will bounce off the cabin roof and hurt your eyes. The days are lonely, just three of you: one on each boat steering, one cycling along the towpath to prepare the locks for the boats' arrival.'

She looked at Polly. 'You are here because we've just lost the second trainee, Phyllis, owing to, shall we say, temperamental incompatibilities.'

'Pardon?'

Verity snapped. 'What Bet means is that Phyllis

and I didn't get on. She was a frightful bore, very wet and irritating.'

Bet pressed her lips together. 'It's too late now, but both girls needed to try harder, and learn to get on. It's essential in such a small space and I think Verity has come to understand that.'

Verity sighed, and turned the page, patting her hair and adjusting her slide. 'If you say so, Bet.'

'Yes I do.'

There was another silence. Polly thought of living in a small space with this girl who seemed impervious to criticism, who verged on rudeness, who . . . Well, just wasn't very nice.

Bet talked a little more about their duties, until finally she paused, as though wondering if she had made it sound as appalling as was necessary. Well, she had, thought Polly, as she finished her tea and picked up her handbag, feeling that perhaps it was time for her to go.

Bet saw, and smiled. 'Before you run away, there are the pubs in the evening, when we tie up along the cut. The boater women disapprove but we go anyway. We justify it by declaring we need to keep our sanity. Now the pubs are a lot of fun, and the sun does shine sometimes. Remember this is the boaters' world into which we are intruding, a world with a definite culture, and we need to tread carefully. But more than anything we have to bear in mind that ours is essential work. Someone has to do it and it might as well be us.'

Verity had laid down her newspaper. Now she grinned. 'At last our esteemed Führer Bet Burrows comes to the light at the end of the tunnel – the pubs. Otherwise, the boss is telling it as it is. Just look at my ghastly hands.' She held up her calloused palms and fingers.

Polly said, 'Heavens, they're worse than my dad's.'

Verity stared at her. 'Not imbued with tact, then?' She buried her head in her newspaper.

Polly grimaced. 'I'm sorry. I didn't think.' She could have kicked herself.

Bet stood. 'And on that note, before I'm breaking up a butty brawl, I think that's everything. Come along, I think we've kept you long enough but have you any questions?'

Polly could think of nothing to say. She looked around the cabin. How on earth could Bet call this home? How on earth did she manage with a girl like Verity? How on earth would she cope with Polly, who had listened carefully but couldn't remember a thing? She shook her head. She didn't know what she thought about it all.

Bet said, 'Don't worry, the information will sink in slowly as you travel home. I'll have a think and let you know, all in good time. We both have decisions to make.' She smiled and Polly said, 'Thank you.'

Verity turned yet another page of her newspaper.

Bet handed Polly her mac, which had not only

stopped dripping but seemed partially dry, thanks to the suffocating heat. Polly placed her handbag on the side bench, put her mackintosh on over her damp clothes, pulling her muffler tight, and picked up her handbag again, thinking all the time of everything she had heard.

'Do you have far to go?' Bet asked.

'Woking. So, not far once I get through London.' She checked her watch. She had been here just over half an hour and her head was spinning. And it hadn't gone well, if Verity's face was anything to go by.

Bet pulled the slide hatch back and shoved the doors open, and almost sprang up the steps to the deck. Polly followed. The rain had stopped, but the wind still blew. Clouds scudded, and the noise from the depot was just as loud as before.

As the wind whipped Polly's hair across her face, Bet said, 'You would need to think a little more about what you say, Polly. I suspect few girls like to be told their hands are like a man's, especially Verity. She's rather prickly, as you can tell, and has had some sort of loss though who knows what – and who hasn't? But she's improving. One does try to be patient.' Suddenly, Bet looked exhausted.

Polly wondered what on earth Verity had been like before and why Bet kept her on?

Bet, leading her back on to the *Marigold*, said, more to herself, Polly thought, 'I do just feel Verity needs us more than we need her. It could all work out, but on the other hand . . .' She stopped, and looked at Polly as though she had forgotten she was there. 'Ah, Polly, you'll be hearing from Mr Thompson, or me. Have a good trip home. Now, head down the frontage, then back through the yard. The lavatory is on the left, just before Enquiries.' Bet held out her hand. Polly shook it, turned and stepped down on to the bank. `

As she was about to head back she thought of the only question that really mattered.

Bet was still standing on *Marigold*'s deck, leaning against the cabin, smoking. The water can, painted with flowers and castles, like the cupboard, nestled next to the chimney. Further along, smoke curled from the butty's chimney only to be snatched away by the wind.

Polly took a deep breath, and called from the towpath, 'Do people get killed on the canal? I'm sorry, I know that might sound like an overly dramatic question, but I need to be able to tell my mum it's safe.'

'My dear girl, there's a war on. No one's safe.' Bet smiled slightly. 'But we're safe enough, as few bombs are falling at the moment.'

Polly dug her hands into her pockets, feeling foolish, but defiant. She looked straight at Bet. There was silence as Bet studied her. At last she nodded, a nod that told Polly Bet knew something of why Polly was so keen to escape to the canals in the first place. It had been on her application form.

'Don't miss your train, young Polly Holmes. We'll be in touch.'

Polly said, 'All in good time.'

Bet's laugh followed her down the towpath.

Chapter 2

25 October – the return journey on the same day

Polly decided to try and clear her head before making for home, so strolled along Oxford Street. She walked the length of it, looking in the shop windows, skirting the sandbags in doorways, trying to sort out her feelings about the training, proud of the spirit of the Londoners who were out shopping, chatting, as their city lay in ruins in many places.

She had a cup of tea at a Lyons Corner House, watching the rain as it ran down the windows. Could she stand blistered hands, freezing weather, Verity? Could she bear being as wet as she was, day in and day out?

She watched the passers-by bearing who knew what losses and heartbreak, then straightened, and finished her tea. She was proud of them, so she should do something that made her proud of herself. She sagged again – what about the bucket? She stared out at the street. Well, she'd make sure she used a proper lavatory whenever she could. But what about living and sleeping in that small space, with Verity? What if she thought Polly was as wet and irritating as that poor Phyllis? She finished her second cup of tea, paid, and left a threepenny tip. The rain had stopped, and she saw her reflection in the window. Her hair was a disgrace. She headed along Oxford Street again, hunting for a cheap felt hat.

Eventually she gave up, and walked to Waterloo Station, arriving at about six o'clock. The train from Waterloo to Woking was crowded but she managed to secure a seat, though the corridor was crammed with soldiers, sailors and airmen, not to mention the odd businessman. Polly ran yet again through the day as the compartment fogged up around her.

She pictured Bet, her energy, that booming laugh, the cabin which was so tiny, Verity who was so snotty. What on earth had Bet thought when Polly asked if life on the canal was safe? After all, everyone had loss of some sort. How could she face her again?

But then, what if Bet turned her application down? She felt a huge wave of relief sweeping over her, and she leaned back, her feet aching. She had wanted to join the Air Transport Auxilliary but her parents had been distraught, so when she'd seen the War Transport advertisement it seemed like a good alternative. Was it? Could she commit to it as Bet wanted?

As the train drew in to Esher a pregnant woman clambered into their compartment. Polly stood, 'Come on. Sit down.'

The woman smiled, 'Thank you. Bit of a day.'

'They tend to be at the moment, don't they?'

Polly slid back the door into the corridor, and squeezed in between a soldier and a sailor. The train jerked as it set off again and the sailor steadied her with his elbow. There was a general murmur of voices, and she noticed that an airman next to the soldier to her left was sitting on the floor, snoring.

The soldier pulled out a packet of Woodbines. ''Ave a fag, love, as a reward for good behaviour.' He jerked his head towards the carriage. She smiled and shook her head. Her mum would have her guts for garters if she smelt cigarette smoke on her.

She said, 'My brother would have given me a boot if I hadn't got to my feet.'

'Ah, he's doing his bit, is he?'

She hesitated. 'Yes, you could say that.'

'Older than you, is he?'

'Younger, by two minutes.'

The soldier laughed. 'Ah, twins. You got that tight bond, then? My auntie's got two lots of 'em. Two, would you believe. She's called it a day now. The four of 'em run my auntie ragged, the little toe-rags. But split 'em up, and they're quiet. Sort of lost. Reckon you feel the same, with 'im away?'

'Reckon I do.'

They both stared out at the darkening countryside. 'When will the lights come back on?' Polly murmured, more to herself than anyone.

'Ah, that's the question, ain't it, but we're doing our best, love. We all are. One day, you'll see, they'll all just come back on and we'll forget they was ever off and start grumbling at silly little things again. You got a bloke out and at 'em?'

His cigarette glowed brightly as he took another drag.

The train lurched, stopped yet again. 'Troop train coming through, probably,' the sailor on her right said.

'Likely it is,' the soldier agreed.

'Well, sort of. I've got Reggie,' Polly said. 'He's on the bombers.'

'Tough one, that.'

'I know.' For a moment Polly felt even more weary.

The soldier squeezed out the end of his cigarette, and tucked it into his uniform pocket and no one spoke. As soon as they'd trundled into a station, they were out again within minutes. Along the corridor a GI began to sing 'If you were the only girl in the world'.

At Woking Polly left the train, waving to Tommy the soldier, and Arthur the sailor; the airman was still asleep. 'Break a leg,' she called, never good luck. That's what Will . . . Well, anyway, never say good luck.

She had her torch's meagre slit of light, but she could find her way blindfold to her home on the outskirts of town. She reached the cul de sac of 1930s houses. Theirs was detached, a fact of which her mum was inordinately proud. Her parents had bought it when Polly's dad had been made chief storeman at the factory. It made her mum feel they had at last scrambled into the middle classes, even though it was the bottom rung. She had hoped for better for her children, and when Will had been accepted for an engineering apprenticeship, and Polly had passed her secretarial course with flying colours, she felt that they both had excellent prospects. Polly must work at a solicitor's and might then marry one, and Will would be . . .

She stopped the thought and continued walking to the end of Pinewood Avenue past the semis. There were two lilac trees in the front garden of Jotom, which was a mixture of her parents' names, Joyce and Tom.

The front path was weedless now, thanks to her mum's current need for perfection. Although she had a key, she knocked at the front door, which was as her mum had come to insist on over the last six months; it gave her a chance to put down newspaper to catch any dirt, and to save the lino, but from what? Polly and her dad didn't know. Nor did her mum like them to trudge round to the back door and let themselves into the kitchen, walking mud on to her pristine kitchen quarry tiles.

What the hell would she think of the cabin? Language, Polly, she told herself.

Her mum opened the door of the dark hall, wearing her wrap-around apron and holding back the blackout curtain with her elbow. 'Hurry up, for heaven's sake, you're letting the cold in, and the heat out.'

Polly stepped in, wiped her shoes on the doormat, then stepped on to the newspaper as her mum shut the door, and the blackout, behind her. Polly switched on the light as her mum spun round. She had permed her grey hair during the day, and the smell wafted across as she reached into the hall umbrella stand, and brandished Polly's black umbrella. 'Just what do you call this?'

Polly was taking off her soaked court shoes. 'I know, I forgot, sorry, Mum.'

'Sorry isn't good enough. I shouldn't have to remind you at your age – and just leave the shoes on the newspaper.'

Polly did, stepping on to the lino in her bare feet. Her mother dropped the umbrella back into the stand with a clang, her voice shrill. 'Just look at those blisters on your heels. I told you to wear ankle socks.'

She picked up the shoes and shook them over the newspaper. Polly said, 'I'll carry them,' but her mum bustled to the kitchen calling over her shoulder, 'Take off that mackintosh too, and bring it through. It needs to hang on the airer if you're going to use it tomorrow. I hope you wore your vest or you'll get a chill on your chest and kidneys. I'm just putting the kettle back on. I don't know what time you call this, I really don't. It's not safe to walk alone in the blackout.'

Polly sighed at the never-ending stream of words. What had her mother planned for tomorrow? Had she forgotten that Polly was working on a daily basis at Mr Burton's solicitor's office while she waited for war work and she was expected at nine in the morning? Her dad came out of the back room, his unlit pipe in his mouth, wearing his Air Raid Precaution overalls. Shutting his *Daily Mail*, he bustled over and kissed her. He smelt faintly of pipe tobacco, though he only had enough on the ration for a brief smoke every other day.

'Your mother took a phone call from a Miss Burrows at four o'clock but you know how she doesn't like the telephone so she came to the depot and I rang this Miss Burrows, with Mr Wendle's permission, of course. You've been accepted for canal work, and must head back tomorrow, getting off at Hayes Station, near Southall. Be there at ten in the morning, she said, most specifically. She also said that your medical was quite acceptable, and that you will be expected to complete the training satisfactorily. That is, of course, if you decide that "the canal passes muster with you".'

He raised his eyebrows, and smiled at Polly. 'She will telephone the house at nine o'clock this evening. I rather liked her. She's brisk, no nonsense, says what needs to be said, and then nips off. No long dithering goodbye. She just put the receiver down. Click, it went.'

Suddenly all doubt left Polly. How could she have thought she didn't want to go? She said, 'Oh Dad, oh I thought . . . Well, I couldn't think of many questions, and I didn't feel she'd want me, and then I wasn't sure I wanted it. But I do, I know I do now. I really do.'

His smile reflected hers. 'Yes, I can see that. Well, young Polly, just as you've passed, I'm now passing you on my way to my night shift. Get the camping mattress down from the attic. You'll need that, apparently, for your bed, but you're to keep your clothes to a minimum as Miss Burrows was most stern on the matter of storage facilities. And you'll need some money, but you've saved some, haven't you? I will add to that, until you receive your pay at the end of each trip, a mere two pounds or so, but there's a war on. Take your ration book too. Toodle pip for now, love.'

He was edging towards the front door, stepping on the newspaper. Polly reached out and held him back. 'Can I do it, Dad?' she whispered. 'Really, do you think I can? It will be cold, hard, and Verity and I have to live and sleep in a tiny cabin, and she might think I'm irritating and wet.'

He hugged her so tightly she could hardly breathe and whispered in return, 'A Holmes can do anything, and you're not irritating, though no doubt you'll be wet.' He chuckled. 'You'll do it well. So what if you have to share a small space – that's what soldiers do, and this is war work, you'll make us proud, I know you will. But don't tell your mum too many details. She won't like hardship for you, or things like that, not at the moment.'

Her mum was rattling around in the kitchen and

called, 'Don't forget your sandwiches, Thomas, they're only Spam, but beggars can't be choosers, and have you got your flask? I put two biscuits in, one for Anthony Burton too, though how he can concentrate on his soliciting after a night without sleep I don't know. Don't be late in the morning, back by seven-thirty, though I know you'll pop into the allotment first. But no later than seven-thirty, do you hear? I don't want to be worrying, I really don't.'

Polly's father called wearily, 'Now, Mother, I won't be late, but there're no bombs and not likely to be, because the Blitz is over, and the Boche are too busy fighting Russia. It's boys like Reggie who are taking the raids to them now, so don't fret.'

Her mother said nothing, but the slam of the oven door was comment enough. Polly closed the door and curtain on the heels of her dad.

Her mother called, 'Polly, get those wet clothes off and bring them down for washing. You're to wear trousers, of all things, that Miss Burrows said, so I asked Aunt Olive at Number 16 and she's let me have three pairs of her daughter's, the one who's no better than she ought to be. I gave them a good boil, just in case of germs. I had to pay for them, but not a lot. And Miss Burrows said boots, but you have some wellington boots. You can pack two of your father's sweaters. It's a shame I threw away your sailing sweater but it was torn something shocking. But hurry, your pie will be on the table. There's a bit of bacon to give it some taste, but you like parsnips, don't you? Of course you do.'

Polly started up the stairs and called, 'I'll be down in a minute, and thank you, Mum, for having a meal ready. I really need it.'

Her mum didn't answer but just continued her babbling which Polly allowed to wash over her as she had done for these past six months. It felt as if the more her mother chattered, the less Polly spoke, and it had become something they both hid behind. Polly stopped on the stairs and leaned over the bannister, waiting for a pause. It came, and she cut in, 'I could perhaps use one or two of Will's sweaters?'

Her suggestion was met with a rare silence, so Polly continued upstairs, stripped off her clothes and changed into her dressing gown, before carrying her clothes on to the landing, hesitating outside Will's room for a second longer than she ought. She continued downstairs.

At the kitchen doorway she said, 'I've brought them down, Mum. I'll wash them out later, then put them through the mangle.'

'You'll do no such thing as to put that poor skirt through the mangle, for goodness' sake,' her mum called. 'It's wool. I'll do it. It'll be dry by morning and you can take one of my hats. You're not going to be on the boat all hours of the day or night, surely. Go into the dining room. Your supper's on the table. Then go up into the loft and get the mattress down. Miss

Burrows said army blankets were provided. No sheets, mind, or she didn't mention them.'

Polly sat at the table. The stew was steaming, just as everything seemed to have done today. Suddenly ravenous, she dipped her bread in the gravy.

Her mother called, 'I hope you're not dunking your bread? You'll be with smart people, or at least that Miss Burrows sounded high class, so don't let yourself down. Remember, it's lunch, not dinner. Remember your knife is not a pen . . .' Polly sighed. Her mother had read all the books, and brought her and Will up to 'know better'.

On the wall over the mantelpiece there were just blank squares on the pipe-smoke-stained wallpaper, and the mantelpiece itself was empty of photographs. She knew her dad had most of them in his shed on the allotment because her mother couldn't bear to face such a harsh truth yet.

Later, Polly searched through the loft and found the mattress, the one that was used for camping, though it was what Will also used when he went sailing here, there and everywhere with Uncle Sidney. She was only suitable for day trips, Will had said, pulling her pigtails, but one day . . . He had left the mattress behind when he joined up but her one day was here. Tomorrow she'd be on water, on the canal. She would be going forward and it might help her begin to heal.

Will had chosen to go into the Tank Corps, or

41

whatever its name was. His friend Simon Barston had called a month after they heard he was dead. He had told her and her dad that Will's tank had received a direct hit, and there was nothing left of any of them.

Her mum had snatched the cup of tea she had given to Simon, telling him that, in that case, no one could know that it was her son who was dead. She had fled to the kitchen, and her dad had followed. When Polly had led the poor lad to the front door and he'd put on his boots again, she said, 'I'm so sorry. Mum is . . . tormented. It will take time.'

The lad, Simon, had nodded. 'For you too. Twins are closer than any other sort of relationship, I think. You are sort of almost one person, or so people say. I'm sorry, Polly. He talked a lot about you.'

She had shaken his hand, but could not speak. She had pulled back the blackout curtain and opened the door. 'Break a leg,' she'd said and he had grinned. 'Will used to say that.' Then he was gone.

That evening her mum had talked and talked, until she had suddenly screamed, again and again, and rushed into the dining room where she had stared at all the photos, running her finger around the face of her son. Going from photo to photo, and then to her bed.

The next morning all the photos had gone. Her dad rescued them secretly from the hole her mum had dug in the night, close to Will's favourite rose, because they did not have Will himself to bury. 'So,' her dad had said. 'So, at least she has accepted it.'

Her dad had given Polly her favourite photograph, of herself and Will together when they were twelve, in their school uniforms. She had hidden it in the third of her bedroom drawers.

Now Polly sat in the loft with the mattress Will would never sleep on again. But she would make sure it was used.

Polly stood up, and dragged it to the loft hatch.

'You need to get to bed,' her mother called from the landing. 'You've an early start in the morning, and no doubt you'll go to see your father after his ARP shift at the allotment. Heaven knows what he thinks will happen to his veggies if he doesn't pop in every day. I expect that lady will call any minute so you best get down here, but don't be on the telephone too long. It's expensive.'

Polly rolled her eyes but said nothing. Her mother couldn't understand that only the caller paid.

Later that evening, with all her packing done and Bet's call finished, Polly's mother reluctantly cut her daughter's hair to shoulder length, almost weeping to see the 'lovely chestnut locks' on the newspaper spread out on the kitchen lino. Polly had begged her mother to make her life easier in what would be endless wind and rain, and give her a bob, but Mrs Holmes refused to go shorter than shoulder length.

'It's not proper, and people might think you're "fast",' she told her. 'And what will Reggie think?'

Later, when her mum was asleep, Polly crept into Will's room. She pulled open the second drawer where his sweaters were folded, some knitted by their mum, and lifted out one of his old white sailing sweaters. It was too big for her, but that didn't matter. He was bigger than her; stronger, too. He always had been when he put her in goal at the recreation ground and he and his friends kicked the ball into the net. She tried to stop one, but it stung. She was hopeless. He yelled, then laughed, 'Move your blessed feet, girl.'

She did and blocked the next one, and the next. That had shown him.

She buried her head in the sweater, and there he was: that indefinable sense of her brother, the other half of her, the loss of whom had left her with a great void, a great nothingness where no feeling lived any more. Yes, she could talk, smile, laugh, but it never touched her, though that wasn't quite true, because today she had been truly pleased when she knew she was to join the narrowboats.

She hugged his sweater so tightly that it made her arms ache. She listened to check that her mum was nowhere around, then crept out of the room, carrying it. She put it in her kitbag, her father's from the previous war, which her mum had cut down to half its size. Then at last she slept.

Her alarm clock woke her early. She listened to

the sounds of the house. Her mother in the kitchen, up with the lark as always. Mr Bridges next door was leaving early for London. Soon she would set off for the train too, she thought. She was torn between excitement and nervousness and couldn't stay in bed a moment longer. She dragged on her clothes, including the trousers which fitted like a glove. She put on the light, standing in front of the full-length mirror on the back of the wardrobe door. 'Shoulders back, stand straight. You can do this.'

After a cup of tea and toast Polly hurried to the allotments in the darkness of early morning, finding her way along the mown path to her father's shed with the help of a shaded torch. There was a curtain over the window, but he'd be there. She knocked. 'Dad, turn the hurricane lamp down, I've just popped in to say goodbye.'

'Give us a minute, pet.'

The door opened and he ushered her in, saying, 'Oh my word, you look just like . . .' He stopped, then said, 'I like your hair shorter, pet, and you've pinned it up. Suits you. Now tell me why you've had it cut?'

She explained as he sat back down in his deckchair, and she on the stool. He puffed away at his empty pipe and when she'd finished he tamped down the memory of tobacco in the pipe bowl. 'You make the most of this, you hear me. Try to enjoy it, try to start filling up again, if you know what I mean. Try to care, because I know you don't – not about anything, not really, since he went.'

Polly looked anywhere but at him, unable to bear the grief in his eyes and the sudden tremble of his hands. All along the shelf were the photographs he had taken from the house. Every time Polly came to the shed, she looked at this record of the pair of them growing up. Always together even when they were with friends. They had even had their own language when they were only about four, her dad had said. A few years later they had ridden their bikes and fished for minnows, had picnics. They were part of a gang by then, which Will led, but she was his lieutenant. Later they had sailed, he had a girlfriend, she a boyfriend, but it was Will she talked to about Robin, when he had not turned up at the cinema but had gone out with someone else instead.

She said, answering her dad at last, 'I do care, Dad. I love you and Mum.'

Her dad said, 'You've got to cry one day.'

The hurricane lamp was spluttering. Polly lifted the window blackout a fraction. Dawn was breaking. She had a train to catch, a war to win, a narrowboat to steer, and many loads to collect and deliver. She smiled at her father. 'Dad, I love you. I'll have leave after every two trips apparently, so I'll be back in a month, I promise.'

He stood, turned off the lamp, opened the door. 'I love you too, and thank you for choosing something safe, sweet girl. The ATA could have been dangerous, perhaps? I just don't know, but it got your mum in a fret.' He patted her shoulder. 'I will see you soon. Be good, and write to Reggie. He's a nice chap, your mum likes him.'

'Well, he's been to a posh school, he's on the bombers, and likely a good income when the war is done,' said Polly. 'It's what she's always wanted for me.'

Her dad just looked, then murmured, 'You could do worse, and it will make her happy. Well, happier.' He stood on the path, holding the door open against the wind. The sky was clear, there were birds flying high, riding the thermals, and others were singing, guarding their space. Bert from the Crescent was pulling up his runner bean poles. It was all as it always had been but today she was leaving.

'Look after Mum,' she said as she left. 'She's still talking too much.'

He pulled Polly back, and hugged her close. She rested against him, just for a moment, but she must not for long, because she was so nervous she felt she would not let go. Inside, though, she wanted to leave.

Releasing her, he said, 'Come and see us when you can, and write. But I'm glad you're going. You need this, and never forget that.'

'Bye, Dad.' Polly was torn between relief and guilt. Perhaps she should have stayed to help? But her dad wanted her to go. She clung to that.

*

47

Her mum came on the bus to the station, and stood in front of her as they waited for the train, along with many others. She smoothed Polly's dry mackintosh. 'There, that's better, and you have your vest on?'

Suddenly she hugged her daughter as though she'd never let her go, but it was then that the train came chugging into the station. It stopped, doors opened, people rushed from and to it.

'I'll be home on leave,' Polly said as she disentangled herself from her mum's embrace. 'I'll write to Reggie, I promise, to tell him where to write to me.' It was what her mum wanted, and Polly didn't really mind, one way or the other. Was it because what she and Reggie had was not important, or was it because . . . well, what? It wasn't the right time? He was Will's friend, one of those who had kicked balls into the goal, and had come to offer condolences. Things had gone from there, but what things?

'If you have the time, Mum, write as well. I'd love to hear from you.'

Her mum shouted as Polly clambered on board, 'You must be safe. I won't have that Mr Hitler taking both my children, I won't, do you hear me? Do you?'

After the train pulled out of the station Polly's arm felt as if it might fall off from waving. As she made her way towards the corridor, the seated passengers who had heard her mum looked at her with pity. She clutched the rolled mattress and kitbag to her. For the first time ever she was leaving home.

Chapter 3

Tuesday 26 October – the canal at Hayes, near Southall

Miss Bet Burrows had instructed Polly to arrive at 10 a.m. at Hayes Station, near Southall, and so she did, to be met by Verity who was wearing a navy sweater with a hole in the left sleeve. On top she wore a pair of faded blue overalls, and wellington boots. 'Come along, chop-chop.'

'Hello,' Polly said, adjusting the rolled-up mattress under her arm; at least it wasn't raining, or she'd have been sleeping on a soggy mess tonight.

Verity stormed ahead, leaving Polly struggling in her wake, jostled by others who were leaving and entering the station. She called to Verity, 'Any chance of a hand?'

Verity didn't hear, or perhaps pretended not to, but flung over her shoulder, 'Bet's waiting on *Marigold*, the motorboat. She thought we should introduce you to the joys of life à la cut, hence meeting you here, and taking the motor along to the depot.'

Almost immediately, it seemed, they were at a steep bank that led from the station level to the canal side where Bet stood smoking on the deck, the slide hatch pushed open, the breast-high tiller at her back. She was reading a book that lay on the cabin roof next to the water can. Polly could hear the engine ticking over, pat-patter. Verity called, 'Ahoy, sailor.'

Bet spun round, and flicked her cigarette butt into the cut. 'Yet again I remind you, Verity, that it's the deepest insult to call anyone on the waterways a sailor. If one of the boaters heard they'd think you were mocking their culture.'

Polly heard Verity sigh and mutter, 'Everyone's so damned touchy.' She raised her voice and said, 'Sorry, I suppose I forgot. Here's our lost soul, with bag and baggage.' She headed down the slope to the motor, leaving Polly to follow.

Bet stood legs astride on the deck waiting for Verity to approach, and then she put up her hand as though stopping traffic. 'Listen, Verity. You've chased off one vulnerable girl, and as I said, I won't tolerate much more. Now go back, and help Polly by taking the mattress. We're a team, and you simply must get that through your head.' Though Bet had spoken quietly the wind carried her words to Polly.

Bet lifted her hand to Polly and raised her voice. 'I like your hair, Polly. It suits you a bit shorter and won't be such a nuisance. Very well done. Nice cut, too.'

Polly reached up. Her hair had come free from its grips, yet again, and fell in waves to her shoulders. Verity stormed up the slope and snatched the mattress. 'Who's a smarty-pants, then?' she hissed.

Polly followed her to the motor with her kitbag, calling to Bet, 'My mum's a hairdresser and I convinced her it was necessary, or I'd be combing out knots all the time.'

Verity said, for Polly's ears only, 'My word, father a store-man and mother a hairdresser, how one's heart sings.'

Polly stepped on to the *Marigold*. Verity's words should have wounded her. They didn't.

Bet was standing on the far side of *Marigold*'s deck. A narrowboat with a butty at its side pat-pattered steadily alongside. Bet said, 'I'm glad you're here, and while you are, please note that passing traffic slows to go by any boat at its moorings, or the wash could suck it away from the kerb and break the mooring strap. If you hear anyone using that term it means a rope. That passing butty and motor are strapped abreast. Strap, got it? Might as well pick up what you can, when you can, but don't worry about it. Rope will do, or change and change about. It's how you work that matters.'

Polly nodded as Bet added, 'Stow your bedding and clothes in the locker beneath the side-bed, which is to be yours. As you know from your visit yesterday, it is narrow but will be thine own. Verity has the cross-bed as she was here first.'

She checked that Polly was listening before continuing, 'You'll find pots, pans and army blankets in the locker as well, so move those to one side and put your mattress and towels and that small kitbag to the other side. How clever of your mother – she told me she'd adjust the size. The Grand Union Canal Carrying Company has fixed a shelf into every cabin. of every boat or butty that we women are to crew. They feel that our books and trinkets are all that's needed to keep us happy. That is, if anyone should have such things as trinkets. The regular boaters on the Grand Union boats don't have a shelf because, of course, they can't read. Why is that? It is because there's no time to stop anywhere long enough for regular schooling. They just pop the children into school for the odd day and then these children have the unmitigated pleasure of being mocked and derided as scum of the cut.'

Bet's fury was evident, and she took a deep breath before continuing.

'Sorry about the rage, but they're, on the whole, such startlingly good and worthy people doing a really tough job that to be derided as they are by bankers – or landsmen – is intolerable. Now, we've already winded the boat, Polly, and so we'll head to the lay-by to give you a tiny taste of life on the water. We're going there because that's where we receive our orders, as I said yesterday.'

'Winded?' Polly asked. As she waited for the answer she heard a train draw in, and on the other side of the bank a dog walking with its owner barked as a duck flew off from the cut.

Bet shook her head, lighting up another cigarette, shielding her match and resting an elbow on the huge tiller, which she had swung towards the bank to make more room. 'Ah, sorry, to "wind" means to turn it round. Hurry up now, tuck everything away, put your ration book in the drawer, and ten shillings in the kitty jar, then come out on to the counter. I'll give you a running commentary.'

'Counter?'

'The counter is the deck. Don't worry, Polly Holmes, you'll get the hang of it far quicker than you think. Verity, help her, if you please.' Bet smiled at both the girls. They ducked down into the cabin, unpacked and stored Polly's belongings, then while Verity began to make cocoa on a Primus stove Bet called for Polly to join her on the counter. Polly put ten shillings into the kitty jar and her ration book into the drawer, then joined Bet on the stern, or rear, deck. No, she meant the counter.

The doors had been opened wide against the cabin walls, and Polly stood close up to them, looking over the length of the *Marigold* right to the front of the boat, and then on, down the length of the cut. Bet held the breast-high tiller behind her. 'Polly, go on to the kerb and let go the fore-end, or front mooring strap, then the rear, if you would, in that order.'

Bet was tapping off the ash of her cigarette into a saucer lying on the roof and staring up at a flight of birds. Polly leapt for the bank, pretty sure this would be just like releasing the sailboat. She ran to the end of the long narrowboat, unwound the rough wet rope from around the fore-end or prow mooring stud, and threw it back on to the tiny fore-end counter. She ran back and did the same for the stern rope.

Bet nodded. 'Just coil it, if you would.' Polly leapt on to the counter and did so. 'Well done.'

'It's much the same as when we sailed,' Polly said.

'We?' Bet stubbed out her cigarette, started the motor and they pat-pattered along the cut, steering towards the centre. Polly shrugged. 'My brother and I.' She said nothing more, and all Bet said was, 'Ah, yes. I have no siblings.'

They were motoring along the centre of the cut, and Bet was staring down the length of the *Marigold*, over the cabin top and the hold, when she almost whispered, 'Polly, stand tight against the cabin for the moment, and watch all I do. But while we're alone – I do hope you can rise above Verity. I know I've mentioned it before, but I think her – well, what shall we call it – abrasive attitude covers a basic lack of confidence, and a measure of unhappiness. If you find it is too much, then come to me, but she truly is improving.'

Polly nodded. 'Each to her own,' she said.

She too stared along the cabin and engine roof, and over the huge length of hold where top planks rested on stands.

Bet said, 'You can see the headlight on the iron stand erected on the fore-end counter, can you? Of course, because of the blackout, the light is shaded. I hope you brought a hat, woollen or not, because the head is the greatest area of heat loss, and believe me, there will be heat loss.'

Polly had, and it was still in her kitbag. What would Verity make of the over-large pom-pom her mum had created, determined to use up the whole of the spare wool? Well, let her say what she liked.

The wind was in their faces as they chugged along, and the water rippled either side; the slapping sound was soothing. Bet said, 'When steering I like to stand in the "hatches", here where the slide hatch is.' She indicated the position. 'I have my hand on the tiller behind me like this, rather than standing alongside it. Everyone does. It makes sense if you have to suddenly swing to one side or another or you'll find yourself in the way. I'm in the centre of the cut as well, where it is deepest. I move over, obviously, when there is other traffic.'

'I'm coming up,' Verity warned them from the cabin.

Hand on the tiller, Bet stepped away from the opening.

'Here you are.' Verity handed cocoa to each of them. 'Rest it on the roof, Polly,' she advised, and disappeared back into the cabin. Bet resumed her previous position, taking a sip and, with eyes on the cut, said, 'Normally we snatch a piece of toast at five-thirty when we rise, and once we're under way we'll have porridge at nine-thirty or so. You'll put your bowl on the cabin top, if you're steering.'

She called down into the cabin, 'You could give

the shelves a clean, and the range bar needs some enthusiastic rubbing, Verity. We'll keep using the Primus for today, and only put the range on this evening. We need to replenish the coal when we come back through Coventry on the next run. Now, Polly, do you remember the gunwale alongside the motorboat cabin?'

Polly nodded.

'All right, then nip along it, and have a look in the hold to see just how big it is. You need to know everything about both our boats. You'll pass the engine room at the rear of the cabin and then the back-end lean-to. Call it the back-end, we all do, There's also some coal for the range in there, though we keep some in the coal cupboard beneath the bottom cabin step. In the back-end you will find brooms, rope to be spliced, something and everything. Don't worry, I'll show you how to splice – join two ropes – if you haven't done it while sailing.'

Bet watched ducks fly low along the cut ahead of them. 'As you go along the gunwale you'll notice that the cabin sides slope inwards so you shouldn't fall off, but if you do, don't scream. Just keep your mouth shut, and we'll hook you out with the shaft, otherwise called a boathook.' Bet pointed to the two shafts lying on the cabin top between the water can and the dipper.

Ahead, a motor and butty were approaching in the centre of the cut, but they began to steer right, just as Bet was doing, so eventually they'd pass left side to left side. Polly set off along the cabin gunwale. The oncoming motor and butty were set low in the water, with a tarpaulin covering the loads, and planks running over the top of the load from the cabin to the fore-end. 'They'll have come from the east London Limehouse Basin after loading, heading on to Birmingham.'

Polly clung to the cabin top with one hand and waved to the man steering the motor. He ignored her, his face shaded by his hat. 'He's towing the butty on a long snubber, or in other words, a tow-rope,' Bet called.

The woman steering the butty continued with her crochet, the tiller guided by her upper arm. A toddler sat on the cabin roof with a chain running from the chimney to her waist presumably to stop her crawling overboard. Another, older child sat further along, legs dangling down the side of the cabin. He must have been about five. He was doing something with a rope, or was it two? He wore a cap and long trousers. Bet called, 'He's splicing the two rope ends together.'

'I wondered – but he's so young,' Polly called.

'Go on,' Bet called back. 'Get moving, you haven't even reached the engine room.' Polly edged along the gunwale, clinging to the edge of the cabin. She reached the engine room and the back-end, then stared into the depths of the hold: apart from the top planks there were others lining the base. They were coal stained. Water slopped beneath the planks.

This was her new home, her new job, and the hold was so huge she couldn't imagine loading, unloading, or even handling the boats and getting to Birmingham safely. As for locks . . .

Bet shouted, 'Stop looking so worried. You needed to see the whole thing to sort it in your head. Come back and finish your cocoa.'

Polly felt her way back, but before she stepped on to the counter Bet said, 'Right, now you're getting the hang of it, stay on the gunwale or sit on the roof, like those children you saw. It'll give me more room to steer.'

Polly hopped up on to the roof, as the wind tore through her hair. 'The gunwale round the holds? When do we use it?'

Bet smiled. 'When I tell you. Until then we use the top planks. Now, relax.' Polly dangled her legs over the side of the cabin, her mackintosh flapping in the wind. On the left-hand side there were views of fields but on the nearside they passed a series of wharves and warehouses, with a range of smells, noise and smoke. She reached for her cocoa, smiling back at Bet, who said, 'Don't look so confused, it will all fall into shape.'

Polly hoped it would be soon. She drank her cold cocoa, which was vaguely sweet.

Bet said, 'I have a friend with bees, so we usually have honey.' She waved ahead. 'We're travelling at about five miles an hour, but with a load or towing the butty it will be about three miles.'

Verity called from the cabin, 'It's not in the least fun clearing out the hold after a load of coal, let me tell you, or clearing grain. We have to get every little piece of coal out, and as for the grain . . . If we leave any, we start to sprout wheat, for goodness' sake.'

Bet laughed, and continued, 'So, to get from Limehouse where we're loaded to Birmingham we head uphill most but by no means all of the time to the Midlands and finally Birmingham via approximately one hundred and fifty locks. Just think how you will enjoy opening and closing, not to mention filling and emptying, them.'

One hundred and fifty? Polly was unable to absorb the number. Bet was running on, 'We pick up another load immediately we return. Not glamorous but necessary. This, Polly Holmes, could be your life for the next few years or however long it takes to end this bloody war.'

The motor pat-pattered onwards, there was the slap of water, the sound of shouting from the bank, a jackhammer whacked down, a saw screeched from a multi-storey workshop with very dirty windows. Or was it a factory? Polly was feeling pulverised by the sights and sounds. Would she ever get used to this?

Bet said, 'If there's no chance of being given an order by the depot today we'll maybe head out to Cowley Lock. It will give you a bit more of an idea before the long run.'

Verity called again, 'You did put your ration card

in the drawer and your share into the kitty? Ten shillings. We'll be shopping at the depot. Everyone contributes the same, you know.'

'Yes, I did.' Polly lifted her face into the wind. She was here. Her mum would be queuing for rations that had arrived at some shop or other. Her dad would be at his Stores Department in his overalls, trying to stay awake after being up all night. So, there they were, and here she was, sitting on a cabin roof, her shoulder-length hair whipping her face, sipping cocoa instead of typing for Mr Burton. It hadn't been what she originally wanted, which was to be in a uniform doing something more obvious, but it was something, and already she thought it might be a very good something.

Chapter 4

'Coming into sight is the depot you visited yesterday,' Bet called. 'We're mooring *Marigold* at the kerb of the concrete lay-by. I'm cutting back the throttle now, slowing steadily.'

Bet looked alive, fizzing with a sort of joy as she fixed her gaze ahead, over the *Marigold*'s length, the tiller almost a part of her. The sun had come out, clouds scudded, the wind was increasing. Leaves that had fallen early were floating on the cut. Polly's dad would have those out and on the compost as soon as look at them.

Bet kept *Marigold* to the right as a laden motorboat and butty headed past them slowly in the opposite direction. This time, the man at the tiller of the motor nodded, and called, ''Ow do.'

'How do you do, Steerer Ambrose,' Bet called back.

The woman steering the butty continued with her knitting, and merely nodded.

Polly saw the dry dock, and the same three

narrowboats tied up parallel to the frontage. Men were busy on the hardstanding which fronted the workshops, while the tannoy was still playing tinny music. Sparks flew from a workshop with an open front. The men in boiler suits wore goggles. She heard a sound like chalk on a blackboard. 'So, now we're passing the dry dock, the slipway and oil store; in a moment you might just see the Enquiries office where Alf will be huddling in his lair. Ahead is the lay-by.' Bet raised her voice. 'Verity, out of the cabin, keep an eye out for *Horizon*.'

As they pat-pattered along Polly saw what seemed like even more narrowboats emulating sardines, moored up in the lay-by, their sterns towards the kerb, their fore-ends into the fairway of the cut. In a way they looked like the Venetian gondolas she had seen in pictures, all in a row, bobbing up and down.

'Verity, I repeat, out of the cabin *now* and on to the gunwale, if you please, and find *Horizon* – there're more parked than earlier. Polly, you'll find that the lay-by is constantly changing, with arrivals and departures, but more of that later. Now, I need you to jump down from the roof and grab a shaft to shove *Horizon* aside when I reverse into the space. Wait until I tell you.'

'Shafts?' Polly shouted, in a panic, slipping down from the roof on to the counter.

'Sorry, Polly, remember – they're the boathooks you'll find lying along the roof. Still can't see *Horizon*.'

62

Polly looked and saw two shafts. Which one? Her panic increased.

Verity shoved past her and eased herself on to the right-hand cabin gunwale. 'There she blows, our *Horizon*, next to Granfer Hopkins's butty, *Swansong*. They're probably having a chat. Oh, if only butties could talk, what tales they'd tell.' She shouted to Polly, 'Nice old boy, is Granfer. Always says '"Ow do", which is more than can be said for his grandson, Saul.'

Bet peered ahead. 'Yes, good idea, Verity. Polly, when we're closer I'll be steering across the fairway of the cut, and then reversing, forcing a parking space, as it were, between *Swansong* and *Horizon*. Going astern there are no brakes, and one's steering is minimised, so the boat is prone to swinging. Therefore I need you girls shafting. Verity, down to the fore-end *now*. If you please.'

'Aye, aye, Steerer.'

Bet sighed, laughed, then raised her eyebrows and shouted over the engine, 'Well, that's a damn sight better than Sailor, so let's be thankful for small mercies.'

Verity grabbed a shaft from the cabin roof, scooted along the cabin gunwale, and then almost danced along the top planks over the hold, skirting the central uprights to the fore-end while Polly grabbed the remaining shaft. It was heavy. She dragged it off the roof, and stood with it, the boathook at the top. Bet nodded at her. 'Get ready. I'm now steering her across the cut. Don't worry, just listen to me.'

63

Bet was straddling the main channel or fairway. She roared, 'Verity, watch it, fore-end's swinging.'

Verity, down at the fore-end, shoved her shaft to the bottom of the canal, leaning into it, correcting the motor. They could hear her language from the stern as she hauled up the shaft, changed sides and plunged it deep down, to stop the boat from swinging back the other way.

Bet yelled, 'Save your breath, just don't let it swing too far. Polly, take a grip on your shaft, stand firm. I'm reversing in.' Polly braced herself, seeing the *Marigold* swinging again, reversing towards the mass of boats. How on earth had Verity spotted *Horizon* amongst all the others?

She took the right-hand side. Bet roared, 'Polly, spread your legs, if I can be so indelicate; push against the butty your side, I'm inching back, there's *Swansong* on our right. As you're on the right too, create a space. Don't fall in. I don't want to have to fish you out.'

They inched back, swinging again. Polly shoved at *Swansong*'s fenders, her heart pounding, and heard Verity shouting from the fore-end, 'Not many of us women can park a boat first time, Polly, look and learn. Bet's a diamond.' There was real admiration in her voice, and for a moment Polly saw a different Verity.

Bet yelled, 'Keep us straight, Verity. Come on, Polly, get bloody on with it, one poke's not going to do it.'

Polly braced herself again, legs apart, pushing again at the fender on the fore-end of the *Swansong* butty. She kept her weight behind the shaft and shoved, shoved, and *Swansong* edged away, into the motorboat the other side, which also moved slightly. Bet slowly, slowly backed *Marigold* into the gap between *Horizon* and *Swansong*. Polly's arms ached, her shoulders too, and her hands slipped on the shaft. She took a breath, and tightened her grip as *Marigold* eased further and further into the gap.

Her thighs strained as she pushed harder, and the small of her back ached as they eased more and more of *Marigold*'s seventy feet between the two butties until Bet pushed the throttle to neutral and let *Marigold* glide the rest of the way. With a jolt, their fenders hit the kerb. Verity danced back along the planks, then dropped down to the cabin gunwale, slapping her hands on the cabin roof. 'My word, the girl might have managed it, Bet, but why, for the Lord's sake, didn't she go to the left and shove *Horizon*, instead of poking and prodding someone else's butty?'

Bet chuckled, 'She landed on the right-hand side, so I didn't like to mention it at the time. But something to consider, Polly, eh?'

An old man popped his head out of *Swansong*'s cabin. ''Ow do,' he nodded at Bet. 'Yer new boatee, she giving oos a push 'n' shove?'

'She is indeed new, Granfer, but willing. Shafted quite well, given it's the first time. Next time she'll choose *Horizon*.'

'Aye, no matter. 'Appen she'll be as good as one of the young 'uns oop the cut in time.' He crossed on to the motor the other side of *Swansong*, and disappeared into the cabin.

Bet called as she held the tiller, 'Replace your shaft then, Polly. The young ones Granfer talks of are all of eight years old, before you get too cocky. They can manage a cut-down shaft and much more besides. Now, tie us up with the mooring strap, if you will.'

Polly heaved the shaft up on the cabin roof. She pressed herself against the open cabin door and was wondering why the other narrowboats had removed their tillers, or turned them the other way round, when a young man came out of the cabin of *Swansong*. He was dressed in cords, a waistcoat, and checked shirt, its sleeves rolled up. He had a red cotton kerchief tied at his neck, his hair was black and curly, his cheekbones high, and his smile warmed his whole face when he gripped the shoulder of the young boy who followed him. 'Get to school then, Joe. Learn 'em lessons while yer can. Then come on 'ome, but only at t'end of the lessons, no bunkin' off early. We got no orders today.'

'Aye, scuttle along now, and no messin'.' Granfer was now standing on the counter of their motorboat, the other side of *Swansong*.

The boy, his cap pulled down, and wearing a worn dark red sweater over his baggy trousers, pulled away from the young man's hand. 'Yer din't go, so why should I, Uncle Saul?'

'Cos the world is changin', and no talkin' back. On with yer. Got yer grub?'

The boy turned as Polly stood facing *Swansong*, stretching, trying to ease her back. He sneered, 'What yer gawpin' at?'

Polly turned to Bet, who was doing something to the tiller. 'I wasn't looking – really, I wasn't.'

Bet shook her head, and said quietly, 'Privacy is all important when we live so close together and you were facing their way, so whether you were looking or not, it doesn't matter. It will be assumed you were. You turn away, should others be talking or working on the neighbouring boat. You only look if invited, you only visit if invited. I'd never come into your cabin unless I knocked for permission. You will never come into mine unless you do the same.'

Verity tutted from the gunwale. 'It comes down to manners, so try remembering yours.'

Polly stared at her hands, which were rubbed red from the shaft, and frozen. She eased her shoulders, and turned to Verity, who had slipped from the gunwale and was squeezing past her, heading for the cabin. 'Mind your own . . .' Polly said under her breath.

There was a sudden shout from further down the lay-by, 'Watch it, you bugger.'

She heard the sound of a revving engine, as *Swansong* and *Marigold* and all the motors and butties began rocking and jostling one against the other. Within seconds the *Marigold* was sucked from the kerb, by the wash, but as Polly had not yet tied up, nothing snapped.

Bet jumped on to the gunwale, and then the cabin roof, balancing as she yelled, 'Cut your bloody speed, you blithering idiot. You're passing the lay-by.' A narrowboat and butty seemed to be accelerating past the parked boats, heading for Limehouse. The rocking grew worse. 'Get down, Bet,' yelled Polly.

Verity emerged from the cabin. 'What the hell?'

Bet jumped to the counter, revved *Marigold*'s engine. She shoved it into reverse and *Marigold* crept astern again, struggling against the wash from the speeding narrowboat, which was now dead ahead. The whole of the lay-by was in turmoil, with boats jerking, and even the washing hung on lines over the hold danced like dervishes. Cries and curses echoed around the lay-by, and the crashing of crockery.

The *Marigold* heaved, tossing Polly to one side. She reached for a handhold on the cabin top, slipped, and was thrown against Bet, then into the tiller with a thwack before she crashed to the counter, nudging Bet off the tiller. Bet regained her position within seconds, but Polly lay at her feet as *Marigold* knocked into *Swansong*, just as *Swansong*'s mooring strap snapped.

Polly scrabbled to her knees, her side hurting, and saw the boy was safe on the kerb. The wash continued to tear at the boats, and now the *Marigold* swung away to port, while *Swansong* lurched to starboard. Saul pitched into the gap, whacking his head on *Marigold*'s fender, then sank into the water.

Polly screamed at Bet, 'Stop revving astern. Man in water. Go forward, get out of the way.'

Bet yelled back, 'I can't, it's Saul's brother-in-law, Leon, dragging his bloody butty past the lay-by at a rate of knots and now it's dead ahead, I'll hit it. He's such a bastard. Get on, girls, what do you think the shafts are for?'

Polly scrabbled to her feet, and leapt for the shaft, dragging it off the roof. She fended off *Swansong* as it swung towards them in the turbulence, threatening Saul, who was surfacing, floundering, blood streaming from his head.

'Verity, help me.' Polly's shout was high-pitched. The pain from her side caught her. All along the lay-by she heard the clashing of boats, the bellows of the boaters as they cursed Leon. Below her Saul was splashing, his eyes rolling, but then they closed, and he sank again. On the bank the boy screamed.

Verity scrambled to the counter, grabbed a shaft, and kept the gap open as Polly threw hers back on the roof and lay down, her hand outstretched. Saul reappeared, coughing, his eyes open. 'Take my hand, take it,' Polly shrieked. But the *Marigold* was too high, and Saul disappeared again, then struggled to the surface, thrashing the water, spitting, his face streaming with blood.

The boy screamed, 'Uncle Saul.'

The *Marigold* swung towards Saul again. 'Shove it back, Verity,' Polly, shouted. Verity did.

Polly was about to leap in, when Granfer tore

across from the motor, his shaft in his hands, and held it down to Saul, who clung to it as the wash sucked him towards the fairway. Granfer braced himself, shortening and shortening his hold on the shaft, dragging Saul back and shouting all the time, 'Damn yer, Leon Arnson. Yer a bloody idiot.'

The boy was screaming again from the bank, 'Leave oos be, Da. Just yer leave oos be. Cut yer speed. Uncle Saul he be drownin'. Granfer, 'elp him.'

'I am, lad.' Granfer kept hauling Saul against the current. Polly got to her feet, grabbed the other shaft, and shoved the boats apart as Verity was doing. She also stared towards the cut. A man yelled, 'How's yer like that, you bloody sailors. Yer should keep yer bloody noses out me business and give oos back m'boy.'

Polly turned back, to see Saul heaving himself on to the *Swansong*'s counter, where he lay still for a moment, his body heaving as he gulped in air. Cool as a cucumber Granfer picked up the shaft and returned to *Seagull*, his motor, setting straight the painted water can he had knocked aside, checking the *Seagull*'s mooring strap, which had held. He used the shaft to keep the *Seagull* clear of the boat to port.

Meanwhile, Saul clambered to his feet, water pouring from his clothes, blood dripping from his cut forehead. He rubbed the blood from his eyes with his arm, an arm which Polly saw was shaking. His tanned face looked pale. He looked hurt, frightened, and she reached out a hand.

He coughed out water, then turned towards the kerb laughing, but it was strained and unreal. 'Get yoursel' to school, Joe. Now. Nothing's 'appening 'ere. Nothin' cept me 'aving a bath I probably needed. You get on now, quick. Leave everything else to me 'n' Granfer.'

Polly dropped her hand; that man was brave, and kind, and he didn't need her, he had his own kin, but something flickered inside her, and then was gone. Bet called, 'All clear, Polly?' Polly nodded. 'You can go back now, Bet – steady, though.'

Saul's butty, *Swansong*, was floating forward, swinging this way and that, its stern counter on a level with their cabin. Verity was squatting on the roof, fending it off. Saul snatched up a new long rope, secured it to the stud on *Swansong*, then leapt with the other end coiled over his shoulder on to their gunwale. He rushed along, then down to their counter, brushing past Polly, who was handling her shaft in tandem with Verity.

He leapt on to the kerb as Bet reversed *Marigold* against it. He let the rope uncoil, catching it round his back, and then began to try to haul *Swansong* back with both hands, his muscles bulging, the strain showing on his face, calling again to Joe, who was slouching down the lay-by. 'Stay till t'end of school, yer 'ear. I'll be there, so don't come 'ome on y'own.'

Saul managed to stop *Swansong*'s forward float, his legs braced, the strain showing in his face as he heaved the butty back to the kerb. Securing the rope round a mooring stud and checking that the motor was secure, he then stood on the kerb astern of the *Marigold*.

'Give us your strap then,' he called. Bet threw it to him without a word. He tied the rope through the iron ring embedded in the lay-by, then checked *Horizon*'s mooring too, before leaping back on to his motor, springing on to the cabin roof and running down the hold planks, almost swinging round the uprights, to the fore-end, watching Leon disappearing along the cut towards Limehouse Basin.

Slowly the waters were subsiding. Granfer nodded across the *Swansong*'s counter to Bet, before hurrying along *Seagull*'s planks to the fore-end, also watching the departing butty and motor.

Suddenly, all was calm. Polly turned to Bet. 'Not even a thank-you?'

'He tied us up. What more do you want? That's a big thank-you in this world. Now let's get the kettle on while I check for orders, and if there's nothing for us yet, we'll head off for the lock at Cowley. Use the Primus again, Verity. We won't light the range.'

Verity heaved her shaft on to the cabin roof. 'Why me?'

'Because I want to check Polly's ribs before I go; that was a cracking collision with the tiller, not to mention the counter. What's more, I thought she was going to be christened in the cut on her first morning. She almost had to leap in, but you reacted well. Both of you were quick and efficient; it was good teamwork. Well done.'

Verity slammed into the cabin. Bet was reversing the tiller. 'Why do that with the tiller?' asked Polly.

'Look at the extra room it gives us on the boat. Some actually remove it temporarily but this suits me, especially if we might be off. Let's have a look at you, then.' Bet poked and prodded but found nothing cracked or broken, though it hurt Polly to breathe.

'So, you'll have the first of your many bruises by tonight. I'm heading for the office to see how the orders are looking. Don't relax, either of you. We're off one way or another.'

Then she left. The boy had gone, the red, white and blue colours of the Grand Union Canal Carrying Company boats gleamed in the sunlight, the flowers and castles of the water cans on the cabin doors were riotous; so, too, the wooden helms and sides above the high-water mark. It was as though nothing had happened.

The weathered women from the other boats were heading along the lay-by with shopping bags as they had yesterday, or washing clothes on the bank, the water boiling in the large pans on grills which rested on brick sides over fires. Some were cleaning, and turning to shout at their children or husbands, their washing already hung out, flapping gently. Bet bustled back, calling from the lay-by, 'No orders today.'

Polly nodded. Leaning against the cabin, she was

looking only at the towpath, trying to calm down, as well as making sure she did not turn to watch Saul and Granfer returning over the roof of *Swansong* after cleaning their hold.

Bet smiled at her, leaning back against the cabin too. Dragging out her cigarettes, she offered one to Polly, who hesitated but then accepted. Her mother wouldn't approve. But what would she like here? She cupped the match Bet held out, sucked in on the cigarette and coughed, because she hardly ever smoked, but she needed something. 'What on earth was that all about?' she said, before coughing again.

Bet dragged deeply, then exhaled. 'It's none of our business. These people live in their boats year in, year out. They travel all the time; feuds occur.' She gestured to the boats. 'Generations ago, in the canal's heyday, they lived on the bank, as they call it, and ran their cargo boats. Then times got hard, they couldn't afford the rent, so they moved on to the boats. The cabins are small because the load is their livelihood and they need the biggest holds they can get. It's a different world to that of the land. You will be away from your "real" world, Polly, for a while, but you will one day go back to that world.'

Polly nodded. Bet continued, 'So you won't gawp, you won't question, you won't pry. Neither will you expect thanks, because they don't give it except in very exceptional circumstances. But what you do to help won't be forgotten, and will be repaid, never fear, as we've just seen.'

Polly inhaled; the end of her cigarette glowed. This time she didn't cough but neither did she like it. Verity called, 'Three mugs of tea down here.'

They squeezed out their cigarettes, put them in their pockets for later, and ducked down the steps into the cabin. Polly and Bet sat on the side bench, and Verity on the cross-bed. Verity pointed to the small bookcase up above Polly. 'Why have you brought *Winnie-the-Pooh* and *The Water Babies*? They're children's books, and *Pooh* looks as though it's ready for the dustbin.'

'How about minding our own business, eh, Verity?' Bet said wearily.

'Because I like the books,' Polly answered. 'Do you have a problem with that?'

Verity flushed. 'Of course not. I didn't mean anything by it, I was just making conversation.'

But it wasn't conversation, it was point-scoring and, what's more, Polly's ribs hurt and she'd had enough for the moment. But then she shook her head. The girl wasn't to know that that copy of *Winnie-the-Pooh* was her most prized possession.

Bet gulped down her tea, reached across the eighteen inches of floor space and placed her mug in the painted bowl on the range rest. She stood, as though restless.

'Drink up, and off to Cowley we will go,' she said. 'You, Miss Polly Holmes, are about to have a lock-wheeling lesson.'

Polly drank her tea to the dregs, wondering what

on earth lock-wheeling was. She felt determined to somehow break the difficulties with Verity, and announced, 'No, first I have to use the depot lavatory, and I bet you did, Bet, while you were checking orders? What about it, Verity?'

Bet looked from one to the other and roared with laughter. 'I think we'll make a team of you two yet. Off you go. See you in ten minutes.'

They left the *Marigold* together, not quite walking in time, but close to it.

Chapter 5

26 October – Saul and Granfer at the depot on the same afternoon

On *Seagull*, as the kettle simmered on the range, Saul sighed and poured water into the bowl on the hinged-down cupboard door in front of the cross-bed. He'd been born in that bed, his mum before him, and probably Granfer too.

Already there was clean water from the water can in the bowl. It had to be clean to wash the smell of the canal from him, as well as the shame, and while they were near the water tap, why not? He'd hit his head as he fell and that's why he couldn't sort himself out, that's why his hands were shaking. He hadn't been scared, course not. He dragged the red check curtain his mother had made across the port-hole, just in case them on *Marigold* forgot to keep their eyes on their own boat. Bloody foreigners, didn't know what was what. He stripped off and stood naked on the towel. He sluiced himself, then scrubbed himself dry with the second towel, which was ragged but enough.

He dressed in his only other pair of cords, a shirt

and a leather jerkin, slinging the stinkers into his towel. Ma Mercy, from the *Lincoln* motorboat, had said she'd boil 'em up nice with her own, as she had her washtub brewing on the kerb already. He'd pay, course he would. The kettle was still simmering, always was. He strapped up his boots, which were still wet and cold, but when weren't they, as autumn loomed?

Granfer called down, 'Sling me them dirts. I'll trog 'em down to Ma.'

'Yer all right, Granfer. You make oos tea.' Saul picked up the bowl, closed up the table, running his shaking hand over the flowers he had painted, and the castle on the cupboard front. But the shaking would stop. It must, he had a water can to paint for the *Headingly*. He stopped, and called up the steps. 'Ma Mercy could want some paintin' doin', Granfer, 'stead of paying. Yer could sluice the bowl for me, if'n you don't mind.'

He sprang up the steps and bounded on to the bank, taking the clothes to Ma, who tipped them into the simmering bucket. Her old chap had made up the brick surround but mortar was never used, so it could be taken down and put in the back-end to be brought out at the next stop.

'Granfer'll set oop our own on the run back from Coventry if'n we 'ave an order for coal,' he said. 'D'yer need a kettle to be painted, Ma, as yer obliging me?'

Ma wore the long skirts and wide belt like a few of the women, though no one wore the old black bonnets. Granfer said Grandma had worn 'em but she'd died when some sort of cold was going round the world after the first war.

'No, lad. I needs nothin',' Ma said, drawing out a skirt from the tub with her tongs. 'Yer shafted the motor oot of the mud for us before Alperton, 'tis enough.'

Saul smiled. She said, 'Yer watch that Leon, nasty that one is. He be after yer now, but yer done right by Joe. Your dad and mam woulda done same.'

'Aye.'

He dug his hands into his pockets and strode back to *Seagull*, still shaking, but less so. Granfer was making tea and they sat in the motor cabin, he on the side-bed where Joe slept, Granfer on the cross-bed where Saul slept. Granfer had the butty cabin; it was where he and Saul had lived while Mam and Da had the motor.

Granfer slurped his tea, pulled the cupboard front down again, then placed the enamel mug on it. He looked up, cleared his throat, and asked the question neither knew the answer to, 'What we to do 'bout our lad? Got to keep 'im safe from Leon. He only just be talkin' again, sort of matching the going of his bruises, yer seen that?'

'Well, we just keep him safe, is all, Granfer. I'll fetch 'im today, and keep him under me eye. We'll be all right once we're on the cut, cos we can keep an eye on 'im all the time. I's going to ask 'round Southall shops again if anyone's seen our Maudie.'

Granfer nodded. 'I just don't know how yer sister would've just run away from the bugger without takin' Joe, but the more I sees in the world, the less I damned well know. What with that bloody bomb dropping on yer ma and da as them was walking to the shops, an' all. We need 'em here, now. Maudie needed them. She needed us, but wouldn't let oos do nothin'.'

Saul felt the great weight on his shoulders that had been there since his parents had died. But it was Maudie who had it harder, married to Leon who bashed her bad, just cos he liked doing it, Saul reckoned, and hit the boy too. She'd said no, Saul, stay out of it, I'm sorting it. She must of meant she was doing a bunk, and who could blame her, but to leave the lad alone with Leon? That wasn't Maudie . . . or was it? Now he was twenty he should know about these things but was it like Granfer said, the older you got, the less yer knew?

Now Granfer said, 'Anyways, lad, we 'ad to take the boy when we heard his cries. Had to. I reckon that bugger'd 'ave killed him, if'n we ain't. We 'ad a right. We's family.'

They'd had the conversation time and again, but they had to, because of the worry about his sister. Where the hell was she, when the boy needed her? There'd be no letter, cos she couldn't write, like the rest o' them. Saul drank his tea. His hand wasn't shaking, no; steady as a rock, it was. Had that girl seen him shaking, she that'd tried to pull him out?

He could see her clear as day, as she shouted 'Take my hand'. He'd thought she'd cared, but she was a foreigner, a landsman, whose children spat from the bridges, and called boaters names, and the landsmen themselves weren't much better so he didn't want her in his head, but she bloody well was. She had no right there, neither. He'd do better to think of Leon – that'd keep them safer instead of all this meandering.

Saul remembered the time back in September when they'd left the lock on their way down from Birmingham, just before the gates were shut for the day. They'd seen Leon tied up for the night, his butty and motor abreast, parallel to the bank, waiting for the lock to open come morning as the bugger headed up Birmingham. They'd heard the lad crying and crying above the pat-patter of *Seagull*, and acting fast Granfer had rammed the *Seagull*'s engine astern, slowing, and staying on the throttle as Saul had leapt from the motor and run along the towpath.

There'd been the sound of laughter from the pub, which was set back. He bet Leon was in there. He'd run over the bridge, and back down the towpath t'other way. He jumped on Leon's motor, *Brighton*, and slammed back the doors. No, no crying in that cabin. He'd leapt across on to the butty, *Maudsley*, and found the cabin doors chained shut. He grabbed the shaft off the roof and crashed it down, and again, breaking the chain near the padlock, hearing the boy start to scream now. 'No, Da, no.'

Saul had called, 'It be me, yer Uncle Saul. It's just me.' Silence fell. Inside he found Joe, curled into a ball on the floor, lying in the blood streaming from his poor broken nose.

He'd picked him up and, once on the counter, he'd thrown him over his shoulder and headed off down the towpath again then over the bridge, and back along the towpath. He'd wanted to run but he didn't want to hurt the boy any more. He could hear Granfer revving the motor, which started moving slowly towards him, then stuck on the mud. Oh God. He'd snatched a look at the pub. No change.

He'd thrown Joe across the gap into Granfer's arms, leapt the gap himself, grabbed the shaft and shoved the motor off the mud, sweat pouring from him, though it was a cool September evening. Granfer had laid the boy down on the counter and was revving the motor, and they were away, close towed, with no one stopping them. Several though 'ad seen them as they stood on their counters, but they'd turned to watch the pub, their hands on their horns should Saul need warning.

Saul thought they'd stopped Leon. They had a right. Cruelty cut through the code of privacy.

Granfer picked up his mug, saying, 'Reckon I'll collect t'lad from school. Yer go and check for orders at t'office, remind 'em we's here. We needs the pay more'n ever now we's got him, but at least we won't have the school 'tendance bloke round again, cos he'll have been ticked off the list by the teacher

82

today. Yer fetch the rations too, and yes, 'ave a chat around about Maudie and we need some pheasant and a rabbit or two once we's got going on up.'

Saul took their ration books checked at the office, and headed into Southall, where he collected a couple of eggs, a bit of meat and whatever else he could find, asking, always asking, because one man selling shoelaces from a tray, who'd been lounging against a wall a couple of weeks ago, was pretty sure he'd seen a redhead heading for the station, a big old bag over her shoulder. That sounded like Maudie. Ma Ambrose had said another old chap, Alperton way, had seen a lass like her and all. Did he believe them? He didn't know, because there was something squirrelling way deep in his heart, but he didn't want to see it, or hear it. Course she was still alive, just fleeing, for now. Leon wouldn't have hurt her worse. No, not that.

He bought bread, and a bit of lard that a bloke was selling down a side street, and cabbages, which'd make the cabin stink but was good for a growing boy. No one knew anything more of Maudie, though they wished they had. He hurried back to the lay-by, nodding at those he knew, ignoring them he didn't, which weren't many.

Granfer was on the motor when he returned, making toast for the boy. 'Where's he gone?' asked Saul.

'Just to the lav. Don't take on, Leon's not in t' lay-by, and our boy ain't lost his voice again, like he did when 'is Da 'urt him so bad, so I reckon he's all right.'

Saul stowed the shopping and cleaned and polished the engine as he waited for the boy to return, walking along the lay-by more than once, but when he returned to the cabin, Joe was there, with the cupboard front down, colouring in some flowers he'd drawn.

'Where'd you get those?' Saul asked, looking at the packet of coloured pencils beside Joe on the cross-bed.

'Teacher gave 'em to me, Uncle Saul.' The boy sounded sharp. His eyes wouldn't meet Saul's but he was shook up, course he was. 'What d'yer think?'

He showed Saul the flowers. Saul smiled, 'Your grandma, my mam, was good with paint and you're like her.'

Joe put his head down, and coloured in a red flower. He had also drawn a castle. All of these were as a boater would do it, an artist boater, that is, Saul thought, wanting to paint the land they passed on their travels, and the way the shadows played on the fields, and the— But there was no time, never.

'I'm like you too, not just 'er, Uncle Saul,' Joe said, his tongue slightly out, his fingers tight around the red pencil.

'Have you learned your words in school?'

Joe put the red pencil down, and chose a blue one. Saul watched as he coloured over the red and produced a deep purple. Yes, the lad was good.

Joe said, 'I can't see letters. I can see flowers, but not the shape of letters. When you talk I can hear you, but I can't see it, so how can I write it, how can I read it? It just be squiggles, same goes for numbers. I can't see 'em but I can count off me fingers and in me 'ead.'

Saul nodded. He could understand, cos he couldn't read neither but he wanted to, he needed to cos the boats weren't going to last, there were trains and lorries and once the war was over, he, Granfer and Joe would be too.

'Well, we're going to have to find a way so that you understand, and I moost too. I just don't know 'ow.'

'You know everything, Uncle Saul – don't 'e, Granfer?'

Saul checked over his shoulder. Granfer was at the stove now and said, 'Reckon 'e knows a fair bit, but what 'e don't know is whether you're bothered at seeing yer da again, what with all that fuss and fandangle?'

Joe didn't falter in his colouring. 'Oh no, not with Uncle Saul 'ere, and you, Granfer. You'll stop 'im getting to me, till she gets back 'ere. I reckon she knew she could go, and yer keep me safe till then.'

Chapter 6

26 October – Bet, Polly and Verity on the same afternoon

Polly steered their butty, *Horizon*, which was short-towed by *Marigold* as they left the lay-by for the lock at Cowley almost immediately after the excitement. Verity stood close up to the cabin, as there was no gunwale. Both boats were unloaded, so rose high in the water. The tiller was unwieldy and it was strange to be steering something high and behind her, but Polly was getting the hang of it.

She already knew that if you steered right, the boat turned left; Will had shown her that much but the sailboat was quicker, this was a carthorse ... Polly stopped the thought. She must move forward with this canal, these women, and the strange boaters.

Verity said, 'It's a straight run through to Cowley. Bet does it with all her trainees, though usually with just the motor unless it's a fine day. You don't actually need to steer very much because the butty will follow the motor on such a short tow. So you're superfluous, but I would think that's not an unusual situation for you.'

Verity hauled herself up on to the cabin roof and edged away, sitting looking at the view. For two pins Polly would grab Verity's leg and flick her into the cut. The thought made her smile, and she said, 'Oh come on, you can do better than that pathetic insult.'

Verity ignored her, and sat reading her book, *The Thirty-Nine Steps*, but then Polly felt a screwed-up handkerchief hit her. She brushed it aside, leaving it lying on the counter. 'Hope that was clean?' she asked.

'Spotlessly so, darling,' Verity said, ducking her head down to her book again. Polly had read and enjoyed it a couple of years ago. 'I know the ending,' she called, 'I'll tell you "whodunnit" if you don't perk up.'

'You won't live to work the lock if you do – you'll suffer a miserable and vile experience, the planning of which I will spend time perfecting.' Verity gave a faint laugh.

Silence reigned while Polly wondered what on earth was really going wrong in this girl's life. She said, 'Saul and Granfer sound as though they're from Birmingham, or a bit like that, anyway.'

Verity lifted her head. 'I know, and you're right, it's a funny accent the boaters have, a bit of a mixture.' She returned to her book.

Polly looked at her. That was the first proper conversation they had had.

In no time at all, the *Marigold* slowed, heading towards wider water where beech trees lined the cut. 'We're tying up to walk to the lock,' Verity said.

The *Marigold* dawdled through the wide still water, disturbing the reflection. They finally stopped when the lock gates were just ahead.

'You could turn a boat around here, with this width of water, couldn't you?' called Polly.

Verity leaned back on the roof, her weight on one elbow. 'It's called winding, idiot. Not turning around. Go on, tie up. The lock's been left ready, so you're lucky. Left by someone who came through heading towards Limehouse.'

Polly leapt to the bank, feeling that at least she could tie up but horribly aware of the uphill lock just ahead. The lower gates were open and the water was at the same level as their cut. Verity followed her, checking the butty mooring strap, then handing her a windlass. 'This is yours. You'll lose it, we all do, and the bottom of the cut must be full of them, rusting quietly, but try not to. Stuff it in the belt of your trousers. We're taught to wear them down the front, like mine.'

Bet joined them, and they walked along the towpath to the top of the lock and looked down into it. The slimy walls reflected the sunshine of the cool day. The top gates were massive, and seemed to sit on a sill looming over the lower level; Polly imagined she could hear them groaning as they held back the water of the upper cut. Their balance beams stretched across the towpath, with a narrow platform running along the top of both. Polly stared, not knowing the first thing about opening the gate, or filling the lock to lift the boats so that they could continue up the hill. Alongside the lock was a small building, with an Office sign above the door.

Bet stood beside her, a cigarette behind her ear. Polly's mum would be appalled. Bet said, 'You'll be nipping along that platform, but not yet, and there's a railing – see? – which will keep you safe.'

There was more of a breeze up here, and it rustled the beech leaves. She continued, 'Paddles are very small gates, I suppose. The paddles are below the water, by the hinges of the gate, can you see them?'

Bet pointed them out. 'In order to fill the lock, you must bring in your boats, and then shut the lower lock gates behind them. Then you need to open, or raise, the paddles by winding up the ratchets – over here on top of the top gates – using your windlass. This will let the water through in a controlled way and lift the boat to the height of the upper cut. You will be climbing a staircase, by taking a step at a time – can you make any sense of that? – then you open the gates and Bob's your uncle, off you go.'

Verity stood the other side of Bet. 'You don't need brains, you just need brawn, darling, so that shouldn't be a problem.'

'I'll learn from you,' Polly shot back.

In between them Bet smiled. Polly had no idea how on earth she was going to move the balance beams to open and close the gates. Did she shove with her bum? But wouldn't that, in time, wear a hole in her trousers?

She sighed.

They seemed to be waiting, and she wondered why, but then a lad of about thirteen ran along the towpath and stood by the lower open gates. She heard a pat-patter approaching, and swallowed as Bet winked at her. At last she understood. Round the bend came a pair of boats and now both Verity and Bet laughed. Bet said, 'No, relax, not you this time, but watch the lock-wheeler; the lad who's run on ahead of his boats, just as you will cycle ahead of ours. Well, just as we'll all take turns doing.'

The motor reduced speed and glided slowly into the lock, keeping close up against the wall, its fender nuzzling the sill of the top gate. The butty followed on a short tow. The motorboat steerer lifted the short tow-rope from its stern stud, throwing it on to the fore-end counter of the butty as it glided slowly, slowly alongside until it too nudged the sill. Now, with the boats parallel, the steerer of each, one a man, one a woman, clambered up the narrow steps of the lock wall, each carrying a mooring strap attached at one end to the stud of their boat. They secured these to mooring studs along the lock kerb. The boy shut the lower gate on his side, then ran up to the higher front lock gate, crossed by the platform, and closed the other lower.

The lad then used the windlass he flicked from the back of his belt to raise the paddles on the top gate. Polly fidgeted with hers, down the front of her belt. She might move it to the back as it felt so awkward. Water gushed into the lock through the opened paddles raising the level. The woman climbed down the wall and on to the cabin roof, and then the counter. She disappeared into the cabin and they heard a clatter of pans.

Bet said, 'Not a moment is lost. She's cooking while the water does the work for a change.'

'We haven't eaten since breakfast,' said Verity.

Polly realised she was ravenous. Bet murmured, 'Sandwiches back on board, or you can always eat your fists.'

Verity frowned. 'She always says that.'

Ignoring her, Bet said, 'Watch the office, Polly, if you please. You too, Verity.'

The door of the office opened and the boater handed the officer some paperwork, which was ticked, then reclaimed.

Bet said, 'The lock-keeper's noting that they've been through the lock. It's a way of keeping tabs.' The lock was filling. As the boats rose with the water, the steerer waited on the lock kerb, shortening the mooring strap, while the lad altered the strap on the other side. When the cabin roof was level with the steerer, he stepped on to the roof of his motor cabin, and then the counter, waiting until the lock water was on a level with the upper cut.

Once this happened, the boy looked down the cut the way they had come, then at Bet, who nodded. Whatever message passed between them was one Polly hadn't understood, but she knew better than to ask. She would wait to be told.

The boy leapt on to the motor, the steerer reattached the tow-rope to the butty and revved the engine, as the lock-keeper opened the gates. 'Leading his duckling,' Polly breathed.

Bet nudged Polly, 'See what's coming.' A motor and butty appeared round the bend from the Limehouse direction, wanting to travel up the 'staircase'. Polly said, 'The lock's full. They'll have to empty it first.'

Verity sniggered. 'Wrong, darling. We'll have to do it.'

Bet said, 'I told the lad. Didn't you see?'

Polly shook her head. 'That's what the nod meant?'

They shoved the beams with their bums until the top gates closed. Then Verity, her windlass at the ready, helped Polly to fix the windlass on the end of the paddle spindle of one top gate, before doing her own. Together they half turned the ratchet. They snatched off the windlass as the paddle dropped down, blocking any more of the top water from entering the lock.

'Now to let the water out of the lock, ready for the approaching boats,' Verity yelled.

The three women hurried to the bottom gate. Polly fitted her windlass on the spindle by herself this time, and wound as Verity ordered, huffing and puffing and struggling. It was hard but she got her paddle to open fully, and the water started emptying out of the lock into the lower cut. Polly watched the swirling, turbulent surface as the water drained through the lower gate paddles. Finally all was still. In the lock the water was at the lowest it could go, on a level with the lower cut.

'What now?' called Bet.

'Open the gates,' answered Verity, just behind Polly.

'Why?' called Bet.

Polly nodded. 'To have it ready for the boats that are waiting, parked up by the side now in front of ours,' she replied.

'Gold star for the girl,' called Bet. 'This is why we like one pair to go up, and then another pair to come down, taking turns for ever and a day. That way it's always ready for the next boat. However, it seldom happens, so don't get your hopes up.'

All three of them opened the gates, and watched as the pair of narrowboats repeated the actions of the ones before, with the steerer nodding and calling ''Ow do.'

'That's it,' Bet shouted and waved the girls back on to the boats. Once on their home-bound way, Bet insisted that Polly took the motor tiller. 'I'll be beside you, so come on, we haven't time for you to be precious. There's a war on, you know.'

Polly stared ahead, listening to the pat-patter, the slap of water against the sides, the cool wind in her face. Of course she knew, and for the first time in her life she'd worked a lock. She found herself smiling.

Chapter 7

Wednesday 27 October – at the depot

The next morning Polly stirred, her shoulders and back aching, her hands sore, her lids heavy, her ribs painful. She groaned, then lay still, wondering when her dad would knock on her door on his way to her mum with the early morning tea tray. 'Up you get, don't be late for the office.'

She felt her hair lift in a cold, cold breeze. What? She opened her eyes, wondering where she was. She turned on to her side. A mere eighteen inches from her the ashtray of the range was cold and dead. Above and behind her the slide was open, the source of the breeze. She shivered, and remembered – of course.

For a moment she shut her eyes again, her head throbbing, and looked up and backwards at the slide. Why on earth hadn't she shut it? A cold draught always gave her a headache. She thought back and ah – she had cooked scrambled eggs on toast for supper for the three of them before they went to the pub and on their return the smell of cooking had hit them. As Verity fell into the cross-bed Polly had decided to leave the slide open to clear the cabin of cooking smells.

At the thought of the food, her stomach heaved. Oh, the pub, what had possessed her? How many beers? She hardly drank. So, maybe it wasn't the draught. She struggled to sit up, shoving back the stiff army blankets, feeling sick, her head worse. Well, that would teach her, and she'd never, ever drink a whole pint so quickly again. Her mum would be shocked. Half a pint in a woman's glass was the thing, if indeed a lady drank beer at all. But she'd bought two pints, hadn't she? Did she drink them both? She must have been mad, and was obviously no lady.

They'd returned along the hardstanding of the lay-by, past the tied-up boats, Bet hushing Verity, who had wanted to sing 'The White Cliffs of Dover' – Verity, who was well on the way to being plastered – and Polly who was feeling not quite in control of her legs and a million miles from wanting to sing. She had just wanted her bed.

Polly swung her legs on to the floor, in a panic now to get dressed because she needed to run for the toilet. She dragged on her clothes, refusing to even think of sitting on the bucket in the back-end. She pushed open the cabin doors, crossed the counter to the bank, and rushed as fast as she dared the quarter of a mile to the depot yard and the lavatory, where she sat, her head in her hands, wanting to go home, to lie in a bed, to have a wardrobe, and a kitchen downstairs with her mother doing the best she could with the ration.

Someone knocked on the door. A man. 'Are you building the damn thing?'

'So sorry, sorry.' She dragged up her trousers and hurried out. He shouldered past her in his blue overalls, saying, 'Go and make a cuppa, you look like hell but you can throw a mean dart, I'll say that for you.'

He slammed the door shut behind him. She groaned and headed back to the butty. Darts? Then she remembered that Verity had picked up the darts from the shelf in the public bar, thrown a few and she couldn't have been drunk because they hit the spot. Soon there had been a bit of a match between the depot boys and the *Marigold*, for Bet could play too, but not as well as Polly, because Will had taught her. He had learned at Scout Camp, and on returning home had created a cork dartboard which he had set up in the shed, and dragged her dad in to play with him.

Together they had taught her, in between laughing hard enough to make their mum come out to stand and watch. Then they had given her mum the darts and she had thrown three bullseyes in a row. Into the silence she'd said, 'I had a brother too, you know. A twin as well and he taught me to play. He died in the war, at Ypres.' The laughter had faded, but her mum said, 'He wouldn't want me to mope, and I feel he's still with me. You never really lose your twin. Life's for living, don't you forget that.'

They had played on all summer until something else took their fancy.

Polly had forgotten all of that, and her mum had forgotten to live. But the memory of those days made her feel that her mum would remember, one day, and so, too, would Polly. She hugged the memory as she hurried through the yard. All around, men were busying themselves. She ducked and wove through them. What on earth was the time? She tried to hurry once she reached the start of the lay-by, but steadied down as her head swam.

As she walked she looked down at her dirty trousers, grubby red jumper, muddy boots, and became painfully aware of her unbrushed hair.

The boats she passed were alive with activity. Women were washing down the cabin sides. The tillers had been removed from some, and others were turned like theirs; children and men were splicing rope while their wives made breakfast or washed clothes. Polly kept her eyes on the way ahead.

Bet had reminded her how to splice when they returned to the lay-by from Cowley yesterday afternoon, reversing into their spot. Polly had felt she'd shafted like a professional, but Verity had put her right, muttering, 'Don't butter your parsnips yet, ducky, you've a long way to go.'

Now she passed the *Seagull* and *Swansong*, but didn't look. She hopped on to the *Marigold*. Verity was up, laying kindling on to the cold ash, calling to Polly as she stood on the counter. 'Kettle's on for a pot of tea. I have a mouth like the bottom of a birdcage so I fancy something tasty. We'll have bread and your mother's marmalade – so quaint of her to beaver away doing little things like that. I bet she knits too, probably that sweater? Well, watered-down beer or not, the pub did the job. I slept the night through, and now I'm off to the lavatory, which I imagine is where you've just been. Get your bed put away and finish laying the fire.' She dusted off her hands, leapt up the steps, across the counter and off down the lay-by.

Polly took her place in the cabin. The smell of the Primus, and its hiss as it heated the kettle, reminded Polly of a charabanc journey to the seaside with her mum. They'd sat behind the windbreak and Mum had pumped up the pressure on the small camping stove. Polly cleared her blankets and pillow, wishing it was Verity she was stuffing in the cupboard beneath the bed with the bed covers.

She shovelled coal from the coal-box beneath the bottom step of the cabin, washed her hands in the painted bowl, brushed her hair, cut the bread, dug out the marmalade from the cupboard, checked her watch. It was 8 a.m., much later than the 5.30 a.m. Bet had spoken of last evening.

The kettle had finally boiled, so she turned off the Primus and poured water on the tea leaves they were reusing from yesterday. She smeared a minuscule portion of the rationed butter on her bread, and showed the knife to the marmalade so it would last longer. If there was a complaint, Verity could go and boil her head.

She poured her tea, adding evaporated milk, carried her breakfast outside and left it on the cabin roof, then dashed down the steps and found her pen and paper. She must write to Reggie, and to her parents. This she did, leaning on the cabin top as the wind flipped the corners of the paper and she sipped her tea. There was little she could say except that everything was going well, though they hadn't yet been given orders, and that she hoped they were all right. On Reggie's she added, 'and do try and be safe'. Then thought what a daft thing to say.

She put both letters in envelopes, licked them down, and stuck on a stamp. She turned Reggie's envelope over and over. Reggie's presence in her life lifted the shadow from her mum a little and, after all, he was nice and kind, but Polly didn't know if that was enough. Shouldn't you miss the man you were stepping out with? Shouldn't you go to sleep dreaming of him? But that was probably because she didn't really think of anyone . . .

'Writing home, that's what I like to see, Polly.' It was Bet, who was dragging her hand through her hair as she stood outside the butty, *Horizon*'s, cabin door. 'I felt we could all do with a bit of a break, so I let us sleep on. It's the last late morning we'll have until the end of a second run, when you will both have a couple of days' leave, while I interview a few more trainees.'

Polly was quiet for a moment, then said, 'But that means Verity will do three runs before she has leave. Is that fair?'

Bet grinned. 'She had two days while I sorted out Phyllis, so it's quite fair, don't worry, but nice thought. Now, may I join you? We usually eat together.'

'Of course. Tea is brewing,' Polly said. 'There's bread and Mum's marmalade.'

Bet stepped on to *Marigold*'s counter. 'How scrumptious. I love home-made marmalade, and I bet it's been hoarded for a couple of years, and will be heavenly. Clever woman, your mother.'

'Yes,' Polly agreed, though she had never thought of her mum like that, and it cheered her.

As the next couple of hours wore on there was still no order for them, though the tannoy boomed out every so often, calling for Steerer Mercy, Steerer Stennings, Steerer Ambrose, and so it went on. Polly was half relieved because the whole thing seemed so daunting and Verity so difficult, but was also half disappointed because she wanted to learn.

While they waited, Polly was given another lesson in splicing rope, weaving the strands together, binding them until her fingers felt on fire, but at least her head was clearing. Then it was time for both trainees to polish the brass in the cabin – the range bar again, the horse brasses, the knobs on the stove – and wash down the walls and the ceiling. They dusted the pierced plates, and cleaned the porthole. They heated water on the kerb and washed their clothes, hanging them on the line behind the back-end. They refilled the water can.

At 10.30, Verity made porridge, which they ate on the counter, putting the bowls on the roof. Verity said, 'You'll normally be eating mid-morning breakfast as we go along, so enjoy a moment of peaceful grub while you can.'

Bet called from the butty, 'I've put together a shopping list. Verity, you nip off into Southall please, while Polly is introduced to the delights of wiping down *Marigold*'s external cabin walls.' She waved the list, and sent it across from the *Horizon* as a paper dart. It landed at Verity's feet. 'Good-oh,' Verity muttered. 'Anything to get off the bloody boat on to terra firma. My head is still swimming.'

She nipped down to the cabin, and Polly heard the rattle of the kitty jar, then a bellow, 'Get down here, Polly.'

Polly left her porridge, which was cooling rapidly, and leaned through the doors. 'Can I help?'

'I think you already have, but not me – you've helped yourself to the kitty money, haven't you? It's short.' Verity brandished the jar containing the coins at her.

'Hang on, what do you mean?'

'Some has been taken.'

'Well, not by me. Why on earth would I?' Polly made her way down the two steps and, feeling suddenly strange, sat on the side-bed.

Verity shook the jar in her face. 'We're five shillings short and you said you couldn't afford to come to the pub, and then you came, and I believe you bought two pints. What's more, the kitty hasn't ever been short in the past. Work it out, why don't you.'

There was a heavy silence, which was broken by a knock on the cabin door. Bet stood there. 'If I can hear you from the butty, Verity, so can others.'

Verity shook the jar at Bet. 'But Bet, no one locks their doors, because there is a code of no stealing, so it has to be—'

'Let's just sort this out quietly, Verity.' Bet looked from one to the other, but her gaze lingered on Polly, who said stiffly, 'I have never stolen in my life. I have money, but I have to make it last, which is why I said that last night. I brought money from the locker.'

'Calm down, Polly. I was just thinking, not accusing.' Bet was in the cabin now, her back against the unlit range.

Verity grabbed a bag and pushed past Bet. She dashed up the steps to the counter. 'Bugger that for a load of rubbish.'

Bet shouted, 'Verity, come back and let's just think this through.'

Verity stood at the entrance to the cabin. 'Well, go on then. You stood up for Phyllis all the time, and now you're doing it with Polly.'

Bet looked from Polly to Verity. 'I'm not standing up for anyone, Verity. As I've said so often before, I'm just trying to think it through. You're right, the boaters don't steal, neither do the blokes in the depot, but who knows, there's a war on, we never know who anyone is and the depot takes on new people all the time. But what we don't do is turn on one another. Verity, you must stop seeing favouritism where there is none. You simply must or how can we pull together as a team? You simply do not accuse people, you wait—'

But Verity had gone. Bet shook her head, and climbed up the steps on to the counter. Polly heard her say to herself, 'I have to try harder to make this work. She's scared off one girl, and I'm not having it again. What on earth is it that has made her so defensive, so volatile, so angry?'

Polly's head throbbed. Poor Bet, how could she be so patient with them all, how on earth could she keep giving chances, and yes, what was wrong with Verity? Or perhaps she, Polly Holmes, was just bloody wet and irritating? Language, Polly, her mother would say, and quite frankly, Polly couldn't care less because her head ached, she felt sick and who on earth took the money?

By the time Verity returned there was still no call for Steerer Burrows, only the scratchy music the tannoy played in between calling others to the office. Verity packed away the shopping, what little there was of it, while Polly washed the outside of the butty cabin as well, to keep out of the way, shoving up the sleeves of her red jumper. Bet stayed in her cabin

103

doing paperwork and then headed for the depot at midday without a word to either of them. At midday Bet called to them from the bank, 'I've been to the office. No orders for us yet awhile, so we'll eat in the canteen. Chop-chop, let's get in the queue.'

Just then a call came over the tannoy for Steerer Hopkins and almost immediately Saul and Joe left the *Seagull* and hurried towards the office as Polly joined Bet on the bank, pulling Will's white sweater on top of her red one. She needed the barrier it would provide between herself and Verity. 'I could do with some dinner,' she said.

Verity jumped down beside her. 'Dinner? Surely you mean lunch.'

Polly flushed. She had forgotten her mum's lessons. It must be the headache, the sense of every noise being too loud. Bet said, 'Verity, remember you're not the only one struggling to cope with the fallout of the war, or a headache from too much beer. You know very well it's called dinner at the depot, so, please, just go ahead and save us a place.' Bet turned away, but not before squeezing Polly's arm while Verity flounced off.

Quietly they traipsed past the boats, and the women washing down the cabins or hanging up washing. Bet said softly, 'I'm right in thinking the kitty is nothing to do with you?'

Polly said, 'I'm sorry you feel you had to ask.'

'As a trainer that's exactly what I do have to do, and I have already asked Verity, though I am absolutely sure there is quite another answer to all this. I just don't know what.'

Silence fell between them. They strode into the ever busy yard heading towards the canteen, just as Saul and Joe came out of the office, talking together. Saul nodded to the two women, hands in his pockets, his red kerchief tied at his neck. His eyes stayed on Polly for a moment, his disgust visible. Joe's hands were also in his pockets and he studied the ground as he hurried to keep up with Saul.

Polly lifted her head, ignoring them both, just saying to Bet, 'So, people did hear. How very lovely. And now let me answer your question loud and clear so there is no misunderstanding by anyone. The loss of money from the kitty has nothing to do with me, but if you think it has I will leave.' She was shouting, because she wanted Saul and Joe to hear, but why? What did it matter what they thought?

Bet said, 'Then the matter is completely closed, and it will be written up as such. There are procedures I have to go through, you see.'

Nothing further was said, but Polly thought of Mr Burton's office, the calm and courtesy of the work, the conveyance documents and wills she had typed up. She almost turned around and headed to *Marigold* to pick up her things, but somehow she kept on walking. Why should she give this lot, especially Verity, the satisfaction of chasing her off?

Polly dug her hands in her trouser pockets and lengthened her stride, her head up, but she couldn't rid herself of Saul's expression, those dark eyes, his thick hair, so curly, his strong tanned arms, his sleeves rolled up as though he was impervious to the wind. She turned and snatched a look. He was almost at the lay-by turn-off, walking with that easy stride that was almost a prowl. Suddenly he turned, and for a moment their eyes met. She spun round, feeling the heat in her face, and nearly stumbled.

'Steady,' Bet said, reaching out a hand.

'I'm fine,' Polly snapped, confused.

Bet patted her arm. 'Yes, you are, of course you are.' They walked on. The yard was quieter as it was lunchtime, and they headed straight for the canteen, seeing Verity emerging from the lavatory, more lipstick on and her hair tidied, the tortoiseshell slide in place.

Bet sighed. 'She's been dawdling, so I'm afraid there'll be no place saved.' She shoved open the door into the canteen and they were met by the smell of cabbage and a blast of warm moist air, overhung with cigarette smoke.

There was a long table down the middle of the room, at which sat mechanics, carpenters, and painters too, from the look of their paint-spattered overalls. Alf, from the Enquiries desk, was sitting at the end of the table, head down, shovelling in his dinner.

They picked up trays, Verity pushing in front of Polly but staying behind Bet in the serving queue, which moved remarkably quickly. Soon, the women in hairnets and white overalls behind the food counter were slapping liver and bacon, and a great mound of cabbage and mash, on to their plates. 'There you are, ducks. Home away from home.'

One grinned at Polly. 'Still pale around the gills, are you, eh? I heard you thrashed our old buggers in the pub.' To Verity another said, 'You threw a few good darts too, I hear, though if I were you, I'd have made 'em 'ave a bet. Adds a bit of spice, it do. Surprised you won, especially you, Blondie, after you downed more'n the blokes, or so it's said.'

Verity snapped, 'It's like as living amongst a load of gossiping old women.'

The woman said, 'Less of the old.'

Bet raised her eyebrows. 'I'm running a kindergarten here,' she said.

The women roared with laughter, and Verity shrugged. Perhaps, thought Polly, she'd just made a mistake counting the money because of her hangover? She hadn't thought to check the jar herself, she'd been so shocked. Looking down the table when she took her seat, she thought that there were so many who could have nipped into the cabin, or could even do so now, and they hadn't locked the doors. But how could they? It would intimate that they didn't trust the boaters.

She ate her liver though she had little appetite, finished, and laid her knife and fork together, while her headache thumped. The man next to her said, 'There's sponge and custard for afters, duck. Go on, do you good. And I want you on my darts team next time. You've got a cool head, and a steady hand. Who taught you, then?'

'Oh, someone I once knew,' she said, and then, out of the blue, added, 'My brother, actually. My Will, he was really good.'

The man, old and grizzled with paint around his cuticles and across the back of his hands, said, very quietly, 'Was?'

She nodded, suddenly feeling unutterably lonely. 'Yes, was.'

'I have a son who "was". Now go and get some pudding, and you take care of yourself, you hear. Life goes on, and some day you'll join it again. Or so the missus tells me.'

He stacked his empty pudding bowl on top of his dirty plate, and stood up. 'You remember that, because you ain't there yet, but you will be. See you when you're back from your run. You might have come on a bit by then.' He nodded, and was gone.

She watched as he put his dishes on a trolley and left the canteen, and just for a moment she felt something real stir, not just fleeting irritation, not . . . Then it was gone. She looked down at the gravy-smeared plate. Verity leaned forward. 'What was that about?'

Polly said, slowly and clearly but quietly, 'Yet again I must tell you that something is none of your bloody business.' She rose, to fetch three bowls of sponge and custard. 'You can take my dirty bowl when you take your own, Verity, as a thank-you.'

Verity stared, shocked, but Bet nodded. 'Fair exchange,' she said. 'And I'll take the dinner plates.' Someone called from the canteen door. 'Tannoy for Steerer Burrows. Steerer Burrows to the office.'

Bet flung her hand in the air. 'Coming.' She nodded to Polly. 'After my pudding, though. Chop-chop, if you will, Polly.'

While Polly hurried to collect the pudding, Bet piled up the three plates and took them to the trolley. Polly asked a burly man in grubby overalls if she could jump the queue, because the tannoy had called them. He nodded and gestured her before him. 'Can't get in the way of someone with a strong throwing arm, can I?' He laughed. She smiled, collected the pudding, hurried back to the table. Bet, still standing, snatched it, gobbled it down, then slapped the bowl back on the table. 'Verity, don't forget the bowls. See you both back at the motor. Chop-chop.'

She was gone, followed by Polly, who wanted to see what was entailed. She waved to the women behind the counter, and then opened the door, striding through the yard, her hands in her pockets, the wind riffling through her hair. She looked down at Will's sweater.

One day, Will, I will feel really alive again, and so will Mum and Dad. I think I know that now, but when, and how?

Chapter 8

27 October – after lunch the same day at the depot

Polly passed the short queue of boaters filing slowly into the office. Bet stood, arms crossed, tapping her foot, at the rear. 'You go on,' Bet called. 'When Verity comes along, make sure the boats are absolutely ready to go.'

Polly nodded, but didn't know what that meant, though she'd be told by Madam Clement in short order. 'On second thoughts,' Bet called, 'wait here with me.'

Polly stopped, walked up to her, hands still in pockets, and whispered, 'Why? So I'm not alone with the kitty?'

Bet raised her eyebrows. 'Don't be childish, Polly, it's so you know what to do when you're a steerer. It's time to grow up, and park that nonsense until we understand quite what happened. I'm not having a couple of kids on the scheme playing silly buggers.'

Polly could think of nothing to say, so stayed quiet as the queue shuffled forward, while the hammering from the sheds and the hoarse shouts of the workmen carried on all around. She saw Verity leave the canteen and saunter towards them, but Bet waved her in the direction of the lay-by.

'I'm just showing Polly the ropes as I showed you, and if the wind changes your face will stay like that, so you can stop being silly, too. As I said to Angie in the canteen, it's like running a kindergarten, so just get on as per usual, and make sure the ropes, water can and dipper are all in place, and that we have some spare windlasses. If not, pick some up from the blacksmith.'

Steerers were coming out of the office door every couple of minutes carrying sheets of paper, which they stuffed in their pockets. Each time that happened, the queue shuffled forward a few feet until finally Bet and Polly reached the innards of the office. A man eyed them as he finished a telephone conversation, slammed the receiver down and reached towards a pile of papers. 'Tell me your boat's ready, Bet? Bit of a rush on, all of a sudden.'

'Ready and able, Ted, but don't know about willing.'

Ted grunted, checking his list. 'Well, ready and able will do if it gets a couple of boats run by daft women to toddle along to Limehouse Basin, or Regent's Canal Dock, whichever you like to call it – and pick up from there a load of steel billets to Brum. And trust me, they will be rusty, having come from our Yank friends across the sea. Thank the Lord that particular merchant vessel escaped the U-boats, but I gather the same can't be said for lots more in the convoy.'

'See, Polly, there's no damn time for nonsense,' Bet said, taking a card he handed her. 'The trip card,' she told Polly. He added her loading orders, and several pink cards with North Bound on them.

She stuffed it all in her pocket, and turned on her heel as the telephone rang again. She headed towards the door at a rate of knots. 'Chop-chop, Polly. We're supposed to drop the pinkies off at certain points along the way, and usually forget.'

Ted called, 'I bloody heard that.'

Bet laughed, and waved without turning. 'Get back to the telephone, and break my heart by talking to your fancy woman.'

'Nah, don't give the game away, the missus'll have me guts for garters,' he yelled. Then yelled again: 'Next steerer, come along now, we ain't got all bloody day.'

Once out in the yard Polly diverted to the toilet, hearing Bet's laugh in her wake. Polly called back, 'You go on now, boss, we ain't got all bloody day.'

Bet laughed again, 'Hurry, and brace up, because you're on the motor with me.' Polly did hurry, and once on board the *Marigold* she saw the tiller was returned to its rightful position, looking very much like a swan's neck. She joined Bet in the engine room as she fired up the engine, which promptly died. Bet clicked her tongue. 'Watch closely, this'll be you coaxing the beast one day.'

Bet pulled the choke, fired the engine again and, finally pat-pattering, the engine caught, but died once more. Bet swore, and shut down the choke a fraction. 'Come on, you ruddy thing, I've polished you till you shine, so stop buggering about.'

The engine clearly heard, because it fired, and held. Bet backed out, wiping her hands down her trousers. 'Come to the counter. You'll need to cast off both boats, and then be ready to catch Verity's tow-rope and slap it over our counter stud. It'll be a short tow until we get a load up, then we'll go to the long snubber.'

Polly followed her along the gunwale and on to the counter, leaping to the bank, where she cast off the mooring straps for motor and butty. Verity caught hers, and coiled it. Bet took the tiller and Polly jumped back on board the *Marigold* as it eased from the kerb, while Verity ran the planks and crouched on the butty's tiny fore-end counter. 'Don't drop the ruddy tow,' she yelled at Polly, and threw it. 'Hook it over your counter stud.'

Polly did. There was a jerk, and then the butty slid in behind *Marigold* as Verity ran back along the butty's top planks. They were off. It was 2.30 in the afternoon.

Bet said, as Polly stood on the gunwale, looking over the length of the boat to the cut beyond, 'Well, time for tea, and light the range while you're about it, if you will.' Polly did.

They pat-pattered until they reached the fork to Limehouse Basin along the Paddington Arm of the Grand Union Canal via Alperton. While Polly lit the range she heard Bet blowing what sounded like a hunting horn. Polly stuck her head out through the doors. 'Seen a fox, have you?'

Bet was staring ahead, as they approached a bridge. She blew the horn again. 'It was my father's. He enjoyed hunting when he was younger. He and my mother would do it together but I was an odd little thing and preferred the fox. I could have understood it more if he had been a military man, charging about on a horse, but he was in the navy until his ship sank in the last war and he spent too long at sea on a raft, all alone. He was never quite the same again and the only thing he enjoyed was the hunt. Now watch, Polly, I'm heading to the centre of the cut, where the bridge is highest and the cut is deepest.'

Bet steered into the middle, heading towards the bridge while Polly watched carefully. 'We have an electric horn on *Marigold*, Polly, but this is better, especially for tight turns like this fork. If the oncoming boaters can't hear this, they've no right to be on the cut. If they do hear it, they'll wait for us to come through this upcoming bridge hole. It's also how I get your attention on the butty, so be warned. No doubt Verity's mother has a bell which has the same effect on the butler.'

Only now did they enter the bridge hole, and Bet pointed up at the worn stones. 'This is where the horse-drawn boaters would walk the boats through while the lad took the horse over the top and down to the towpath the other side.'

Bet then peered to look behind her in the dim light of the bridge hole, and then to the front again. 'Verity's steering through really well. Once we're out of the murk, and heading on a straight course, you can steer. We'll be going up to Alperton where we'll tie up for the night. You and Verity can take the Tube into Piccadilly, or wherever you like. Do you good to spend some time together, in view of the dust-up, and I trust you to be a good influence, and get her back upright and tickety-boo. Hard as it may be, try to be a friend to her, and remember how much she drank last night in the pub. It happens far too often and can't go on, and if we're to be a team we must help her, somehow.'

For an hour or two they drank tea, or cocoa, and took turns with the steering. The butty was on a short tow and Verity could be seen resting her book and her tea on the cabin roof, reading, because so little steering was needed. 'Once it's on the long seventy-foot snubber with a load on board, it will be a different story. The butty-steerers have to stay alert. It's a heavy load to handle, remember.'

A pair of boats were approaching, and as Bet steered to the right, so did the others. They passed left side to left side, or port to port, the sailor in Polly translated. The engine pat-pattered on and on, the water slapped against the bank. Bet didn't steer right up to the edge of the cut. 'We need to be careful we don't ground her, or you'll be shafting again. The cut is always shallower at the edge, or as the boaters would say, the bottom is too near the top and it's so often a very muddy bottom.'

Another laden boat and butty passed by. Twins, Polly thought, and then stopped. She looked ahead, standing on the gunwale, leaning in, feeling safe and strangely at home. She was on the water; a quiet artery, not the surging sea but it was enough. There were two golfers on a fairway and a factory, grey and high, with a pitched roof appeared to the left. Then the country opened out into fields, and there were hawthorn trees by the towpath. It was her turn to steer, and now Bet was on the gunwale, ready to step to the counter and take over if need be.

Polly steered round a long bend, and snatched a look behind. Verity was watching, her hand behind her on the tiller. The wind was cold; more leaves had been blown into the cut and floated alongside, sucked from the bank by their wash. They approached another bridge.

'Bet,' Polly called.

Bet turned to look at the bridge as she sat on the roof, and smiled.

'Well, sound the electric horn, or blow mine, and take it through. I can reach you in less than a second.'

On the bridge children were leaning over, shouting at them. 'Dirty bloody boaters. Gyppos, scum, the lot of you.' Polly sounded the horn. One of them jumped back, startled. She sounded it again. There was nothing coming so she steered to the centre, and as she entered the bridge one of the children spat, and the gob landed on the counter between her and the cabin.

Polly looked at Bet, who insisted, 'Keep your eyes on the cut. This happens all the time, try and ignore it, or put an umbrella up.'

Verity's voice rose behind them. 'How dare you, you little guttersnipes,' she called. 'You need a damned good spank. It's just so disgusting.'

As they exited the bridge hole another gob landed, this time on the cabin roof. Bet muttered, 'At least it missed the water can, and me.'

Polly felt quite sick.

'That's just so disgusting,' she echoed Verity. 'She's right, they need a good smack.'

Bet shrugged, looking back at the bridge. 'You're right, and they're so wrong to despise the boaters, but they do, as do their parents, probably. Can't they see them, day after day, taking loads up the cut in all weathers, their faces chapped, hands bleeding from the cold, their blisters septic, their kids unable to go to school because they're not in one place long enough. Standing out in all weathers, soaked through . . .'

Polly stared at her, then groaned. 'Oh, Lordy, time to stop talking, Bet, if you don't want to scare the pants off me, because I rather think you're explaining my fate.'

Bet laughed loud and long.

Polly continued, 'No wonder Verity's hands are as they are, and then to be spat at, it's an absolute disgrace. Is it every bridge?'

Bet was smiling. 'No, sweet child, not every bridge, but some, and remember you are only here for the duration. The boaters live with it.'

Polly heard the sadness in her voice and said, 'You like doing this, don't you, Bet?'

Bet stepped on to the counter as they passed some beech trees, from which starlings flew in a cluster. 'I love the sound of the water lapping against the hull at night, the owls hooting so near us, the herons, otters, voles, passing towns, tying up at pubs, where we're part of the place for a night, then somewhere else the next day. I feel free on the cut.'

'Did you start on narrowboats with the war?' The tiller was steady in Polly's hand, though the wind was so cold her fingers were numb.

'A friend introduced me long before. She lived on one, can you believe? She bought *Blossom* and chugged her to a shipbuilder. He put in a deck the length of the hold, though he thought she was mad. Then he built cabins to her specification. I used to join her for school holidays. I taught at a girls' boarding school, English actually, before buying into the motorboat, and making it my home too. We still have it, but only for holidays. We are on terra firma now, but near the canal. Keep your eye on this bend, Polly.'

Bet jumped down on to the counter and took over the Grand Union red, white and blue tiller. 'She had a canal artist paint her narrowboat red, with a riot of flowers. *Marigold* will always be G.U. colours but

I got Saul to paint the roses and castles on her door. He had his own boat, or his parents did, and that was quite a picture, but being independent is too difficult now. The loads are far more regular working on a company boat.'

They pulled in to the bank at Alperton in the early evening and while they tied up Polly wondered what had once bound Bet so tightly that she needed such freedom. Had school got to her?

The tie-up was close to the Tube station, with the Piccadilly Line taking passengers straight to Picca-dilly Circus. Verity put on her glad rags, but pulled a face when Bet insisted the girls went together; still, she could not object when Bet pulled her 'trainer' card, and added, 'I'm happy for you to have the evening out, but only if you both go and you must stick together, because it's not safe in the blackout; you never know who is around. What's more, we must press on tomorrow, so I want you to be each other's keeper, and make sure you don't miss the last Tube. Walk back from the station to the cut with all senses alert. And please, please, no hangover. After all, miracles happen and we could be loading some time tomorrow.'

Polly felt far too tired but if she didn't go, Verity couldn't, and she still hadn't posted her letters and there was bound to be a letterbox somewhere along the way. She pulled on her wool skirt, licked a brown pencil and ran a line up the back of her legs in lieu of stockings. She dragged a comb through her hair, and slung on her mackintosh. Verity pulled on her stockings, adjusted her suspenders, eased her dress over her hips, held up her handbag mirror and applied lipstick.

She peered at Polly and grimaced. 'Do, please, put some slap on, darling, you look fresh from the farm. As we're to stick together you will have to come with me to a place in Piccadilly without sawdust on the floor, and no whelks for sale at the bar. Surely you have a better skirt, and perhaps a shawl rather than that ghastly old mac? You resemble a poor church mouse, and are as dowdy.'

Polly eyed Verity's silk dress and light wool coat that must have been expensive because there was not a crease to behold, even though it had been stowed beneath the cross-bed. 'No, I have nothing better here, and I look like most other people who restrict themselves to the clothes ration and save their best, for best. And that's at home.' She wasn't going to admit that there was absolutely nothing better hanging anywhere else in her whole world.

Verity put on high heels, staring all the while at Polly's court shoes and shaking her head. 'Oh, I do wonder if you're feeling too tired? You do look weary, darling. How about an early night, eh?'

Bet said from the doorway, 'Not a chance, Verity, it's both of you, or neither. I want you back bright-eyed and bushy-tailed, unlike last time you hit Piccadilly.' She disappeared again, and Polly followed.

Bet was waiting on the counter, leaning against the

cabin, smoking a cigarette. The tiller had been reversed. Bet mused, 'I think we will take it out next time. It would give us just that bit more room.' Polly stood, watching the searchlights stabbing the early evening sky. Her dad would have left for his ARP duties by now, her mum would be turning on the wireless to hear another voice, since she wouldn't have anyone to talk to.

She watched the searchlights more closely. Was Reggie heading off somewhere tonight? Would he be back to read her letter or . . . She sighed at such stupid questions, to which there were no answers. Somewhere a siren wailed. Was that a stray bomber dumping his load, or an ARP exercise?

'Penny for them,' Bet said.

Polly smiled. 'They're not worth a penny.'

Bet inhaled again, then stubbed her cigarette out on the saucer. She said softly, 'Mind what I said. Stick together this evening, cargo-carrying is important, and so are my crew. Keep yourselves safe.' She sighed. 'In fact, be her friend. I believe she needs one, and after all, that's what being a team means.'

Chapter 9

27 October – evening

Polly followed Verity as they emerged from Piccadilly Circus Underground and turned left down Regent Street. In spite of her high heels Verity tore along, weaving in and out of the other pedestrians, all of them holding their practically useless torches. Taxis, buses and cars with similarly inadequate lights picked their way along to Eros at little more than walking pace. Verity suddenly jerked to a stop, stood on the kerb and waited to cross. Three GIs joined them, talking loudly of New York as they looked for a gap in the traffic. Verity was doing the same. Polly waited with her.

A GI sergeant turned to Verity. 'Hi, gorgeous girl, let me see you across. Who knows, we could be heading in the same direction.'

Polly stared ahead because it wasn't safe to talk to strangers, but to her horror, Verity took the GI's arm. 'Just to cross the road, then, in the spirit of transatlantic friendship. I've been to New York too. Those skyscrapers, so high, but the streets can be so windy.'

A gap developed in the traffic and they had all

begun to cross when one of the other GIs turned, waiting in the middle of the road for Polly to catch up. He grinned in the gloom and walked beside her. She ignored him. 'I'm Al, and you're . . . ?'

'Verity's friend.'

'You Brits,' he sighed, 'are as cold and grey as your little island.'

'Our little island feels a bit colourless after the battering we've had. Just look around and imagine your own home town in smithereens.' Her tone was as cold as the month.

'Here we are, 'n' all, helping you, and still you don't like us,' he grumbled, ambling beside her. They reached the pavement just as a bus swept past, hooting. Polly jumped. He said, 'You're safe on the sidewalk, honey.'

Verity was charging down Regent Street again, and her companion seemed to change gear effortlessly, lengthening his lazy stride to keep up with her. Polly heard Verity's laugh, but it was one full of screeching falsehood. The GI who walked alongside Polly said, 'My mom writes and asks me if I'm safe, I tell her yes, but that I'm cold and that I miss her and Boise, in Idaho, and so I do. Don't you feel sorry for a li'l ole stranger in a strange land?'

Ahead, Verity had stopped at the entrance to Jermyn Street and was shaking her head at the other two GIs. 'No,' she was insisting. 'So sorry, it's a private party, but another time.' She waggled her torch at Polly. 'Do come along.'

Al grabbed Polly's arm, pulling her to a stop. He dug in his pocket and pulled out a packet. She flashed her torch over the cellophane, and saw it contained silk stockings. 'Here you are, Miss Polly.'

Polly stepped back, appalled. 'No, I'm not that sort of girl.'

He did not release her arm. 'I know, Miss Polly, that's why you should take them. Your friend's wearing some, and you ain't. All you've got is that line you girls draw up the back of your bare legs. I saw it in the miserable ole lights of the buses. You're a nice girl, so you should have some too.'

Again she pulled away. 'That's kind, but no.'

She followed Verity into Jermyn Street, and then called back, 'Don't break your mum's heart, Al from Boise, Idaho. You get home safe, and make sure the others do as well.'

She waved goodbye, then ran after Verity, who was hurrying along the street, her torch playing over the pavement and flashing dimly up on to the house numbers. Polly caught up with her outside a terraced house with at least three floors. 'I thought we were going to a pub?'

Verity pulled her camel coat tighter around herself. 'It's similar, but very much more upper class. It's what's called a club. You can find a pub if you'd feel more comfortable.'

She waited for Polly's answer. Polly remembered Bet's words.

She said, 'I'll stick with you.'

'Come in as my guest, but do try and act the part. These are my smart friends. I don't want them to think I'm . . .' She stopped.

'Slumming?' Polly finished.

Suddenly Verity's eyes filled. 'Oh, do shut up, Polly,' she whispered, and lifted the brass knocker, banged it twice, paused, and then banged it once more. Polly stared at this girl. What had she said? A shutter in the door slid open, then slammed shut. The door opened. 'Good evening, Lady Verity, I trust you are well.'

The high voice of the huge muscular man in the dinner suit sounded inappropriate. 'Most well, thank you, George. This is Miss Polly Holmes, who is on my team. Hush-hush, you know.' She tapped her nose, in control again. George gave Polly the once-over. Verity stepped closer to him and whispered, 'Beggars can't be choosers, but she's nice enough.'

Polly heard, but had also heard Verity called a Lady – and why the glint of tears? why the whispered 'Hush-hush'?

'Of course, Lady Verity. Your friends are as usual in the blue room, I believe, and are expecting you, as the gin cocktails have been ordered.' He nodded them through into a long passageway with cream walls and brown and cream tiles on the floor. Verity led the way to the cloakroom desk at the end of the hall, where they handed over their coats to a young woman dressed in black. The lining of Polly's mackintosh was torn, and she waited for one of Verity's comments, but she was too busy straightening her seams to notice. Before the cloakroom attendant hung Polly's mac on the hanger, she shook it slightly and something fell to the ground.

Verity saw, and leaned over the counter. Polly craned her neck to see too. On the floor was a packet of silk stockings. Al of Idaho must have put it in her pocket. Oh well, how kind. She started to tell Verity as the attendant picked them up and replaced them in the pocket, but Verity was staring at Polly.

'So, not just the kitty, but my stockings too?' she muttered through thin lips.

Polly shook her head. 'You're wearing yours, so don't be absurd.'

Verity shook her head. 'I have other packets. Or had.'

The attendant held out a ticket. 'Your ticket, Lady Verity, for reclaiming your coat. I still 'ave the scarf you left behind at the time of your last visit. Incidentally, the GIs give these stockings to all the girls. I expect that's where these came from, as well as the ones you're wearin', Lady Verity. You obviously know a lot of GIs.'

She gave Polly her ticket, raising her eyebrows.

Polly smiled, and said, 'How interesting. Verity met three GIs at Piccadilly Circus, and they escorted us here. Al from Boise, Idaho offered me a pair, which I refused. But he must have put them in my pocket. I'll have to keep them now, not that they're much use on the canal boat.'

126

Verity had flushed, and now her colour deepened and she swung on her heel. 'Don't use the code here, Polly. No one is supposed to know our HQ lingo. Follow me, for heaven's sake.'

Verity almost ran up the stairs while Polly followed, calling to the attendant, 'Thank you, and keep the stockings, I won't need 'em.'

The girl grinned. 'No, I'll put them back in your pocket. I 'ave enough of me own from tips.'

Polly followed Verity. She had taken no notice of the accusation, beyond feeling a surge of irritation which had quickly died. Bet believed her, but what nonsense about codes was this ridiculous woman talking now? At the top of the stairs Verity was waiting, and pulled her to one side. Double doors were open to the right of them, and inside a swirl of people danced on a gleaming pale oak floor to the soft sound of a bass, saxophone and piano. Verity waved to someone who sat at a small circular table, several of which were dotted around the dance floor. She kept a bright smile on her face as she whispered, 'My friends think I'm in something secret. I have French, you see. They wouldn't understand the canal, and would be appalled.'

'Well, why are they your friends, in that case?' Polly said, and pulled free.

Verity looked suddenly at a loss and, once more, her eyes filled. After a moment, she muttered, 'Because they are, you silly girl, and always have been.'

'Then, if so, you can tell them, because they'll be interested for your sake, surely.'

'Oh, shut the hell up, Polly. Don't be so . . .' she paused. 'Simple. Just do as I say, for heaven's sake, or I'll never ever forgive you.'

'Of course I will. I just want to know why.'

But Verity was walking away, erect, her smile in place, her blonde hair immaculate. At the entrance to the room, she waved madly to a group gathered around a table, some standing, some sitting. The men were in officer's uniform, the women in silk dresses, or WAAF or some such uniforms. After only half an hour in their company Polly understood exactly why Verity had created a fiction, and also completely understood that these friends found her woollen skirt offensive, and stockingless legs beyond the pale. Nothing was actually said, but it didn't have to be.

They had made space for her at the table, of course, and a cocktail was ordered, but no one asked her to dance, which was a shame because she could jive with the best of them, courtesy of one of Will's friends. Was it Reggie? She didn't think so. Ah yes, it was Geoff. His regiment had been ordered to Singapore. Had he been killed or imprisoned?

She played with her cocktail and watched Verity dancing a sweeping quickstep with an RAF lieutenant. A girl, who had previously mentioned she had grown up near Verity in Sherborne, came back from the dance floor. Slumping down she fanned herself, her beau bending and laughing, and whispering in her ear.

She giggled, slapped at him, and said, 'Heavens, I'll be delivering a plane at dawn, flying who knows what, to who knows where. Quite frankly, darling, the Air Transport Auxiliary is exhausting but someone has to do it.'

Polly thought she was talking to her lieutenant, but he had turned to speak to a passing army officer, and it was to her that the girl was chatting, and she was offering her a cigarette from her gold cigarette case. 'Thank you, no,' Polly said.

The girl took one herself, tapped it on the case and waited. Her beau interrupted his conversation, leaned across and held out his lighter. 'There you are, Jeanie.'

'You're an angel, Brucie.' Jeanie inhaled, and blew the smoke into the air to join the general layer that hung like a mist below the ceiling. 'So, you're in the hush-hush thingy, Dolly. So strange that you have the same name as my maid.'

Polly avoided Jeanie's next exhale and replied, 'No, my name is Polly.'

She stared at Jeanie then said, 'It's not hard to remember the difference but satisfactory to forget if you're trying to diminish someone.'

There was silence, while Jeanie stared at her, then flicked some ash into the crystal ashtray. 'Not sure I understand you. But as I was saying, Polly, we're so pleased that dear Verity has picked herself up after her bit of foolishness, as the saying goes. We thought she'd end up in the WAAF or something else as useful, but no, though she says this hush-hush is something important?' It was a question which Polly allowed to hang between them before saying, 'Hush-hush means just that, Jeanie, but you should surely understand the term?'

Brucie was making hand signals, and Jeanie glared at Polly before smiling as Brucie made his way over to the bar with the army officer.

But Jeanie wasn't yet in retreat. 'It must mean she has to mingle with all sorts. I expect you feel a little awkward, being here, but don't. It's a good experience for you.'

Polly felt a hand on her shoulder. 'Hey, Miss Polly, fancy a turn around the floor?'

Polly stared up at Al, the GI. 'Good heavens.'

'Indeed, Miss Polly, good heavens. We dropped a pile of dough into the penguin's outstretched hand, and here we are. Hey, little lady, you with the cigarette, how about shifting that toosie of yours, so I can sit in your place and get to know Miss Polly a bit better? I'm sure you'll be happy to let us Yanks join your little group. About time we all got to know one another as we're helping to fight your war, don't ya think?'

Clearly the little lady being asked to move her toosie along didn't think it was a good idea at all, but by that time the other GIs had sat down, and the sergeant flicked a finger. Miraculously, within two seconds a waiter appeared. 'Give us another round of these drinks for our little Britishers, and don't forget some for us Yanks from across the sea, the ones with the dough.'

He threw a ten-bob note on the tray. 'For you – give us the check at the end. Just keep the drinks coming and your eyes on us, eh?' The waiter's eyes nearly popped out of his head, just as Al pulled her to her feet. 'Come on, honey, let's have a dance. Sounds to me as though it's to be a jive.'

It was, and Al threw her around the dance floor most successfully in spite of her pencil skirt, silencing the chattering of the upper classes, which seemed to be torn between appreciation and disapproval as she was twirled, thrown over a shoulder and beneath the legs, and generally loosened up. It was as good as a hot bath, and at the end there was a patter of applause. Patter, she thought. Pat-patter. They must be away before midnight.

She explained to Al, who asked why. Remembering her promise to Bet, she said, as Al swept her into a foxtrot, 'Our senior officer needs us on duty bright and early.' They danced, she drank water, Al drank some sort of cordial, while the others downed copious cocktails. The sergeant monopolised Verity, and together the two of them danced, and drank.

At eleven Polly rose, beckoning to Verity, who shook her head. Polly hurried around and whispered in her ear, 'We must, Bet needs us.'

Verity sighed.

Polly insisted. 'Come on, let's get our coats. I'll wait downstairs.'

Al walked her to the double doors and then down the stairs to the attendant. The girl found her mackintosh, and then Verity's coat. 'I have yours here too, madam,' she called, looking up.

Polly turned. Verity was not behind her but on the stairs. Al murmured, 'Well, you're both going to be on morning parade after all, little Miss Polly. Thought perhaps you might be the only one to make it.'

Verity was uncertain on her feet as she joined them. She stabbed the air, and slurred to the cloakroom attendant. 'Put it back. I'm not ready, the night is yet young.'

Polly tried one more time. 'It isn't. It'll be late, anyway, by the time we get to the canal. Oh, come on, Verity.'

The slap knocked her head back. The sound was loud, the pain sharp. For a moment Polly didn't know what had happened.

'I said, not a word about the canal. Are you stupid?' Verity was red with fury.

Polly was confused, her face hurting, her tongue sore where she'd bitten it. Then she remembered.

'I'm sorry, but the canal could just be where we're based, or your damned code. You've got to stop this. You're drunk. Come with me.'

As Polly turned she saw Verity bringing her arm

back to deliver another slap. Al caught it, and forced Verity's arm down.

'That's not going to win you any stars, little lady, hitting a friend like that,' he said. 'I reckon I should get you both a taxi.'

Verity turned away, and slowly walked up the stairs. 'Get on back but one day you should learn to enjoy yourself, because we could be dead tomorrow.'

Polly murmured, 'Don't tempt me.'

At midnight Polly crept on to the *Marigold*, and fell into bed. Al had given her yet another pair of stockings; because he'd never had such a good night, he'd said. 'Never knew you British girls could be such fun.'

They'd never meet again, they both knew that, but Al from Idaho, please please survive, and have lots of little Als in Boise, Idaho, and make your mum a happy grandma, she thought, and fell asleep.

The alarm woke Polly at 5.30, just as Verity tiptoed down into the cabin, looking pale and stinking of booze. Polly slammed her hand on the clock she'd put on the floor by the side-bed, silencing it. She leapt from bed, grabbed Verity. 'Stand there.'

She stripped off the camel coat, the dress, the laddered stockings, then tore on to the counter in her pyjamas, checking there was no movement from Bet's butty cabin. The coast was clear. She unchained the water can and carried it to the cabin tipping some into the bowl.

She washed the girl down as though she was a child. Verity struggled, and now it was Polly who slapped her, whacking her arm, whispering, 'Stand still. You reek of booze. Bet'll be here any minute, so sluicing will help. You're a damned fool. I'll find you some clothes, then if Bet looks in she might think you've been here all night and are simply drowsy.'

Verity vomited but Polly was ready with a towel on the floor. '*You* can rinse that through when you're dressed.'

She finished washing her, and towelled her dry while Verity shivered, saying, 'You missed a good night.'

Polly handed her the towel. 'Finish, while I find you some clothes.' She shoved the dress and coat in to the cupboard beneath the cross-bed, which she'd made up for Verity on her own return. She bundled up the unused bedding and shoved that in too, digging out underwear, socks, trousers and sweaters from the other end of the storage space. 'Get these on while I sort myself out, but before you do that, fold up that towel with the remnants of the disgusting cocktails you've thrown up and hide it for now.'

When they had dressed, Polly hissed, 'Check for Bet, then tip that water from the bowl into the cut while I get the kettle going on the Primus, and for heaven's sake, pretend to feel human or Bet will have your guts for garters.'

Verity, still shivering, and saying nothing, staggered up the steps on to the counter. There was a pause, and lowered voices, but Polly heard Bet saying, 'Well well, I am prepared to accept that you are upright, and alive, and therefore perhaps able to play your part today, Verity Clement, but all the loyalty of friends who wash you down to stop you stinking of stale booze will not keep you on the team if it happens just once more.'

After a pause, Bet's voice, louder this time. 'Polly, get that kettle going. I need a cup of tea, fresh tea leaves. Do not – and I repeat, do not – give me used tea today or I will throw you both in the cut. Polly, you woke me when you came home at midnight, so another time, be quiet.'

The Primus was hissing, the kettle too, and Polly heard the sound of Verity's water being tossed into the cut, then a thud as the dipper was taken from the roof, the sound of feet slipping along the gunwale to the back-end. A moment later, she heard the clink of the bucket.

Finally, Verity appeared back in the cabin. 'The towel is soaking in the bucket. And don't feel too pleased with yourself, no one likes a Goody Two-Shoes, particularly me, especially when you and I both know you aren't. Kitty, kitty, eh?' She was as white as a sheet and sweat beaded her forehead.

Polly paid no attention, but it was then that she noticed the letters to her parents and Reggie she had intended to post sticking out of her handbag. Oh, damn. She made the tea, and then shot into Alperton, searching for a letterbox and finding one. She started to head back, then stopped as she passed the entrance to the Underground, with its dog-pee-smelling sandbags at the ready. Perhaps that would be her abiding memory of the war, if it was ever over?

Though it was early, people were heading into the station and for a moment Polly was tempted to join them. It would be so easy just to leap on to a train and find her way back to Woking, and get away from Verity, the cold, the damp, the accusations. In the distance a siren wailed and a few searchlights probed the gloom that had not yet been lifted by dawn.

She shrugged and continued to the cut because not even a slapped face bothered her, or made her care. Nothing yet had made her really angry, sad or happy, but the bloke in the canteen had said it would, one day, and she remembered feeling that he was right.

Chapter 10

28 October – heading along the Paddington Arm to Limehouse Basin

As they headed away from Alperton to Limehouse Basin Bet steered, while Polly made cocoa. The butty, *Horizon*, was close towed so Bet blew the horn and yelled, 'Run over the planks and have cocoa, Verity. You are forgiven for now, and probably could do with some sweetness.' She leaned into the cabin and said, sotto voce, to Polly, 'If you didn't find out last night, our hung-over friend is Her Ladyship, but this is not used on the cut. Can you imagine the feeling amongst the boaters? They'd never accept us. Besides, no one is better than anyone else here and, to be fair to her, she never, ever uses it.'

Polly thought of last night, and Bet was right – it wasn't Verity who had used the term, just everyone else. She watched from inside the cabin as Verity made her way along the planks and dropped down to the butty's fore-end deck, then leapt on to the *Marigold*'s counter. As Verity stepped on to the gunwale Polly emerged from the cabin with the cocoa, but at the sight of Verity's face, pale and drawn, she ducked back down the cabin steps and added another spoonful of honey. She turned to see Verity peering down at her from the cabin doorway. 'I'm perfectly sweet enough, thank you very much, Polly.'

Polly merely handed her the mug. Verity backed out, then turned to lean against the cabin door, gulping it down quickly while Polly placed Bet's cocoa on the cabin roof. She took her place on the gunwale, sipping hers. Verity slammed her empty mug down on the cabin roof and leapt back on the butty.

Polly called after her, 'Drink lots of water – lots of it.'

Bet snapped, 'Here, take the tiller for a bit and don't tell me a word about last night. You should have made her come home. I'm cross with you both.'

Polly gripped the tiller. Bet said, 'The cut from here to the loading dock is a rehearsal for the Birmingham run. It has everything, but in a truly acceptable form. I will lock-wheel, you will steer.'

The motor pat-pattered as Bet pedalled away on the bike. They met locks which Bet dealt with. Some were ready, some had lock-keepers taking over the paddles. Polly manoeuvred alone round S-bends, and as the early morning became just morning, the tunnels cut out the sun, not the breaking dawn, and the pat-patter seemed to echo in the darkness. Even the bridges were miraculously free of gobbing children. Instead, London red buses trundled across them, and pedestrians hurried, looking neither to left nor right, quite unaware of the canal world beneath them.

There were narrowboats in front of them, and behind, riding high in the water, and others passing, heading heavily loaded to Birmingham. Some steerers called, "Ow do.' Some didn't. Some boats were pulled by horses, some weren't. They passed houses, factories, warehouses, allotments. There was the smell of smoke from the belching chimneys, there was the noise of machinery, the revving of buses and lorries across the bridges. Polly steered throughout, gripping the tiller less tightly as the hours passed.

Bet returned, and sat on the roof, smoking, as the lock-keepers did their bit. 'See the barges, big and ugly, and too wide for where we go, but you know that, Polly,' said Bet, waving to one of them. 'How do you do, Steerer Evan,' she called. "Ow do, Missus,' called Evan. The barge loads were massive. Polly muttered, 'I expect their cabins are palatial.'

'No doubt,' Bet muttered back. She had not stopped coughing in the cold, damp wind.

They passed a few independent boats in colours of their own choosing, festooned with flowers and castles, all on a black background with one or two who had broken the tradition and inserted birds or animals, and Grand Union boats in the same red, white and blue colours as *Marigold* and *Horizon*. Slowly, Polly realised she was beginning to feel part of something huge, something that she vaguely understood.

On the towpath children on bicycles waved and it was as they entered a tunnel that Polly, on Bet's instruction, slipped the bike from the cabin roof. As Bet edged up to the side in the gloom, Polly dragged the bike on to the path. 'Your baptism of fire as a lock-wheeler,' Bet called. 'Keep calm and remember Cowley Lock. Get pedalling, fast, reach the lock before we do, get it ready if no lock-keeper's on duty. Once we're through, get on to the next, and do the same thing. Time is important.'

She cycled like a woman possessed towards the locks, trying to still her nerves. The back tyre was flat, the saddle split and pinching her bum, and she was tossed over the handlebars into the hedge within twenty yards of leaving the *Marigold*. The branches dug into her, and broke under her.

Verity's laugh reached her as she dug herself out, kicked aside the branch which had somehow found itself on the path and brought her down. She headed off again, leaves in her mouth as well as her hair. Will's sweater was no longer white, it hadn't been for some time, and the fall had finished the job.

She heard the trams, the trains, noted the blocks of flats, factories, a hospital. She nodded thanks to the lock-keeper who sorted the first lock gates and sluices, as he called the paddles, winding the ratchets with his windlass. She cycled on as the *Marigold* entered the lock, leaving the lock-keeper to finish the job. She cursed the saddle, and the dog that yapped at her heels then sank its teeth into her trousers. 'Go and pee on the sandbags, why don't you,' she yelled, kicking it away.

A woman walking towards her with a lead in her hand called, 'Your sort shouldn't be allowed on the footpath. Leave my Rover alone.'

Polly snatched a look behind. *Marigold* had left the lock – she must hurry. She pedalled harder, swerving past the dog walker as a laden boat and butty pat-pattered along going in the opposite direction. The woman shook her fist and called her a hooligan. She shouted back at the woman, 'Why do you think there's a towpath in the first place – for *my* sort, you silly old bag.'

Her mother would be mortified.

She looked ahead, leaving the outraged walker and Rover behind, but within fifty yards her front wheel caught on the edge of a pothole and she flew over the handlebars, skidding along the muddy path. She lay for a moment winded, but then heard barking. She leapt to her feet, gathered up the bike. The front tyre was flat too, now. She mounted, snatched a look behind. It was a tiny dog this time, but it was gaining on her, ignoring its owner who was whistling to it. Polly pedalled and left the dog behind, every part of her sore. She wiped her mouth on her sleeve, and her runny nose. Her mother would be even more mortified.

After an hour or so, she changed places with Verity, taking over the butty tiller, steering when it was so close-tied that it was really not steering at all. Without the engine noise the butty was so quiet that there was just the breeze, and time to watch the world that carried on above them, hurtling over bridges, or alongside them. It was a world that continued to ignore the cut. It suited her.

After another hour Bet blew her horn, and slowed the *Marigold* as she entered a bridge hole. On the towpath Verity waited, threw the bicycle on to the motorboat's cabin roof and jumped on herself, as the *Marigold* continued to glide on slowly. Polly changed hands, easing her shoulder as she steered, but then heard a thumping along the top planks and Verity appeared on the butty cabin roof, panting. Her colour was better. She sat on her heels, slapped down some sandwiches on the roof, and an enamel mug of tea. She also handed Polly a newspaper from two days ago. 'Wrap yourself round the sandwiches and you can borrow my newspaper. Borrow, I said.'

She turned to run back. Polly said, 'Thanks. And Verity, I respect you for not saying you are a Lady. It must be difficult.'

'Why should I want to remember where I came from?' Verity snapped. 'And don't, for God's sake, ask me why I said that. And don't you dare call me by that title. It's in the past, got it?'

'Absolutely.' Polly knew about not wanting to think about things.

Not long after midday they were heading for the lock at the entrance to the docks, and Bet chatted to the lock-keeper, nodding and laughing as a second bloke did the work. Polly waited on the butty's counter, realising that the last couple of days had given her an understanding of locks, mooring and steering, or enough not to feel totally lost, anyway. Finally, and at last, they headed out of the massive gates into the huge pool with its cranes, its buildings, its boats and ships, overflown by crying seagulls weaving in and out of the barrage balloons.

Verity appeared, having run along the top planks. 'Your turn to run the planks – the boss wants you on the motor. Chop-chop.'

Verity took the tiller while Polly told herself there was nothing to it. After all, lots of pirates had done it, and *she* wasn't having to jump to her death, she hoped. She set off across the cabin roof, and then the planks, though not running, conscious of the drop to the bilges. She reached the stern counter of the *Marigold*.

Bet was looking ahead. 'Well done, Polly. Now concentrate. We're to head for E wharf as instructed back at the lock. Did I tell you we were picking up steel billets?'

'Rusty steel billets, Ted said.'

The massive pool was quiet and as Polly looked around, Bet said, 'The lads are off on their lunch break, so even the cranes are taking a nap.' They were, indeed, Polly thought, as the arms were still, their chains and hooks dangling uselessly. What on earth would the troops think about a dock stopping for lunch?

All she heard was the pat-pattering of the *Marigold* as they headed towards E wharf, passing many other wharfs containing narrowboats, some half loaded, some not at all. They passed a merchantman which threw them into shade as it waited to be unloaded, and then a medley of barges, some half unloaded. Finally they reached their destination, where they moored, and climbed up the iron ladder on to the wharf. 'Dinner,' Bet announced, pointing to a canteen across the yard. She set off.

Verity groaned as she caught up with Polly.

Polly said, 'My bro—' She stopped. 'People say food helps a hangover, something to do with blood sugar.'

Verity said, 'Be quiet, will you.' But there was no venom. Polly grinned. Not for one moment had Verity slackened or complained on the way to Limehouse. She nudged Verity. 'Well done.'

'What the hell for?'

Verity strode after Bet, her hands in her pockets. Polly followed as Bet gestured for them to hurry. They followed her in, to the familiar smell and noise of a workers' canteen. Verity groaned again. Bet muttered, 'Be a man, Verity.'

The dockers wore overalls and white kerchiefs round their necks. The talk, the smoking and the scrape as they shoved back their chairs or the bench was the same as at the depot. Verity slumped into a space on a bench, waving her hand at Bet, who was staring down at her. 'Would you please just bring me something hot, which doesn't taste and doesn't smell?'

The men sitting at the table laughed. 'Ah, one of those days.' Verity sat with her head in her hands and said nothing. Bet raised her eyebrows at Polly and jerked her head towards the queue. Polly said, 'For a friend in need . . .'

'Just go,' snapped Verity. Polly and Bet did.

The three of them ate sausage, mash and bacon, and slowly Verity sat up straighter, and even smiled, though she shook her head at Bet's offer of a cigarette. 'A step too far.'

As they walked back to their boats they saw Granfer and Saul on *Seagull* and *Swansong*, moored further along E wharf, washing down the cabins. Many narrowboats were queuing, and right at the front was Leon on *Brighton*, and his butty *Maudsley*, the steel billets half loaded. As one, the women looked elsewhere. Polly whispered, 'Do Granfer and Saul know that Leon's here? Will there be a do?'

Bet shrugged. 'None of our business, you've got to get that through your head, Polly.'

As they headed for the *Marigold*, the dock was awakening again as the dockers' lunch hour ended. They passed the foreman, and when Bet asked when loading would begin on the *Marigold* he said, knocking his cap back, 'It'll be tomorrow now, ladies.' He sauntered off, shouting to one of the crane drivers, 'Get a move on, Will, for Pete's sake.'

Polly swung round. Will? She saw him suddenly, as he'd been on their fifteenth birthday, leaning down with her, blowing out the thirty candles, and laughing while their mum said, 'No spitting on the cake, mind.'

She swallowed, her eyes stinging. Bet called, 'Come on, slowcoach.' Verity was climbing down the ladder to the *Marigold*, Bet following. 'Coming,' Polly called, astonished at the swift pain she had felt, the need to swallow, the stinging of her eyes. Would she cry one day?

Bet called again. 'Polly, no point in cluttering up the place, so we're off to a bed and breakfast I've used before but only after we've given the old dears a good wash-down, and covered up the hold to stop it filling with rain. Look at the clouds.'

The next morning, they overslept at the B & B they had reached after walking through bomb-damaged streets. All three had shared a room, all three had used the bath in turn, soaking for half an hour. They had thought they might go for a drink, but instead had slept from eight until eight, and then run to the dock, past the policeman on the gate, waving their loading instructions as he grinned. 'You're not the first to be late, and won't be the last.'

They tore towards the boats, clambered down the vertical iron ladder, and stripped off the tarpaulin sheets. There had been a bit of rain in the night, which slid off into the pool. Above them the foreman called, 'Come on, ladies, you're holding up the war.'

Polly snapped, 'Nonetheless, we never, ever stop for lunch on the cut, and shouldn't think the merchantmen bringing in the loads do either. They're too busy dodging the submarines.'

The foreman stared. Bet raised her eyebrows at Polly and whispered in her ear, 'Steady, we don't want them all out on strike.'

Polly felt the tremble that had taken over her body, and the heat, and for a moment she couldn't recognise what was happening, but then Verity said, 'You look so angry and I thought you were Miss Stony-heart.'

That was it, it was anger, but before Polly could examine the feeling, the waters closed over it, the trembling stopped, and she was blank again. The foreman stomped off. Bet said, 'Come on, we need to finish the job.'

The three of them dismantled the planks and stands from the hold and then did the same on the butty as the crane swung inland and a team of men fastened chains around the first bundle of rusty billets. These were swinging over the *Marigold* in no time, and being lowered into the hold where four men shouted, pushed and waved their arms. The billets were laid to rest with a clang. With each bundle, the *Marigold* sank further into the water, while on the kerb, Polly, Verity and Bet slackened off the mooring straps.

'Why are you doing this?' Bet challenged them for the third time.

'If we don't, we'll tip and sink,' they almost

screamed back in unison, then smiled at one another, panting.

Polly stretched her back, hearing the sounds of men and machinery at work overlaid with the calls of gulls and the siren of a merchantman that was moving away, unloaded. She watched it head off, soon to be out at sea in convoy, destined for America most probably, to reload with necessary cargo. Every second its crew would be facing possible death and disaster. All around the basin was the pat-patter of motorboats towing butties, in and out. Heading to the basin she saw Saul steering *Seagull*, the tail of his red kerchief fluttering, his eyes on the forward passage, as he towed Granfer on *Swansong*.

He'd be heading back past Alperton, and the depot lay-by and, finally, the start of the Birmingham run. Joe was sitting on *Seagull*'s roof, and it looked as though he was colouring. Polly waved. Granfer had turned to check a motorboat that was edging out from the side. He saw Polly and nodded in reply, but he was the only one who did.

Bet called, 'Polly, get on board and light the motor's range, will you? Might as well make tea.'

She did, and by eleven they were loaded, which was when the work really began for the three of them. Polly watched the other two as they replaced the beams across the boat, and drew the rigging chains across the holds to keep the sides of the boat together. Then the stands were dropped down to carry the top planks, which were screwed and tied into position. Now, Polly thought, she'd know how to do it next time.

Bet called, 'Time for the side sheets, girls. Polly, you copy us.'

All three of them clambered over the cargo, untying the ropes and unrolling the tarred canvas resting on the gunwale before tossing the tarpaulin side sheets over the top planks. Bet and Polly threaded ropes through eyelets to secure the sheets, while Verity did the same on the port side.

The top sheets were heaved up next, and secured, and only now did Polly see that they were stencilled with the company initials, GUCCC, and the *Marigold* number 109. For this they had to stand on the four-inch gunwale which was close to the water, now that the load weighed so heavy.

Polly's fingers were raw and blistered from the rough, hairy ropes, and there was still the butty to do. Opposite, she could hear Verity's swearing and she learned new words every few moments, while Bet chuckled beside her.

It was past three when they set off, Bet and Polly on the *Marigold*, and then had to wait outside the lock for the gates to open. Eventually, when the lock was free, Bet called, 'Take the tiller, Polly, feel the difference steering with a full load on, and ease her into the lock.' Polly's heart almost beat out of her chest. 'I'd rather not,' she said.

Bet shook her head. 'That's a shame, little one, because you're doing it anyway. Come on.' She stepped to one side. Polly took the tiller and Bet shouted, 'Aim the prow to the wall, then it will swing round, tight against the lock-side. Reversing will keep her from headbutting the gates. You just need to get used to the elephant you're handling after the gazelle of the empty motor.'

Polly couldn't quite picture *Marigold* as a gazelle, empty or not, but under the lock-side's looming shade she forgot the image while she did as ordered. The stern automatically swung over to lie against the wall, leaving the *Marigold* to drift towards the gates, until it nudged the sill. 'Smoothly done, Polly. Slam it into neutral.' Polly did, her hand slippery with sweat.

Bet had unhooked the short tow-rope from the stud behind Polly, and was coiling it before throwing it on to the bows of the butty as its fore-end slid past. The *Horizon* glided under its own momentum into the lock alongside the motor.

There was a slight thump as its fender hit the sill at the far end of the lock. 'Good girl, Verity,' Bet yelled, and leapt on to *Marigold*'s cabin top, with the mooring strap coiled over her shoulder, and then up the steps on the lock wall, calling, 'Up you come, Polly.'

Polly followed her. Bet roared, 'Tie her up, take out *Marigold*'s tiller, if you please, Verity. We should have been doing this from the start, Polly, but it was a step too far for a trainee's first trip.' Bet ran to the lock gates behind them. She was shoving at the beam, closing it, as Verity yanked the tiller from the *Marigold* and stood it by the cabin, before removing the tiller from the butty.

Polly was mooring *Marigold* as Verity rushed up the steps of the lock wall and wrapped the butty's strap around the nearest bollard. Then she ran across the narrow bridgeway on the front gates, to reach the rear gate on the other side and close it. Polly followed and together they shoved the beam, pushing, until finally the gate closed. 'What now?' Verity panted.

'Open the front paddles,' Polly shouted.

'Go on, then. She got it right, Bet,' Verity called, and followed Polly, who took the windlass from her belt. Together the girls worked, and it was not until then that Polly realised what a tough job Bet had, trying to teach them everything the boaters absorbed from the moment they were born.

Bet was on the other paddle, and shouted across, 'Not bad at all, Miss Verity Clement and Miss Polly Holmes.' Verity turned to Polly, grinning. Her tortoiseshell slide had fallen out and her blonde hair hung over her face. 'Only another one hundred and forty-nine to go,' she hollered.

When the paddles were open, she and Polly searched and found the slide on the kerb between the gates. Verity put it in her pocket.

Polly said, 'It's too nice to lose.'

'It cost someone a lot of money, when he didn't have much.' Suddenly Verity's face was inexpressively sad. 'I think I'll leave it in the cabin. It'll be quite safe.'

She smiled at Polly, nodded, but said nothing more.

Polly watched her head back over the front lock gates. Did that mean she was off the suspect list? Who knew, with Verity.

Chapter 11

Friday 29 October – heading for the depot lay-by

The *Marigold* towed her butty, *Horizon*, past Paddington, Willesden, Park Royal and stopped again at Alperton overnight, with the butty on a short tow. While Polly moored up the boats, she heard Bet ask Verity to replace the vegetables Bet had used to bulk up the rabbit stew simmering in the butty range. 'You know where the shop is from last time, don't you?'

'More or less – it's next to the pub.' Verity stood on the counter of the motor, calling across to Bet on the butty counter.

Bet smiled, and said gently, 'Of course, silly me, this is the girl that navigates by the pubs, not the shops.'

Polly stood quite still, the mooring strap in her hand. Would this set Verity off again? There was silence for a moment but then Verity laughed. Relieved, Polly finished the mooring and came back on board the *Marigold*, ducking down the steps into the cabin. She hunted for some cleaning cloths beneath her side-bed. Verity slipped down after her, counted out the money in the kitty, once, and then a second time, but said nothing as Polly watched. She merely checked the amount against figures in her notebook, nodded, grabbed the shopping bag and headed off.

Left behind, Polly set about wiping down the bike on the towpath after she had mended the punctures, as per Bet's instructions, but it had been on her mind to do so anyway, because already the routine was becoming normal life. Tonight, they were to eat in Bet's butty, a tradition apparently, to have a change of scene before leaving London behind. She moved on from the bicycle to the *Marigold*'s chimney, buffing up its brass bands when Bet called her to the counter. Bet was lugging the flat battery. 'You need to know how to charge this, so follow me to the engine room, if you would.'

In the engine room, she handed it to Polly and heaved out the charged battery from beneath the engine. 'Polly, if you'd just pop yours into place, please.'

Polly smiled. 'Not sure about "popping" it any-where. It weighs a ton.' Bet laughed, then coughed, and banged her chest. 'Damned thing,' she muttered.

'The battery or your chest?' Polly groaned, as she bent her knees as Bet had done, and lowered the battery beneath the engine, watching as Bet connected it, and wondering just how her back and abdominal muscles would ever recover. Finished, Bet stood, stretched her shoulders, then slapped Polly on the back. 'Right, we're done for the day. Come into my cabin and let the heat of the range do its bit towards relaxing those muscles you never even dreamed you had.'

Polly sat on the *Horizon*'s side-bed, relaxing in the cabin's warmth, which was all-encompassing, even though the slide was open for fresh air. Bet's cabin looked far more like a home from home than theirs, festooned with pierced floral plates, a crocheted cover on the small shelf, and a far more intricate crocheted curtain hooked up beside the cross-bed. There was floral paintwork wherever possible, and a photograph of Bet with two older people. Her parents? They stood in front of a great big house, with a spaniel at the woman's feet. 'Is that your mum?'

Bet, who was making a pot of tea at the range, merely nodded.

'You look alike.'

'I like to think so. Now, I'll let the tea stew for a moment. Verity should be back soon and I expect she'll like one too.'

Verity returned at 6.30. There was no smell on her breath and Polly realised she had feared there would be. Bet seemed to breathe easier too, as they ate the stew and then drank the tea. When they had finished, they didn't head for the pub, but fell into their beds, and slept. Polly dreamed of a cabin with photos of Will and her together on the wall, and another with her mum and dad. In her dream cabin there were

155

pierced-edged plates, horse brasses and crocheted curtains.

The next morning, 30 October, they were off before dawn, still on a short tow, one behind the other. Bet steered the motor while Polly pulled up her muffler against the bitter wind, which chapped her lips and made her eyes and nose run. Her mackintosh was flapping in the wind, and she drew up her collar. It was Verity who was cycling this morning, but as they approached the lay-by at the depot she deviated into the yard. What on earth? thought Polly, her elbow on the tiller, as she watched Verity disappear. 'Now what?'

But within minutes Verity was back again, cycling along the towpath, brandishing letters. 'For us all,' she yelled.

Bet called from the tiller, 'Well done, Verity. Pass 'em over at the next lock.'

Once past the depot they swung right, pat-pattering along, and through the Cowley lock where she had vaguely earned her spurs, but it was only the start of the long climb up the staircase. At the next lock, she and Verity changed roles, and Polly was the one tearing along the towpath lock-wheeling and her hands, already blistered and sore from the previous days, grew worse. She had tried wearing her woollen gloves, but they had caught on splinters and worn through in no time.

As they headed towards distant Watford she was almost beyond pain as she dodged potholes along the towpath, swerved round the odd pedestrian, not to mention fallen branches. Why the hell couldn't a boat come south, and move away from the lock, leaving it ready and making her totally redundant? As she rode along she found herself using the swear words she was learning from Verity.

Polly threw herself off the bike at the next lock gates which were, yet again, shut against her. This time she yelled the rude words, because there was no unsuspecting civilian to hear, and right this moment she felt she was fighting her own wretched war.

It began pouring with rain as she rode along the towpath, and her two sweaters sagged, the red one underneath, and Will's no longer white one on top. By the next lock they were both weighed down almost to her knees, even though she'd wrung out the hems. The cut wound from Denham, through Rickmansworth to Croxley Green, and finally through Cassiobury Park, where the beeches were beautiful, and the sycamores were shedding more leaves. At the next lock even the oak leaves, such late shedders normally, were being torn from the branches in the gusting wind. She flung the bike down and tore up to the beams, ratcheting up the paddles, to release the water, checking that *Marigold* and *Horizon* were not having to wait.

There was a lock-keeper on duty, who hurried out from his house, and helped her, offering eggs, as his hens were laying well. 'Strange, cos they don't really like the dark mornings, but here I've got six, just waiting for someone who'd like 'em.'

As the *Marigold* entered the slimy lock and Verity drifted the butty alongside until it nudged the sill, the lock-keeper closed one of the gates while Polly closed the other, yelling down to Verity, 'If the kitty can stand it, we have the offer of eggs, off ration.'

'There should be enough. In fact, there should be fifteen shillings and fourpence farthing. Jump down to the motor and take some.' While Polly waited for the *Marigold* to rise just a bit, before jumping, Verity yelled across as Bet wrenched out the tiller. 'Check it with her, Bet.'

Polly shook her head but said nothing, because Bet said it for her. 'I'll do nothing of the sort, you silly girl.'

Polly jumped on to the motor counter as the *Marigold* rose, and pounded down into the cabin, snatching up the kitty. She grabbed a shilling and raced out on to the counter, up the lock steps, then across the narrow platform of the gates. She haggled with the lock-keeper, who complained she was ruining him. She stuck to her guns and got eight for eightpence.

These she handed to Bet when the lock was full and left the pink docket in the box near the lock-keeper's house, to show that they had been through. The paper was so wet it almost disintegrated. Then she was off again on her bike, and passed a boat coming towards her. When it was within earshot, she balanced her bike between her legs and called, 'How do you do. Is the lock, by any wonderful chance, ready for us?'

The steerer nodded, then called, 'Seagull's ahead o'yer, by quite a ways, but I's been through the last few behind 'em so they is ready. How many yer left ready for oos?'

'Most of them – no one else has passed us going south.'

He nodded, touched his hat, and went on his way, butty and motor riding high, both with no loads. Perhaps he'd offloaded coal on the way, Polly thought, but he wasn't a Grand Union boat, so maybe he'd been out of luck for any sort of return cargo, poor man.

As she mounted her bike and cycled along the towpath the rain was easing and Polly was aware of the beauty of the canal they'd passed through, the countryside, the fields, and trees, the bridge holes where once so many men had walked their boats through. In this weather the parapets were free of children gobbing them, or throwing whatever they could find, so perhaps she should be grateful.

The next lock-keeper stayed inside his house, but so what? She shrugged, shivering, waiting for the *Marigold* as it entered, and closing the gates behind it. Once she'd ratcheted the paddles and the lock was filling she jumped down on to the counter. Bet said, 'I've cocoa on the go.'

Verity grinned across at her from *Horizon*. 'Tough old shift. Bad luck. Don't know where the lock-keeper is today.'

Polly searched for sarcasm and found none. She

smiled back as the boats rose. 'He's probably hiding from the bloody rain.'

Verity raised her eyebrows, and said quietly, 'I'm not a good example, Polly. Don't change yourself.'

Polly laughed, 'I'll bloody change if I want to, so there.'

The girls grinned at one another. Verity shouted, loud enough for Bet to hear, 'We won't need our trainer soon.'

Bet came out from *Marigold*'s cabin with three enamel mugs of steaming cocoa, into which the rain spattered. She handed the mugs to the girls. Polly warmed her hands, sipping as the steam warmed her face and the cocoa warmed her stomach.

So it went on, taking turn and turn about until the afternoon became evening as they headed north and the gathering gloom became darkness, though the rain still hadn't stopped. Exhausted, they tied up where Bet always did, alongside many others at a spot between Kings Langley and Berkhamsted, near a pub. Polly could make out a few scattered houses near the cut, but as she looked more closely she could also see a built-up area fading into the darkness.

They ate a rushed supper of Spam fritters, cabbage and baked potatoes, and listened to the rain on the cabin roof. Suddenly it ceased. 'Just like that,' Verity muttered. 'I can hear the rain god saying, let's make them utterly soaked, utterly miserable and then, when they're in the dry and warm, I'll call a halt to it.'

Bet and Polly laughed. Bet brought out her cigarettes. 'Here, little storyteller, have one of mine and be thankful it's not going to be soaked before you can draw breath.'

Polly shook her head, then accepted one. Verity tutted. 'You're so easy.' Again, there was no venom. 'Always,' Polly murmured.

Chapter 12

30 October – evening, moored north of Kings Langley

After they had washed up, Bet insisted they went to the pub set back from the canal. 'Life can't just be work, girls. We need a life, however tired we are.'

As they emerged from the cabin Polly saw that there was a bombers' moon, and by its light they spotted the *Seagull*, Granfer Hopkins's motorboat with its butty, *Swansong*, moored a bit further along, beyond another Grand Union boat and butty. And surely that was Leon's right at the front of the queue?

Bet saw too. 'Oh joy,' she said. 'Let's hope he stays on board, or in the other bar at the very least. We really don't want to be in the middle of another to-do.'

The distant hills looked like dark shadows and the pub would have melded against them, hidden, had they not heard music and laughter as they approached along the path leading from the canal to the building. The summer-time chairs were tilted up on the tables. The three of them had not changed clothes, but they were only slightly damp after sitting in the heat of the cabin. Bet led the way into the pub, via a dark lobby. 'Shut the door, quickly. Verity, check the blackout curtain.'

Verity called, 'Got it, boss.'

Bet laughed softly. 'Let's try and weave our way to the fire Bob usually has going by now.'

Verity was just behind Polly, and sighed. 'I know, he's a lifesaver.' Bet shoved open the door into the bar, to be met by even more sound, light, cigarette smoke, and the clash of billiard cues on balls. To their right was a dartboard, with two teams playing, grim determination on their faces. Bet nodded towards the chimney. 'We'll get a pint and then force our way through the scrum. I expect we'll steam, but who isn't?' She was right. There was a layer of steam coming off most of the clientele.

They squeezed through the boaters to reach the bar, and Bet hollered, 'Bob, three pints when you're ready, or even if you're not, if you please.'

'Yer tell 'im, eh Bet?' It was Granfer, holding a pint glass up in the air to avoid being jogged, as he slipped past them. 'Off to check the lad. He's out in Mrs Bob's kitchen, being spoilt.'

Bet laughed. 'Oh, I doubt very much that's all you're checking, Granfer. I expect there's something in the oven that Mrs Bob wants you to test.'

Granfer smiled, winked but said nothing. In the blink of an eye he was gone, though how, Polly wondered, because he hadn't pushed. People had simply parted to let him through. The same did not happen for them as they held their tankards high and tried to get to the fire. Verity led the way, to no avail, so Polly edged past her, nudging the elbows of the men who blocked their path. As their beer slopped, they turned, and Polly dived into the space this created, shouting, 'Sorry, so sorry.' She did the same to the next man, until the message got through and a way magically appeared as they headed to the fire. Once there, they stood, their backs to the roaring logs, steaming along with the rest of them.

'Who taught you that little trick, may I ask?' Verity said, sipping her beer slowly.

'You may ask,' Polly said, and nothing more.

Bet laughed and after a moment Verity joined in. But then she said, 'I saw your letter, forwarded by your mother. Who does she think is suitable, as was written on the back of the envelope? *He's most suitable and remember he has a future* were the exact words, I think.'

Polly paused mid swallow, almost angry. It surprised her.

'Oh Verity,' sighed Bet. 'You might have come from a drawer somewhat higher than either of ours, but you have so much to learn. Basic manners, for a start.'

Polly sipped the beer; it was warm but weak. She sipped again, and looked up. To the left of them, Saul was talking, lifting his glass of beer to Granfer who had returned. Together, the pair of them roared with laughter. Again, she was surprised at herself, because she liked to see it; and the way Saul's face lit up, and the sound of it. He looked younger than he had on the lay-by, alive just as Bet did when talking of the cut. Another man flung his arm over Saul's shoulder. 'Come an' give oos a song, Saul boy.'

Saul shook his head. *Oh do, please*, Polly thought.

Near her a man shouted, 'Yon girl sez please, Saul, so 'ow can yer not, man.' The man was pointing to her. Polly realised she must have spoken aloud. She looked at the floor, as Verity poked her. 'Manners, Miss Holmes.'

Saul just shrugged and pushed through the throng of men, making for the bar. The throng closed in his wake. Polly turned to the fire, feeling the heat from the flames playing on her face, and perhaps drying Will's filthy sweater.

Verity moved away and Polly, relieved, sipped her beer. Verity called from the dartboard, 'Oh, do come, you two. I've a darts match for us. Quick, before someone else gets the board.'

Polly didn't want to leave the heat but Bet was forging a path for them through to the darts area, so she tagged along, feeling like the butty following the motor, but Bet was barging through at such a pace that she was reminded of Leon rocking all the boats in the lay-by on her first day. Where was he? Not in here, anyway. She was pleased, because the aggression in the man's voice had been enough to turn anyone's stomach. She pictured Saul's struggle in the water again, his care for Joe in spite of the blood pouring from—

'Do come, Miss Polly Holmes,' called Verity. 'You're holding up play.'

They played against the steerers of *Maiden*, *Letchworth* and *London Pride* and it was Verity's final throw that won the match for them. The men weren't happy, but neither were they cross; instead they asked for another match.

This time Bet bought pints for both teams, using the kitty money, which was a great idea, Polly thought, because who knew when they might need help on the cut, especially if they beat the steerers again.

Verity missed with the final throw, though only just. Polly leaned across and whispered, 'Good manners, or a bad throw?'

'You can ask,' Verity whispered back, nudging her.

Polly grinned, for it had been her answer, earlier.

Bet put an arm around them both. 'Now, my little pair of Cinderellas, time we made our way back, but I need to pick up my winnings from Bob first.'

Verity shook her head. 'I don't believe it. You bet on us losing that match?'

'I bet on your common sense and good behaviour, Verity Clement.' Polly and Verity stared at her, then at one another but Bet was pushing them towards the door. 'Make some cocoa when you get back.'

Polly called, 'Oh no, we'll wait for you, or you'll have another drink and the kitty will be all over the place and Verity will be upset . . .'

Bet paused, looking shocked, and for a moment

Polly wondered if she had gone too far, but then, against the wall of sound and smoke, Verity sighed, 'All right, all right, point taken. Can we let the damned kitty saga rest now?'

'Oh, please do,' Polly groaned. Bet looked from one to the other, and her booming laugh reached them.

With the kitty issue now over, Verity and she left together, abandoning Bet, at her insistence, who claimed that everyone needed a break from the kindergarten from time to time. Mindful of the blackout they made sure the bar door was shut behind them before leaving. The moon was still bright, the air quite dry, and the puddles on the path leading through the garden mainly gone. Probably, Polly thought, people sat here in the summer watching the boats on the cut, envying the boaters their idle, perfect life as they glided along. She sighed. Verity stared at her. 'For heaven's sake, what was that?'

Polly muttered, 'I was thinking of the people sitting here in the sun.'

Verity snapped, 'Not that, idiot. Listen.'

They stood still. An owl hooted, and then again. 'It's an owl,' Polly said.

'Shut up, and listen,' Verity hissed.

Polly heard it then. A groan, a thud, then another coming from round the side of the pub. 'That's the kitchen side,' breathed Verity. They rushed to the corner, and there in the moonlight were figures fighting. Verity held Polly back. There was a movement to their left. Granfer was holding Joe to him, burying the boy's head in his jerkin.

Saul? Polly stared into the gloom at the heaving bodies that tumbled out into the moonlight, then back into the shadows again. Yes, Saul. But who else? There were four. Two against two, or three against one? She saw one man in the midst of three. She could hear Will's voice – three against one wasn't fair. She pulled free from Verity. 'Go and get help,' she urged her.

Granfer called, 'Leave 'em be, girls. 'Tis family – no one's business but our'n. On yer way now.'

'You're sure?' she asked but even as she did, she heard Leon's voice and saw that he was kicking Saul, who was curled on the ground as the other two men laid into him too, one carrying something which looked like a pickaxe handle. Leon landed another kick. 'No one takes m'boy, sailor, yer 'ear me. You're not 'aving 'im for yer runnerabout, cos I needs him. You got that.'

'Leave 'im be, Da,' yelled Joe, trying to wrench free from Granfer.

Verity pulled at Polly. 'Come away, it's not our business, you heard Granfer.'

'I thought you'd gone for help. It's three against one.'

Leon brought back his leg and landed another kick. She heard Saul groan, but then he called as he grabbed Leon's leg, forcing the man to lose his balance, 'Get Joe away, Granfer. Keep 'im safe.'

Leon roared at the man with the pickaxe handle, 'Hit 'im with it, don't just stand there. Kill the bugger.'

The man raised the weapon and whacked it down as Saul released Leon's leg and rolled to the right. The pickaxe handle hit the ground. The man cursed. Granfer dragged Joe towards the garden. Leon snatched the pickaxe handle from his mate, and lifted it. 'Hold 'im,' he ordered. The two men grappled with Saul and held him still. Polly saw the stools stacked ready for the summer against the shed where Granfer had been standing and ran across, pulling the top one free. Verity screeched, 'Don't, Polly.'

Polly yelled, 'Do as you're told and go for help.'

Leon turned at her shout, but Polly was charging at him, holding the stool by the legs, bringing it up, and before he could grasp what was happening she swept it across his side, jarring right up to her teeth. Leon staggered, roaring, 'What?'

She swung it up again. Will had said, if attacked, fight back straight away or you'd lose the initiative. She brought the stool across Leon again, then there was a flurry beside her and Granfer was there, also with a stool in his hands, and they prodded two of the men back as though they were lion tamers while Leon clutched his arm, and sagged down on to one knee.

The other two ran, while Granfer went to Saul. Polly stood over Leon and said, 'Stay down – if you move I'll hit you again. I promise I will.'

Her fury was drowning her, sweeping her to the

chaos of Will's tank as it was blasted to smithereens, but now Bet was beside her. 'Leave it, Pol. Leave it. Time to go. Come along now.'

Will had called her Pol. Her thoughts were drowned by the sound of others pounding along the path, someone shouting, 'What t'hell's 'appening?'

She still brandished the stool. 'Stay down,' she whispered, but Bet was taking the stool, as some of the steerers from the pub arrived. One rushed to Leon, grabbing him. 'Speed by the lay-by, would yer?'

Now Bet and Verity were pulling Polly away. 'Come on, we're not needed.' Together they stumbled back towards the boat, Bet's arm around Polly, whose fury was dying into nothingness.

Bet said, 'Best to let Granfer and the others sort it now.'

They heard curses and then the sound of a man staggering well over to the left. 'That's Leon,' Verity whispered. 'I'm not sure he saw who hit him in the dark, but he heard you. Why on earth did you interfere? Of course he wouldn't kill Saul. It was just a scrap. You should have come with me to get help. What will he do to us now?'

Polly stared at her, exhausted, as they made their way along the towpath. 'Someone had to interfere, there was a child involved, and those three *would* have killed Saul, and it wasn't damn well fair.' The fury was back. 'It isn't fair,' she shouted. Then repeated it in a whisper.

'Oh, don't be absurd,' Verity shouted. 'Whoever said anything was going to be fair.'

They were passing the boats moored along the tie-up. Some women sitting on the counter, knitting in the moonlight, looked round sharply. Bet hushed Verity and said, 'My father killed my mother when he didn't care for the steak pie she had cooked. Insanity, of course, after falling from his hunter, or brain damage, or some such thing from the first war, but somehow one is never free, having seen such a thing. He's in an asylum. I should visit him, but I don't. I also think Leon would have killed Saul, Verity. He ordered those men of his to hold Saul down while he brandished the pickaxe, and there was death in his voice. He's dangerous. We know that, and we must keep clear of him – you especially, Polly, from now on.'

Polly nodded, frightened now, and trembling.

Verity went ahead to the *Marigold*, and by the time Polly and Bet arrived the cocoa was ready. The three of them sat outside on the counter, smoking. Polly's hand still trembled, but here they wouldn't talk for fear of disturbing the other boaters, and that was better for her. They continued to sip their cocoa and smoke in silence. Finally Bet disappeared to the butty cabin, and returned with brandy. She whispered, 'Medicinal purposes only.'

She topped up their cocoa with a shaking hand. They smoked yet another cigarette. Polly looked up at the stars, which seemed so close she could almost touch them. So, she wanted to say to the man at the depot, I think I'm coming alive again, but I'd better not go round bashing up too many people or Mum won't like it. She began to laugh but then stopped abruptly. The other two took no notice, merely drained their mugs. Verity muttered, 'Never a dull moment with you around, Polly Holmes, but time for bed.'

As Verity washed in the light of the cabin's hurricane lamp, Polly took *Winnie-the-Pooh* down from the shelf, tracing Will's message with her finger. She knew it by heart and it was her most precious possession. He had given it to her for their tenth birthday. There, in his rounded writing, were the words 'We will right all wrongs, make unfair things fair, because we are invincible. Forever, and ever.'

It was the motto of their gang, which Will led, but Verity was right: life wasn't fair. Fair was for children, for a boy with hair the same colour as hers, with brown eyes like hers, a boy whose socks always fell down around his ankles, his plimsolls as battered as hers, plimsolls which smelt like hers after they had put whitener on them, leaving them overnight to dry.

She turned down the lamp once Verity was in bed, latching the already closed cabin doors: it was safer that way. She shoved the slide open for fresh air as it was not a cold or wet night. Clutching the book to her, she slept.

Chapter 13

**30 October – later that evening, Saul and
Granfer**

In the *Seagull*'s cabin Saul stripped, then dipped his
hands in the bowl of clean water he had poured
from the water can, because the water from the cut
wasn't at all the thing for open wounds. He sluiced
his face. The cut over his eye stung, his lip too, and
he'd a lump the size of a swan's egg on the back of
his head; not that he'd seen one of them for many
a long day.

Eyes closed, he reached for the clean rag torn from
one of Granfer's shirt-tails, patted his face dry, then
sluiced off the rest of his body. He twisted and saw
that Leon's boot had gashed the skin over his ribs.
He could see the bone. Granfer'd have to stitch the
bugger.

He dragged on clean trousers, for his legs weren't
cut, sat on the side-bed and waited for his granfer
to settle the boy in the butty cabin for tonight. Best
that way cos Saul reckoned to tossing and turning a bit, with the pain, and that'd keep the lad
awake. Granfer'd chain them doors shut an' all. The

hurricane lamp flickered. The kettle whistled. He leaned forward and splashed the boiling water over the needle and knife he had made ready, then laid them on the plate with the catgut.

It was one of his ma's pierced-edge plates, the one they used for cutting and stitching. Seemed to bring them luck, for never had cuts turned nasty, yet. Inside, he felt as if he were shaking, because this tumble had been different; death had been in Leon's eyes but no way was that bugger having back the boy. Never. Somehow they had to keep Joe safe, keep him under their eye. It were all right while they was on the cut because they could steer on past Leon if he were coming down when they were going up, or keep behind him if they were going the same way. It were at the lay-by and so on they had to be careful. Then the boy needed to be close by, till him was grown. Where the hell were Maudie? Had his sister seen the look in them eyes? Had a pick-handle come down on her? What had the lad seen?

He heard Granfer on the counter of the motor and was glad because it stopped his thoughts going away from sense, but he heard Joe's footsteps too. Stitching weren't a thing for a lad to see, but better he were here, Saul supposed, if he weren't wanting to go to sleep. Safer.

Granfer knocked. Saul called, 'Bit late fer manners this evenin', don't yer think? There's work to be done.'

He and Granfer laughed. It weren't funny but it

lifted the whole bloody mess up off the floor. Saul said, as Granfer pushed Joe before him into the cabin, 'You bring that book t'colour, our Joe? I want to see how your castles is comin'. I got paint, so next lay-by I'll get yer a pan or plate to paint.'

Joe's eyes lit up, and Saul gestured to the cross-bed. 'Sit yersel' down, and pull down t'cupboard door, and put yer colours on that table.'

As Joe passed him, he snatched a look at his uncle, but Saul kept his elbow against the cut on his ribs because there was no need for the boy to see things close up. Later, he'd have to learn to sew cuts, but not with his dad so close and downright vicious and his mam Lord knew where. Yes, she'd be out there somewhere. Course she would.

Granfer poured the water over the catgut, then threaded the needle. He looked towards the lad, saying, 'Come on now, our Joe, 'ead down. 'Tis late but I reckon that's when you'll 'ave the time to paint when yer busy on the cut, so best give it a try.'

Joe looked from Saul to Granfer, then lowered his head, picked up his coloured pencils, and began. Saul marvelled at the way he could draw straight lines, just like that. The lad were better than he'd been. He kept his eyes on that as Granfer began to sew. He did a running stitch, the one Grandma had taught him, then later he'd pull the whole line out if it hadn't softened and disappeared as the cut healed.

Saul let the pain wash over him, let it take him

where the sun shone, so he could feel it on his face. He'd go poaching when they tied up. He'd set the traps under the moon, and fetch the booty in the morning, and sometimes, in the summer, when the grass were dry and daisies was out, he'd lie, close his eyes and see the red of his lids, and his body'd soften. He'd hear the larks. Yes, them larks, sky-larks they was called.

The pain was building and taking him away from them sky-larks, but he dug his nails into his thighs and went back, feeling the sun on his face, the smell of the grass. Sometimes he thought he'd like the life of a banker, them people who lived on the land. Is that what Maudie had done, taken to the land? He'd like to run a pub on the cut, cos he could see the day when they'd not cart loads no more, but them'd be taken by trains . . . He could paint, an' all.

He groaned. Granfer said quietly, 'Sorry, son.'

Saul nodded, his eyes shut, lying on the grass, the daisies wobbling. Yes, p'raps he'd take to a pub, when the loads was taken by trains, and lorries, cos they said the cut were too slow. He'd even seen some boats turned into homes. Holiday homes, but what was an holiday? What'd yer do on an holiday?

He opened his eyes as Granfer set about the stitching business again. 'What yer do on an holiday, Granfer?'

'Yer rest, son, on 'oliday. See other places, have fun, so Bob at the pub reckons.'

'Fun?' Joe asked.

'Seems so. No work, just fun.' Granfer was almost done, the rag he'd been dabbing at the wound was red right through.

'What's fun?' Joe asked.

Saul said, 'Don't rightly know, but them's we sees cluttering up the locks in boats made into 'omes have fun, Bob says, or did afore this war. Eating, drinking, going oop and down t'cut 'aving a look at everything, and not doing their jobs. I reckon there'd be work for us in that, when t'war is done. Sometimes I wish they'da let me fight 'stead of stayin' on the cut. The more who does, the quicker it's done.'

Granfer patted his shoulder. 'Reckon yer done yer fair share tonight, lad, and we's needed taking stuff about the place. Time for thinking of after, when after comes.'

Granfer poured simmering water over the needle, and took the bowl out on to the counter. There was the sound of water being poured into the cut, then a scratching on the roof as he took down the dipper, to collect cut water. They heard him swill the bowl out before returning and pouring boiling water into the bowl, then up the steps and into the cut with it, again.

Saul leaned forward and flicked his clean shirt off the range bar. Granfer collected the kettle and took it out on to the counter. 'I'll top this oop, then we'll 'ave a mug o' tea and get our 'eads down.'

He was back in seconds. Saul was leaning on the side-bed, his eyes shut, listening to Granfer bustling.

It was a good sound. A warm one. Saul said, 'You finished yer castle yet, Joe lad?'

He turned. Joe was staring at him. 'You're looking white, Uncle Saul.'

'Tired, Joe. Just tired. Thinkin' too. I reckon yer needs to spend more days at school. Need to learn yer letters and numbers.'

'Yer can teach me.'

'Wish I could, but I don't know 'em neither, and we needs t'know letters these days. The world'll change quick when the war is done, if'n we win. If we lose then we'll do as them damn Germans command.'

'Will Mam be back then?'

Saul didn't answer but looked at Granfer, who was watching the kettle. 'It'll never boil if'n yer do that,' Saul said.

'Yer got to answer me, Uncle Saul. When'll Mam be back?'

Granfer kept on looking at the kettle. Saul nodded slightly and seeing there was to be no help from his granfer turned to the lad. 'I don't know, Joe, that's the 'onest truth. But there's naught t'be done about that, 'cept going on until she do.'

'Will the Germans come?'

This was easier. Saul shook his head. 'I don't reckon them will now. They done their worst with the bombs. Now we's just got to keep knocking 'em down till they stop getting up.'

The tea was ready. Granfer handed a mug to each

of them, looking at Joe's picture and handing it to Saul before coming to sit next to him. 'Reckon it's as good a castle as I've seed,' Granfer said approvingly.

'Good enough,' said Saul. 'Reckon we got to find a plate for our lad to paint soon as we can. See how 'e gets on with it.'

The boy said nothing, just held his mug and stared into it. Now Granfer did look at Saul, who knew they were thinking just the same thing. Was the boy going dumb again, like he was when they fetched him to them, so bruised and beaten?

Saul said gently, 'Yer drink up, lad, then we'll get yer to bed, eh. New day tomorrow.'

Joe looked up. 'He kicked yer, like he kicked me and Mam. 'Urts, don't it? Really really 'urts. Yer'd a seed him off, wouldn't yer, Uncle Saul? Yes, yer would, but that woman, she made 'im angry. Real angry. 'E'd get angry when Mam 'it him back, and he learned her not to. Learned me, 'n'all. It were better then, cos 'e got over it quick. But that woman, she made him angry. I know it. A woman banker 'itting 'im. He'll want to 'urt oos more. She were a bugger to do that. He'll get 'er, and 'e'll get oos, yer see if he don't.'

Saul walked across, keeping his head low or he'd hit it on the ceiling, and he'd had enough bangs today. He sat next to the boy, fingering the crochet curtain his mam had made. He put his hand on the lad's knee. 'See this 'ere curtain. It drops between me and yer on the side-bed, don't it? I will be between yer and 'im, you 'ear me? Granfer and me will always be between yer and 'im, even when yer mam comes back.'

'But I 'ates that banker woman, because she's made it worse, 'itting him like that. 'E'll have plans. That's what 'e says when yer makes him mad. 'E'll have plans.'

'Don't yer worry about her, she looks well and good at lookin' after 'erself.' Granfer was cackling, as he looked into his mug of tea. 'I reckon she did yer Uncle Saul a good turn, I do too. I don't know if yer da saw who 'it 'im, anyway. It coulda been me for all 'e knows.'

Joe drummed his heels on the cupboard beneath the cross-bed. 'He'll know,' he muttered. ''E knows all things.'

Chapter 14

Sunday 31 October – heading away from Kings Langley

Polly and Verity were knocked awake by Bet at 5.30 in time to hear a boat pat-pattering off. As Verity eased from the cross-bed she muttered, 'It'll be that Saul Hopkins setting off to get to the lock first and not even a thank-you.'

Bet knocked again, and said, 'Tea on the roof. Get it down quick, and I've done you both a slice of bread and honey, then we'll set off. And Saul's not the first to leave, Verity. Leon set off in the dark, thank the Lord. We'll do our best to avoid him. He'll be raw for a while but get drunk and hopefully forget it was Polly, if he even realises it. It was dark, remember. We've a long way to go, and— saints preserve us, that's quite some bonnet, Polly.'

Polly had clambered out on to the counter. Verity followed saying, 'I think perhaps it was knitted as a tea cosy, and you nicked it.'

Bet laughed, and handed Verity her tea. 'You're on the butty again today, Verity, for some of it anyway. I'll take a cycling shift when we see how

Polly settles after her fisticuffs. But Saul will leave the locks ready, no doubt, especially if he knows it's us following, so it could be easy-peasy. Chop-chop, got to keep up with the boaters. Got to prove yourselves, ladies.'

'Wasn't last night enough?' Verity called as she made her way on to the butty, munching her bread.

Bet was hurrying along the gunwale to the engine room and called, 'Ah, word won't spread. Saul will keep quiet, Leon certainly will, and so will we, and the men from the pub saw nothing, or that will be what they say. Least said, soonest mended.'

So, that's that, thought Polly as she took the post of steerer once she heard the engine catch, and start. Bet leapt on to the roof, and from there to the bank, letting go the mooring rope. Polly eased open the throttle, feeling *Marigold* take up the strain of the tow. She snatched a look to the left, at the pub set back from the cut. Would she ever look at it without feeling the thud of a stool on a body, the vibrations up her arm into her jaw? Rage? It was so long since she'd felt anything so strong that she felt invigorated, and almost grateful to that vile man and his vicious kicks.

Bet was on the gunwale. 'Good girl, ease her into the centre,' she said. '*Horizon*'s on a short tow today, but we might put the snubber on later, when we get to a long pound – or in banker language, Polly, a straight long run between locks. But we've more than a few short locks to get through again before

Fenny Stratford, where I reckon we'll tie up for the night.'

They passed an oncoming motor. 'How do you do, is the lock ready?' she called to the boatwoman steering.

The woman nodded. ''Ow do,' she called. 'I'll buy that 'at off you, if'n yer like.'

'I'll knit one for you,' Polly called, keeping her eyes ahead. The boy steering the butty looked over at her. She called to him, 'How do you do. Not sure if your mother heard. Tell her I'll knit her a hat and leave it at Bob's pub north of Kings Langley next time we're coming through.'

The boy stared ahead, not acknowledging her.

Bet jumped on to the counter, then ducked into the cabin. 'I'll make some porridge a bit early. You can eat it on the move. Verity will make hers in my cabin. Take note of all of this. Incidentally, got your knitting needles, have you? On the cut you can't make promises you're not going to keep.'

The wind was tearing at wisps of hair that had escaped from Polly's hat, her nose was running, her hand on the tiller was freezing. She dug the other into her trouser pocket. Maybe she would put her mackintosh on today after all, she thought, but then shook her head. No she wouldn't; the boaters didn't bother, neither did Verity or Bet so she'd look a fool. 'Well, have you?' Bet called up.

'Yes, not to mention my crochet hook, and wool, in the bottom of the kitbag, but there's been no time. We're

either working or drinking. My mum would understand the working, but not the drinking.' She stopped.

She shouldn't have said that when poor Bet had
seen her mother killed. What must that be like, especially when it was your father who did it? She
wanted to know more, but to ask would be rude.
Was Leon really capable of killing? If so, the army
should have snatched him up. She made herself grin
at her pathetic joke, but it wasn't funny. *Leon* wasn't
funny. Poor Joe, how could his mother have left him
with that monster? Because that was what seemed
to have happened, or so Verity had heard.

She steered through pretty countryside, beneath
tumbling clouds, and was soon approaching the lock.
A queue of boats and butties had lined up along the
edge of the cut, waiting. The *Seagull* and her butty were
there, at the back of the queue. Polly steered closer to
the bank, putting the engine into reverse, the propellers
churning up the water as the *Marigold* slowed. Bet leapt
out of the cabin and on to the gunwale, watching
Polly's every move. Finally they were 'parked' and Bet
tied up. The butty parked behind her, and Bet tied her
up too, almost before *Horizon* had stopped.

Verity jumped onto the *Marigold*, and poked her
head into the cabin, with Bet in her wake. 'Oh, well,
if you're brewing porridge I'll have some too to save
myself the bother. It will line my stomach so I can
better face the Berkhamsted to Tring locks. I hate
them with a passion.'

They hunkered down in the cabin while Bet stirred

the porridge that was thickening into a glutinous mass on the Primus. Verity said, 'Saul and Granfer are the next in the line. Will he come and thank us?'

'Just stop obsessing about it, you know he won't,' Bet said. 'And who knows if Granfer even told him? We say nothing, remember.'

They stood on the bank, spooning down the glop, as Verity called it. 'So it really was a tea cosy, wasn't it?' queried Verity.

Polly flicked her with porridge. 'I've had an order to make another, so very there. I'll knit you one as well, if you like.'

'I'd rather die,' Verity laughed. She stopped, and looked sideways at Bet, then shared a look with Polly, who wondered if they might one day be real friends not just a boating team. She also wondered if there would ever be a time when someone or other hadn't lost someone or other, and those around didn't have to watch their words.

They were on the move within half an hour, following Saul and Granfer as the convoy of boats used the locks, with oncoming boats feeding through alternately, leaving the locks ready. Consequently they rose relatively swiftly.

'It's a bit like clockwork,' Polly said. Bet nodded. 'It doesn't happen often, but when it does it's seamless, and you feel you've won a prize. But we're not through yet, and once we are, we're on a downward slope, so it's the same thing but in reverse.'

*

185

In the early afternoon the sun was out, the wind had died, and but for the trees with their turning leaves, some green, some edged with red or yellow, it could have been spring. Bet made fried egg sandwiches, and they dripped soft yolk down their sweaters as they moved along and up, and swigged tea and didn't give a damn as they pat-pattered along the pound.

It was then that Polly realised it was Sunday. Her mum would have been to church, her dad too, but he would have snoozed through the sermon. Then it would have been a rationed apology for a roast, and later for tea it had always been crumpets and celery. She and Will had not been allowed out to play on a Sunday – to show respect, her mum had said. The rest of the road thought they were daft, but in a way Polly understood. It kept them close as a family. It made the day an observance of things other than everyday affairs.

Polly removed her hat, and shoved it in her trouser pocket and realised that – yes, she was happy; not happy as she had once been, but vaguely happy, and knew without doubt that she really was slowly, so slowly, healing. Would Will mind? Would he wonder how she could go on without him, when he'd been her other half even before birth?

They travelled on through more locks with slimy walls, and water with a dank stench, and beams that rubbed their hands and bruised their backsides as they shoved, because they all took turns to roar along on the bike, and to open and close the gates.

At last they were at the top and coasting the long pound towards Tring, which they passed, and then Bet called, 'We're at Marsworth Junction, so flex those muscles for the delightful locks on the way to Leighton Buzzard, dear hearts.'

Polly thought she'd never be able to work out where she actually was in England while she was on the cut, because it seemed an entity that was enough in itself with no point of reference. So much of the scenery looked the same: the banks, the locks, the towpaths, the tunnels, the bridges – one of which she could see in the distance – the fields, the few dwellings, or the backs of towns.

And what about the warehouses and factories, and the farms, and backs of gardens, allotments . . . But hang on, was that an aeroplane landing? She shaded her eyes and stared into the distance, seeing it circling, then dropping. Yes, it was.

Bet said, following her line of sight, 'RAF Leighton Buzzard over there but then there are airfields all over the country now, aren't there? And there are prisoner-of-war camps for Germans all over the place too, of course. I often fear the prisoners will escape and grab an aeroplane, and get back to the war to cause more havoc.'

Ahead Polly saw another bridge. She was so used to them now she never gave them a second thought, just ducked the manure, gob or whatever descended from them. The children were fair-weather, anyway, and the rain kept them in, and so did school unless they were playing truant. She smiled. She and Will had dipped school only once. It had been the most boring day of their lives, and they'd never done it again. Polly sounded the horn well in advance and only now did she remember Bet's concerns. 'The airfields are guarded though, Bet, so that wouldn't work.'

Bet laughed. 'Forget about that. Look ahead, and be ready to duck, we might be in for some gobbing. It's a day off school, remember.'

There was a child on the bridge, leaning over. Damn, Polly thought. She'd have to wash her hat free of spittle once they tied up at Fenny Stratford if their aim was as good as this morning. Yesterday there'd been a few out but she'd ducked well. She concentrated hard, knowing she must take the centre line through the narrow bridge or she'd knock into the sides. She sounded the horn again and looked up, to pinpoint the enemy. The child, a boy she thought, had disappeared and there was no answering horn either so she could enter.

'All clear,' she called to Bet. 'But I'm going to buy that umbrella you spoke of before too long, and it's not to keep the rain off. The little toe-rags.'

Polly steered the fore-end dead centre into the bridge hole. The walls were as always so close to the motor that a mere couple of feet separated the boat from the towpath. She kept her eyes glued to the exit though the stern hadn't yet entered, listening hard for a warning hoot. As she was about to go beneath the bridge she looked up again, just as Verity yelled from the stern of *Horizon*, 'Polly, Polly, brick. It's a brick.'

It was too late. The brick hit the bobble on her hat, slid off and caught her forehead, then crashed to the counter. The pain crashed her mind, she had bitten her tongue, her ears rang, everything went dark and she felt sick, but only for a moment for then she heard Bet call, 'Pol, Pol.'

Polly shook her head, Will called her Pol. Will? Her head cleared it, but something was running into her eye. The tiller was snatched from her hand and Bet said, 'Get in the cabin, wash that blood out of your eye.'

Polly shook her head, brushed the blood away, and instead leapt from the counter on to the towpath. 'It's got to stop, he could have killed someone. I'll catch you up.' Her legs were shaking, but still she ran.

Bet called, 'You can't keep fighting everyone's battles.' But in Polly's mind was Will's voice: *We are invincible.*

She heard Bet yelling, just before the butty entered the bridge hole, 'Oh well, no concussion, obviously. It'll give him a scare anyway.'

Polly was scrambling up the horse track which led up to the road. Verity whistled, and yelled, 'Atta girl, Polly.'

She reached the road, looked, but saw no one. She tore over the cut, then searched from left to right, her chest heaving; she could taste the blood trickling into her mouth but could still see no one. For a moment, she stood, then yelled, 'You could have killed someone. Don't you dare hurt a boater again, do you hear?'

Of course there was no answer. She ran back and down the horse track on the other side of the road to the towpath. The butty was halfway through. She ran to catch up with the *Marigold*, which Bet was steering as close to the bank as she dared, and leapt back on board. Bet said, 'He'd gone, no doubt, but equally no doubt you feel better charging about like someone who is determined to set the world to rights.'

It was then that Polly's legs gave way and she sat on the counter, all the fight gone out of her, feeling very sick and utterly ridiculous. 'I wanted to stop just one of them, and it hurts and I feel sick. He could have killed someone. Little devil.'

'Get down into that cabin and stop making the place untidy,' Bet urged her. 'Sit on the side-bed. Don't fiddle about or you'll drip on the floor and we'll have to mop.'

Polly laughed. 'You're so sympathetic, I'm underwhelmed.'

Bet grinned. 'I'm tying up the tiller on a straight line once we get round this bend, and I'll check you. I seem to have to do this with you too often, my girl.'

Polly let the tiller swing over her as Bet steered them around the bend. Ahead, quite a way, was

Saul's boat and butty. Had they been hit too? That'd be a bit much, after being whacked by Leon. She laughed when she recalled telling her parents it was as safe as they had insisted, then slipped into the cabin and sat down with a thump on the side-bed. She closed her eyes, knowing she'd been lucky. Thank the Lord for the bobble, but she wouldn't tell her mum. Anyway, it was only some blasted toe-rag, and was what the boaters had to put up with every trip, year in and year out. What the hell was the matter with people?

Behind *Seagull*, the butty, *Swansong*, was swaying slightly in the wind that tore across this part of the cut.

'Granfer.'

On *Swansong*, Granfer Hopkins spun round, trying to trace Joe's call. He looked back on the towpath, and there was Joe, gaining on the butty. Another bridge hole was coming up. Had the boy been trying his hand at poaching? There were too many houses around, and dogs, so he needed to learn the ropes a bit more. The *Seagull* was entering the bridge hole, towing the butty, and now Joe had caught up and leapt from the towpath on to the counter of the butty. 'Where yer been, young 'un? I says yer to stay close,' Granfer said.

Joe climbed up on to the cabin roof. He was panting. Granfer said, 'We're supposed to be lookin' after yer so I can't 'ave yer losing sight of us, you 'ear me.'

Joe drew some leaves out of his pocket. 'I got these. Nice colours, Granfer, just on the turn, they is. I'm goin' try and make the colours with me pencils.'

Granfer looked, then saw Joe's hands. 'What's that? You been muckin' with our boiler bricks? We need 'em left alone, to boil our clothes. I told yer before, them's not for throwing in the cut to see the splash. Yer too old for sech things.'

Joe nodded. He'd only used half a brick, but he wanted to get the woman, the one who'd made his dad so angry; he wanted her to be scared, like 'e was, but Uncle Saul was right about her, she weren't scared, but narked.

He sat on the roof, next to the dipper. Yes, Uncle Saul was right. Something inside him settled cos she chased him and he weren't so angry, nor so scared just for this minute. He heard her voice, saw her run so fast. He'd not seen women in trousers, really, not seen 'em run at someone, only away. She were strong, so if she were strong, he could be, and all. He was sorry he'd hurt her now. She were bleeding. Sorry, he was.

'You got chores, lad. Go and get the range fire laid. Go on now.'

Joe nodded, dusted up his hands, put his shoulders back. She couldn't half run, but somewhere, inside, he were scared and angry again, and it were partly her fault. Cos of her he'd have to keep looking over his shoulder.

Chapter 15

3 November – nearing Birmingham

The Hatton locks were the ones Polly thought she'd remember most as they slogged on towards the environs of Birmingham three days later, and that was not because of the flight of twenty-one locks but the rushes, rank upon rank of them. Rushes that bent low into the water at their approach, the water of their boats' wash swirling and eddying around the bowed heads.

Polly said, as she stood on the *Marigold* cabin gunwale, 'It seems to be some sort of homage to our survival.'

Verity was on the tiller of the motor, reading *The Count of Monte Cristo*, the pages weighed down by her windlass, and she snorted. 'You've gone mad.'

'No, I mean it, our survival as we lock-wheeled, beamed, and—'

'Oh come off it, we're hardly on the front line, ducky. Anyway, I'm trying to read.' Verity checked ahead, lifted the windlass and turned the page. 'Actually, how's Reggie?'

Polly, knitting a red hat in rib stitch, stared at

Verity, her wool in a pudding bowl on the roof. 'I forgot all about the letter.'

She finished the row, stuck her needles in the wool, and scrambled from the gunwale as Verity tutted and moved aside to let her scurry down the cabin steps and search on the bookshelf, trying to remember where she'd put it. Then she remembered she'd used it as a bookmark in *Winnie-the-Pooh*. She found it, read the letter, and was putting it back when Verity called, 'On your marks, some allotments coming up. Might be leeks for sale on the old table someone set up last time.'

She slipped on to the counter, and then the gunwale, bringing her knitting with her, but would she recognise the woman to whom she had promised the hat, if she saw her again? Well, if she didn't, Bet would. Anyway, she could leave it with Bob and he could hang it somewhere. 'Where are we?'

'We're heading towards Knowle but we won't be there until tomorrow. You have to learn how to place yourself by things like these allotments.' Verity waved to the bank. There was no table, and no leeks, but there were men, or were they women? Either way, they were working on their plots, hats pulled hard down, and wearing trousers and old coats. On the nearest plot the string of the runner bean poles seemed to have perished and some canes were falling. A man waved on his way to the bank with a bucket on a bit of rope. Surely, after all the rain, the vegetables didn't need watering?

She watched as he rinsed out the bucket in the fading daylight. What looked like manure was dumped in the cut. Well, they did much the same, so who was she to sniff and tut.

'So, what did Reggie say?'

'Not a lot.'

Verity closed her book with a thwack. 'Oh come on, he must have said something.'

Polly started knitting two together to create the top of the hat as she replied, 'He's well, hopes I am, and Mum and Dad too. That his mum and dad are, that sort of thing.'

'Not the Oscar Wilde of Bomber Command, then?'

Polly looked at her. 'I hope not, for the sake of a satisfactory sex life.' She dropped a stitch. The light was fading, making the recapturing of it tricky.

Verity stared, then said, 'Polly Holmes, I'm totally and utterly shocked.'

They laughed. Polly said, 'You've taught me well.'

They laughed again.

A fly-boat, the sort which she had learned carried beer, was approaching, storming along the cut on its way to deliver manna to the thirsty Londoners. *Marigold* lurched in its wash. These young men would work throughout as many days and nights as were necessary, with no stops anywhere, to get to where they were going. 'Well paid, too,' murmured Polly.

Verity was steering towards the bank as another narrowboat and butty approached. Ahead, on the left, was a red-brick pub. Behind them, Bet sounded the horn. Verity sighed. 'What does the boss want?'

'Time to moor up, I expect. She said we needed to change the batteries around, so we'll probably do it here, won't we? The light's going, after all.'

Ahead were several boats already moored, and they joined them. The canal was wide enough for them to moor abreast, so Polly took the strap from Bet and secured the butty to the *Marigold*. For some reason they had passed Saul and Granfer tied up outside a lock the day after the Leon debacle three days ago. Bet had called as they passed, 'How do you do, Granfer. Need a shaft, or a tow?'

Granfer had shaken his head. ''Ow do, just got an engine playing around.'

The *Seagull* had followed on behind them ever since, like a shadow. Polly grimaced. Was Saul hurt so badly that he was taking it easy? But no, they had seen him leaping from the motor to the towpath when they passed them. Well, whatever it was, he hadn't thanked her, but he wouldn't. The boaters didn't, and she didn't know why she cared. It was too damned silly – and why did she dream of him, and that kind voice to Joe when Leon rocked the boats.

Bet called them over to the butty for a stew that had been simmering in her range all day; mostly vegetable, but with some bacon. Replete, they headed for the pub, leaving the door unlocked as Leon was well ahead, or so the lock-keeper at the Radford lock had told them a while ago.

As they walked along the towpath some of the boater women were on their counters, the tillers of which were removed. Some were brewing washing on the brick boilers. Instead of ignoring the *Marigold* trainees or pulling a face at their wantonness in wearing trousers or going into pubs, they nodded; some even smiled. Several called, ''Ow do?' This included the old ones, who sat on old stools on the counter, smoking clay pipes.

'It's acceptance,' Bet said. 'We've done well, and kept up with the flow, and not got in their way, more to the point. Perhaps word has got around about lovely Leon and your, and our, part in the tumble, Polly? Who knows.'

In the pub there was the smell of beer, the usual fug of smoke, and the thud, thud of darts on a board.

Almost immediately, while Bet made her way to the bar, Polly led Verity to the darts area and the two teams playing. 'Two bob says we'll win, if we play the winner of this match?'

There was a cackle of laughter. 'Yer'll clean oos out, so yer will. Reckon yer cleaned out the lads last night, or was it the night before, past Buckby.'

Another man, Thomo, or so Polly thought she heard him being called, shouldered his way through. 'I'll give yer a run for yer money.' He spat on his palm and held it out. Verity nudged Polly. 'The pleasure is yours, ducky.'

Polly sort of spat, and shook his hand, Bet whispering from behind her, 'The brothers Thomo,

Timmo and Peter who run the *Venus* and *Shortwood*, and there's no need to let them win. They're the cut champions so we'll need to throw well.' Polly looked at Verity, who edged over, talking into her beer, 'They've no wives or children so we can go in hard as we're not taking food out of the mouths of babes and sucklings.'

Bet was between them now, reaching for the darts on the shelf, feeling their balance before passing them to Verity and Polly. 'Only if you're ready to lose all previous winnings, girls,' she muttered. 'Even if they win they always want to play again.'

The men were beaten but lost with aplomb, finished their beer, and surprisingly Thomo didn't want another match but headed towards the door, passing Granfer who was making for the bar. Bet asked, 'Joe in the kitchen of this pub too?'

''E is. Just got 'ere, we 'ave. 'E wanted a bit of a scamper with the other childers but all them do, if they're on the boat all day. So we watch over 'im and then likes 'im to come in 'ere. The missus helps 'im with his letters.'

'That's good.'

Polly asked, 'Saul's well, is he?'

Verity nudged her. Granfer nodded. 'Getting on, gal. Gettin' on. What's with yer 'ead?'

'Bit of a do with a bridge hooligan, but Bet's pulled the cut tight with a plaster. She was going to stitch it herself, but we'll try this first. It's already getting better.' Actually it throbbed from time to time, and

198

she had felt sick for twenty-four hours. Today it had been better, though. Bet held the door open. 'Come on, we have to change the batteries.'

The girls followed. Verity muttered, 'I still think they're bloody rude. No thank-you – nothing. We could have been killed. Saul could have been killed.'

Bet spun round. 'I don't think you were in any danger, Verity Clement, whereas Polly—'

'It's still bloody rude.'

Bet looked from Polly to Verity and asked, 'Why do you think Saul and Granfer lost ground and are now following us?'

They were nearing the towpath, and Polly could see her breath billowing in the light from the dying boiler fires. What would the ARP wardens say about that? Probably yell 'Put those bloody lights out', but Bet had said that during the Blitz the boaters only washed in the daylight. The washing was already flapping on the lines strung at the rear of the butty cabins.

'Because they had engine trouble, of course,' Verity said. 'Come on, let's get the battery.'

It was Verity's turn to heave out the newly charged battery and shove it out to Polly, who lifted it and groaned, saying, 'I don't need this after a pint of beer.' Verity took the flat one from Bet and connected it.

'How often do I have to say – bend your knees to lift things?' she said.

They stowed it beneath the butty side-bed while Bet coughed. The cold weather seemed to irritate her chest, and she was coughing more and more. Polly was sometimes woken in the night by it.

Once it was all done they fell into bed, leaving the slide hatch open but closing the doors. Thunder woke Polly at two in the morning, but it was too late. It had been raining for hours, from the feel of her blankets. Her face and hair were drenched, her plaster was off, the cut open and bleeding. She swung out of bed on to a wet floor, dragging her soaking blankets and throwing them on to the counter, hearing the slap of the water against their bows, the roar of the rain driving on to the surface of the water, the flash of lightning which lit the sky.

She lit the hurricane lamp, slid shut the slide hatch, towelled her hair dry, dropped the towel on the floor and stood on it while she dressed in her socks, trousers and both her sweaters. She put on her boots, grabbed a clean towel from beneath the side-bed, held it to her forehead and lay on the part of the mattress which had escaped the worst of the wet and all the time Verity snored. There was normality in the noise, and it almost drowned the storm. She fell asleep, not even wanting to be home, because home seemed another world, and nothing to do with this one.

Chapter 16

4 November – arrival at Birmingham

They rose at 5.30, with Bet tutting, and slapping another plaster on Polly's forehead, taking a moment to show her the needle and catgut which would have to be used if it didn't improve. Polly grinned. 'I can feel it healing already. I did start Reggie's letter by telling him that. Not sure why, really. I'm sure he has bigger things to think about.'

'You're such a little teacher's pet. You'd tell Bet it was healing even if it wasn't. Sucking up isn't nice, you know, it's often a lie,' Verity snapped. Polly and Bet ignored her. As they set off, Polly could tell by the set of Verity's face that she had changed back to the girl Polly first knew. Polly sighed and braced herself for a day of it.

She took the tiller, while Verity cleaned up the cabin, on call for the next lock. Dawn had brought an end to the rain, Polly wrote to her parents, leaning on the roof, thinking Braunston Tunnel was worth a mention in her letter home. She explained that they should reach the unloading dock today, or perhaps tomorrow if things went very wrong.

At eight they were still climbing the five Knowle locks, and Polly knew she'd hate them more and more as the months or years went by but she felt that was because they were almost at the end of the journey, and she was extraordinarily tired. For the sake of peace she lock-wheeled because the set of Verity's face was too irritating. In comparison the tranquil pound once they were through was a taste of heaven. 'We'll be gliding along this for two and a half hours,' Bet soothed her as they laid out the snubber to tow the butty. 'I will join Polly on *Marigold* while you, Verity, can have some peace on the butty.'

While Polly made an early lunch of sizzling bacon bought off ration from last night's pub, mashed carrots, swede and potatoes, she used the hinged table to write to Reggie, telling him they were not far from Birmingham, that a pound was a stretch of water without locks; a pound, she said, was something they worshipped and adored. He would smile but she realised she couldn't really remember that smile. She tried to think back to the boys kicking the ball into the net when they were children, but she still couldn't. The lads were just a blur, really, one the same as the other, except for Will.

She added the information about the pound in her parents' letter. Her dad would smile, but what about her mum? Perhaps, but not if she was still talking like a maniac, as she had done since the news of Will's death. It was a ploy which gave her no time to absorb anything other than her torrent of trivial words.

Polly looked up from the table, her pen to her lips. Should she tell her mum that she had known anger, the first for such a long time, and that she had laughed, and not just once, but several times? She reached forward and turned the bacon. What was Verity's loss? A lover, a parent? Why had she resorted to a sharp tongue again? Was it something Polly had done this morning, or to do with the 'loss'? It was then Polly realised that none of them really talked about their lives, they just lived from day to day. Would they ever?

She fried eggs, and bread, and finished her letters after asking Reggie if he played darts for money. She explained that they had won sufficient to buy extras off ration, or off the back of a lorry, then she crossed it out because perhaps the censor was reading it and they'd all be carted off in a Black Maria. She put the food on to plates, placing hers and Bet's on the cabin roof. Polly then jumped off at a bridge hole, and back on to the butty to deliver Verity's meal, curtseying as she did so. Verity muttered, 'Don't hang about, you're not good enough for a tip.'

Polly laughed, but Verity did not. Polly jumped off and ran back to the motor, wondering when the wretched girl would stabilise.

Traffic became more and more congested and they had to wait for oncoming pairs to come through bridge holes before they could continue. They passed under the branches of trees, and between shrub-covered banks, and pattered through a carpet of leaves in one winding spot. It was here that Bet said, as the wind rifled through her hair, 'Believe it or not, we're a mere half a mile, so about half an hour, from unloading this load of rusty billets.'

Polly didn't believe her, as there was no sign that they were near such a big city, but steadily as they pattered on the traffic thickened even more, until – there it was, Tyseley Wharf, Birmingham. They were not alone; there were other pairs of boats moored up and waiting, some of which they knew, some they didn't. Leon was not visible and a great weight dropped from her shoulders.

The wharf was almost on a level with the boats, rather than looming over them as had been the case at Limehouse Basin, and they tied up for now, waiting to be told where to go. Polly felt almost as though she'd dragged the boats all the way, so dog tired was she as she stood at the tiller and breathed in the sense of industry and commerce, then noticed both horse-drawn and motorboats pulling away, heavily loaded, some with coal.

Polly said, 'I thought coal was loaded at Coventry?'

'It is, sometimes, but stop nit-picking and think about your darling Reggie,' Verity said.

Polly ignored her, it seemed the least tiring thing to do, so she continued to watch the toing and froing as they waited on the counter of the *Marigold*, and Bet smoked on *Horizon*. Instead of trees there were great smoking factory chimneys, and huge mounds of rusty iron. There were corrugated-iron sheds, and stained stone sheds, and men bustling, unloading, shouting, laughing. Some smoked, some obeyed the instructions others gave, others waved their arms and bellowed because someone was doing something wrong.

Ahead they could see the *Venus* having steel billets unloaded. Thomo, Timmo and Peter would no doubt be cleaning up *Shortwood*'s cabin while they waited, and would have another darts match tonight. Perhaps they'd be on better form. Lorries were grinding their gears as they drove into or out of the yard. One lorry pulled up near Thomo's boats; the crane driver and dockers continued to unload the steel billets from the *Venus* and lowered them into the back of the lorry. Once it was full the driver roared towards the exit, but screeched to a halt outside the office. Wearing a muffler, he kept the engine running while he jumped out and ran in. Was there an Alf or a Ted in there? Polly wondered.

Bet was standing on the wharf now, slapping her arms against her sides to keep warm. She said, 'The lorry will have to go over the weighing platform, and it will be noted down. Over there is another lorry delivering a load – but of what, I can't see. Machinery of some sort, perhaps. It's a seamless machine, girls, and we are part of it. Now, time to stop gawping and clean up our little darlings, and then we'll clean up ourselves, eh Verity?'

'Oh joy,' said Verity. It had been one of her most overused comments today. Her face was tight, her voice cold. It was as though the closer they got to Birmingham, and journey's end, the sadder, or more angry, she became. Was it because she felt nothing mattered quite so much while she was on the move?

Bet said, 'Miss Clement and Miss Holmes, the hatches will be scrubbed, the floors and the steps of both boats too, while I find out when we're likely to be unloaded.'

It transpired that it would not be until the next morning. All three scrubbed and cleaned, as boaters' wives were doing the length of the wharf; then, not content with that, they polished and Polly wondered if her hands would ever recover; not just from this, but from everything entailed in being a boater.

Clearly they must never bet on winning the housework race, for they still had work to finish by the time the boaters' wives were off shopping to find food wherever they could, ration cards in hand, their string bags hanging empty. Bet wondered if Saul had managed to snare any game. If so, maybe they could make him an offer he couldn't refuse, using their winnings, because they still had some in the winnings jar.

'He's not at Tyseley, yet,' said Polly.

'Been watching for him, have you? What would Reggie say about that?' Verity snapped, her blonde hair streaked with dirt and sweat.

Polly stood back to check the shine on the range bar. 'I can see my lovely face in it, so all is well, grumpy chops.' But was that the problem? That she had someone to write to whereas Verity never wrote to anyone? She had no more time to think about it, because Bet came to inspect their work, running her finger along the bookcase, opening the range oven. 'It'll do, this time,' she said. 'Now for ourselves.'

Mystified, Polly followed the other two, who insisted she brought her clean trousers, pants, socks and shirt on to the wharf, having locked the cabin doors. She asked, but they wouldn't share their secret. Instead they hurried to the tram stop near the entrance to the depot. A tram came and they jumped on. Polly had to stand, along with many others, and it seemed so strange to be here, in a city, bumping and lurching along, with so much noise, so many people, so much traffic, and to top it off, surrounded by the accent of Brum. It was even more obvious that the boaters' speech owed much to this region.

They arrived at a stop near a smoke-stained red-brick building and Bet hopped off, with Verity pulling on Polly's arm. 'Do hurry, can't you.'

In the foyer they paid ninepence each and were given a towel and soap by the woman in the payment booth. She pressed a bell, and a plump grey-haired female attendant in a white cotton coat pushed through swing doors, beckoned, and led them back the way she had come, walking down a white-tiled corridor. This opened on to a large white-tiled hall divided into cubicles. It echoed as Polly asked, 'So, it's a swimming pool? But we're filthy, we can't—'

'It's a public baths,' Bet said.

'We're spotless,' the attendant said. 'But yer not, because yer off the boats.' She looked at Bet. 'You was 'ere before, Missus, and you too, Blondie, I recognise yer. I had to scrub the baths right hard afterwards. Slimy, yer left 'em.'

The woman's forehead corrugated into a scowl.

The three of them looked at their feet, and shuffled. But the woman then said, 'Good work yer do, so I don't begrudge yer. Couldn't do it meself, bloody hard.'

She opened the first cubicle door and the women crowded round as she unlocked the taps and filled first this bath, then the baths in two more cubicles, with piping hot water. 'I won't chain 'em taps oop again, so yer can let it out and top 'em up for a second time. It'll be my part towards 'elping this whole mess of a war. My old chap says you women are doing well. 'E didn't think yer would, but yer does. He's on the cranes, 'appen you saw 'im. Felt bad t'other day, chains broke, sack o' wheat fell, killed a boater while 'er children watched. Don't leave yer feelin' good, it don't.'

She left. Verity said, to no one in particular, 'Well, it wouldn't. I expect the wife, husband and family didn't feel that marvellous about it either.'

The women were quiet for a moment, imagining the scene, the aftermath, and knowing that the boater family would somehow carry on, just as the crane driver was doing.

'Oh hell,' snapped Verity. 'I'm not wasting this

hot water. We'll tip the attendant as she's given us two for the price of one. Last time she didn't and just gave us five inches.' She looked into the cubicle. 'Just look at it – must be a foot. Maybe dropping a bag of wheat on some poor sod should be factored in to every visit we make.'

She slammed into the cubicle. Bet and Polly looked at one another. Bet whispered, 'I thought she was over the hump of whatever it is that's dragging at her, but clearly not. If we knew we could help, perhaps. Maybe you could try and find out, Polly. She won't talk to me.' She raised her voice, 'I'm heading for mine, too. No singing in the bath, anyone. I want to lean back and relax. I don't need foghorns bellowing out.'

Bet chose the cubicle to the right of Verity. Polly was left with the one on the right. She entered, shut the door and leaned back against it. A bath? A heavenly bath, and no nonsense about five inches either. Verity was right, it was a good foot. She undressed as the steam rose. The attendant called, 'Everything all right, ladies?'

Bet called, 'More than all right, it's well past perfect. We can't thank you enough. It makes such a change from sluicing off the worst with cut water, and fiddling about with a little bowl. I fear we smell.'

The attendant said, 'Ye fear right, but then, that's not the worst sin in the world.'

Polly lifted her arm and smelt herself. Her mother would die if her daughter was anything less than fragrant.

'I'll leave you for an hour. Give yer time for two baths, and a brisk towel down. I'd be 'appy if you'd give the bath a swirl round after the last lot of o' water goes down plug 'ole. There's a bit of a cloth behind the taps which I can choock away after. Makes me job of cleaning a bit easier.'

'Of course,' Bet and Polly said. There was silence from Verity.

Polly listened to the squeak of the attendant's wellington boots on the tiled corridor floor, then lowered herself, wondering why she had never realised the sheer luxury of lying full length in piping-hot water. For a while she almost floated, as the water took on the colour of the mud into which she had repeatedly fallen when the bike skidded, not to mention the oil from the engine when it was her turn to clean it, or the cabin roof . . . She closed her eyes and fought to stay awake.

Reluctantly, she stirred when she heard Bet swear, 'Damn and blast.'

Verity called, 'Are you in trouble, boss woman?'

'No, the soap skidded out of my hand, on to the floor so I'll have to get out and find the damn thing. It has a life of its own.'

Polly called, 'Life is unbearably hard.'

They all laughed. Polly hoped Verity was coming round again. After a good soaping Polly let the water out, standing as the slime slid over her feet and accumulated near the plug. She was disgusted with herself. Her mum would pale, and fuss and talk about germs.

She sluiced the slime down the plughole, fitted the plug, ran the tap for a moment until there was an inch in the bottom, before letting that out also. She picked up the enamel mug Bet had advised them all to bring, and washed her hair over the bath. That water too was disgusting. She sluiced it, and finally ran another bath, but only up to the five-inch mark, then sank into the water, rinsing herself again and again, scrubbing her nails with the brush she had brought with her.

Her father had been in the first war, and ever afterwards had a thing about shiny shoes and clean nails. He'd been a stretcher-bearer, one who refused to bear arms but had saved a life or two, he once told her as he sat at the kitchen table polishing the household's shoes to a high gleam and dabbing the twins' plimsolls with Blanco to start the week clean and tidy. It was his Sunday evening chore, while her mum listened to the Home Service on the wireless.

She sluiced off the last remnants of the soap as a buzzer sounded and she heard the returning squeak of wellington boots on tiles. She stood, pulled the plug, and watched the water disappear with a final glug.

The attendant called, 'Are all you ladies awake? Your time is over.'

'Just dressing,' Polly called back, and knew from the flurry of noise from the other cubicles that the same was happening with Bet and Verity.

The attendant wasn't finished. 'I rung me old chap

at the wharf office. We feels so bad about the boating woman we wants to do something to make oop for it. The boater wouldn't take nothing, cos he 'ad family at Buckby where them go to retire on land, but we has a big 'ouse, cos we has a big family, only they's at war. Why not use their beds as you won't be loaded until tomorrow? They's freshly laundered, cos we put up the theatre folk when they comes doing plays, and there ain't one this week. One room each. Bathroom at the end of the corridor.'

'How much?' Verity snapped.

Bet called, 'That's a really nice idea but we just wonder how much? I'm sorry about our friend, she's very tired, and sometimes forgets how to put things nicely.'

'We was thinkin' that it's just something we'd like to do, something we'd like to give. It'd make my old bugger feel better. Never killed no one before.'

Polly said, not sure she had enough money, 'He mustn't feel bad. It was an accident, but we must pay something.'

Bet took over again. 'We can't keep shouting through the door, it's so rude. Give us ten minutes and we'll come and find you, if that's all right.'

'I'll be at end, in the 'tendant's cubicle. You 'as a chat about it. You needn't stay, just thought it a nice rest from the boat, and the noise. Them fly-boats carrying the beer come and go all night. Them's on a quick-return schedule. And . . . well, up to you.'

Polly listened to the fading squeak of the wellington

boots, then the shutting of a door. She sluiced the bath, finished dressing, dragged a comb through her hair and all the time she thought of a bedroom to herself, a bathroom down the corridor, and no bucket. Oh glory be, no bucket.

Bet knocked softly on the cubicle door. 'May we come in?'

Polly shot the bolt, and opened it. 'You may enter my domain.'

The three of them huddled together. 'I can't bear the thought of some ghastly old dive,' Verity said. 'We'll have to walk out, and I don't care if it's rude. At least my cross-bed is full of my dirt, my smell and not some jobbing actor's, who hasn't made it.'

'Do you have to be so unmitigatedly difficult and unpleasant? It's such a kind thought,' Bet snapped.

'But only to ease a conscience, so no – it's not kind. It's not that easy and neither should it be.'

Polly stared at Verity. What had gone on in her life? What? Had someone hurt her? Was that the loss Bet had spoken of at the beginning of everything? Perhaps he left her? She thought back. She'd been writing a letter to Reggie when Verity started to get in a bate, so could it be . . . She said nothing, but pulled out her purse. 'I could offer five shillings. We must pay something, and Verity, if you don't want to give it a try, I'll come with you back to the boat, and then meet Bet wherever the house is. That's if Bet wants to stay in a warm room. Or I hope it's warm, or at least aired.'

For a moment there was silence, the only noise the sound of a knocking in one of the pipes that ran along the back of the cubicle, through a hole and into the next one. It was probably the water heating up again, Polly thought.

Bet crossed her arms. 'I most certainly do, Miss Polly Holmes. It's manna from heaven and I've never known it to happen before. It's worth a look, anyway. So that's two of us. What about you, Verity? You've made it clear it's not up to your usual standard, but who the hell cares. A bed, not a board with a skimpy bit of flock pretending to be a mattress to lie on.'

She opened the door, ushering the girls before her. 'Verity, make up your mind before we reach the attendant's cubicle, and watch that sharp tongue of yours, if you please, or even if you don't.'

By the time they'd reached the end of the corridor Verity murmured, 'Well, if you are game, you needn't think I'm standing guard on the *Marigold* on my own. Leon could be hanging about, just waiting, for all we know.'

Polly did know that he wasn't. He had been at least a day ahead, and was probably on his way to Coventry to pick up coal by now. But if it saved face for Verity to blame her acceptance on safety concerns back at the wharf, it didn't matter.

Mrs Green, for that was her name, insisted that no money must change hands because that would mean that her old bugger wasn't paying penance. 'It's for oos, not yer. For oos. That poor young lady.'

She gave them the address, and told them of the hidden key. 'There's a nice little pub where y'can eat sausages and chips on the corner. Just you lets yoursel' in after your tea and pop on oop to yer rooms since we'll likely be asleep. Top floor, rooms one, two and three, there's brass numbers on the door. There's coal and wood in the grate, my old bugger gets it off the wharf when it's dropped by the carts and lorries.'

'Or even off the lorry when no one's looking?' Verity said. Bet sighed, and dug her in the ribs.

Mrs Green looked at Verity curiously. 'That'd be something my old bugger wouldn't do, ever. The priest wouldn't like it, and neither would God. Perhaps you're another that should make penance, or is it summat else hanging over yer, or someone who done yer wrong, to be so sad and nasty?'

Verity coloured. Bet stepped between her and Mrs Green and said, 'We'll be up really early but will creep out. We'll leave some money by the beds.'

Mrs Green said, 'No you won't. Or we won't be giving it as a gift. I said before, so yer got to understand?'

Polly said, 'Yes, I'm sure we do understand.'

Chapter 17

4 November – evening, Birmingham

They headed through the blackout towards the Bull and Bush, the pub Mrs Green had suggested. Searchlights probed the skies as they skirting bombed-out buildings. Somewhere nearby a beam crashed to the ground, and rats ran across the road ahead of them. 'Flushed out, but they'll just go to another,' Bet muttered, keeping her torch with its reduced beam directed to the pavement which was also damaged here and there.

They turned left, and the next right, and heard singing and a cheer and knew that they were close to the pub. They followed the noise, and there was the Bull and Bush on the corner. Inside there was the usual fug of cigarette and pipe smoke, the rumble of male voices, and the looks of surprise and distrust as they, three women on their own, entered. Three women, however, who clearly weren't on the game, or didn't know how to play it, dressed as they were in trousers and sweaters, not to mention one in a woollen hat.

A man called, 'Reckon my old lady'd like yer 'at for her teapot, yer with the whopper of a bobble.'

Polly snatched off her bobble hat and waved it at him. 'It'll cost you a round of darts later. Winning team has the hat, and a bob on top of that.'

His mate nudged him. 'Favour the lady, why don't you, 'arry.'

There was a shout of laughter.

Bet was forcing her way through to the bar. Once there, she shouted over her shoulder, 'Sausage and mash, you two, or mutton stew?'

'Stew, please,' Verity added. 'Don't forget the beer.'

Bet leaned on the bar in deep conversation with the barman. She called back, 'It'll be sausage and mash, the stew is off.' She gestured over to a table near the fire. 'Sit there and behave,' she ordered.

The men parted for them and as they sat Harry called, 'Yer on for a game, lassies? We'll play yer, Chris, Archie and me.'

Polly took one of the pints of beer that Bet brought over even before she had put the tray on the table. Bet said, 'The barman thought we might be a comic turn at the theatre, as we're staying at Mrs Green's. He wasn't impressed when I told him we were off the cut. Now they know we're staying at the boarding house, don't fleece them, or poor Mrs Green might get it in the neck.'

Verity sipped her beer. 'Don't worry, we'll be kind.'

Polly muttered, 'Well, there's a first time for everything.'

Verity stared at her, slammed her tankard down and turned to Bet. 'You go on at me, but she's got

217

a tongue like a lash and you never say anything, but come down on me like a ton of bricks.'

Bet nodded, looking from one girl to the other, then burst out laughing, shaking her head, trying to stop. She waved her hand in front of her face. 'I'm so sorry,' she spluttered at last. 'So sorry, don't know what's the matter with me. Verity's quite right. You must not lash your tongue so much, Polly, it causes a draught and both of you, please remember I am not running a kindergarten. Seriously, don't, Polly. It's not helpful.'

Polly sipped her beer, knowing she'd say it again if she was pushed, so there. The food arrived borne by an elderly woman whose cigarette, held in the corner of her mouth, had an inch of ash. The three women snatched the food off the tray just as the ash fell where Verity's plate would have been. Bet started laughing. Polly kicked her, but then Verity was laughing, so it was, for heaven's sake, thought Polly, all right again.

The sausages were mostly bread but the gravy was thick and brown, and the mash surely had some butter in. Polly hoped that was all there was, and poked around for ash. Bet leaned forward. 'Don't fuss, just think where we've been, the water we've travelled on, the filth we've just washed off, the bucket . . .'

Verity stared at Polly. 'Bet Burrows is a mad and cruel woman. Here we are, finally clean, sitting in front of a fire, eating food we've not had to cook on a tiny Primus stove or a miniature range, and she brings up the ruddy bucket.'

They were all laughing and Polly ate in the warmth, and the light from the flickering fire, absorbing the strange steadiness of the ground which had made her feel quite sick when she walked from the public baths to the Bull and Bush. She said, 'I've only been a trainee for a few days but I can't quite remember what life on the land is like. It's just been so busy, so different, so far away from—'

'The war,' interrupted Verity.

'Not to mention, your lives,' added Bet. They finished their meal. There was still half a pint left in their tankards. Bet offered her cigarettes. Polly and Verity shook their heads, Verity saying, 'There's enough smoke to breathe without puffing on a fag. Why don't you save them for the cut? Not sure it's helping that cough of yours.'

Bet nodded, swinging round in her chair. 'Perhaps you're right. The dartboard looks as though it awaits, ladies. Now, we must be gentle, it's their first experience of the Terrible Trio.'

Later, at closing time, they left the pub with six shillings in their pocket but no woolly hat, because Polly had felt guilty and let Harry have it for the missus. She had told him to be gentle with it, because it had probably saved her from having her head bashed in by a brick thrown from a bridge, but at least it was free of gob, because she'd washed it. He'd looked from her to the hat and placed it on the table, quickly. 'Little buggers, them kids are. We 'ear of such things, but it ain't right.'

As they set off down the road, they heard the sound of someone running behind them. It was Harry. He thrust the hat at her. 'Can't take this off yer. Yer need it on the cut and make sure yer dodge 'em bridge missiles and don't fall in.' He walked back, coughing. The door opened into the pub.

Polly said, 'That's so kind. But hey, I thought it was closing time?'

'Not for the regulars, don't you know anything? It's a lock-in.' Verity was searching for the key beneath the stone in front of Mrs Green's boarding house, just down from the pub. The sign in the window said FULL.

Polly followed Verity and Bet as they crept up the front steps. 'How do you know about lock-ins? I wouldn't have thought you spent your time in pubs, only clubs.'

Verity stopped turning the key in the lock and said, 'You know nothing about me.'

She sounded angry again, but this time there was something else, something—

The door swung open. It was Mrs Green, who smiled, and looked quite different without her white coat. She gestured up the stairs. 'Waited up for yer, after all. Seemed polite. I changed my mind and 'ave given you the best ones as you left your baths so clean. So it's rooms three, four and five.'

Bet dug into her pocket, and held out the six

shillings they had won. 'We want you to have this. We won it at darts tonight, at the Bull and Bush. Really, save it for your children, for when they come home from the war.'

Mrs Green looked at the money for a moment, and took three shillings. 'For the children, then. Thanking yer, so now each of yer take a bob for yourselves.' She let three shillings drop into the large pocket at the front of her wrap-around floral apron. 'Only for the children, mind, and I thank yer. I lit the fire in your rooms. Breakfast at six? Time for yer to get to t'wharf for unloading. My old bugger says yer'll be early on. Go on to the second landing.' She pointed the way. They traipsed up the stairs.

Verity stopped at number three, opened the door, and slammed it in her wake. Polly and Bet stared at each other. Bet nodded, that was all, and took number four. 'See you in the morning, sleep well.'

She shut the door quietly. Polly opened the door to number five and entered into the dry warmth and the soft light from the fire, and the silence. There were no owl hoots, no sound of the wind, or a child's cry from another boat tied up close to them, no sound of a man talking to his wife, no pat-patter of a fly-boat at all hours of the night as it transported beer, or whatever it was this time, down to London non-stop. Most of all, the room didn't move. Neither did it have Verity, snoring.

She pushed the thought of Verity from her, and bounced on the bed; the mattress was soft, the bed seemed so wide. It was a lost world of comfort and luxury, and quite strange to her, as though here she was, out of place on the land, alone in a room. Alone.

She stripped off her clothes, scrambled into bed, and slept immediately, waking only to a knock at the door and Bet saying, 'Breakfast in ten minutes. Chop-chop.'

They made their way back on the tram, hopping off near the wharf, with Verity buying *The Times* from the newspaper stall, rolling it beneath her arm and running to catch up as Bet and Polly reached the policeman at the entrance. 'Good morning,' they said, in unison. He flicked a salute. 'Nice one, too.'

They hurried through the yard, dodging the puddles left by the overnight rain which they had not heard. Behind and around, chimneys were belching dark smoke, men were hurrying as they did at the depot and Limehouse. The women scrambled on to *Marigold* undoing the tie-strings, gathering up the tarpaulin, getting drenched with its stained water. Verity swore and almost sobbed, 'I hate this life. I bloody hate it. We were so wonderfully clean for a moment.'

Polly looked away, saying nothing. Bet was starting on the planks, calling to them to hurry, and Polly could see the crane lifting out the remnants of the steel billets from the hold of the *Letchworth*'s butty, which was tied up just in front of them. It was then that she looked behind, and there was the

Seagull moored behind *Horizon*. It must have come just before the last lock closed. Bet saw her looking. 'They arrived early morning, the foreman said.'

Verity muttered, 'Who the hell cares.'

Polly untied the last of the top sheets on her side and threw them back, with Bet the other side, folding and folding them. She helped Bet stack the top planks while Verity rolled down the side sheets, leaving them tied up in pipe-lines tight on the gunwales. Together they stowed the top sheets away in the *Marigold*'s cratch, or store at the fore-end, just as the *Letchworth* moved off with the usual pat-patter. The crane was already swinging into position over the hold. Gulls were calling though they were miles from the ocean.

Bet yelled, 'The unloading will begin any minute.'

'All done,' called Polly.

Just then, three dockers jumped on to the top of the steel billets and the crane swung into position. Within two minutes the unloading began. Polly followed Verity and Bet to the butty and tackled its tarpaulins, the planks. In front of them the *Marigold* was rocking as the billets were removed by the men who were unloading from the fore-end far side. Polly looked again, because the motor was still heavy with billets against the wharf side, and surely the weight was dragging *Marigold* down, sinking it?

'Bet,' she called, but just then the foreman yelled, 'Take from the nearside too, you silly buggers. Keep her level, for Gawd's sake. You'll have her over.'

The men rushed to fix the chains to nearside billets, while the girls rushed to loosen off the mooring straps. The crane began to take billets from the nearside as Polly walked towards the butty. As she did so, a boy ran past, coming from the yard. It was Joe.

'How do, Joe,' she said.

He just looked at her, then away, heading full tilt for the *Seagull*. As she carried on, Saul overtook her, with that long-legged loose stride, his hands in his pockets, his wide leather belt shining. There were loose vegetables in a string bag over one shoulder. He had a yellow kerchief on today. She called, 'How do?'

He turned and nodded in reply, and for a moment she thought she saw a smile, but then it was gone. His hair was flopping over his tanned forehead and he looked so young; too young to be looking after an old man and a boy. She said, as *Marigold* began to settle, 'It's a nice day.'

He looked at her again, and nodded, again, and now there really was a smile. 'Good wind across the water. It cleans t'air summat grand.'

Verity was with her now. She said, 'I've a newspaper in the cabin, Saul. Perhaps you'd like to read it? Oh, I forgot, that's not something you can do, is it.' It wasn't a question.

By now on the butty's top planks, Bet lifted her head. 'Get down here at once, Verity,' she ordered. There was a terrible rage in her voice that mirrored that of Polly, who for a moment couldn't breathe, she was so furious at Verity's cruelty. Saul looked at Verity, and then Polly, the smile gone, his jaw muscles tightening. He glared at them and strode on towards the *Seagull*, his head hard down, his windlass in the back of his belt. Verity muttered after him, 'Well, don't thank me, whatever you do. We only saved you from Leon, after all.'

Bet shouted again, 'If you don't get down here now, and into the butty cabin, I will come up there and get you. You too, Polly.'

Polly gripped Verity's arm and hauled her on to the butty counter while Verity struggled, shouting, 'Let me go.'

Polly did, thrusting her away, scared she would shake her if she held on to her any longer. Verity stepped back. Polly ground out, 'How dare you be so rude, so cruel, to anyone? How bloody dare you?' Bet was on the roof, sitting on her heels, a cloth in her hand. 'Indeed, Verity, I've finally reached breaking point, I—' Verity glared from one to the other then said, 'You have no idea what I'm going through.' She swung away, and lost her balance.

Polly reached forward. 'Care—' It was too late. Verity fell into the dock, screaming as she went. Some dockers walking past stopped, but seeing Bet jumping down on to the counter, they walked on.

Polly rushed to the counter edge, reaching out a hand. Bet snatched a shaft off the roof, and held it out to Verity who was splashing, coughing and spluttering. Verity ignored the shaft. 'Take my hand,' ordered Polly, 'and keep your mouth shut.'

Bet murmured, holding the shaft close to Verity, 'You might like to add, Polly, keep it shut the rest of the time too, if what's going to spew out is so vile.' She raised her voice. 'Come on, Verity, calm down, don't swallow the water, grab the shaft or Polly's hand. Your choice or we'll go about our business.'

To Polly, talking quietly again, she said, 'I fear she must go home. I can't have this. She's only got the return trip to pull this around, and why would she?'

Polly stared down at Verity as she dog-paddled to the butty, her mouth tightly closed, real fear and despair in her eyes. It was the despair that caught at Polly's heart because in it she recognised her own after Will's death. 'Not yet, Bet,' she whispered. 'Let me talk to her, I think I might know what some of it is about. I was writing to Reggie and that's when she started. There's a good girl under all this, perhaps. Besides, we can't let her loose on society without trying everything. It wouldn't be fair on it.'

The two women smiled at each other. Bet nodded. 'All right, but only one more chance. I can't have the boaters upset. That sort of remark does great damage.'

Verity had reached the hull. Bet dropped the shaft, and together she and Polly dragged Verity on board, hauling her to her feet, where she dripped, and coughed. Verity said, shivering, some straw caught in her enamel hair slide, 'How bloody dare you, Polly Holmes. He's a rude, common little man. He's never thanked us, and I know the boaters don't but they damn well should. It's time people like this learned some manners and stopped just taking.'

Bet had been replacing the shaft on the roof but at this she turned, reached forward, gripped Verity's arm. Verity flinched, staring wide-eyed at their trainer. Bet said, 'You listen to me, and listen well, you silly child. That young man has held back, and tucked in behind us, shepherding us all the way – guarding us, in other words – for daring to help him escape damage from Leon. Why the hell else would a boater give way to a bunch of bloody women, one so rude and bullying she deserves a damn good spank. Now, I'm leaving you to Polly because I can't do this any more. And don't think Polly did anything to you. You overbalanced, and that's that.'

Bet turned to Polly. 'Get her back on that wharf, dripping or not, and both of you cast off the mooring straps because I need to run the *Marigold* ahead now she's unloaded, and tow the butty forward. You will moor up *Marigold* again, and do the same with the butty. Then, when the unloading begins, loosen off the ties.' She set off walking on the billets to the fore-end of the butty, and jumped on to the *Marigold* before disappearing into its cabin.

Verity wailed, 'But I can't go on the wharf looking a fool.'

Polly said, 'But you are a fool, so get up there, and later we're going to sort this out, once and for all.'

*

227

Polly and Verity had cast off and tied up again in stony silence. They obeyed Bet and traipsed to *Marigold*'s counter, while Bet stayed with the rocking, clanging and banging of the butty's unloading. Verity stood dripping and shivering on the counter.

Polly said, 'Stay there while I put your newspaper on the floor for you to stand on, while you wash.'

Verity said nothing, just leaned against the cabin, shivering, hugging herself against the wind with her head bowed. Polly poured clean water from the water can on the roof into the bowl and put *The Times* on the floor of the cabin. 'In you come,' she called.

Verity came, and stood on the newspaper. Polly said, 'We've been here before, when you mucked up and came in at dawn. This time, you wash yourself, and dress, and then we talk.'

It was Polly's turn to stand on the counter, in the rising wind. She gave Verity fifteen minutes, but after ten Verity called, 'I've finished.' She sounded like a child. 'I've made a drink for us as well.'

Polly joined her. They sat on their beds clutching mugs of tea. The silence continued. Finally, Polly spoke. 'There's something wrong, we all know that. You've talked of loss and I can recognise despair when I see it, and rage, so we need to talk about it. I don't want you to leave. I want to work with you, and come to know you.'

Verity looked down at her tea. At last she said, 'Just drink your tea and leave me alone.'

Polly didn't know what to say. Verity's real world was not one of which she had knowledge. Wealth and privilege and spoilt to the gunwales . . . It was all so different. Perhaps it wasn't despair she had seen?

Verity said, 'Why should I be despairing, you idiot? Even now, in spite of the war, my family and I have servants. I have a groom to look after the horse I love. We have a cook—'

'But you *can* cook so why pay someone, when you don't need to?' Polly interrupted.

'Ah, that's a typical "Polly" remark. We also have a family tree, and a position, and the importance of that, dear Miss Holmes, is carved in stone on my heart. "We have a position, Verity, and you will not besmirch it. I have paid off your bit of rough."'

As she looked at Polly, tears were streaming down her face. 'She called the boy I love a bit of rough. He was the chauffeur, and I thought he loved me, but he just disappeared one day and left no note. I kept trying to find him, going to all "our" places – the pubs where he taught me to play darts, the woods where we walked. But nothing.

'One day he was cleaning our Rolls, the next he was gone. Mother said, in the drawing room, when I asked, that she knew not where. She said that he appeared to have packed his bags the previous evening and was gone by morning, and why on earth should I care? Well, I wasn't going to tell her, was I? Then six months ago, Mother called me into that same drawing room, shut the door behind me, and said that she couldn't stand this "ghastly mooning around", and then told me she had offered Tom three hundred pounds to leave because she couldn't have her daughter making a fool of herself.'

Polly reached out to Verity across their cabin but Verity shook her head. Polly started to rise, wanting to comfort this girl, but Verity snapped, 'Don't be kind, I can't bear it when I've been such a bitch; just let me finish. Mother said, "Verity, now can you see just how much you were worth to him, and how I have saved you from a disaster?" She then said he'd told her he would have taken two hundred pounds, which was all he had been after the whole time. Leading me on, he said, in order to get money to set up some business or other. The look on her face, Polly. I will never forget it. Such contempt and not for him, but for me.'

Polly could hardly believe any of this but it was written clear as day in the pain on Verity's face. But no one must think they had only been worth money to the person who said they loved them. To have to experience this seemed to Polly almost worse than the death of Will or a lover. It was dirty, without honour, and left one no consoling memories, even. No wonder Verity was so hurt and angry.

Polly insisted, 'You are beyond price, we all are. If the person you love took that money, he is not your love. If your mother told you all of this, then you must somehow put it to one side, and perhaps be better than the person she is. You must find the girl that your friends like, you must . . . oh, I don't know, make something better for yourself.'

'I was rude, and unkind to Saul. I just have this . . .'

'Anger, which is perhaps grief?' Polly suggested but it was to herself as much as Verity. The two girls nodded. Of course, thought Polly, it is grief. Poor Mum and Dad, poor Verity, poor herself.

'I joined the boats because we keep on the move, in a separate world, and one which Mother can't be proud of, and won't come to, as she would have, had I been a WAAF or something. My friends would be shocked if they knew what I am doing, and she won't tell them and I promised I wouldn't. I pretend I am in intelligence. I just feel I have to be what she thinks I now am: a person beyond the pale. I have to be as different to her as I can.'

Verity stared at her hands, which were gripped into fists. 'Polly, Tom bought me, or she sold me. I can't quite work it out, but what I do know is that she let me look for him, trawling the pubs, asking, always asking. Everyone must have been laughing. He wanted to start a garage, we talked about it, and I would live with him in a flat above and do the figures. I would have put up with the ridicule of my friends, but all the time he must have been looking at me, and seeing the price of a garage.'

She laughed, harshly, her voice still thick with the tears that were falling. 'But it's not your fault, or Bet's or Saul's, or Reggie's, who you write to, and

231

it's time I stopped wanting to kick out all the time. I want to stay on the cut, and not just because if Bet sacks me I have nowhere to go any more. I just want to stay.'

Verity's eyes were red from weeping, the straw was still stuck in her hair slide.

Polly shook her head. 'Just pick on someone your own size before you insult a person who can't read, and who is shepherding us.'

Verity half sobbed, then laughed. 'He's a fine figure of a bloke, I reckon he can look after himself.'

Polly shook her head. 'No, he can't. Words hurt a bloke like him because he isn't as articulate as you. Well, they'd hurt me if I wasn't used to you by now. He has his pride, it's almost all he has. His sister's gone, his parents are dead and, what's more, this is his world we've barged into, and he will now think we are sneering at him, at everyone like him. You've done what the chauffeur did to you, in a way.'

The two girls held their mugs of tea, which were cold now, and silence fell. Finally Verity whispered, 'Should I apologise to Saul, and thank him for looking after us?'

Polly looked doubtful. 'I don't know. It would then mean that we really know he can't read, when you didn't quite exactly say that. What was it? – "that's not something you can do, is it". It might have meant he needed glasses or something. Perhaps we should all thank him for being our shepherd, but on the other hand, let's be like the boaters and accept it as paying off an obligation. The obligation he might feel he owes us for helping *him*. The question is, will he go on guarding us now?'

Remembering Mr Green, who might be swinging the crane around outside above their heads, Verity said, 'I hope Mr Green feels he's paid his penance. I can't imagine how it must feel to kill someone or even to have seen it happen.'

They looked at one another, remembering how Bet had seen her father do just that. Verity said, 'Bet's such an admirable woman. I can't think how you get used to that. Do you think she will ever visit him? Will he ever improve?'

'He had a fall from a horse, and was damaged, she said, so I don't know.'

'You know she left teaching – the whole thing made her walk away, first to a narrowboat, but since the war, to a house at Buckby, and now she's back.'

'It's so awful, really truly awful.'

Verity sighed. 'Yes, you're right. *That* is awful, mine is just grubby, and one day I suppose I will forget, but she never will. It makes me think that I've lived inside my head for too long. Self-pity is never good.' She put her shoulders back. 'Hey, Polly, this unloading will take for ever, or at least most of the day, then we head for the ghastly Bottom Road, hell bent for Coventry.'

Polly smiled at her. 'Where else have you got to go? Relax, and tell me about the "ghastly" Bottom Road.'

Verity rose, took Polly's mug. 'Can we be friends in time, do you think?'

'I think we probably already are, don't you?'

'On the way to it, Polly, if I don't mess it up.' She took the mugs to the range and placed them on the rest.

'If you do,' Polly said, 'it's into the water with you again, if only to keep your mouth shut.'

Verity flicked her with water from the bowl. Polly shrieked and leapt up the steps, with Verity in pursuit. Bet, who was on the kerb talking to the foreman, turned at the noise. 'I'm still running a kindergarten, I see, girls,' she said. There was a question left hanging in the air. Verity called, 'I'm sorry. It won't happen again, really it won't.' She clearly meant more than chasing Polly.

Bet just nodded, and said, 'We'll see.'

Chapter 18

5 November – Tyseley Wharf, Birmingham

It was early evening and Saul felt exhausted. The motor, *Seagull*, had been unloaded after the *Marigold* and *Horizon*, and was riding high while the butty, *Swansong*, was still slung low in the water. They'd get to it in the light of day, the foreman had said. Granfer had quarrelled with the foreman, pointing his finger, saying the *Seagull* had money to make and loads to pick up; besides, didn't they know there were a war to win?

The foreman had said, 'Look 'ere, we're only human, and don't do miracles every day. Them's take a bit longer, so yer calm yersel', Granfer Hopkins. You'll be off by lunchtime tomorrow.'

Saul lit the hurricane lamp in the *Seagull*'s cabin and hung it from the ceiling hook, because there was no way he wanted to charge the battery again. He could hardly sit still, though he were so tired. He should have been heading to Coventry by now, having picked up his load of coal, hot on the heels of them girls. They'd be way ahead of him so how could he protect them? Especially that Polly.

Granfer stuck his head through the doors and said, 'Don't yer fret, our Saul, them's safe enough. The bugger went through a day afore them. 'Sides, you cain't keep 'em safe for ever. Something'll 'ave to 'appen, and mayhap 'e'll forget.'

Granfer pushed the slide shut, and the doors, in case they were yelled at for breaking the blackout, and Saul stood there, listening to make sure Granfer made it on to the butty counter, and heard the slap of the cabin doors closing after him.

Young Joe looked up from the book given to him by the teacher at the school he had gone to today. 'Them women was rude, you know, just before school 'ttendance bloke called. Them taunted yer with t'newspaper. Don't know why yer hold oop our loads for 'em.'

'We's obliged, is why. Besides, it's just the toffee-nosed one who is, not t'other one who hit your da.'

'She be called Holly, or summat like that.' Joe kept his finger on the picture in the book, the one he'd been tracing with his finger because he liked the shape of the bear. 'She's the one who made Da savage with oos. She be the one who make it worse.'

Saul shook his head. 'I told yer since, and I'll tell yer now, she stopped it being a damn sight worse, you daft lad. After 'e finished with me, 'e'd 'ave been after yer granfer, and Lord knows if 'e'd ave survived, then 'e'd a took you off with 'im. Yer got to listen to me, Joe, and give credit where it be due.'

Joe put his hands over his ears. 'I don't want to,

cos it means yer can't keep me safe on yer own. Then I be scared all the time.'

'I told yer, and so did Granfer, that I won't be caught like that again, so stop yer worrying.'

Joe just looked at him as though he was thinking of something else. After a while he said to Saul, 'Her 'ead is better. Got cut, didn't it, going into a bridge 'ole?'

Saul was surprised. 'I suppose so. Yes, it were raw and now it's fadin'.'

Granfer stuck his head through the slide. 'Time the lad was in bed, our Saul.'

'Right, Granfer. I'll come on up on t'counter and give 'im some peace.'

Joe called up to Granfer, 'The warden'll 'ave your guts if yer let the light show them bombers the way. Is that how the bombers found Saul's mam and da?'

'Who knows why they found 'em. It's life, in't it,' Granfer said. 'Anyways, what's that book you got given from school? Did they show you the letters in't?'

Joe shut the book, and traced the letters on the front. 'I forget what they said.' He traced his finger around the last big letter. 'I likes these shapes. These circles.'

Saul, who had sprawled on the side-bed, rose and came across. 'That's a nice picture,' he said and flicked open the book. 'The teacher writ summat 'ere. What do it say?'

Joe flushed. 'Can't rightly remember, but summat like "To Joe, to help with yer letters".'

Saul nodded. 'I reckon I needs to go and see 'er, give 'er some money for it. Get 'er to read it to me, then I can 'elp yer, maybe.'

Joe snatched up the book and held it against him. 'No, no, I did work for 'er. I . . . Well, I emptied them bins where they put the paper and things like that. And she'll 'ave forgot by the time we come again, won't she, Granfer?'

But Granfer had gone, and the slide hatch was shut. Saul sat down on the side-bed again, as he watched Joe reopen the book as though it held treasure. The pictures were grand: a little lad and a bear, and a honeypot, and summat that looked like a donkey. The lad had to learn to read. It'd open up the world to him and then no one could say what that girl said today. He dug more coal from the coal bin beneath the second step, feeling his stomach churn with such a sorrow that it made his eyes sting, like they had when that snooty one had said he could read her paper. He looked across at Joe, thinking about the snooty one. Then he thought that . . . that . . . p'raps she thought he needed eyeglasses.

He gripped that thought, swallowed and said, 'Yer must go to school, when we stop at depot for orders. If yer can go at the start of a trip, and at Birmingham, and then at depot again it's sort of reg'lar, and yer'll get the 'ang of it, Joe.'

'I don't want to go. What if Da gets me on the way?' Joe turned a page, not looking at Saul, but the furrow between his brows told Saul he was sizing up the pictures. Would he draw them?

Saul replaced the coal tongs his mam had bought off the blacksmith in the depot, and murmured, 'If 'ttendance officer don't come to take yer, then one of us'll do it. Like I's said before, the cut runs won't last, and we needs to think of land jobs, or so I reckon. So did my mam and da, they wished . . .' He stopped.

They had wished they'd sent him off to the live-in school, but he hadn't wanted to go. He wanted to stay with them, on the cut where the birds flew over as they travelled along, as the otters slid in and out of the water, as the owls hooted, and the night sky showed through the open slide hatch. He was glad he hadn't now, because the bomb had taken them when they was walking near the depot. If he'd gone to the live-in school like the teacher had said, cos he was clever, he wouldn't have had that growing-up time with them, or been able to help Granfer and Joe now cos he just wouldn't have wanted to.

But he wished he'd been at the school with every bit of the rest of his heart, because most of the time his head was buzzing with thoughts that ended nowhere, cos he didn't have the learning to take them on to somewhere. He'd tried to teach himself, resting a book on the cabin top, but he didn't know where to start, and he didn't want to ask no one, or they'd have a good laugh.

Joe looked up from the book and said, 'Maybe

that's where Mam is, getting herself a banker's job.'
Joe yawned, the hurricane lamp spluttered, and
shadows danced.

Saul shook his head. If he let the lad start thinking
on Maudie, then there'd be no sleep for either of
them, for he'd toss and turn, and then Saul's stomach
would turn too, cos he'd go and sit with the lad, all
night, but had no answers for him.

'Maybe she is,' he answered, chasing around
inside his head to find another thing to talk about.
He closed his eyes and let the pictures come, and
the first made him smile. He opened his eyes, and
said, 'D'you see 'ow that snooty one went in t'cut.
Did that Polly toss 'er in, or did 'er fall? It's Polly
yer see, not Holly. I reckon that Polly gave 'er a
piece of 'er mind, whatever, so I reckon she got a
right good 'eart. Your grandma, my mam, said that
people who 'elp have a good beat to their heart,
which is why we need to 'elp back. Them might not
be the best boaters, but them're different. Yer never
know what they going to do.'

Joe was smiling, but then his face clouded, and
his lips thinned. He stared at the book and pushed
it away, lying down, his eyes open, staring up at
the hurricane lamp which shifted slightly as the
Seagull drifted to and fro, tethered though she was
by the mooring rope.

Saul saw and sighed. Where was the lad going in
that head of his?

He leaned back on the side-bed, watching the

flames in the grate. There weren't much coal because it got too hot with the slide closed. He heard Granfer's footsteps, and the slide was shoved back again. Granfer looked in. 'Time the lad was in bed, I said, Saul. Use the lav in t'yard, and your Uncle Saul'll go with you.'

Saul and Joe sauntered into the yard, and while the lad used the lavatory Saul looked out at the chimneys, the crane, the warehouses, black against the starlit sky. Somewhere he could hear men and women's laughter from a pub. He wanted to be there but he was a father now, at least till Maudie came back. He turned on his heel and stared out over the water. A queue of laden boats waited behind the *Swansong*, mostly Grand Union too, they were, as the days for the independents were closing, and the horse-drawn nearly gone and all.

There were bitty bits of light on the counters as the women smoked while their men drank in the pub. Bitty bits that were like pinheads.

It were the same, always the same, hour after hour on the cut, standing, working, lock-wheeling, loading, unloading, never a day off. Them women worked their guts out. Had Maudie had enough o' that, on top of being belted black 'n' blue by the bastard? They'd all tried to stop it, but Maudie wasn't having none of it. 'I love 'im,' she'd say, 'and after, 'e always be sorry and lovin'.'

Saul loved the cut, and he hated it. With the war he thought he could escape – he could learn to fight proper, but then he weren't allowed because the war needed the boaters. Then they brought in the women cos some men had managed to go early. He laughed aloud again when he saw Polly having a right go at the blonde one till she fell in, and then that Polly'd helped her out.

He could tell Bet liked her. Bet? The women had thought her strange, teaching women to run the boats cos she'd lived in one herself. What would make a woman live like that, without a man, without kids? A nice woman too? It were different for the young like Polly. It was just for a while. The thought churned, but life was what it was. They had other lives, the young ones.

He dragged his cigarettes from his pocket, lit one, let the match burn for a moment, expecting, and hearing, 'Put that light out.' Then a laugh. It was the policeman at the gate.

He drew deeply as the searchlights began their stabbing of the night sky, dimming the stars. Joe came out of the lavatory, slamming the door behind him. Saul said, 'Did you do your teeth?'

'Course. I don't want 'em falling out like Granfer's.'

They walked back to the boat and were hailed by Mrs Wakely who was sitting on the cabin counter of the *Norfolk*, just behind them. 'You keeping up with yer washin', young Saul? Joe, I haves a nice biscuit for yer.'

'Just about on top of the washin', Mrs Wakely.'

Joe hopped on to her counter while Saul stayed on the kerb. 'Tom at the pub be 'e?' he asked Mrs Wakely.

'Oh aye. 'E was 'oping those lasses'd be there, to win back a bob or two at darts. Done 'im good to lose to 'em. I weren't sure about lassies on the cut but they's all right, pull their weight and don't hold up the boats too much at the locks. Mark yer, they've got Bet with 'em just now, but after a trip or two she'll be training others. Then we'll see what's what with them two on their own boats. Maybe they won't stay though, lots don't cos young lassies on the cut get lonely, and tired and too wet and cold, and give up.'

Saul nodded. 'Goodnight, Mrs Wakely.'

They walked back to the *Seagull*. Mrs Wakely called after Saul, 'Don't yer be lonely being an uncle and grandson, our Saul. Yer got to have a life, an' all.'

He waved his hand and said 'Goodnight' again.

The two of them stepped on to the *Seagull* where Granfer was on the counter, leaning against the cabin and drinking a mug of tea in the darkness. He ruffled Joe's hair. 'Yer get yer 'ead down, for the 'undreth time of saying. We'll be towing them boats through the bugger of a Bottom Road tomorrow, so we'll need yer muscle.'

Joe turned and pressed himself against Saul, who put an arm around him and held him close. Joe said, 'Sometimes we do things wrong, don't we, Uncle Saul, cos we gets so angry and it takes a mite of putting 'em right again.'

Saul squeezed him. 'You have to stop worrying about your da. It's up to 'im to put things right, and maybe he will. Now get to bed. We'll be busy tomorrow.'

Granfer had doused the hurricane lamp and Saul watched while Joe made his way by the starlight from the slide. Granfer called, 'I pulled out yer bedding. Yer sleep well.'

They shut the slide and the doors behind the lad, and Saul flicked his cigarette stub into the cut, watching it arc and die. He was lonely, but when did he see girls, except when they passed on the cut, or tied up at the lay-overs?

'Yer all right, lad? It's a lot, taking on t'lad, and t'boats.'

'I's always all right, Granfer, but I don't know what's right to do, if'n yer know what I means, with the lad, an' all. I just want to know where Maudie is, an' when she's comin' home. I want Leon t'stay away, cos what rights 'ave we to the boy? He's Leon's, not ours.'

Granfer slurped his tea. 'That's yer all over, boy. Stop your mind, make it be still. He's 'ere with oos, that's enough for now. We'll keep him safe, or die trying, cos we do 'ave a right. He's our Maudie's flesh and blood, and we couldn't 'elp her when she was 'ere, so we will help 'er now.'

But how? Saul wanted to ask.

Joe lay on the cross-bed. He should use the side-bed, because this 'ad been Uncle Saul's, but here he felt safer, because he could pull the crochet curtain across. That way his dad wouldn't know he was here, and would have to get past Uncle anyway. His mum had always said his dad didn't mean it, that it was the drink, but he did mean it. He had heard him shouting at her the night she ran away. Dad had pulled her off the boat and said he'd see her off, see if he didn't, and he 'ad. He saw his mum's face as she had said, when Joe asked her one Christmas, that she'd never leave him or her lad, but she had lied.

She'd said he could always trust her, always.

He couldn't.

Well, no one could trust him either, not really. He touched the book he had put under his blanket. He loved the pictures, and the shapes in the words, and he shouldn't have it, not really, but he had thought she was bad. She really wasn't so he should put it back on her shelf in *Marigold*.

He turned on to his side again. But she hadn't said nothing about missing it to no one, so she hadn't noticed, not yet. He'd have heard if she had, but grown-ups didn't read children's books. And on the bridge hole he hadn't really meant to hurt her with the brick; besides he were angry at her, then, and scared.

He turned to face the wall of the engine room. He was like his dad sometimes, but he couldn't think that. No, he was like his mum, and Uncle Saul, and Granfer cos he hadn't meant it. But that was what his mum said about his dad. He wished he could forget it all, and have an empty head, but it never happened. Tomorrow, though, they'd be real busy and he'd have to help to tow the boats through the Bottom Road locks, and that'd make him tired, stop his mind, and one day he'd know what he should do. He'd pay back the money from their jar too, when he could – somehow.

Again he turned on to his back, and fingered the crochet curtain. His grandma and grandpa were nice, like lovely old Granfer, the head of their family. Saul and Mam were nice too, like them. Well, he would be from now on, if he could, but he feared it were in him not to be, like his da.

Chapter 19

6 November – Tyseley Wharf, Birmingham

The next morning the three women cleaned the holds of debris and rust fragments from their unloading, coughing as they swept and the dust billowed, undoing all the good the baths had done. Verity, though, leaned on her broom, shaking her head at the other two as they all stood on the hold's wooden boards. 'Right, now you'll stink as badly as I do after my "cut" bath, so stop your moaning.'

Bet and Polly snatched a look at her but saw the smile. 'Yes, ma'am,' Bet replied. 'Anything you say, ma'am.'

It was Polly who saluted but all three of them who laughed.

Bet poked at one of the boards. 'Damn and blast, three broken, and since the order is to pick up coal from Coventry we're going to have serious bilge-cleaning once we're unloaded. We won't pump out the water, because it'll help stabilise it as we ride high. Come on, chop-chop.'

They chop-chopped for the next half hour and

then set off for the Bottom Road, with Verity and Polly on the butty, being towed on a snubber, past the shunting yards and Birmingham backstreets.

'Why don't we go back the same way?' asked Polly, who sat on the butty cabin roof threading wool through the centre of the card circle she had cut to make the pom-pom she would sew on to the finished hat. 'Why not just wheel the boats round if it's such a pig of a cut and go back the way we all came? There's plenty of room.'

The morning breeze cut through her sweaters and thrashed her own pom-pom from side to side. She continued to thread wool through the hole, and work her way around the circle. She'd done about three layers, so a few more should do it. Soon the job would be done, and then she just needed to remember who it was she had promised it to. It would help if she could remember the name of the motor and butty but she couldn't, so no point in ruminating any more. She'd leave it with Bob at the pub.

'If only going back was an option,' Verity ground out, as she steered. 'But the powers that be have decided this cut must be used. They might change their minds in due course, I suppose, because we're all bleating so much about the filthy route.'

A dog walker on the towpath waved, and the dog barked. Way ahead of Bet's motor was a boat and butty but they'd left the *Seagull* and *Swansong* behind with the last bit of unloading still to be done. Polly missed them, but she doubted Saul would want to be too close to them any more. Why would he when he'd just been mocked?

'Why not change over, Polly? It'll be good practice to steer us out of the wharf.'

It was not an order but a suggestion from Verity, so Polly smiled, and shoved the wool and card into her pocket, and they changed places. Verity leaned against the cabin, her arms crossed, looking out at the smut-stained warehouses, houses and offices that overlooked them, casting the canal into shade. Polly held the tiller with a loose grip. It was quieter here, without the pat-patter of the engine, and protected from the cross-winds. In the distance was the banging and crashing of a busy industrial zone.

They glided on, and in spite of herself every so often she looked round, checking, consumed by a momentary fear. But no Leon. He was well ahead. Had Will felt fear?

As Polly steered the unloaded butty behind *Marigold*, she could feel deep within her the beginnings of something . . . Then, as they passed a wharf, she realised it was pain. Verity was looking at her. 'You all right?' she asked.

'Cold, that's all. So what's so bad about the Bottom Road except the view?' She nodded towards the washing that was hanging out of windows of the apartments they were passing. Some were bomb damaged, and showed the charred remains of rooms.

Further along Verity waved to someone at a window. 'Wotcha,' the small girl called.

'Wotcha,' Polly and Verity called back.

'Canal scum,' the girl called again before disappearing back into the room.

'Another one who needs a good spanking,' sniffed Verity. 'Can't she tell the difference between them and us?'

Polly murmured, 'I suspect you sound very like your mother at this moment.'

There was total silence as Verity stared at the window, then tugged her woollen hat down over her ears. It was one she had brought out from her kitbag before they set off. She turned to look ahead at the motor. Polly's hand on the tiller was freezing, and she dug her other into her trouser pocket. Her windlass was tucked in the back of her belt, as Saul's was. It really did make more sense, she'd decided.

The butty glided through the thick dark water and knocked aside a car tyre floating amongst the debris. 'It'll be a Dunlop,' Verity said, quietly. 'They're made in Birmingham.'

The tyre rocked; there were clusters of straw stalks trapped within it, and a headless doll. Ahead, a pair of fly-boats were moored at a wharf. 'It's the Guinness wharf,' Verity muttered. 'Soon we'll be into the crème de la crème of the canal world, and, yes, I am joking. Bet has been a wise old bird and taken the motor today, and probably will tomorrow, but why shouldn't experience count for something.'

She slid down on to the counter. 'I'm going to put the kettle on the range, and check the rabbit stew.

We're all fed up with it, but without it we'll be eating our fists later.'

'Why?' Polly said, stepping aside, leaving room for Verity to squeeze through to the cabin.

'Because we'll be hungry in a way you will not believe, and tired, so tired you will hardly be able to breathe, let alone start cooking. And you're right, Polly,' Verity said as she ducked into the cabin. 'I did sound like my mother. You have my permission to pitch me into the cut if I ever do it again, or I'll pitch myself, like I did before.'

She popped her head back up. 'Only if I sound like her, though. I don't want it taken as open season on Verity Clement, is that totally clear, or I will rip out your throat with my teeth.' She laughed, but her blue eyes were full of tears.

Polly reached forward and pulled Verity's woollen hat down over her face. 'Perfectly clear, so I will just deluge you in water instead, from the cut.'

Verity laughed, and disappeared. Then called up, 'Just to break it to you, as you are probably feeling enormously smug at the thought of dousing me, the butty has to be hauled by hand along the short pounds between locks, and then hauled by hand into and through the locks. You might also think you've seen the last of debris in the cut? Wrong – the tyre was just the beginning. The Bottom Road, or Brum Bum as I call it, hasn't been dredged for years, so we're likely to get the propeller tangled in some disgusting muck or rope – or even dead dog, on one memorable and awful occasion. We will have to spend hours trying to untangle the damned thing. Or, perish the thought, go in and really get to grips with the obstructions. If you should fall in, keep your mouth shut even more than ever.'

Polly kept her eye on Bet who was steering along the middle passage, while Verity continued, 'Or, darling, we might ground on the mud because the bottom is too near the top. In other words, it's shallow because it's just so silted up as to be a menace. This experience, my dear girl, will be a vital part of your education. As I say, you will need rabbit stew.'

She dipped back into the cabin, and reappeared, grinning. But then added, 'If that's given you a headache, just let me say I'll try and be good, and kind, and nice from now on.'

Polly laughed. 'Crikey, it'll wear you out, and then who will pull the boat?' She paused, then said, 'We don't really pull it, surely?'

'Oh indeed we do. It's something to do with the fragile nature of the cut here. No two boats are to be in a short pound at the same time so the motor goes on ahead.'

As conditions grew worse she and Verity gulped down their tea, standing on the counter, following *Marigold* and trying not to smell the cut, hoping nothing tangled in its gear to hold them up, not here. Bet finally gestured that soon they'd be in the first of the short pounds and she'd let go the snubber.

The canal wasn't the only thing that was filthy.

The towpath was black with coal dust, not to mention dung from the horse-drawn boats, and that was just the identifiable filth. It was like a nightmare as they glided, still pulled by the *Marigold* through bridge holes which stank, and above which buses or trains passed, while a medley of factories belted out smoke with windows so thick with grime that no one would have been able to see out. The air was stifling and turgid.

Polly kept thinking of the fields they had travelled through on their way to Birmingham, the distant hills, the kingfishers darting on the bank, the otters, the men fishing. One day she'd live in the country where she could see for miles, and count the narrow-boats as they plied along the cut.

Soon the locks began to appear and Bet uncoupled before the first of the short pounds, and waved as she headed off. She'd have to lock-wheel herself through, as there were no lock-keepers, but there was no sympathy, because at least she had an engine.

Polly lost the toss and while Verity steered it was she who had to haul the weight of the seventy-foot butty along the pound, dragging it, the rope over her shoulder cutting into her flesh, her legs quivering with the effort. Once she got going it wasn't so hard but, still, the sweat was pouring not just down her back, but her legs, face and arms as well. She kicked up soot, she squelched through horse manure and dog mess. She slip-slopped, and outside a warehouse skidded heavily on to her side, jogging the aching ribs from her first fall which seemed years ago but wasn't. 'Quick, for heaven's sake,' called Verity from the stern. 'Don't let her go aground, we'll never shaft the madam off.'

Polly struggled to her feet, took up the rope again. *Horizon*, like a good girl, had kept going at a snail's pace, heading onwards to the flight of locks. Polly left her to glide, and ran up to the lock which Bet, God bless her, had left ready. Into the lock *Horizon* went; Polly yanked the windlass out of her belt. Everything she touched was black and greasy. As the water emptied through the raised paddles, taking them down to the next 'step' of the downhill staircase, the level lowered, the lock-sides were exposed as filthy. Then she shoved at the beams, opening the gates, taking up the slack and hauling *Horizon* on to the pound. At the next one she jumped down to take Verity's place at the tiller as Verity leapt on to the towpath and, once the gates were open, hauled the butty along the short stretch to the next lock, repeating the process.

So it went on, each taking turn and turn about until their boots and trousers were covered in grease and soot, their shoulders raw from the rubbing rope, the blood from their burst blisters mingling with the soot. Polly remembered her mother saying one could clean one's teeth with soot. Not this soot, Mum, she thought.

After four locks they met a horse-boat coming in the opposite direction; a child steered the butty, and both boats were loaded with glistening coal. The horse pulled at twice Polly's speed, if not three times. She turned to watch as Verity steered towards the towpath to allow it passage, and realised for the first time what one, two or three horsepower meant. It was there, as the horse doggedly threw itself against the harness, the breath from his nostrils visible in the cold air, step after step, after step.

''Ow do,' called the boater as he let his cotton-line go slack in the water, and allowed the *Horizon* to float across it.

''Ow do,' she replied.

The young girl steering looked little more than six or seven. Polly and Will had been in school at that age, coming home at three and sitting or playing until teatime instead of standing on a box on the counter, the tiller in safe tiny hands. Was there such a thing as childhood on the cut? She doubted it. Had Joe, Saul's nephew, known a childhood with that awful father? Had Saul? And what about Granfer?

She remembered the children who had spat from the bridge on her first day, and many times since. She felt her forehead, where the cut had scabbed up into her hair. She'd like them to have a day on the cut, and just experience the lives of those they were insulting. Would it make any difference? Well, a clip round the ear might.

At the end of the flight, Bet waited. They linked up again. On the long pound, life improved because the butty could be tied close up to the motor and they no longer had to haul it. Instead they steered, and shared out bread and cheese.

Then it was time for more short pounds. Polly's legs felt as though they wouldn't carry her a step further, but they must, and so they did, because there was just the cut, the wind, the wet and the filth, and these two women who were beginning to be part of her life and she wished Will could meet them.

At the thought of Will, the second of the day, she felt, at last, a sob building, first in her chest, and then her throat. But as she lock-wheeled it faded, and again there was nothing deep down. A horse-drawn boat was waiting to come through. ''Ow do,' she called, and smiled.

Yes, there was a way of functioning but, as the boaters would say, for so long the bottom had been too close to the top: the functioning was shallow. Nearby the whining of trams could just be heard, advertising hoardings seen, torn and drained of colour. Through bridges they went and down the flight of locks until they came to a narrow neck of water where the *Marigold* waited. 'At last,' breathed Polly, while Bet waved.

Polly left the butty to give their trip card to the old man at the office, just past the lock. He stood shivering in his dark jacket, and a cap that was too large. He grimaced as he marked the soiled card, which looked as though it had been nibbled. Perhaps it had. Perhaps along with everything they had rats, Polly thought. Well, if that was so, the buggers hadn't left so the *Marigold* and *Horizon* weren't sinking ships. She smiled at her joke. Will would—

No, not Will, not again. Why was he in her thoughts today?

Verity called up from *Horizon*, 'Let me have it back, Polly. Then I can return it to the drawer and we will forget it again and again, as we have been doing.'

The man called down, 'Ain't no laughin' matter. Rules is rules, and there's a war on, you know.'

Polly slipped her arm through his. 'Indeed we do know, which is why we've just hauled this butty as though we are horses – just because there are rules. So I don't think you need to tell us about rules, do you?'

He patted her hand and said, 'There ain't no need to take on so.'

'Oh, but she does take on,' Verity called from the counter. 'I ended up in the cut because I annoyed her. I'd stand back if I were you. Oops, she's got her arm through yours. Bad, bad sign . . .'

Polly gripped the official's arm tightly as he tried to pull away. He tugged, and she gripped, laughing. Finally, she let him go and he laughed, heading for the cottage. 'Trouble with you incomers is that you don't 'ave no bleedin' manners. I don't 'ave this with the proper boaters. Bloody cheek . . . Make sure you come and say hello next time you're coming through though.' The door slammed on his laugh. Polly winked at Verity, who crossed her arms and scowled at her. 'Get yourself down here, Polly Holmes. You're getting too cocky by half.'

Bet blew her hunting horn in a tally-ho from the *Marigold*, then they heard her great booming laugh.

They forged on and soon the factories were left behind and they tied up overnight beneath trees and by allotments, guzzling the rabbit stew, using water from the kettle to wash their hands. It was useless; the oily soot was too embedded. The blisters and cuts on the hands stung, and Polly even had blisters on her shoulders and round her waist from the cotton-line, but so probably did the others, so why mention it?

They fell into their beds, not bothering to undress, knowing that they would make the blankets black, but the rain had begun so there was no way to wash clothes. Besides, tomorrow they'd become as black again so they could wash everything at the end of the nightmare.

The rain stopped within an hour. Polly turned over and slept again, though the cold oozed through the cabin walls. They were awake with the dawn and set off as soon as they could, cutting through a frost-bleached land, leaving behind the allotments carved as though in white marble, and so too the trees. 'A hoar frost,' said Verity. 'My mare loves it. Father said he'd look after her.'

The wind froze their hands and faces as they continued along the pound, aching all over, but at least they were now on the flat land heading to

Coventry and able to remain together more often than not. Never had the pat-patter been so welcome.

As Verity and Polly took turns at the tiller of *Horizon*, the wind gusted across flat country, and before long, while Verity steered, Polly found herself shafting frantically as the butty caught on the silted-up cut bottom. It happened again and again, straining the snubber as the *Marigold* kept up its pace. Verity used the electric horn, ran down the top planks and yelled from the fore-end, 'Motor down, Bet,' then ran back, grabbing a shaft too. 'Oh Polly, shove, shove. We can't be splicing a snapped snubber on top of everything.'

Each time the two girls dug down with the shafts, punting the butty free, the water splashed back over them, freezing but marginally cleaner now. They headed into a bridge hole and only in its shelter did Polly realise how loud the wind had been whistling. They emerged and Polly found herself looking behind for a sight of the *Seagull* and Saul, because surely with his strength he could have caught them by now – if he'd really wanted to. She also found herself peering ahead more often, in case Leon was waiting round a bend – for them.

The short pounds had not finished with them though, and still Polly and Verity took turns acting as pack animals, hauling, and hating the wind which was icy and gusting, and loathing the needle-like rain. When the pounds were longer and they could both come back on board and enjoy the luxury of a tow, Verity washed some clothes on the range top while Polly steered, and stood by to shaft if needed. It was Polly who pegged the clothes on the line at the rear of the cabin and the bucket shed when the rain had stopped and Verity who took the tiller and hoped she wouldn't need to shaft. For the next hour, wherever they were on the butty they could hear the washing cracking like whips in the wind.

They pat-pattered towards a bridge, over which marched a squad of soldiers. Others were marching two abreast along the towpath. A dog walker stood aside to let the men pass and the old man yelled to the girls, as his dog yapped, 'You keep going or they'll be 'aving them boats off you for their little war games, you see if they don't.'

One of the soldiers called to Polly and Verity on the butty, 'Give us a lift.'

Verity replied, 'Strip off and swim over, then.'

The men laughed until the sergeant bawled, 'This is a bloody war, not a bloody picnic.'

The butty headed under the low bridge in *Marigold*'s wake, and as the fore-end entered the gloom, Verity and Polly, both on the counter now, with cocoa in their hands, ducked, then looked at one another and laughed. Polly said, 'If I look like you I know I am black, with bags under my eyes in which I could carry the shopping.'

'Yes I can see that, but please, please, tell me I am still blonde.' Verity tore off her woolly hat. Polly shook her head. 'Nope, and we'll need detergent to get all of this stuff off, I reckon. We're little soot babies, that's what we are. I'm chewing the stuff.'

They were being towed along a pound between ploughed fields now, and while Verity steered, Polly washed down the cabin roof and the sides with water and soda heated on the range. She wiped down the inside of the cabin with fresh hot water, the ceiling too, then mopped up the water that had dripped from her clothes on to the floor and thought she hated this awful cut.

She made tea and took it up to the counter, where the two girls clasped the hot enamel mugs, warming their hands as slag heaps appeared, and the odd cottage. Soon more and more cottages grouped into hamlets huddled alongside the cut. Many more dog walkers were in evidence, and cyclists, heads down, pedalling like mad things while the wind whipped their macs. Single-track railways ran parallel and coal trucks chuntered along them.

Verity called, 'Coventry isn't far.'

The bridges were more frequent, always a sign that a town was in the offing, with roads carrying buses, lorries, cars and pedestrians, rather than the odd track leading from one village to another. But then the locks reared their heads again, and they had to shoulder the tow-rope. Polly feared that the sight of a lock would one day cause her to strangle whoever was standing next to her.

They were towed past a coal mine, and saw miners coming off-shift, their faces black, their shoulders slumped with exhaustion, and were ashamed, because dragging a butty every so often was nothing in comparison.

The day passed quickly and now there was actual coal on the towpath, not just dust, and it even floated on the cut so when they had to queue at the locks, they collected as much coal as they could. Polly still looked behind from time to time, but Saul was not there. She checked ahead. Leon was not approaching – but of course he wasn't. He wouldn't have had time to reach Limehouse and set off back again.

The temperature continued to drop, and they kept both boats' ranges going with impunity, knowing that they could pick up coal from the cut-side.

They reached the top lock of the last flight as the afternoon drew to a close. There was a queue again. They moored up for the night, and asked to refill their water cans from the pub which was set back. They were not invited in but waved round to the back, where there was an outside tap.

The three of them lugged the water cans back in the freezing gloom, without speaking. They banked up the grate, absorbing the warmth, and ate bread and cheese; now it was dark they stripped off their coal-smothered clothes, shaking them over the side, not caring if anyone saw their naked frozen bodies in the gloom. Too tired for the pub, they sliced as much of the dirt off as they could and went to bed in their pyjamas, feeling that the filthy trousers and jumpers piled in a heap between the side-bed and range would stand up on their own and walk out. Verity dozed, while Polly thought through the day and, in need of comfort, reached over Verity for *Winnie-the-Pooh* in the light from the range grate.

It wasn't on the shelf. She looked again, tearing the books down. Some hit Verity who sat up, shouting, 'Hey, what are you doing? It's night-time, for goodness' sake.'

'Have you had it?' Polly shouted at Verity. 'Have you?'

Verity grabbed Polly, who was frantically searching. 'Have I had what?'

'*Winnie-the-Pooh*. Will wrote in it. It's gone.' She pulled away from Verity, who was looking through the books too. 'You're right, it's not here. Did you take it down earlier? Is it in your bed, or beneath it?' Verity lit the hurricane lamp and held it up as Polly dived down and searched the cupboard. Still on her knees she wailed, 'It's gone. Someone's taken it.'

'You can buy another,' said Verity, placing the other books back on the shelf before turning off the lamp. 'Come on, into bed. We'll find you another at the depot.'

'We can't find another, not that one. There can't be another of that one.'

The tears were flowing now, hot and endless, carving their way through the ingrained soot and the grime, and Verity was on her knees beside her, holding her as at last she sobbed for Will. Someone had taken the last thing she had of him, the only words she had written by him, the only thing she still had that they had loved, and now she was alone. Now she felt the awful pain of understanding, and accepting, that she would be only half of a whole for a lifetime. That Will would never return, he was truly gone, and it was too much to bear.

Verity soothed her, stroked her hair. 'Oh Polly, don't cry. It's a book, that's all. I promise we'll find who's taken it, or find another. Oh, please.'

'But it's not just a book. I've had it for so long and he wrote in it.'

'Who wrote in it, Polly?'

Polly couldn't say, she could only weep. Verity rocked her, soothing her, whispering, 'There, there. Whoever it was . . . Whatever it is about, you can bear it. You are brave and kind and strong. I will help you. Let me. Talk to me when you're ready. Until then, I'm here.'

Polly rested against her and still she couldn't say the word, Will. But one day she would, she knew that now. Her tears were quieter, Verity's arms around her were strong, and she let herself be held by this girl, who also knew pain.

Chapter 20

7 November – arrival at Coventry

In the morning Polly's eyes were sore from crying, but when Bet knocked on the motor's cabin door she called as usual, 'Come in.'

Bet just looked at Polly, and said nothing. Verity said nothing either then or when they had woken. Now, however, as she made morning tea, with extra honey for Polly, she gave it to her, patting her shoulder. Now, when Bet took hers outside for a smoke, Verity said, 'When you need me, I am here.'

Polly nearly cried again, but instead sipped her tea, and ate the bread and honey that Verity shoved into her hand. 'Eat the crusts, it'll make your hair curl,' Verity said. 'It's what Nanny used to say, and look at mine.'

Her hair was straight, with just the same two looped curls she manufactured with grips. Polly laughed, her throat raw. Verity grinned.

They approached Coventry on a cut whose only view was of slag heaps either side. When they were almost at the loading yard Bet sent Polly cycling along the towpath, saying, 'Go ahead and pick up our orders, if you would, Polly.'

Many boats were tied up along the bank, and she pedalled past checking their names, looking for Leon's *Brighton,* or his butty, *Maudsley.* Neither were to be seen, and her hands relaxed on the handlebars. She checked for Saul's but again, no, of course not.

Her back tyre was soft, but it would have to stay so. She stood in line outside the office, keeping her bike with her, moving it along. The boater behind said, 'Yer can rest it against office, Missus.'

She smiled, pulling her hat down round her ears against the chill wind, but told him, 'I'd rather hang on to it.' She didn't know who had stolen her book, or the kitty, and she wasn't going to lose anything else.

She dragged it through the door into the office. The manager, still wearing his hat, shook his head. 'That should stay outside.'

'Well, it's here now.' Polly rested it against her hip and blew her nose on her sooty handkerchief. She had never felt as filthy as she had during these last heaven knew how many hours. It felt like a million. The manager looked at her. She put her handkerchief back into her trouser pocket, and stared at him. In the end he raised his eyebrows. 'You trainees get more arsey by the day.'

'Indeed we do. Must be something to do with the bike saddle.'

The man flushed, and looked down at the form he held. She dragged the nibbled trip card from her pocket. He took it, checked the names, and handed her a packet of letters. 'Here you are, post for Holmes, Burrows and Clement, sent to the depot and forwarded to us. We do our best to look after you, arsey though you are.'

It was Polly's turn to flush. 'Thank you,' she muttered. He gave her a loading order. 'You're one of Bet's babies, but growing up quick, eh? The cut, especially the Bottom Road, makes you fight your corner, or if you don't it'll take you down, sort of drown you, but not with water, if you get my meaning. You'll do all right, I can see that. Bet'll be reversing up the arm right this minute, so remember to turn off the main cut on your bike, not to mention that uncomfortable saddle.'

She laughed, and left, then following directions cycled alongside the rails which were carrying coal trucks. Across the narrow cut, threadbare hawthorns carved by the wind into hunchbacks lined the path. Her hat was riding up again. She pulled it down, clutching the loading order in her teeth. She passed some men with shovels. 'My old lady'd like that for her teapot,' one called.

She snatched the loading order from between her teeth, and called back, 'You'll have to join the queue because it's reserved for the first person to come bearing a fur hat in exchange. Until then this little miracle of a tea cosy stays on my head, pom-pom and all.'

She cycled on, followed by laughter. Coal dust was everywhere. Black gold, it had been called, but she remembered the exhausted men they had passed who paid the price. She coughed as she passed the trucks piled high with the stuff, crunching the grit between her teeth. The workers must live all the time with this grit in their throats, between their teeth, and probably breathed it in. She saw Bet then, shafting the *Marigold* into place, and Verity doing the same with *Horizon*. Polly waved the loading order. Bet shouted, 'You can wipe that smile off your face, you'll be shafting next time we're here.'

Polly laughed. It was a deep, real laugh and surprised her, as had her sound sleep last night, after those hours of crying all over patient and caring Verity. This must be the real girl, so Tom was a fool, and Mother Clement horrid. This morning, as she slung the bike on to the towpath, Verity had repeated, 'Remember, I'm here when you want to talk.'

She had accepted Polly's nod, and as Polly had mounted the bike and set off along the towpath she'd called after her, 'I'm sorry about the kitty and the fuss I made. Whoever took the book, perhaps took the money.'

Bet had swung round asking, 'What's this about a book?'

Polly had left them to it. Now she waited on the wharf and caught the mooring straps that Bet threw, winding them around the stud. She then caught both straps that Verity threw from *Horizon*, and tied up, then lifted the bike on to the roof of the butty before joining Bet on the *Marigold*.

Bet said, 'You're feeling like an old pro, aren't you?'

Verity landed on the counter beside them. 'I beg your pardon, boss?'

'An old professional,' Bet laughed. 'Not an old—'

'Enough,' shouted Polly just as trucks of coal arrived, with four men covered in coal dust riding them. They set the trucks alongside *Marigold*'s hold, where a chute was positioned. Coal gushed out and the men guided it into the chute with the backs of their spades. Polly thought she'd experienced all that coal dust could throw at her, but she was wrong, and from the counter she breathed black dusty billowing air.

One of the men was smoking. Polly just stared. How could he breathe, smoke and shovel?

Another crew had begun loading the butty. The noise, the dust, the rattle and roar of the coal, and the occasional shout, created a frenzy of noise.

Bet yelled, 'Polly, pump up the Primus and produce a mug of tea for the lads.'

Polly opened the *Marigold*'s cabin doors but didn't slide back the hatch. Anything to keep the dust out. She doubled up and almost crawled into the cabin, but the hatch hadn't kept anything out, she realised. She poured methylated spirits around the Primus gutter, trimmed the wick and lit the stove. While the kettle heated she sat on the side-bed, looking at the bookshelf.

She could remember him writing in it. Remember the way his tongue stuck out. It was then she pictured herself writing in *The Water Babies* for that same birthday, for him. Her mother had bought the books, and asked them each to write the dedication, as a surprise. It would be something to treasure, she had said.

The kettle was simmering. She dug her hands in her pockets; in the left one was the packet. She opened it and took out a letter for Verity, and another two for Bet. Polly had one from Reggie, and another from her parents. Later. She laid them all down on the cross-bed, then remembered the letter she had left in *Winnie-the-Pooh*. Thank heavens Reggie hadn't put in anything the censor could care about.

The kettle was boiling. She made six mugs of tea, as those were all they had. Verity looked into the cabin and said, 'Chop-chop.'

Polly pulled a face. 'Go away. Incidentally, today I'm the postman, and you've a letter on your bed.'

Verity slipped down the steps and past Polly, picked up the letter, glanced at it, and tore it in half unopened. She picked up three of the mugs and headed back to the counter, calling over her shoulder, 'Bring up the others if you will, the lads are gagging with thirst.'

Polly called, 'Hey, why tear it up? You can stick it together. I'll put it on your bed, shall I?'

'It's from Mother, so what else should I do with it – perhaps light the range?' With that, she was gone, out on to the counter, and then the kerb, handing out the tea.

Polly did the same, returning to the cabin to wipe

down each surface, feeling the *Marigold* tilting more with each load. She headed up, calling to Bet who was already on the kerb arguing with the foreman. He shouted, 'Calm yerselves, it'll settle with the rain, look at that sky, Missus. I can't do more'n we're doing, and you're nearly done, anyhow, so let's put a sock in it, shall us? We'll give it a quick level at the end.'

For once in her life, Bet was silenced. Verity and Polly looked at each other, impressed.

Another hour and the loading was finished, and levelled, and as the rain started in torrents the three of them laid the planks along the top of the coal, which wasn't tiered as high as the billets had been. They started to tie up the side sheets but there was no need for the top ones, Bet told them. 'Coal will always dry out.'

Verity muttered to Polly as they continued lashing the side sheets. 'Thank heavens for small mercies.'

Just then, they heard Granfer calling from the kerb. 'I'll show yer a better 'itch.' He was up on the planks before they knew where they were, kneeling, showing them an easier knot, making them repeat it twice. 'That be it.' He eased himself to his feet. Polly said, 'Where did you spring from, Granfer? I thought you were way behind?'

'Well, I knows the cut like the back of me 'and, so we can keep going when t'light goes. Saul wanted to keep—' He stopped. 'Saul, 'im wanted to get a move on, is all. We is way back in the loading queue, so yer ladies will be off in front, but don't yer worry about that Leon, he be a day or more in front o' yer.'

Verity nipped off with the ration books and a string basket to gather up what she could from the shop, while Polly and Granfer stepped on to the kerb. The rain had begun and was drenching Polly. Granfer said, 'Still got it, then?'

He nodded to her hat.

'No one's offered me anything better. You all right, Granfer?' Polly had felt herself relaxing the moment she saw him.

They were here. Saul was close. She was safe.

'Aye.' He dug his hands in his pockets and Polly and he stared at the coal, which glistened, but at least the rain had damped down the dust. Them men were running around through the rain, just dark shapes, their faces undefined.

Polly wondered how long she and Granfer were going to stand there but it seemed rude to walk away, though she had rather fancied a walk to the shops to try and get Verity to pick something other than rabbit. Surely there was just a nice piece of cheese?

The rain was dripping through her hat, and her bobble could only absorb so much. Will's sweater was filthy, her trousers were stiff with coal and dirt. 'I don't want any more rabbit,' she said, though she had not meant to.

Granfer nodded next to her. ''Aving a lot, is yer?'

'Seem to be growing ears under this hat. But it's off ration, so yer know.'

He laughed. 'Yer talking like oos, just then.'

'I suppose I was.'

It was cold, she was shivering. She said, 'Shall I put the kettle on, Granfer? Will you have a cup of tea? It'll warm us.'

He moved then, tipping his cap. 'Keepin' you, ain't I? Best away back to the *Seagull*, only I was wondering . . . you reads, don't yer?'

Polly kept her eyes on the hawthorns across the way. Did he want her to look at something for him – a letter, a form of some sort? Should she ask? 'Yes, I do.'

Granfer said, taking off his hat and kneading it in his hands, 'Only I were wondering if yer read books with pictures, sometimes? Does grown-ups like 'em, or only little 'uns?'

She said carefully, all her senses alert, 'What sort of pictures, Granfer?'

'Nice 'uns. Mostly animals, but this'n has a boy in, too.'

Again carefully, she said, 'You have a book like this, do you? Or perhaps you've seen one?'

To the right of them Bet hauled the bike off the butty roof, slung another string bag over the handlebars and pedalled away, calling, ''Ow do, Granfer.'

''Ow do, Missus.'

She called over her shoulder, 'Back in five minutes, Polly, then'll we'll be ready to press on. Fire up the engine.'

He turned to her. 'Best be getting back, then. Only

our Joe, 'e said the school done give him a book. That's what he said, only . . .'

He scratched his head. Polly saw Will, his tongue slightly out, writing. She could smell the ink. Oh Will, she thought, that boy has stolen you from me. How bloody dare he? She felt hot, and seething, and crossed her arms to hide her clenched fists, wanting to rush to the *Seagull* and rip the book from Joe. He must have sneaked in. He probably took the money too. She stared at the glistening coal, felt the water trickling down her neck.

She swallowed. Granfer had said no more, neither had he moved, but as she looked at him she saw the worry on his face. She asked, 'Why does he want the book?'

It wasn't what she had intended to say, which was, 'Tell him to give it back, the little thief.'

A coal truck passing behind them drowned out Granfer's reply. She shouted, 'I didn't hear you.' It felt good to shout when she was so angry.

Granfer repeated, ''E likes the shapes.' He stopped, then continued, ''E thinks in shapes, but not letters. 'E likes drawings, 'e copies good. He's been left yer see, by 'is ma, our Maudie. She's gone, we don't know where, and 'im, the boy, 'e's been beaten good and proper by that da of 'is, like 'is ma was, and it makes 'im muddled, and scared. Right scared 'e be. I reckon the book gives 'im summat. We got no books, see. But I's not sure where 'e got it, and we need to do what's right, what's fair.'

Will had written in her book, *We will right all wrongs, make unfair things fair, because we are invincible. Forever, and ever.*

She felt her throat hurting, her heart aching. We are not invincible, lovely Will, my dearest brother. But then, as she stared past Granfer, thinking hard, a formation of geese flew overhead, circled, one at the head leading them, as always. They came in to land downwind of the busy, noisy cut. How like Will, who led their gang, all of whom had to pledge to right all wrongs, and make unfair things fair.

She said, 'I had someone, Granfer, who wrote in a book of mine when we were ten. He said that we would right all wrongs, make unfair things fair. We thought we could do anything then, that the world was ours for ever, but we can't, and it isn't, is it?' She wasn't ready to tell anyone that her brother had died. Bet knew because of her personal details that were on file, but she couldn't get the words out, even now.

Granfer looked sad, and nodded. 'Our Joe, 'e be ten. 'E's never 'ad a book and I'd take it 'ard if 'e died, cos if I'm not mistaken, you said "had someone" so I 'spect your someone has gone. I'm sorry for your loss, my lass. Like part o' your life goes missing, ain't it? My girl, Saul's ma, she died by a bomb. Saul's sister, Joe's ma, is gone, running from that Leon. Gets 'ard to bear but we 'as to, cos what else is there to do?'

She said, laying her hand over his, as he twisted his hat, 'You'll mash up that hat, Granfer, and that would be a shame. I think, don't you, that we should make something unfair fair, I think we should try and make something that is wrong, right. You tell him to take good care of that book, Granfer. Will you do that for me? Because it is precious, it has a place in my heart. Then later . . . Well, never mind that. Books are precious, tell him, wherever they come from. Who knows, Granfer, he might like to give it back one day, to make it fair, and right.'

Granfer nodded, and his look was one of relief, and gratitude. He tipped his cap at her. 'We'll be following on after you, lassie, so don't you fret. You won't be alone, our Saul'll see to that.'

He walked back along the wharf, the coal trucks careering past. Somewhere a factory hooter sounded. She watched that kind old man who was looking after a poor beaten boy, and doing his best for Saul, while Saul was doing the best he could for them, too. She knew she had done what Will would have wanted the gang, and her, to do. She watched the geese that were clustering against the opposite bank. So, Will, it's done.

One day she'd have a talk with Joe. If he'd taken the book, which of course he had, he'd have taken some of the kitty too, but the money didn't matter any more. The boy mattered, his safety mattered, and the safety of Granfer and Saul, and Bet, Verity and her. The boy must feel some joy in the book, until he found it in some other way, but only when he was ready.

The geese were already leaving, their leader pointing the way. They flapped and almost ran along the cut, lifting, lifting, almost, and yes they were airborne, climbing, following their leader, free of earthly bonds, soaring, circling, and away over the treetops, heading who knew where. But they had been here, just as Will had.

She stood for several minutes as the ripples they had made died, but then began to walk towards the motor. Soon Bet, Verity and she would move on down the cut. The cut— She stopped, felt her forehead. The boy who had chucked the brick had run off when she chased him, off to the left, towards the cut, and it was the *Seagull* that had gone through the bridge hole before them. Was that Joe, too? No, of course it wasn't. There was no reason on earth why he'd do that to her. It was some other boy, a banker.

She looked around at the men, who were so busy, and at the boats without her team. The geese were gone. For one moment she felt totally adrift, half a person. 'Will,' she whispered, but heard only the rain in reply.

She shook her head and heard running feet. It was Verity, who slipped her arm through hers, drenched just as Polly was. 'Guess what I've got?'

'Rabbit.'

Verity's face fell. 'Oh. Well, that's that then.'

'It is indeed,' Polly agreed. 'Ooops, there go my ears, growing again.'

Verity roared with laughter. 'And, and, I have

bacon, lots of it, so there. Someone's just killed a pig, but we're to say nothing to anyone, because I have worked my womanly wiles.'

Polly smiled. 'Bacon? Oh, wonderful girl. I can almost smell it cooking.'

Bacon, she thought, as they clambered back on the motor to fire up the engine, ready for Bet's return. She could still feel Verity's arm slipped through hers, linking the two of them together. It was a beginning, and as Granfer said, though it's all hard to bear, what else is there to do. Go on, like everyone else was doing. With that, the despair eased, because she really and truly was not alone; others were struggling too.

Verity was chattering about getting the range going, keeping the slide shut, and by the time they moored up along the cut for the night, the rabbit and bacon would be cooked and they could sit in the warmth and dry out at last.

'Sounds good,' Polly said. 'But are you sure you won't read your mother's letter? It might be torn in half but it's still possible.'

Verity said nothing as she threw the shopping on to the side-bed from the cabin doorway before following Polly down the gunwale to the engine room, where they primed the engine, pulled the choke, and fired it up as Bet called from the counter, 'Back to the butty, girls. Let's crack on, chop-chop.'

As Polly followed Verity back along the gunwale her friend said, 'No, I don't want to read it. She can say nothing of interest to me. But what about you?'

Polly had forgotten about Reggie and her parents' letters. 'Later,' she said. 'After I've got the motor range going, the rabbit on. Incidentally, Saul's behind us. Granfer said Leon's still a day or so ahead, and they'd follow along still shepherding us.'

They cast off, attached the tow-rope to the stud and as they felt the slight jerk of *Marigold* taking up the strain, the two girls grinned at one another.

'Cocoa or tiller?' Verity asked.

'Tiller,' Polly said.

'Done.'

Verity disappeared into the cabin. The rain had stopped, and now they were passing the *Seagull* and *Swansong*. Granfer nodded at Polly, lifting his hand in a sort of salute. Saul and Joe were wiping down the cabin roof and sides. Saul straightened, nodded, smiled, and called, ''Ow do.' Beside him Joe looked up at Saul and said something. Saul nodded and put his arm around the boy's shoulders. It was then that Joe looked full square at Polly. He didn't smile, or nod, or wave. He just looked and the sadness almost reached out and touched her. Then she was past and they were heading south.

Chapter 21

9 November – still heading south

They had reached Fenny Stratford, north of Leighton Buzzard, by 9 November, two days later, and Polly felt utterly spent, but so did the other two. Each evening they had washed some of their clothes on the bank, still trying to remove the coal dust and oil, and the smell. The coal dust made their hands even more sore as it scratched and cut when they wrung out the clothes. In the morning, in the heat of the range, they were dry, and slightly cleaner, but by no means perfect.

The clothes situation had become trivial by 11 November, by which time they had been through Leighton Buzzard, and through lock after lock to arrive at Marsworth Junction, because the engine, clearly feeling as exhausted as they were, had begun to cough and splutter. They drew in to the cut edge so that Bet, bottom up in the engine house, could fiddle and sort out the problem. She cursed, and finally kicked. Verity said, 'It's fed up, caught it from us.'

They laughed. Bet shouted, 'Shut up.'

She kicked again, which didn't help, but it

obviously made her feel better. She fiddled again, then, covered in grease, gave it a go. It started again, and pat-pattered for another mile, then stalled. This time it was Polly up to her armpits in engine grease, following Bet's instructions, pulling, pushing and finally kicking as Bet had. And so it went on, as they limped through the locks to Berkhamsted, though they had found time for one minute's silence at 11 a.m., which had reminded them why they were doing what they were doing.

Hourly, it seemed, they waved past those they were slowing down, including the *Seagull* and *Swansong*. Granfer nodded, and called, "Ow do?'

Bet yelled back, 'The engine is buggering about, but will get us back.'

Granfer continued on, towing the coal-laden *Swansong*, which in its turn drew alongside the *Horizon*. Saul, at the tiller, nodded at Polly, tipping his cap, the wind lifting and tossing his dark hair. "Ow do?' he said.

"Ow do,' Polly called.

Saul smiled, and for a moment his face was alive. He called, 'T' day be fine.'

She shouted, 'Indeed it is.'

'Yer need oos?' Then the butty was past and Polly saw Joe emerge from the cabin to stand beside Saul.

She called, 'We'll make it, Saul, but thank you.'

He turned, tiller at his elbow. 'We might be at t' pub, come evenin'?' There was a question in his voice.

Polly grinned. 'If we get that far we might be too, but if not there are other pubs, other evenings.'

He waved his hat, then turned back, as Joe tugged at his jerkin, said something, then ducked into the cabin, leaving his uncle at the tiller. Polly watched the butty as the water rippled in its wake. Saul turned, looked at her and smiled again. She lifted her hand. He faced forward. Verity called from the roof, 'He never smiles at me. I really should apologise.'

Polly found she was still smiling, still watching as the *Swansong* carried on. She said, 'Well, we might all catch up at the pub.'

She wondered how it would be. Would he sit with them, or just nod and say "Ow do?' Did he smile at everyone once he knew them? Did he . . .

Verity said, 'Have you written to Reggie yet?'

Polly said, 'I should but what do I say? That we have boiled our clothes again, the wind is cold, I have chilblains on my toes, corns on my hands.'

'You could say something nice about how you feel.'

She looked at Verity. 'The thing is, nothing seems real that isn't on the cut. I'm not sure that Reggie ever did, except he was one of our gang. I didn't have a boyfriend, and he's very nice – very suitable, Mum thinks.' She paused. 'Thank you for helping me when I cried.'

They had never mentioned it since that time. Verity swung round, looking forward. 'Polly, to help is what friends are for, idiot. If they don't help, then they're not friends. It's something I'm beginning to face up to, at last, especially when I think of our evening in the club . . .'

They fell silent, but it was a good silence. Polly stood, her elbow on the tiller, her woollen hat pulled hard down, enjoying the quiet of the butty. On either side were fields beyond the towpaths, and a gun emplacement. Did they expect the enemy to charge the cut? Well, why not; they were transporting cargo, so the enemy could too. Rooks were in the fields. What were they looking for? The farmers used to shoot them. Did they now, or were all the bullets for the war?

She thought of Saul. What had Joe wanted of his uncle? Was he reading her book? Of course not, he couldn't, but perhaps he was copying the pictures. She'd find out, one day, because she trusted Saul and Granfer. The *Swansong* had disappeared under the upcoming bridge, and Verity eased off the roof. She thrust her newspaper into the cabin, grabbed the bike off the roof ready to disembark as they edged through the hole. She murmured, 'Our shepherds have gone.'

'Ah, but so has Leon,' said Polly. 'He's days ahead by now, and by the time we reach the depot he'll already be on his way north again.'

In the bridge hole Verity slung the bike on to the bank, and headed off for a lock, calling back, 'We're able to look after ourselves, anyway, so even if he's on the way back to Birmingham, and passes us, we're the waterway girls, so we are, and aren't scared. Tally-ho.'

Polly grinned, then laughed. Tally-ho indeed.

At last, on 13 November, they struggled into the London environs, a world of traffic noise, and of red double-decker buses which roared over bridges. Their cargo of coal was unloaded at a factory producing something, but who cared what. All they did know was that they were yet again covered in billowing coal dust, eating it, breathing it, before heading off. Instead of finding it easier, now that the boats were lighter, the engine grew worse and soon it was stuttering, grinding, rasping until at last the depot came in sight. Never had Polly been so grateful to reach a familiar port of call. They backed into the lay-by and moored up. Polly wound the strap around the stud in tandem with Verity who was doing the same for the *Marigold*.

Bet jumped off, and headed for the yard. 'I'm going to have a word about the dear old girl's engine. I thought it had been sorted, but patently not. Be back in a minute. Polly, I'm surprised you haven't run off to use a proper lavatory.'

Polly was too busy trying to spot the *Seagull* but, at the suggestion, felt the need, and walked off past the boats, knowing her face was the colour of coal, or as near as dammit, if Verity's was anything to go by. She heard Verity running up behind, felt her arm slip through hers. 'We could do a bit of a minstrel show, and make our fortunes.'

'You do that, but I couldn't kick up in the air if you paid me right this minute.'

It felt good to be walking together, in step, a team.

They were entering the yard, and now Verity snatched her arm free and set off running. 'Race you,' she said.

Polly shook her head even though it was just like something she and Will would have done. 'Not with that head start. I'll wait outside.'

Verity continued running, while Polly looked to the right, where Joe was coming along carrying a string shopping bag from the town. He saw her and hesitated, but then kept on, his head down.

Polly walked across to intercept him, barring his way. He stepped to one side, but she blocked him, and then again as he sidestepped the other way. He stood quite still, lifted his head and stared at her. 'What ya gawping at?'

Polly smiled. 'Just wanted to talk, Joe. Let's walk back together, shall we, a little way.' It wasn't a question.

He set off at a rush, but she kept pace. He slowed, and she slowed. Finally he stopped again.

'So,' she said, 'I think perhaps you have something of mine. In fact, I can see it behind the carrots in your string bag.' Joe clutched the bag to him and stepped back. She smiled. 'It's all right, I don't bite.' He looked confused, and then stared hard at her mouth.

'Oh Joe, I'm sorry, it's just a saying which tells

you I'm not fierce. But my book is precious. It was given to me by someone when we were both children and he even wrote in it. He's dead now and his writing is the only writing I have left of his. I can see him holding the pen, as clear as day.'

They were walking on again, side by side. Joe said nothing, and did nothing more than clutch the string bag. They were on the towpath now and a dog rushed past them, followed by a girl of about seven or eight. A temporary brick edifice held a boater's boiler and the fire beneath burned fiercely. Polly felt the heat as they passed. 'I wonder what your mother would think about you going into someone's cabin and taking not only money from a kitty, but a book. And what about dropping a brick from a bridge, because I do think that was you too? Have a look at the mark you made.' She shoved back her hat.

He glanced up, but then down, muttering, 'Can't see nothing, yer so dirty.'

She sighed. 'But answer me, what would your mother think?'

The boy stopped, and kicked at a stone with his battered boot. 'She'd 'ave said, Oh Joe, 'ow could you?'

'So, how could you?'

He kicked the stone towards the cut, and she stopped it with her wellington boot, which had once been pristine. 'Cos . . . cos I wanted pencils to draw, and that meant money, then I wanted to 'urt you, cos you made my da angry and that made me scared, so I threw the brick, but that was then. Then

I took the book just cos I wanted it. I like the shapes, the animals. I wanted to draw 'em. To try to learn some letters.'

'May I have it back now, or at least the page with the writing?'

He put the string bag down on the towpath, eased out the book. It had his small dirty fingerprints on the jacket. He opened it at the inscription. He traced his finger along the writing, then tore out the page. 'There, yer got yer writing.'

She looked at the page, then squatted beside Joe. His hair was parted on the left, and she wanted to reach out and touch him, soothe him. Instead she said, 'Will you give me my book back, when you think it is the right thing to do?'

Joe stuffed it back in the string bag, and ran off. 'Yer see, I did it, so I'm like me da. I'm like me da cos it just burst out o'me, in a nasty great billow of muck. That's why I threw it, the brick, that's why I took the book, cos I'm nasty, not nice like Mam.'

Polly watched as he ran, the string bag banging on his leg. The boater woman wiping the outside walls of the cabin of her butty looked at her, and shook her head. 'Kids – who'd 'ave 'em?'

Her toddler was chained round the waist, the chain attached to the range chimney. Another child of about five was cleaning the cabin doors which were painted with flowers and castles. The tiller had been removed. Polly smiled. 'I don't know what goes on in their heads,' she said, and waved as she turned on her heel and set off for the yard again, meeting Verity on her way to the lavatory.

'Where on earth have you been?' Verity asked. 'I expected you to be breathing on the hinges telling me to hurry up.'

When Polly returned she stepped on to the butty counter, the cabin doors of which were open. Smoke came from the range chimney. She called, 'May I come in?'

'Yes, the kettle's on, and I'm just putting Verity in the picture.' The warmth was welcome, but the smell of them all was not: a mixture of sweat, coal and, quite simply, dirt.

As Bet told them that the *Marigold* was going into dry dock Polly sipped her tea. She could still taste the Spam fritters they had fried up in the *Marigold* cabin at lunchtime. Perhaps the taste in the air had been absorbed by the milk.

Bet finished by saying, 'So, I think you must take your two days' leave now, and not wait until the end of the next trip. I'll stay with the boats, of course, but first we'll give them a bit of a clean.'

It took an hour of hard work, and then they washed themselves as best they could in the lavatory sink. Polly packed up all her clothes, and one of the blankets to launder at home. She threw on her mackintosh over the clothes she was wearing, stuffing her hat into the bag as well, while Verity sat on the cross-bed and finished *The Times*.

'What will you do?' asked Polly when she was almost ready and trying to drag a comb through her filthy hair.

'Who knows, darling. Catch up with some friends, or people I know might be a better way of putting it, as I've come to realise. Or just bunk up in the butty. Bet says I can share, just this once.'

Polly put down her bag. 'Look, why not go to your parents', and try to sort it out?'

Verity didn't even look up. 'Darling, you know I can't possibly do that.'

Polly hesitated, then climbed up the steps, toting her bag. 'I'll see you in a couple of days, then.'

She stepped on to the towpath, and walked away. As she did so, she heard running feet behind her and turned, expecting Verity. It was Joe. He held out Reggie's letter, which she had put into *Winnie-the-Pooh*. 'This yers too. It's got writing on't.'

She took it, realising she had not only not missed it, but had also forgotten to read his latest. 'Thank you, Joe. You see, I don't think your da would have given it back to me, but your mum would, so what does that tell you?'

He looked at her, then shrugged and shook his head, and ran back to the *Seagull*, which had backed into the kerb two boats along. Granfer was standing on the counter. He waved. Saul stood on the butty roof with a broom. He nodded, then mouthed 'Thank you'. She forgot about Reggie, just looked back at Saul, and nodded. He'd said thank you. The cut folk never did. She felt a rush of such warmth, such pleasure for the first time since Will. She waved, turned, and tucked the letter into her pocket and walked on.

Back on the motor, Granfer followed Joe into the cabin. 'You sure she said you could keep the book?'

'She said t'give it back when oos felt it right to give it back. Just as I says, Granfer.'

Saul jumped down to the counter and stood behind Granfer, looking all the time at his nephew. 'When d'ya reckon that will be then, Joe?'

Granfer pulled Saul with him on to the towpath. 'She be a wise one, lad, like yer ma. No point in rushing 'im. 'E 'as to come right by 'isself.'

'And if 'e doesn't?' Saul said, feeling angry and embarrassed, and something else. Something deep in his chest.

'We try summat else, cos we don't want 'im to give up on 'isself and believe he's like that bastard Leon.'

Saul looked down the towpath as Polly turned the corner, swinging the bag as though it were as light as a feather, her head held like she always held it, strong and into the wind. He wanted to run after her, because the lad had taken something precious but she hadn't torn into him, like she could have, and he had this feeling he didn't recognise, which grew worse as she went from his sight.

*

Once on the train Polly thought that she'd telephone her mother from Waterloo Station and warn her that she was coming for two nights, that she would need to wash her clothes and have a bath, or even two; and that her mum must try not to mind the sight and smell of her daughter. She stood, because the people near her were looking anywhere but at her, and some had their handkerchiefs to their noses. She smelt her arm. Her mac was nothing like the horrors beneath it, but there was, without doubt, a sizeable echo. She watched one station go by, and then another, wondering how she would have the energy to get home.

She thought of Verity, going to stay with 'people', and somehow knew that this would not happen because, Polly sensed, she had seen them for what they were.

As the train drew into a station and people sidled past her on to the platform, looking back surreptitiously, Polly knew beyond a doubt that Verity would stay in the butty, because there was nowhere else to go, not really. Yes, she had Bet, but she would be busy. That was no way to spend her leave.

At the next station, she pressed herself against the side as others passed her, and she remembered the feel of Verity linking her arm in hers, and laughing as she had not done when they first met. Well, had Polly? No. So together, somehow, they were helping one another. As the guard blew his whistle, she leapt off, and caught the next train back. At Southall she ran from the station into the yard, waving to the policeman at the gate, and down the towpath, powering past a woman carrying back her shopping, and others washing clothes or chatting. Panting, she leapt on to *Horizon*. She dumped her bag on the counter. The tiller had been removed and Verity was smoking as she leaned on the cabin, staring into the cut and looking lost.

Polly called, 'Oh, come on. Come back with me, and slum it at Woking, why don't you? You'll have to share my room but at least we can form a united front when Mum spreads out newspaper just inside the front door, looks at us, smells us, and thinks all her worst nightmares have come true.'

Chapter 22

13 November – heading to Woking

Her mother was all of a flutter when Polly telephoned in the early evening gloom of Waterloo Station, explaining that she had been given unexpected leave, would it be possible to come home for a couple of days?

'Goodness me, leave? For two days? Well, of course, but what will we give you to eat? Oh dear, let me think . . .'

Polly interrupted the familiar torrent, her heart sinking, though she grinned at Verity as though all was well. 'Mum,' she interrupted, 'Mum, listen a moment. It doesn't matter what we eat . . .'

'"We", what do you mean "we"? How many is "we"? Oh, how can I feed "we"? It's wartime . . .'

Her father must have snatched the telephone. His voice was hearty and pleased. 'Of course you must come, and how many others? We'll just have more vegetables, and we've a spot of cheese. I'll take it out of the mousetrap.' Polly laughed, hoping it was a joke, as he continued, 'I brought some leeks from the allotment and we have cabbage. All will be well.'

Then she heard her mum in the background. 'No, *we* is too much.'

Her father reassured Polly. 'Don't worry, Polly, we'll manage.'

Polly sighed. 'Oh Dad, do tell her it's Lady Verity Clement,which should thrill her. Polly's making nice friends again, now all the others, even my friends from school, are in the war effort.' He laughed and said, 'Just don't worry. Leave it with me. We'll make up the other bed in your room, if you can bear to share. You know she won't countenance using . . . Well, you know.'

'Of course I do, Dad. But be warned, we smell, and look like nothing on earth. We're also very tired, so food isn't an issue, but please, please stoke up the furnace for hot water. Have you extra logs?'

As the pips started she heard him say, 'Yes, to the furnace. Reggie is home on leave too—' The line went dead. She replaced the receiver and walked over to Verity, who was leaning against the wall, smoking. Her mother would tut that it wasn't proper for women to smoke in the street, any more than it was for them to eat. She smiled at Verity. 'Mum's in a bit of a do, but Dad's taking over.'

They checked their watches against the station clock. Even this had anti-blast paper strips stuck across it. There were sandbags dotted about but those couldn't smell as awful as the girls did. 'Come on, seven minutes,' Verity said, taking a last drag and scrunching out the stub beneath her boot. They

294

walked into the Ladies and tried yet again to wash off the worst of the residual coal dust, but it was too greasy. As they made their way to the exit they heard the announcement: 'The train on Platform 4 will be departing in two minutes.'

'Chop-chop,' Polly muttered. They were both laughing as they ran for Platform 4, their kitbags over their shoulders. They showed their tickets at the gate and were waved through. They clambered on to the train, deciding it would be more merciful to everyone if they stood in the corridor. They squeezed in amongst a group of sailors, whose ship must have come in, or they were off somewhere only they knew, for the corridor was lined with them. There were soldiers at the far end, some sitting on their kitbags. Polly said to their neighbours, 'We've just come off the canal boats, and smell to high heaven.'

One of them yanked the window down. 'Get downwind, love, and the breeze'll shoot it on to the pongos, as our army brethren are called – by us, anyway.'

A squaddie shouted, 'I heard that. We'd rather have the smell than pneumonia, so shut it, darlin', there's a good girl, and let the matelots enjoy the whiff. You know matelots are the people God made out of leftovers, so they'll be used to it.'

Verity shoved up the window, laughing at the usual inter-service rivalry. When the train started, the girls also sat on their kitbags. Verity drew out her cigarettes and handed them round. The sailors leaned across one another to snatch one, saying, 'For self-preservation, it'll drown out you two.'

One said, 'That must have been some awful canal.'

'You have no idea,' Polly muttered, inhaling.

'What's been your cargo?'

Polly said, 'Steel billets to the Midlands, coal to London, can't you guess?' She held out her grubby hand.

The train drew into a siding only once, to let a goods train get ahead, so they arrived in Woking in forty minutes. As they stood waiting for the train to finally stop, the sailor next to Verity handed her a couple of packs of cigarettes. 'Take 'em. We get troops' comforts, and you wouldn't want the other sort.' The sailors around guffawed. He said, 'You deserve the fags. We're on the water too, and know the bloody hell of it, day after cold bloody day.'

Verity took them and said, 'I won't kiss you.'

'Thank Gawd for that,' he grinned. The two girls eased their way along the corridor to the door while the sailors flattened themselves, holding their noses. Verity and Polly were laughing too much to say goodbye.

Once on the platform their kitbags seemed heavier than ever, the wind too cold, the walk to the entrance too far on legs that had absolutely no energy. As they dragged themselves out of the station, past the sandbags, two men loomed out of the darkness. The girls hesitated, then in the moonlight Polly recognised her father beneath his muffler and hat as he said, 'Reggie called in, so we thought we'd come to carry your kitbags.'

Polly had almost forgotten what Reggie looked like, but could make out the RAF uniform as her father flashed his torch about the place. As the slit of light played across Reggie's features she saw the deep lines running from his nose to the corners of his mouth, and the thinness of his face. He had changed, but so had she. She felt pleased to see Will's friend, but that was all.

Polly put up her hand in a stop sign. 'So lovely to see you both, but please do not approach, do not think of kissing me, or shaking Verity's hand. We've had a long coal-dusted trip and are utterly disgusting to behold, let alone smell. We'd better carry our own kitbags, as they are pretty much as bad as us.'

Reggie laughed, and that was the same, and there was something good in the familiarity. Verity said, 'Speak for yourself, darling. I am in no way disgusting, so there, but I agree, we'll carry our own filth. We will lead the way, Mr Holmes, while Polly and her Reggie toddle along behind. How's that?'

She set off, and Polly's dad waited alongside Polly and Reggie as they watched her go. Finally her dad called, 'Best if we go the right way, Lady Verity, which is back past the station.'

Verity stopped dead, turned on her heel, and walked towards them. 'Oh, how very unkind, Mr Holmes. You mean I have walked further than I might?' She collected him up as she passed, saying,

'Come along, Polly, stop dithering, and you too, Reggie.'

Polly could hardly breathe for laughing, but Reggie was pulling at her arm. 'Come along then, we've had our orders.'

As her dad walked by Verity's side he too was laughing, and it was a good sound. Verity said quite clearly over the rattle and hiss of the train as it continued on its way, 'Less of the Lady, if you don't mind, all of you. It does so mean one has to behave, so I'm just Verity. Having people curtsey is such a bore. Now tell me about the allotment.'

Reggie, staring after Verity as they scuttled along in her wake, asked, 'Is she real?'

'Some of the time. There's a broken heart under that lot, but she's healing.'

They kept up the frantic pace, which Polly knew meant Verity was trying to build herself up to cope. Reggie held the torch in a trembling hand. She said, 'What about you, Reggie, how goes it?'

'Oh, fine. Just a bit tedious, the same thing night after night. But it's a job that needs doing. It's much the same for you, I expect.'

She kept her eyes on the trembling slit of light that picked out the lamp posts and dustbins, kerbs and bus stops. 'No, it's not like that for us, because we are safe, and you're not. We're camels carrying loads that need to be delivered, that's all.'

His laugh was harsh. 'We're camels too, carrying loads that need to be delivered.'

They walked in silence now. Slowly Polly realised that she was actually back in her world where a war raged. Somehow, on the cut, they were too busy, too tired, too isolated, to really think of the life going on beyond the wharfs, the factories, the buses driving over the bridges. Their enemies were reluctant paddles refusing to budge, children who gobbed from bridges, the wind, the cold, and Leon, who beat and terrorised a child.

In this real world, there were searchlights that probed the sky for Reggie's aeroplane, and ack-ack guns that tried to down him, fighter planes that also tried to down him. And for the pongos there were other soldiers that wanted to smash them or catch them, or if you were a sailor there were submarines that wanted to sink you.

As they turned into Polly's road she stopped dead. 'No, you're not camels, Reggie. You are brave and exhausted young men trying to protect us. There is no comparison, and I'm proud of you, Reggie Watson. Now go home. Get some rest and leave us to sleep until at least lunchtime tomorrow. Does your leave last that long?'

'I'll pick you up at six tomorrow, then, after your tea. We'll go to the Palais which has a special Sunday fundraiser tomorrow night, and take the Lady. She can learn how to slum.'

'Oh, she's already learning that, never fear, and making a good fist of it.'

Polly blew him a kiss as he and his torch headed

back towards his own street a good half-mile away. 'Sleep well, Sergeant Watson,' she called after him, fearing that he probably wouldn't. She waited until he turned the corner, her heart going out to him, but that was all her heart was doing. It didn't do the hops and skips she knew it should, as it had just done on the wharf when Saul had said 'thank you'.

She hurried to catch up as Verity and her dad pushed open the gate of their detached cul-de-sac house, and headed up the path. Would her mother have the newspaper on the floor? Surely not if there was a visitor?

Her dad knocked, though she knew he had his own key. Oh dear, it didn't bode well.

Verity waited behind him with Polly and whispered, 'How is your Reggie? He looked a bit wan.'

'I think he is, but he's walking us to the Palais tomorrow evening, after tea. He'll pick us up at six.' Polly waited. A couple of weeks ago, Verity would have mocked the thought of 'tea'. Tonight she just said, 'I've only got a skirt, not the whole shebang.'

'There's a war on, idiot. Anything goes in our area. It's not like your club.'

Verity was silent for a moment but as the front door started to open she murmured, 'Indeed it is not, but it's like the world that Tom talked of, though we never went to a Palais.' Her voice broke. She laughed, coughed, and murmured shakily, 'Heavens, I must be tired.'

Polly's dad was gesturing them before him. 'Have you explained about the newspaper, Polly?' he asked.

Polly sighed. As Verity started to enter, Polly whispered, 'Think of Tom, and be kind.'

Verity looked over her shoulder at her. 'You have to learn to trust me, Polly. I won't get it right all the time, but I'm trying.' Her voice was steady, and totally serious.

She stepped into the darkness. Polly heard her mum say, 'If you would just wait a moment please, Lady Verity, until everyone is in, then we can close the door and put the light on. It's the blackout, but you'll know about that, of course.' Polly followed, then her father, and they all stood in a line in the darkness until her mum switched on the light.

Newspaper had been spread the width of the hall. Her mother wore her best dress, and Polly was starting to say how nice she looked when she was silenced by her mum's shriek of horror. 'What? What? Father, did you pass anyone? Reggie hasn't seen her, please say he hasn't.' Her hands were to her face and she was shaking her head. 'What do you look like, Polly? You haven't come through London like that? Oh, what will people think? And that smell, oh my goodness. Oh.' She was waving her hand in front of her face. 'Father said you would be grubby and needed hot water for baths, but . . . Oh no, this isn't right, what are we to do? You can't go back. It's not seemly. Oh, and for Lady Verity too. Oh dear . . .'

Polly's dad said, 'Step out of those wellies, girls, before they fall apart, and I'll try to do something about them before you go back. Then straight up those stairs, and Polly, show your friend the bedroom, and I'd wait there while she baths, as many times as she wants, and then you nip into the bath-room. Got it? I'll help your mum with the food. Then it will all be tickety-boo.'

He had already eased his feet out of his boots, and now carried them through to the kitchen, leading her mum firmly by the arm, so that they were left to drop their kitbags and take their filthy feet out of their boots. The smell was appalling. Verity whispered, 'There's not much to choose between my socks and my boots, and I daren't take my socks off because my feet will be horrendous.'

Polly was mortified, and muttered, 'I'm sorry about Mum. This is how her grief shows.'

Verity was already tiptoeing up the stairs. 'Oh, don't worry about that. If I was at home I'd be in the dogs' room until I was presentable.' She called over the bannister, 'You're looking quite lovely this evening, Mrs Holmes. I adore your frock.'

She continued up, and started to enter Will's room. 'No,' shouted Polly. 'Not that room.'

Verity closed the door. Polly opened her own bedroom door. 'We're in here. We can't use the front bedroom yet.'

Verity tiptoed into Polly's bedroom. There was a fire in the grate throwing out warmth and the blackout blind was down. Polly switched on the light. Verity said, 'It's huge. Do you find everything is huge, and busy, and war-ish? It's not like the cut, not at all. We're separate from all this, aren't we, but it's just as damned hard I think, only safer.'

Polly's mother called up, 'I've just been up to the bathroom and changed the towels for brown ones, girls, so don't feel embarrassed. Everything can be washed. I fussed. I shouldn't have done, but you both look so tired as well as dirty. Tired, and thin, and it upsets me. You're young and lovely, and your lives are too hard.'

Polly listened, and realised that there was a slower pace to her mum's speech, almost a tiredness, rather than the frenetic awful busyness. Was this good, or not? Then she absorbed the actual words, and they touched her and she feared she would weep. It was so long since her mum had been her mum.

'You go first, Verity, as Dad said. I'll stand here until you're done. If I sit on anything it will never be the same again, so don't hang about.'

Verity squeezed her shoulder and whispered, 'You are lucky with your family, you know.'

After an hour and a half of bathing the girls pulled on pyjamas from Polly's drawer. Her mother had left her own dressing gown on the spare bed for Verity. They pulled on socks and walked downstairs with wet, but clean, hair tied up in brown hand towels. The dining-room fire was red in the grate, the room was warm. Polly and Verity ate large baked potatoes filled with cheese and leeks while at one side of the fireplace her mum listened to the wireless, and her dad wrote up his allotment diary.

It was as it had been with Will: her parents doing this while she and Will played Snakes and Ladders or tried to do the *Daily Mail* crossword. Her mum looked up and said, 'You must go straight to bed when you have finished, and I don't expect to see you until lunchtime tomorrow, is that quite clear? I can't have you girls looking so tired, and that's that.'

Polly's dad winked at them. Verity said, laying her knife and fork together on her spotless plate, 'There, how rude, I haven't left any for Mr Manners, but with rationing one doesn't. You know, Mrs Holmes, I feel I wouldn't have done anyway, because it was so delicious. Were they your leeks, Mr Holmes?'

Polly listened as Verity talked to her parents, her dining chair turned towards them. She had a silvery tongue, she really had. The warmth was making Polly relax, she felt her eyes closing, the talk grew fainter, then she came to with a jerk. Her mother was behind her, her hands on her shoulders. 'You have become thin so quickly, little Polly, but then a bit of hard work never hurt anyone. And at least you haven't anyone wanting to hurt you, and for that I am grateful. Now, up to bed, girls. There is a hot-water bottle in each, though probably only warm now. Remember we don't want to see you until lunchtime. No point in going shopping or anything like that, but you can't anyway. It's Sunday. I will go to church, but you must stay and rest.'

Verity stood up, smoothing her dressing gown and looking up at Polly. 'Good heavens, Sunday. Days mean so little on the cut. You see, Mrs H, we only get paid a couple of pounds a trip, and when you're trundling along on the water, it's all like a different world, so we only buy food, really. Or the odd pint of beer at the pub when we moor up.'

Please don't, Polly urged, but Verity sailed on. 'We play darts and bet on winning, and we're good, which brings in a bit more. Perhaps we can spend it at the Palais tomorrow evening, Polly.'

Her mum was looking from one to the other. Polly cut across Verity as she was about to blurt out even more, and perhaps include Leon, 'Come on, we must get to sleep.'

She kissed her mum on the cheek, and her dad who had come to join them. 'We'll see you at the allotment, Dad, when we're up and about. You'll be taking your sandwiches for lunch?'

He nodded. They left the room, and hurried up the stairs. Once in the bedroom Verity said, 'I shouldn't have said anything about the beer, should I?'

Polly was throwing her dressing gown on the bed, but kept her socks on. The fireguard was in place. 'You should not, but at least I cut you off at the pass before there was any mention of cigarettes, or Leon.

Now, last one in bed's a cissy, and as it's you, you can turn off the light.'

Verity did, and as she felt her way back in the dark there was a thud. 'Damn, I stubbed my toe.'

'Serves you right for snitching,' Polly said, through lips that were almost too tired to move.

Chapter 23

14 November – on leave in Woking

When Polly woke, the room was still dark, but once her eyes adjusted she could see that Verity's bedclothes were pulled back and her pyjamas on her bed. Had she done a bunk? Had it all been too much?

Polly felt for her watch on the bedside table. It was almost 12.30. Was that at night, or lunchtime? Drunk with sleep she eased her way to the window and lifted the blind. Midday, and a cold sparkling day it was too. She threw on clothes, and used the blessed and wonderful flush lavatory that should actually be canonised, and headed on down to the kitchen. She feared that Verity was on her way back to London, perhaps to her false friends. Had it been that bad here?

She opened the kitchen door to be greeted by the smell of baking. Verity was standing next to her mother, her hands covered in flour and marge. Her mum looked up. 'Hello, Polly. Verity is showing me how to make cheese scones. They're nice with soup, she says. How clever is that, I would never have thought of it.' She paused. Taken by surprise Polly said, 'Dad will like those.'

She had expected her mother to rattle on, and on, but no, not today. Was it having Verity here, or were things better?

Her mother said, 'Polly dear, would you go into the front room. I left one of Reggie's letters there for you. Since then he's been sending them to your depot, or some such. I think that's what his mother said, at WI.'

Polly did, saying, as she left, that it would be an idea to take some scones to the allotment for their father. Verity called after her, 'All packed up, ready, and enough for us because we need feeding up, your mum thinks. Then we'll be out of your mum's hair for a while. Talking of hair, she said she'll trim my locks a little this afternoon, ready for the Palais. It'll be so much better.'

Polly shook her head; Verity with shorter hair? Would miracles never cease?

She opened the door into the front room, which was always cold and impersonal except at Christmas, when they were forced to sit and gaze with awe at a chicken and eat balls of stuffing, which she and Will loathed.

On the table were piles of clothes, Will's clothes; his sweaters, trousers, socks and shirts. She touched the sweaters, remembering when he had worn each one. Her mum entered. 'I saw you had taken his white sweater. At first I was cross, and then I thought our boy would like you to use his things. It's as if, somehow, he's still here if you do that. You see, I know he's gone. I do know that, I just couldn't bear to know it, if you can understand what I mean.'

She stood by Polly's side, wringing her hands. 'I thought when you went, Polly dear, that there you were, keeping safe for us, not for yourself, but for us. And at last I knew I still had you, and that you would return, *for* us. So, it was time to share his things, but not his room. Not yet. You do see that? I can't do it all at once. I have to believe in little bits.'

Polly slipped her arm through her mum's. 'Yes, I see that, and I think the same. A little longer, don't you think? Just for it to be his and his alone for a while more, for us all?'

As they left the house for the allotment, her mum called, 'Bring back the photos, would you, Polly. It's time. Let Dad keep a couple, but bring back the rest.'

'I will, Mum.' Polly walked ahead, down the path, letting her mum's words reverberate.

'Photos?' Verity asked as they walked along in the bright November day.

'Of Will, my twin. He died in North Africa, in a tank, silly idiot, just over six months ago.'

She could only just say it without the words blocking up her throat.

'Ah,' said Verity after a while. 'Thank you for telling me. I think I can imagine how you feel when someone you were actually born with, lived with, is now gone. Only half of you is left, but it's a strong half, and I think perhaps it's on the way to becoming whole.'

Verity slipped her arm into Polly's and squeezed. Polly squeezed in return. Neither said more.

They turned into the road to the allotment. The milkman was coming along, bottles clattering in his horse-drawn float. He'd be collecting his money for the week's milk. Verity stopped, and stroked Betsy. Polly smiled at Alf. 'All well, Alf?'

'Seems to be, Polly. You enjoying the canal? Any horse-drawn around still?'

His white coat was pristine, his cap too. His leather money bag hung across his chest. Verity answered, 'Yes, a few, but not many.'

Betsy tossed her head and started to pull the float to the next house. Alf laughed. 'She has her own timetable. Oats when she gets back so she won't hang about, even for a fuss.'

They reached the allotment in ten minutes, but Polly pulled Verity back. 'Are you a twin?' she asked.

'No, but I always felt Tom was part of me, and when he left I was only half there. That's love, Polly, brotherly, or romantic. If you feel that for Reggie, then it's enough. If you don't, it isn't. Don't you settle for less, because you, and he, deserve the full packet. We all do.'

At the Palais, there were GIs, soldiers, a few sailors and airmen already dancing with women in uniform, and some who weren't. The band were local, and Polly knew that they worked in a garage and were well past the first flush of youth, but the saxophone player in particular knew his stuff.

Reggie had brought Alan, another RAF bomber boy, with him to walk them into the town. At the door Polly and Verity insisted on paying for themselves, and all were happy to pay extra for the Spitfire the Palais management was hoping to raise funds to build. At the bar the men bought half-pints of beer for the girls, and a pint for themselves.

The music was loud, the beat tempting, so they left their beers on a spare table, Polly and Verity draped their coats on the chairs, and they took to the floor. Reggie was a good dancer, but Alan was not. Verity sorted that out, and within half an hour sweat was pouring down Alan's face and he was throwing Verity over his shoulder as the GIs were doing to their partners.

Polly felt a surge of energy the moment she and Reggie took to the floor; a sort of craziness seemed to take over them both and they danced until they couldn't speak, twirling, whirling, over a shoulder and beneath an arm. They danced like this for an hour and then all four of them flopped into their chairs, drank their beer, talked of the band, of the weather, and then danced again.

It was because, Polly thought, they all realised they had nothing more to say to one another, there were too many subjects to avoid. Where the boys flew; the friends they had lost, like Will, who had been Reggie's friend. The future, the past, the trembling of their hands. After two hours they were all drained of energy and couldn't even dance, so the lads walked the girls home. Alan kissed Verity on the cheek at the front gate, and Reggie hugged Polly, and kissed her on the forehead.

Polly wondered if it was for the last time. Would he live another day? He should know love, but perhaps for now it was enough to have friendship, because that was what she'd seen in his eyes, as he must have seen in hers. She waved to him, and watched him go with a sense of sadness. He was so young. She called, 'Be safe.' How stupid. Verity opened the gate. 'Come on. They might be all right.'

Chapter 24

Monday 15 November – back on the cut

Polly and Verity walked from Southall Station to the depot singing 'Don't Sit Under the Apple Tree', adding a bit of a two-step and twirl at the gates. The policeman waved them through, laughing. 'Go on, get orf that cloud, and get your backs into it again.'

They kept on singing and two-stepping right through the depot. Most of the men ignored them, but some grinned, and one even joined in, making a threesome. 'With anyone else but me, anyone else but me . . .'

He peeled off, heading for the blacksmith's, but not before he'd slapped Verity's bum. 'Oh, I say,' she spluttered, almost dropping her kitbag, which was perched precariously on her shoulder, then laughed.

They reached the towpath, pulled themselves together, and walked sedately beside the moored boats. Then Polly started singing quietly, 'With anyone else but you, you, youuuu.'

Verity laughed. One of the women sponging down *Eastbourne*'s cabin roof turned, wearing her weariness like a cloak. 'You 'ave fun while yer can, lasses.'

Polly waved. 'We're trying.'

Verity murmured, 'Succeeding, too. Your Reggie can swing a girl round like nobody's business, and what about that friend of his, Alan, once he got the hang of it. I had forgotten what it was like to have a twirl, a proper twirl.'

Polly waited for Verity's smile to fade as she remembered all that she had said as she talked late into the night about her Tom, on their return from the Palais. But Verity's smile remained. They passed the *Swordfish*, the *Snowdrop* and the *Fairweather*, all with their tillers removed, all with cleaning in progress, or the washing boiling on the bank, or clothes flapping on the line over the empty hold. Young children played on the bank, running, scooting past them, trying to make up for the days of virtual immobility on the counters.

Polly stopped dead. 'Oh, what if *Marigold*'s still in dry dock?'

'Wouldn't Bet have telephoned?'

They kept on walking, and now Verity hummed 'Chattanooga Choo Choo', doing a double-step alongside Polly, who joined in, until they were singing it out loud as they sashayed along, finally seeing Bet on the counter of the *Marigold*, who called, 'I wondered who was killing a cat.'

Verity stopped, and shook her head. 'Jealousy is a green-eyed goddess that does no one any good.'

They were almost abreast. Just past their boats was the *Seagull*, still moored. Granfer was splicing

as he leaned against the cabin. "Ow do, Granfer,'
Polly called.

"Ow do, lass.'

He nodded and returned to his splicing. She
looked from the *Seagull* to the *Swansong*, and her
heart was hopping and skipping, but she couldn't
see Saul.

Verity was pulling at her arm, and Polly gave her
attention to their own motorboat, and leapt with Verity
on to *Marigold*'s counter. Bet picked up the rope she
had been splicing, and handed it to Polly. 'Dump your
stuff and get to work. We have straps to splice while
we wait for orders. The engine is fit as a fiddle, but
you two need to get back down to earth, you've obviously been spoilt by someone's mum.'

'Don't you mean back down to water,' trilled
Verity as she ducked down into the cabin.

Bet shook her head at Polly. 'That's the last time
you two girls go home together. Can't be letting you
have all this fun, it could make an old maid like me
become sour.'

Polly grinned. 'What do you mean, *could* make . . .'

Bet laughed. 'Go on, Polly, unpack and sort yourselves out. And don't worry, Leon took off for Limehouse yesterday.' She called into the cabin, 'By the
way, I like your shorter hair, Verity. The curls are
sharper, somehow. Courtesy of Mrs Holmes, one
imagines.'

Polly headed into the cabin, amazed all over again
at its tiny size. She shoved her clothes in the

side-bed cupboard. Leon? For a couple of days she'd been able to forget about him. Verity squeezed past her, and up the steps to the counter. Polly heard her say, 'Two days away and this world fades, but any minute now, when we're back to working, it'll be as though nothing and nowhere else exists.'

Bet replied, 'I suppose each day is so intense that it wipes out everything, and so we quickly become part of the world. We have to, it's sink or swim, if I can use that phrase.'

Polly called up, 'I'd rather you didn't.' She headed for the counter, but remained on the top step. Bet was sitting on the roof by now, still splicing.

Bet threw her a couple of rope ends. 'A short splice will do.'

Polly taped the ends, unravelled enough for about five tucks and while she pushed the ends into each other she called up to Bet, 'My kitbag is stuffed with sweaters Mum has handed on to us all. I'll divvy them up when we've a minute.'

'Okey-doke.'

Verity slipped from the counter on to the kerb. 'I'm off to the lav, and I need to pick up another windlass from the blacksmith. I seem to remember we lost the spare on our way back, when a certain someone let it slip.'

'Thanks for reminding me.' Polly pulled a face.

Verity waved as she set off down the towpath, while Polly made the first complete set of tucks in the rope, and then another set and realised she had forgotten how sore it made her fingers. The tannoy from the office was blaring threadbare music, and stopping every so often to call steerers into their portals. Just before lunch and when they were taking a break from splicing they heard, 'Steerer Burrows, to the office. Steerer Burrows.'

'Make ready the *Marigold* while I go and sort it out with Ted. Then I have a surprise for you both.'

Verity was in *Marigold*'s cabin preparing Spam fritters for lunch. 'We're well and truly back, Polly darling, and are left with mere memories of your mother's cooking. It's all too sad. And what surprise will our Bet bear in her hot little hands?'

'Who knows?' Polly headed along the gunwale to the engine room and peered in, hoping it was really in order and giving the engine a pat. Fat lot of use but it made her feel that perhaps it might respond when the time came to start.

They heard Bet's cough before they saw her running back. 'Same load as before, so we head for Limehouse right this minute. Well, I say we, but as a lovely surprise you two will captain the old girl and the butty, while I am your slave. Don't look like that. You just have to tell me what to do, and if you don't, then I will do nothing. It's all part of the training, so let's see how you manage.' She coughed again.

Polly said, as she heaved the tiller into place, 'Perhaps you should see a doctor, Bet. That cough's getting worse.'

Bet shook her head. 'No need, the wind just caught in my chest. It's not a problem.'

Verity stuck her head out of the cabin. 'Are you sure?'

Bet shouted, 'Stop going on about the doctor, because it won't work, I'm not leaving the boat to sit in a queue and be told I'm quite all right while you two sit about thinking you've got away with doing nothing.'

Verity shook her head. 'Foiled again.'

But the look she gave Polly was serious. Polly nodded, because the cough sounded so much worse.

Bet was in full trainer mode, standing with arms crossed on the kerb. 'Verity, you've done two trips, so should be able to do it with one hand tied behind your back, so we'll ask Polly to take over the motor. Start the engine and sort it out.' Bet pulled her muffler tighter and took up a position on the counter, ready to obey orders.

The Spam fritters were taken off the heat, Polly found her woollen hat and dragged it on to her head and then started the engine with the minimum of choke. It ticked over like a bird. 'Thank the Lord,' she breathed. 'And the spare battery is in the hole charging nicely.'

Verity cast off both boats before hopping on to the butty then racing along the cabin roof and the top planks to the fore-end, readying herself to throw the short tow-rope towards the stud on *Marigold*'s counter when her stern drew level.

Polly eased the *Marigold* forward as Bet said, 'I'll be in the motor cabin, then.'

Polly shouted, sweat pouring down her back in spite of the freezing wind, 'No you won't. You'll stay right here and catch the short tow-rope when Verity throws it, and put it on the stud, if you don't ruddy well mind.'

'Language,' Bet murmured, but nodded approvingly, and stood braced, as the *Marigold* eased forward. Polly snatched a look to the left and right. Granfer was standing on his cabin roof, watching. For goodness' sake, didn't he have anything better to do? Clearly not, and what's more she realised that many others had taken up position on the roofs of their cabins. Her hands were shaking as the engine pat-pattered and *Marigold* moved on, and on into the fairway.

'Get ready with the rope,' she yelled to Verity, 'then I can tow you. A short tow, remember.' The depot lunch hooter sounded. Had Verity heard anything she'd said?

'Oh shut up,' screeched Verity from *Horizon*'s fore-end, as the *Marigold*'s stern counter came abreast. 'Now,' screamed Polly. 'Catch the rope, Bet.'

Verity threw it. Polly kept *Marigold* steady, and checked behind her that Bet had slipped it over the stud. There was a jerk as *Marigold* took up the slack, and then they pulled away together. Polly smiled but then another, much sharper jerk, or was it a jolt, thrust Polly forward, into the slide hatch as the fore-end dug into the opposite reed beds. Just then *Horizon* whacked into *Marigold*'s stern, and Bet fell, skidding into the cabin side. She lay there, looking up at Polly. 'I didn't like to say that you should try steering her as well.'

'Oh, no, no.' The engine was revving, churning the mud of the opposite bank.

'What now?' Bet asked before answering herself. 'Maybe you need to get forward to shaft while I . . . ?'

'Yes, yes, so stop lying about and take over the steering, and I'll go forward. Keep an eye on the engine.'

As Bet finished saying this, Polly was on the roof picking up the shaft, her mouth dry with embarrassment and nerves. She ran along the top planks until she reached the fore-end. She thrust one end of the shaft into the muddy bottom, pushing with all her weight. Her hands slipped. Behind the *Marigold* she could see that the butty's rear end was swinging round. She shoved again. 'Come on, come on.' The *Marigold* wouldn't move.

Then she realised that she'd never move it, because the butty was in the way of any backward motion and here she was trying to shift their combined weight. She laid her head against the shaft. How stupid she'd been, how utterly embarrassing, and now what to do? What the hell to do? Then, as she pushed once more, she realised that, even worse, she hadn't given Bet the order to change gear to reverse, so the *Marigold*'s motor was still driving forward.

She groaned, dropped the shaft and leapt on to the top planks, yelling, 'Bet, ease it into reverse, gently, gently go back. Verity, as *Marigold* backs into you, shaft *Horizon*, keeping her as straight as you can.'

Bet called, 'Well done, Polly. Quite right. Are you going to shaft now?'

'Of course I'm going to,' Polly yelled, furious at herself, no one else, as she jumped down to the fore-end counter again, pushing the shaft deep into the mud with all her might. Sweat prickling her back, she gripped tighter and shoved, and again. The *Marigold* barely moved in spite of the propeller now churning in reverse at the stern. The butty, *Horizon*, was swaying from side to side despite Verity shafting first one side and then the other and they were still blocking the cut. They needed more people. Polly rubbed her forehead, hearing the steerers laughing. She snatched a look, then wished she hadn't, because more had gathered. She didn't know what to do. She pulled up the shaft, and turned, shouting, 'Bet, what do . . . ?'

But she was drowned by Bet calling, 'Polly, look to the east. See, it's Leon's motor and butty with a load on, but surely he'll slow?' Polly stared and saw him in the distance, heading back from Limehouse. Bet yelled, 'Damn the man, he's not slowing at all. I think he's increasing speed, aiming for us. That's it, Polly, I'm sorry but I'm taking control. Shaft us back straight. Verity, shaft *Horizon* back straight as you can because I'm going to bump you – that's if between us, Polly, we can get the old girl out of the mud. Quick now.'

Polly was staring, mesmerised, at Leon powering towards them, and there was no way he could miss them, stranded as they were right across the cut.

'Polly, get going, shove that shaft, get us off.' Bet was screaming the order, panic in her voice, and there was no laughter now from the steerers, who were looking from Leon to the girls' boats. 'If it doesn't work, get ready to jump – you too, Verity, and swim for your lives. One more try now, come on. Now, now.'

Polly shoved, her own panic tearing at her. He was mad. He could kill them, he was just like a battering ram with his load on. But then she heard Saul shouting, and she looked around. He was roaring along the *Marigold*'s top planks, shaft in hand. Behind him on *Horizon*, Granfer had leapt from *Swansong*'s fore-end on to *Horizon*'s stern counter, also with a shaft. Saul was beside her now. He said quietly, his hand on her arm, shaking her slightly, 'Yer stay calm, my lass. Push with me when I sez.'

He was watching Granfer, who took the opposite side to Verity. 'Now, my lass,' Saul said, quite calmly. 'Yer push with all yer got, an' we'll all do it together. Gives t'whole thing more thrust.' He roared now, 'Bet, yer keep 'er engine in reverse.'

He leapt to the opposite side of the counter to Polly. 'Now,' roared Saul.

322

They all shoved, Polly feeling as though her eyes would pop out of her skull with the effort, and at last the motor was moving off the mud, and there was a jolt as the butty was bumped straight back with such force it tugged at the *Marigold* for a moment, but then the weight of both was too much, and the butty banged them forward. 'Again when I say,' Saul roared, drawing out his shaft. They all did the same, weeds and mud dripping off the end. Saul roared again, 'Now.'

All four shafted. The motor was free of the mud, backing, backing.

Saul yelled, 'We ain't got time to get both back.' He roared to Granfer, 'Cast off *Marigold*, then shaft the butty back to the lay-by kerb. Bet, keep yer *Marigold* in reverse. Polly, yer stay 'ere, and steady 'er. I'm going back with Bet to shaft 'er round.' He shot a look down the cut. Polly followed his gaze. Leon was close; too close, surely. Saul shouted, 'Still no way that bugger's stopping, so we's got to get 'er abreast t'reeds, this side, and lie in tight, even though we might ground. Don't you let her fore-end swing out. Got it. Remember, we gotta keep 'er tight in.'

Polly nodded and watched him run like the wind, balancing on the planks like an acrobat.

She waited for Saul's call, and when it came she stopped the fore-end from swinging back into the fairway as he shafted the *Marigold* abreast the side, just as the butty was half into a parking space being kept open by some steerers who were shafting

Seagull and *Swansong* apart. Polly snatched a look to the east as Leon's engine sounded louder and louder, then at the *Horizon* which was moored now, with Verity running along the top planks, calling, 'Stay abreast, Polly. Oh Bet, stay abreast. He can't steer to you, it's too late for him to change course. Look, he's going straight past.'

On the lay-by the boaters were shaking their fists at the *Brighton*, as Leon steered it, and his men the *Maudsley*, straight along the cut, their speed rocking all the boats.

Saul held the *Marigold* shafted tight into the side, with Polly stalling the swingback. *Brighton*'s wash rocked the *Marigold* but Polly hung on grimly to the shaft, keeping *Marigold* abreast the bank, struggling against the wash, and the rocking. But her hands were numb, the shaft slipped. As the motor tipped and swayed she felt herself falling into the water, the shaft crashing on to her, sinking as she sank, towards the mud.

She struggled, but her wellingtons had filled with water and weighed her down. The shaft trapped her against the hull as one end caught on a fender, while the other dug into the bottom mud. She couldn't move. She shoved at the shaft. No good. She closed her eyes as the mud churned and stung her eyes. She kicked and struggled, her lungs bursting but she must not breathe. She longed to. No. No.

She kicked, and shoved at the shaft, but the *Marigold* was swinging out, away from the bank into the shaft, squeezing her. She must breathe. No. She couldn't fight, not any more, and so became quite still . . . for a moment the *Marigold*'s hull eased back as the turbulence shifted, and she raised her arms, slipping down and free of the shaft, and with one final effort kicked to the surface, gasping, dragging in a breath and then another.

She reached for a fender, panicking, scared the motor might lurch over her. She dragged in more air, her eyes stinging from the mud. Her hands were too numb to hold on to the fender and she was slipping, but then she caught hold of the rope that held it. Her body was a block of ice. 'Saul,' she whispered. 'Help me.'

He came, of course he did. He came and was above her leaning right down, his arm out. She coughed, choked, dribbled saliva. He gripped her hand, prised her fingers from the rope. 'Let me 'ave t'other.'

She couldn't let go of the rope, her hand wouldn't work. 'Help me, Saul,' she whispered.

'Always,' Saul said. 'Always I will help yer, my lass, and that 'at of yers. 'Tis still on yer 'ead, yer know.' His smile was gentle.

For a moment they looked at one another and something changed in Polly, something became certain, something opened up inside her. He reached down, and gripped her other hand, pulling her free and lifting her from the water, almost throwing her up in the air, then catching her in his arms, to sweep her to the stern counter along the top planks. Bet was holding the *Marigold* steady as the wash subsided.

He let her stand out of the way of Bet. Her legs were too numb to take her weight, and she sank down. He caught and held her against his warmth and strength. Bet had idled the motor. 'I'll get her into the cabin,' she told him.

Saul shook his head. 'Yer needed on tiller. Shall I?' He nodded to the cabin.

Bet said, 'If you would.'

He ducked beneath the slide hatch, Polly in his arms, and sat her on the side-bed opposite the range. 'We'll get that slide 'atch shut, and the doors, and yer be right. But them boots ain't right. Yer need these.' He pointed to his, which were more like leather walking boots. She nodded, her teeth chattering, adding as he went up the steps, bending over to avoid the ceiling and the slide hatch, 'Thank you, Saul. But be careful of Leon.'

He turned, and gave a quick smile. 'He ain't got a gun, and we be warned now, so that's that. You keep a lookout too, cos it was yer boat he were aiming at, and that's down to me, and for that, I have sorrow, and will work more to keep you all safe.'

As he left, and drew the slide hatch closed, she heard Bet say, 'You helped us out of a hole.' Polly took her hat off and threw it into the bowl by the range because it was dripping down her neck.

She heard Granfer say, 'It wouldn't 'ave been no

hole, but for Leon. Anyone else woulda stopped, not roared on at yer. We all done summat suchlike across the cut in oos time. No need for no one to take on like that. 'Sides, you done helped my boys.'

'Boys?' Bet queried. 'I thought we only helped Saul?'

'That's between me and yer Polly.'

Boys? Polly thought, her mind too cold to work. She'd only helped Saul in the fight with Leon – and then she remembered Joe, and the book. It didn't matter, not really. She had the dedication page.

She leaned forward, holding her trembling hands out to the range, frightened suddenly. Granfer and Saul were here, so Joe was all by himself on the *Seagull*. He shouldn't be. Bet came into the cabin. Polly said, 'How will they get back to Joe? They're on the wrong side of the cut. He mustn't be alone.'

Bet gestured to her. 'I want to show you. Quickly now.'

Polly stood on weak legs. Bet pulled her on to the counter. Together they watched as Granfer and Saul stepped from the fore-end of the *Marigold* on to the stern of a lighter heading west, then caught a motor going to Limehouse. Then another, further along, going west again. One of the steerers brought out his motor into the fairway, and the two men stepped on to that.

'Like big stepping stones,' Polly muttered, her eyes fixed on Saul, wondering how she had lived without knowing that he was in the world. She trusted the strength in his hands as he had pulled her from the water, the safety she had felt in his arms, recalled the loss she'd felt when he had placed her on the side-bed and left. She trusted in all of this, because what she felt was love. It was different to Will, of course it was, but it was as deep, or almost.

Polly shook her head, her teeth still chattering as the wind zipped across the *Marigold*'s stern counter. 'I'm sorry, I messed up.'

'You won't do it again. We all do summat such-like, as Granfer said, it's a common mistake with trainees, but most don't have a madman bearing down on them. I should have taken over sooner, it wasn't fair of me but I hadn't quite taken on board the situation. A feud is one thing, but this is absurd. He could have hurt us, or should I say, he certainly meant to hurt us in that moment of time. However he might regret it by now, and there's no point in writing a report for the authorities, because the steerers and Saul won't support it. It's boater business. Still, we must keep an eye on it. You did well.'

The wind was gusting, Polly was freezing. Verity was waving from the butty, putting her hands round her mouth, calling, 'Are you both all right?'

Bet replied, 'We'll be with you very soon.' She turned to Polly. 'Now, change clothes, sit tight for ten minutes to warm through then join me, and we'll reattach *Horizon*. We still need to get to Limehouse.'

Polly changed, splashed cold water from the bowl

all over her, then towelled herself dry, and sat for ten minutes, and all the time she could feel the strength of Saul, and hear his words, and see his face, so calm, his eyes so deep, his quick smile ... It wasn't the range that warmed her.

Chapter 25

Monday 15 November – at Limehouse Basin

While the loading of yet more steel billets was under way there was no chance to go shopping for boots. Verity said as they sat on the *Marigold* with the range oozing out heat, waiting while the butty was loaded, 'We're already behind a proper schedule, what with the engine trouble, Bet, so how about Polly and me nipping into town when we reach Alperton. That's if Polly promises not to hurl herself into any water between here and mooring up.'

Polly sneezed. 'Fine by me and besides, I've washed my tea cosy, which has dried out nicely, with the pom-pom in full bloom. It could do with a bit of an outing.' Bet and Verity groaned. Verity muttered as she sipped her tea, 'You've washed it – given it a new lease of life? You say that as though it's a good thing.'

Polly sneezed again, and coughed. Verity drew away from her and moved to the cross-bed with Bet. 'You can keep those germs to yourself, as well.'

The next morning they were off the moment the dawn broke, with Polly lock-wheeling for the first stage, cracking ice on the puddles as she rode through them on the bike. Her bum seemed to have grown a cloak of immunity, because it didn't hurt nearly as much as it had, though her hands on the handlebars became just as cold, and the windlass on the paddle ratchet just as hard to get going.

There was a great deal of queuing at the locks, because traffic, both coming and going, was heavy. Saul and Granfer had caught up, carrying the same steel billets as the *Marigold* and *Horizon*, but there were a few boats in between them. It pleased Polly to think of her shepherd close by, and that Leon was way ahead, but could not yet have reached Birmingham, so would not be heading towards them for many a day.

They tied up well before Paddington and huddled round the range, and ate yet more Spam fritters, this time fried in the dripping Polly's mother had insisted they bring, courtesy of her friendly local butcher; God bless him, Polly thought. She scribbled a letter to her parents, and another to Reggie, thanking him and Alan for such a good evening on her leave, and telling him they were expected to be early at Alperton tomorrow and would do some shopping, before turning north for Birmingham.

'*We should be there in five or six days, I hope, then it's off to the public baths,*' she wrote, adding that she hoped that he would stay safe. She sat tapping her pen against her lips. She never knew whether that was tempting fate, and almost crossed it out, but left it in the end. She'd post it in Alperton.

Again they were up with the dawn, and now Verity took over the locks while Polly took on steering the motor. They had ordered Bet to remain on the butty and do what butty steerers did, because her cough was raw and frequent. Bet had raised her eyebrows, and given in.

It was a dull and foggy morning and Polly hooted the horn round every bend and through every bridge hole. She was coughing as she committed to enter another, using the electric horn as the London buses drummed over the top. As she pat-pattered along the centre another boat loomed, and how they passed one another she didn't know. 'Didn't yer 'ear me knotting, for 'eavens sake?' the steerer yelled.

'Didn't you hear me hooting?' Polly watched as he whacked a knotted rope on the cabin top. The sound travelled, and it would be even clearer in fog. She called, 'I'll give it a try.' He had gone past, but his wife on the butty called, 'Yer finished that hat yet?'

Polly shouted, 'Oh, I didn't recognise you. Yes I have, and I'll leave it at Bob's pub. It's red, with a green pom-pom.'

When they tied up at Alperton Bet sounded tired, and they left her sipping honey tea. They were both wearing their wellingtons. Polly's hadn't yet dried out, but she was too tired to care. What were damp and freezing feet anyway? It's what she was used to by now. The Tube took them into Piccadilly and they walked to Oxford Street, overwhelmed by the crowds but barely noticing the smell of the sandbags guarding the shops. By the time they finally found a shop selling leather mountain boots and work-men's footwear, the fog was thicker.

They walked around the shop trying on numerous pairs, and then left, with ones that looked very like Bet's, handing the appalled shop assistant their wellingtons and tipping her a bob to dispose of them. They were several clothes coupons lighter, but didn't care, because they were both nervous about repeating Polly's fall into the cut.

As the afternoon grew darker they checked the time, and slipped into a Lyons Corner House for a cup of tea. The nippy, so smart in her black dress and white apron, her hair held off her face by her white cap, looked at their sweaters and trousers, their ruined hands and chapped lips. She said, 'Land girls?'

Polly grinned. 'Waterway girls.'

The nippy shook her head and returned to her station in the corner, keeping an eye on them. 'She thinks we're going to do a flit,' Verity muttered.

'Don't even think of it,' Polly insisted, drinking her tea and eyeing the toast and teacakes two women at the next table were eating. The GIs sitting with them were examining their anchovy toast and looking doubtful.

'Shall we?' Verity asked.

Polly looked in her purse. 'I can, if you can.'

They gestured to the nippy. 'May we have what table 3 is having, please.'

The nippy raised an eyebrow. 'We can pay,' Polly said.

The GIs looked up. One called, 'Hey, put it on our check, all of it; have some of these teacake things too. Any ladies who ask for this fishy thing deserve a medal.'

He winked at Polly, who was about to demur, but Verity kicked her hard and called, 'That's so very kind. We are rather skint, because we help to deliver war materials on the canals, and let's just say the pay is a pittance, and the hours horrendous.'

The GI half saluted. 'We're all doing our bit, one way or another.' He raised his eyebrows at the women, who looked, Polly thought, little better than they ought to be.

Verity whispered to her, 'Don't pull that face, darling. You took stockings, as did I, so who are we to throw stones at those who provide a few comforts of the undeniably physical sort.'

Polly hushed her as their anchovy toast and teacakes arrived. When the nippy had gone she gripped Verity's hand and said, 'Just promise you never will, no matter how homeless or penniless you are. Just come to me. I'll help.'

Verity grinned. 'I do adore you, Polly Holmes. Don't worry, I won't be tempted, I have a lovely big legacy from Uncle Freddy who was terribly terribly rich until he fell under a bus, drunk as a skunk.'

'He didn't?' Polly was deliciously shocked.

'No, of course not. He was killed in Norway, when

our lot were buggering about over there at the start of the war, bless him. He taught me to play poker and fleece people in my early teens.'

The toast, teacakes and tea were finished, and Polly sat back. 'All right then, Moneybags. You can pay, then.' But the GIs had been as good as their word, and had it put on their bill before they left, though neither Polly nor Verity had noticed their going.

On their way to the boat they used their torches to see along the towpath, past washing fires, and the odd pinprick of a cigarette being smoked on the counter. They were just about to board the *Marigold* when they heard a crash, and a woman's piercing scream, behind them. 'Jimmy, Jimmy.'

They spun round, and in the light from one of the boaters' washing fires on the bank saw a woman desperately running up and down the towpath, searching in the water around her motor. They ran back while a dog yapped on the end of a tatty rope attached to a stud driven into the bank. As the woman screamed louder, the dog grew ever more frenzied. Verity caught the woman. 'What?' she asked.

They could hear splashing near the stern of the motorboat which, like all of the boats at Alperton, lay alongside, parallel to the bank.

Polly was frantically scanning the gap between the bank and the motor with her feeble torch. The woman said, 'Jimmy, he's fell between the bank and t'boat. 'E's there, down there, in the cut. Watch for 'im while I gets t'shaft.' She heaved herself on to the counter and dragged off the long shaft, rushing with it to where Polly stood, peering into the water towards the stern of the boat.

The woman shafted the boat, with Polly and Verity shoving at the hull from the bank. Other women came to help and just then they heard a child's terrible cry, a groan, splashing. 'Who's Jimmy?' Polly shouted, using her torch to track along the widening gap at the water's edge.

'My little 'un, five 'e be. Jimmy, Jimmy.'

There was more splashing, and a sort of gurgle. 'Jimmy,' called Polly. 'We're all coming.'

Verity leapt into the woman's cabin without a by your leave and came out with the hurricane lamp, holding it over the water. There were even more women now, and the noise from a pub was all anyone needed to know about where the men were. One of the women called, 'Watch that lamp. There be blackout.'

Verity was on the bank now, scanning the water. 'Not when there's a child lost, there isn't.'

Polly was trying to track the noise. Where was he? 'Silence,' she roared. 'Let's listen.'

Silence fell. It was a real silence, not a sound. His mother started to call. Nothing. Polly shouted, 'Push this bloody boat further away, come on all of you, get your backs into it. Shove. Verity, look again over the stern. Is he near the propellers?'

Several other women arrived with hurricane lamps, and as the boat was shoved further away the wives helped to light up the water. From a distant boat a child cried. Near the rudder there was another splash, a sort of groan, then nothing.

As Polly moved, staring into the dim light cast by Verity's hurricane lamp, the dog lunged once more, broke the rope, bounded past Polly and leapt into the cut. The boat was so laden it was low in the water, which meant the propellers would be deep, but if the dog thought Jimmy might be there . . . Polly sighed, handed the torch to one of the women boaters, and slid down the bank into the water, half walking, half doggy-paddling frantically round the stern then along the hull. She turned, and came back.

As she did so, she kicked something. She ducked down. Nothing. She surfaced, knocking the dog, which was paddling around her and barking. There had to be something there. She dived again, and this time grabbed a coat and hair and hauled, and hauled, but it was a dead weight and wouldn't budge. Was it snagged on the blades? Still beneath the surface she tugged again; the weight moved. Oh God. She surfaced again, spitting out water, shouting, 'Verity, quick, he's here, but stuck. And someone get those bloody men out of the boozer. We need their strength.'

She dived down, trying to see in the murk, the filth stinging her eyes. Verity was in the water now, and both took a breath and sank down below the surface, feeling around the propellers bumping into each other. But no, nothing.

Down they went again, but the seconds were

ticking away. He'd been under a minute or so, but it was cold, bloody cold. There. There – material. She grabbed a little coat, and pulled.

Verity was with her now. Their cheeks bulged as they fought to hold their breath and pull. Someone else joined them, a man. He pulled too, until finally the resistance eased, and they yanked the boy up as one, ripping his coat apart where it had snagged. He was above the water, limp and lifeless. Jimmy's mother screamed. Polly, Verity and the man fought their way to the bank and handed him up to the waiting men and women, one of whom couldn't bear to look. 'Lay him on his front, and pull me up,' Polly demanded as the dog leapt out on to the bank and shook itself.

Verity and the man shoved her from behind as a boater, smelling of beer, pulled her. She was out, dripping. She knelt, her knees either side of the child. What had her dad said?

Head to the side, pump the ribs, pump out the water. Once, twice. Once, twice. Again. Again. Push, push, knowing it was too late, tears streaming down her face, because she had a young child beneath her hands, one dressed in weeds, white, unbreathing. Perhaps someone had tried to save Will. But no, there was nothing left of him, but the boy was still here.

She looked up into Verity's face. She was crying too, and the man, who watched, had sorrow etched into his face and was saying over and over again,

'Jimmy, my last little boy, my Jimmy.' The mother clung to him, silent now, and defeated. But the man was still saying it. Polly pumped again and again. She said, 'My dad said to do this before we started to go to sailing club. He showed us how, just in case.'

She was panting, and now Verity elbowed her to one side, and took over. Then back to Polly, and now it was the father, and then Polly again, and then the mother. All around, in the light of the hurricane lamp, the boaters, men and women, waited, their breath visible in the lamplight. It was Polly's turn again and she pumped, and pumped, and just as Verity knelt to take her place they saw water dribbling from Jimmy's mouth into the frosted earth.

Running through her head were her dad's words. *It helps sometimes if it is cold. The body stops, somehow.* He'd saved a bloke in this way, in a flooded shell hole in the winter, when there was ice on the surface. A padre had told him how.

There was absolute silence. No noise even from the pub, or the father, who had hunkered down, his wife beside him touching her son's head, or the dog that came now and licked the boy's face. Polly pumped again – once, twice. Jimmy coughed, and water flooded from his mouth, followed by vomit. The father dragged back the dog, and it whined and scrabbled to be near the boy. Polly's arms were failing, she was aching with tiredness.

She looked up at Verity. 'I can't,' she said. 'You must, again.'

Verity took over, and the child groaned as Polly crouched beside his kneeling parents. A sigh ran round the onlookers. She whispered, in time to the pumping, echoing the parents, who held back the dog, 'Come on, Jimmy. Come on.'

The voices of all three of them were thick with tears. Polly dragged her hands across her face and said to those standing near, 'Go to the pub, get Sid to telephone an ambulance. Hurry, hurry.'

Granfer called, 'Already done, lass. 'Tis coming. 'Ear it.'

They heard the sound of a ringing bell coming closer, closer. Verity was tiring now, but the child was coughing. Jimmy tried to raise his head. The bells were nearer still. Then they heard the slam of doors, and the crowd parted. The ambulance was right up by the towpath, having driven over the pub garden. The men threw themselves down beside Jimmy, saw the child moving, the vomit and spittle. 'We'll take over,' they said, one of them lifting Verity away while the other wrapped the boy in blankets, and placed him on to a stretcher. 'You coming with us, Missus, and you, mate?'

The men helped the mother to her feet, and it was Granfer who helped the father, dripping and trembling. The man was shaking his head. 'I 'ave to take the billets.' He sounded as though he was in another world. A man came to the girls, who had scrabbled, freezing, to their feet. 'Two o' their lads 'as already gone, drowned. Don't know what they'da done if

340

Jimmy'd gone too. 'Appens a lot. Can't keep 'em safe, not on the water.' He turned away.

Polly said to the steerer, 'The father must go with Jimmy, but he'll be so cold. He's dripping.'

'Him'll go for a while,' he muttered, 'but 'e got to go on with the load in the morning. You best 'ave their dog, will ya? He'll not be able to manage him as well.' He handed Polly the snapped rope which had tethered the dog.

Polly heard Granfer say to the man as he disappeared into the back of the ambulance, 'You'll have our Joe on the butty this trip, to 'elp yer, be yer runabout.'

The man nodded, that was all, because the boaters never said thank you. But Saul and Granfer had.

Verity and Polly walked back to *Marigold*, Polly pulling the dog, their boots squelching, their teeth chattering from the cold. Polly said, 'Well, if the boots survive this, they're worth the coupons. What's more, Moneybags, you won't have to buy us each another pair.'

Verity squeezed her arm. 'I hope he lives.'

'He might, but sometimes they drown later, they've got so much water in their lungs, so Dad says.'

They clambered on board the *Marigold*. Dog, as she thought of him, for she hadn't thought to ask his name, trotted behind as though he knew he had to stay with them for now. Bet wasn't in the motor cabin. Perhaps she was already asleep in the butty, trying to throw off the cough. They stripped off and sluiced themselves; Bet had left the range ticking over for them. They added coal and sat in their pyjamas. 'Where was Saul?' Verity asked.

'Still in the pub, perhaps.' She shouldn't mind, Polly thought, hating the gut-churning flash of misery the thought brought because anyone who went on playing darts or drinking when a child was in danger wasn't worth a sixpence.

The dog sat quietly in front of the fire. 'When on earth are you going to stop hurling yourself into the water, and more importantly, how did you know what to do?' Verity asked.

Polly told her of her father's experience with the man in the shell hole.

'Conchie was he, if he was a stretcher-bearer?'

'Would it matter?'

They were smoking. Verity shook her head. 'Just interested.'

'No, not really, it was just his job, that's all. He didn't want to kill, but wanted to do his bit for the war effort because he felt that if others put themselves in danger to save him, then so should he. The authorities listened.'

During the night, when Polly stirred, she found Dog lying on her legs, and was grateful for the company. In the morning they woke, ready to head off, but there was no sign of Bet. When they let Dog off the boat he ran to Jimmy's motor, and cried. So Polly walked him along the towpath for a mile, and then back, in boots still damp but nowhere near falling apart.

She let Dog into the cabin to eat toast with Verity, while she knocked on Bet's cabin door. There was no answer and, rude though it was, she peered in. Bet was in the cross-bed, muttering and tossing, her face sweat-drenched and ashen. Polly rushed down into the cabin and felt her forehead. It was far too hot.

Bet gripped her hand and whispered, 'I can't go on. Get an ambulance first, then telephone the number in the cupboard. They'll send someone else to help you. You'll be fine. I know you will.'

Polly ran to the pub and beat on the door. The publican, Sid, appeared, his hair uncombed, a cigarette flopping in the corner of his mouth. She explained and he beckoned her in. 'Busy night on the cut? No need to call out the ambulance – if it's Bet, I'll take her. Let me get me old mum's wheelchair and we can tuck her up tidy at the boat and deliver her to the car.'

This is what they did, with no objection from Bet, which was more worrying than finding her so ill.

Verity went with Sid to the hospital while Sid allowed Polly to telephone the vaguely familiar number from the pub. It was the Mayfair office who had first interviewed her. They listened, and told her to stay by the telephone and wait for a return call, which would come within minutes. She waited by the bar for ten minutes, with the clock ticking loudly. Then sat by the fireplace, which was heaped with ash still warm from the previous night. She stuck her feet on the hearth and let the heat dry her boots just a fraction more, her thoughts with Bet. When the telephone rang, Polly hurried to answer it, just as the back door to the pub opened and Verity called, 'Are you here, Polly?'

Polly was listening to the secretary on the other end saying, 'Yes, we have sorted something, we think. A Miss Simpson should be arriving at Alperton very soon. You'll be able to get as far as Kings Langley today. This will be her third trip, so she is a little more experienced than you, and I think on a vaguely similar level to Lady Verity. She is without a team at the moment and can be with you by this afternoon. Once you tell us which hospital, we will stay in touch with Miss Burrows's progress, so phone us.'

The line went dead.

In the kitchen doorway Verity waited. Polly said, 'They need to know where she is.'

'She's in the Middlesex. She's really ill, pneumonia. I said she must have the very best treatment.'

Polly looked at her. 'You're paying?'

'Of course, it's nothing. And she's the sum of so much.'

'And Jimmy?'

'Holding his own. His mum is with him, but we brought the father back and he's taken the motor and butty on, with Joe helping. The father can ring here, Sid said, because he'll keep in touch with the hospital for updates.'

'You're paying for Jimmy too?'

'Mind your own business, darling.' They hugged each other and then sat on bar stools. Verity said, 'She and he must be all right. They must.'

Sid came from the kitchen bearing a tray holding three steaming mugs. 'Coffee, that rare beast, girls, and it's not even Camp Coffee. It's the real stuff and we won't ask where from, and to cap it all, we'll have a little nip of brandy to start the day. It's all been a bit of a do these last twelve hours.' It was more than a nip, but as they sat round the table Sid lifted his mug. 'Cheers, dears.'

The drink warmed them. Polly told them about Miss Simpson. Sid said, 'I don't know, in and out of the water like mermaids, or so Granfer tells me. Him upstairs will give you a few gold stars for this dip, but if I were you, I'd get your heads down while you can. Doing a trip with a strange team can be tricky, or so the other girls who come through tell us.'

Before they left they telephoned the name of the hospital through to the office, shook Sid's hand, and opened the pub door. Polly stopped. 'Sid, did everyone come from the pub to help us yesterday evening?'

'Oh yes, of course. I was there too.'

'That was kind,' Polly said. 'Thank you, Sid, I really think you saved our Bet. I'll buy you one of your own drinks when we're next through here, but what about petrol?'

'No, you're all right.' He tapped his nose. 'It's that

345

strange dyed stuff that a friendly farmer lets me have from time to time, but mum's the word.' His laugh followed them along to the towpath. Most of the boats moored overnight were gone. They watched as others arrived and moored up. It was like a train station, Polly thought. They were about to walk on, but heard Sid call for them to wait. He was panting when he caught up.

He blurted out, 'These boaters lose children too often from the boat: drowning, propellers, sickness, Lord knows what, and it's no fault of their own. It's the life, it's that bloody hard, and they love 'em like they was made of pure gold, but you can't keep kids safe on the counters, and the byways. You mustn't think bad of 'em.'

Polly and Verity looked at one another in surprise. 'We don't,' they chorused. 'Of course we don't.' Sid grinned and headed back to the pub.

The girls linked arms and walked back to the *Marigold*. Verity said, 'You think you're getting to know the worst of it, but we're just scraping the surface. We're so superficial, Polly.'

Polly knew. Dog was waiting, tied up on the counter, and she bent to stroke her. 'Hello girl, come and get warm. We've a bit of a wait, and then it will be chop-chop.'

Verity laughed slightly, but only slightly. 'We should have known Bet was poorly, and perhaps getting too tired. We should write to her.'

Polly remembered then that she hadn't posted

Reggie's letter, but it really didn't matter. Yes, they would write to Bet, and she could post the two letters together.

She looked over at the pub and smiled. So, Saul hadn't been there anyway.

Chapter 26

17 November – on the way to Birmingham

Marigold and *Horizon* had been moored up north of Kings Langley on the evening of the 16th near Bob's pub where Polly and Verity had left the wool hat, but they'd not stayed for a drink. They were too tired, too dispirited, too irritated, too worried about Bet. They felt the same this morning as the wind tore across the fields when they cast off.

As the office had said, Sylvia Simpson had joined them at Alperton, and they had made good time, though the fact that she was a young woman of about their age seemed to be the only common factor. Polly and Verity had shared the lock-wheeling; there had not been a third in the rota. Instead Sylvia had stayed nice and warm, wrapped up against the wind on the butty counter, doing diddly squat except issuing orders.

After delivering the hat, Verity and Polly had tried yet again to make conversation as they ate a supper of rabbit stew that they'd left simmering most of the day. They had told Sylvia of Bet's condition, and the 'no improvement' report from the Middlesex.

They had asked which boat she had transferred from. She had said she'd been on leave and had followed orders when asked to report in place of the trainer, Bet, and presumably take on her role.

Verity had then asked who had trained her, and how many trips she had made, because surely, she said, the Ministry bod had mentioned that she'd only done three so perhaps they were all in this together, rather than anyone taking on a trainer's role. Sylvia had laid her knife and fork together, and muttered something about how important even an extra trip was to the competency of trainees. She had patted her mouth with her handkerchief, and then tucked it back up her sleeve.

On the morning of 18 November Sylvia had again ordered Polly to take the first lock-wheel shift of the day.

'Ordered?' Polly muttered aloud as she cycled, head down, along the towpath two hours later, still furious after lock-wheeling too many locks.

'You sound as though you're ordering me?' she'd said to Sylvia, who had replied that someone had to take the lead. Verity had stood on the towpath, her hands on her hips. 'Bet would share the duties,' she said.

'I'm not Bet,' Sylvia had said, tying up her muffler and waving Polly off. 'Come on, you want Bet to be proud of you when I telephone the office to see how she is, surely.'

Boats on the beer run passed by Polly as she

ground out aloud, 'Ordered, indeed.' The lads on the fly-boats waved, looking more tired than youngsters should.

Polly pedalled on, hearing before seeing the German prisoners of war being marched along the towpath by British guards. She drew off the towpath, dragging the bike hard up against the hedge as they approached. Dog barked at her side. She shouted for silence and Dog obeyed. The Tommy guards whistled at her while the Germans looked ahead as if she did not exist, though one kicked a stone and it hit her shin. It could have been an accident, of course; nonetheless, she hoped the turnips the Nazis had to dig up were frozen solid in the earth. That'd give them something to complain about.

Once they were past she took off again, finally rounding a long bend and the lock was in sight. They'd been stuck behind several pairs heading for Tyseley Wharf, and there'd been only a few returning towards Limehouse, so, yet again, the lock was not ready for them to enter. Instead it was full to the brim with cut water, all of which needed emptying.

Polly dropped the bike and ran to the lock gates, drawing out the windlass from the back of her trouser belt, raised the paddles and let the water out, then opened one of the gates. She ran across to open the remaining gate. It stuck three quarters of the way.

She pushed the beam again, digging her heels into the mud, bracing herself, shoving with her bum. It wouldn't budge. She peered down into the lock, between the wall and the stuck gate. She could see something – but what? Was it a branch? Yes, looked like it, but a bloody big one. The *Marigold* hove into sight, slowed, then pulled in, waiting. Damn. They'd be held up, but what could she do?

Marigold's horn sounded, and then again. Bloody Miss Simpson. How dare she? Verity ran from the butty, shouting as she drew near, 'What's wrong?'

Polly seethed as she pointed down at the water. 'What's wrong is Miss Simpson sounding her horn, for one thing. The other is, the gate's stuck. I passed a load of prisoners who could have helped, but damned if I know what to do.'

'The ghastly Sylvia is going to have to whack the bugger open as she's insisted on running the *Marigold* today. Please please give me the pleasure of telling her.' Verity was off, her face filled with glee, while Polly remained sitting on the beam. Ducks flew overhead. Someone will shoot you for Christmas, she thought, as she watched Verity nearing the butty. Even here Polly could hear her shouting her own order to Sylvia Simpson. Dog was sniffing in the hedges, but keeping a close eye on Polly while she did so.

She made Polly feel safe, as they seemed to have lost their shepherd, though she and Verity thought that as *Seagull* and *Swansong* had obviously had to go ahead, Granfer and Saul would notice should Leon pass them, heading south. She just knew they'd then double back to make sure the girls on the *Marigold* and *Horizon* were all right.

This is what she thought of as she watched Verity gesticulating to Sylvia, whose refusal was clear. In fact, her red hair – so carefully tucked up into loops– positively danced as she shook her head. Polly could imagine the wretched woman complaining that she didn't want to be responsible for reporting self-inflicted damage. It had been one of her frequent complaints yesterday. *Clean that range because I don't want to be responsible for it stopping working because of neglect.*

Polly pulled her bobble hat further down, crossed her arms and laughed to herself as Verity gesticulated once again, pointing at her watch, and the lock, and the sky. In other words, get a move on, or it will be dark before we get to tie up at the Leighton Buzzard pub, though they hoped they would actually make it to Fenny Stratford. Not that she would have mentioned the pub. Sylvia was teetotal and had refused to nip in and see Bob last night.

'Oh, ducks, tell Bet she's simply got to get better and come back,' Polly called after the ducks, as they passed out of sight behind a copse.

At that moment she saw the POWs being marched back. They passed Verity, who stood alongside the *Marigold*, arms akimbo, before beginning to gesticulate yet again while Sylvia in her turn continued to shake her curls. Polly wanted to slap her. Time was of the essence, surely she knew that? As she watched the scene, she wondered, not for the first time, who had been the other trainees unfortunate enough to have her with them until she was posted to *Marigold*.

She suspected her original team had not fought hard to keep her.

As the prisoners and their guards drew nearer, the dust kicked up by the tramp of their feet seemed to increase until she heard the bawled 'Halt'. They were ten yards or so from the lock. Leaving them, a Tommy came to her. 'Just enjoying the scenery, gal, or you got a problem?'

'I am enjoying the scenery of course, Corporal, but also wondering why the damned gate won't open. It looks as if there is a branch stuck behind it.' The two of them went to the concrete kerb and peered down between the slimy lock wall and the gate. 'We're going to ram the gate if we can't budge it but it looks as though we'll have to try to shaft the obstruction out first.'

She could see Verity dragging the long shaft along, while Curly Sylvia just stood on the bank the *Marigold*, watching. Lazy wotnot, Polly thought. Verity carried the shaft past the prisoners and guards and arrived at the gate. 'Right, let's have a go.'

She hooked and then prodded with the shaft.

''Ere, let's be having it,' the guard said.

He took it from her, pulling, stabbing and thrusting. The branch merely disappeared further down. He withdrew the shaft. 'Let's give the gate a try, the ruddy branch might just have changed its position enough.' Together they hauled at the beam, which still wouldn't budge. The Tommy handed back the shaft and said, 'Reckon you'll 'ave to ram it. I'd best get on though, got to get my chicks back to their coop. The ground's too cold and hard, but it was worth a try, and it's been good for them to get out of their huts and away from the heaters, cooking up mischief.'

He saluted the girls, trotted back to his chicks, and ordered them forward. Polly and Verity waited for them to pass by, refusing to drop their gaze and meeting expressions that varied from neutrality, to friendliness, to hate. Bringing up the rear were two who slouched along, out of step, and every inch of them yelled resentment. They were chivvied along but one POW almost stopped and the Tommy thrust him forward with his rifle. The German shrugged him off. '*Schwein,*' he muttered, glaring at the girls. He had a scar on his cheek.

Polly watched as they continued on their way. Verity said, 'I bet he calls that a duelling scar, when it was probably a bar-room brawl.'

The *Marigold's* hooter sounded again, and now there was another boat behind *Horizon*, waiting.

'Come with me, we've got to mutiny and take over the *Marigold* if she won't shift her arse,' Verity said, running ahead of Polly, who pretty soon caught up. Alongside the *Marigold*, Steerer Ambrose, who they'd met in the pub, was on the towpath, scratching his head. He said to Sylvia, "Ow do? Is yer going to ram 'er, or is we going to be 'ere all night?'

Polly nodded at the same time as Sylvia shook her head, saying, 'Certainly not . . .' Polly spoke over Sylvia. 'Yes, we're going to ram her, Steerer Ambrose.

Shove over, Sylvia, or go and make a cup of tea if you can't do something useful.'

Steerer Ambrose shoved his hat back on, and turned, his windlass stuck in the back of his belt just as Polly and Verity wore theirs now, though Sylvia wore hers at the front, as she felt all good and true trainees should. Verity walked with him as far as *Horizon*. 'We'll crack on, don't fret, Steerer Ambrose,' Polly and Sylvia heard her say.

Sylvia disappeared into the cabin as Polly was about to pull the *Marigold* away from the bank, but then Sylvia shoved her way up and on to the top step. Polly kept hold of the tiller as the wretched girl flourished the trip card in her face. She'd written: *Polly Holmes overrode my order not to ram*, and said, 'You need to sign this.'

'And you need to go and make a cup of tea right this minute. That means now.' Polly didn't know she could shout so loud. Sylvia ducked back into the cabin without another word, taking the chit with her.

Polly swung round, shouting to Verity who was at her place on the tiller, 'I'll rev her, and we might skew round. Be ready.' Verity threw the end of the short tow on to the motor counter for Polly to slot over the stud on the deck. Polly waited for Verity to run back along the top planks; the sun was out and shone brightly on the tarpaulin covering the load. She turned to the front, brought up the revs, released the accelerator, and with her hand tight on the tiller she drew away, towing *Horizon*. 'Stand by,

Sylvia,' she yelled. 'Put down any hot drinks.' There was no reply. She drove the *Marigold* at the gate. 'Come on, girl, for Bet. Make a good job of it.'

Her bows hit the gate, throwing Polly forward. There was a crash from the cabin. The gate creaked and shifted a little. With a grinding noise the *Marigold* shoved her hull against the gate for several minutes as Polly kept her going slow but sure, and suddenly the gate whacked against the side of the lock. Polly thrust the engine into reverse and steered to the left, while behind, the *Horizon* steered to the right. It bounced off the right-hand wall, then skewed slightly round. 'Perfect,' Polly shouted. Verity answered, 'Of course.' She threw a mooring rope across to Polly, who hauled back on it, slowing the butty a fraction. The fender glided into the sill of the front gates while the butty came to rest against the *Marigold*. Polly slammed the *Marigold* into neutral, as Verity let out a 'Yeehaw'. It was a cry they had heard a GI on a bridge yell when he waved before disappearing into the bridge hole.

Polly and Verity laughed together, and leapt up the steps on opposite sides with the mooring straps, winding them round the studs. They then snatched out their windlasses, opened the paddles, and the two boats rose like good children while they tightened the mooring ropes. Sylvia stayed in the cabin.

Once the lock was full she brandished the windlass at Steerer Ambrose who was waiting until they were clear and out on the pound. He hooted the

Sunburst's horn. Polly laughed. This was one to tell Bet. They would telephone from the pub, which was why they needed to press on. There were many more locks to climb before they reached the top of that particular staircase.

Finally, as dusk was falling, they tied up, with Steerer Ambrose on *Sunburst* close behind, having climbed the Tring locks, and then on past Marsworth Junction down to Leighton Buzzard. Polly had broken the last two nails that had survived thus far, her callouses had bled, her whole body ached, her lips were so chapped they also bled, but what was new? Verity was much the same; not Sylvia, though, who had polished the range in between taking over the tiller of whoever was designated the lock-wheeler.

Sylvia had pulled on a pristine woollen hat, wound her muffler round the bottom of her face, and hugged her new mackintosh around her. As Verity and Polly finished mooring up they saw her come from the back-end of the butty cabin, carrying leeks, potatoes and a couple of tins. 'Please, not Spam fritters again,' groaned Verity.

It was indeed Spam, but not fritters, it transpired. Just fried Spam. Sylvia said not one word as they sat down at the *Marigold*'s hinged table but then she hadn't spoken since the barging-of-the-gate debacle.

Verity said, 'This is nice. Just what we need after a hard day.'

Polly agreed. 'It's just the thing. My dad grows leeks. Does yours, Sylvia?'

There was just a shake of the head. Polly said, 'We're off to the pub. Come with us, you must know it from your other trips.'

'I prefer not to go to pubs.'

'You will truly need booze later on to set you up for the Bottom Road, which we call the Brum Bum.'

'Do stop being coarse.' Sylvia pursed her lips, and patted them with her handkerchief. Somehow it had remained clean, but, thought Polly, why not. It's not as though the girl had been out actually battling the elements, and the locks. She took a deep breath. Perhaps Sylvia just needed to settle in. It must be difficult filling in as she was doing. The meal finished, they washed up and headed for the pub, all three of them, because Verity and Polly linked arms with Sylvia, and frogmarched her between them, past the women cleaning and washing. Sylvia said, 'We should be doing that.'

'Not tonight,' Polly insisted. 'Tonight we need to telephone the hospital, and have some fun, and a drink. It's been a successful day and we've all learned something about how to open an obstinate lock gate.'

They pushed open the door as Sylvia said, 'I certainly have learned something about you two and I will be lodging a complaint.'

They pulled her into the pub. Verity sighed. 'Of course you will, but not before we have a recuperative brandy.'

For some reason they didn't have to push and

shove their way to the bar; instead a path opened. Verity murmured, 'My word, the sea has divided,' as she led the way. At the bar, they ordered a small brandy each, paid for by the kitty. Sylvia said, as they sat down at the empty table by the roaring fire which normally they had to wait to be free – 'We ought to keep a book in which we write expenditure.'

Verity flashed a look at Polly, then stared into her drink and said, 'I used to think that, Sylvia, but somehow one has to trust the team. If this wasn't part of your training, it should have been. It's the only way to survive all the difficulties.'

There was silence. Sylvia sipped her brandy, then coughed. 'I scarcely drink. In fact, I disagree with it.'

'You told us, but this is restorative, medicinal, whatever you like to call it,' Polly insisted as the flames played around the logs. 'Absolutely,' Verity added. 'And with that in mind I'm going to tele-phone the Middlesex to find out how Bet is. Everyone think positively; we have to know she is beginning to improve. We have to.'

She left Polly with Sylvia, who had taken another sip. The publican came over to Polly, a brace of pheas-ants hanging on a loop over his fingers, and said, 'You were left these by Granfer. Saul's been doing what Saul does. He was out getting one of these when young Jimmy was hurt, and got a few more along the way through to Leamington. Was 'oping to see yer at the pub by Kings Langley, when they came along last night but that's the way of it. A boat a day ahead, stays a day ahead. Reckon these little beauties be nicely hung by the time you cook 'em.'

Polly took them, and smiled. 'Thank you.'

Sylvia tutted and said, 'But they've got feathers on. What on earth do we do with them?'

The publican turned away as Polly said, 'Oh, our Verity's done a course as all young ladies do, or her sort of young lady. She'll manage, and probably rather well.'

Verity was weaving back to them, through the men, who were nodding, and tipping their hats. She smiled at them when she reached their table and sat, and Polly relaxed. Surely that smile meant Bet was improving. Verity gripped Polly's hand. 'Darling Polly, you'll never guess. Bet is out, yes she is, a huge improvement, lots of bad behaviour, so they've agreed she can recuperate at her home, which is, believe it or not, at Buckby. Not that they told me that. I telephoned the office at Mayfair. Miss Fancy-pants had gone home, but I know her cousin, and finally ran Miss FP to ground and dug it out of her. Bet went home by ambulance looking like death, but they waved the bunting to see her go. Such a grump, apparently.'

Polly grinned. 'You are actually totally impossible – poor Miss Fancypants. But that's extraordinary news. Bet's such a tough old bird, I can just imagine what she was like, causing merry hell. She'll do better at home. We'll go, as we pass, shall we? We won't stay but oh, to see her would be so lovely. Any news on Jimmy? Would the hospital say?'

'Not a word, we're not family.'

Steerer Ambrose, nearby, said, "Ow do. Just 'eard I 'ave from Granfer Brown, him with the motor *Golightly*. 'E say that Jimmy Porter'll be back on his dad's motor when he calls in at depot for him, for orders. Bright as a button, 'e'll be.'

'Jimmy?' asked Sylvia, her brandy glass empty.

'The lad these two saved from t'cut. Pumped 'im like an 'andle, them did. Pumped, pumped till the water comed out. We's all pleased for the lad. Yer playin' them darts then?'

Polly and Verity smiled at one another, and nodded at Steerer Ambrose. 'Thank you, all. And yes, we'll be playing darts, indeed we will, and probably winning.'

Steerer Ambrose guffawed. They did play, and win, having bet on themselves. They pocketed the money, putting a third aside for Bet. Sylvia had tutted at the pheasants, tutted at the darts, tutted when the girls had a second brandy, and refused to play, and neither would she accept any share in the ill-gotten gains. Before she left she said, 'I do wish we worked with a better class of person. Poachers? It's not right. We should obey the ration.'

Verity had said, 'I'll remember that when I'm carving it, and you have Spam again.'

As Polly and Verity walked back to the butty, the pheasants hanging from Polly's hand, she said quietly to Verity, 'I wonder what home means with

Bet? Is it where her mother was—' She stopped. 'Well, you know.'

They turned on to the towpath and Verity said, 'I'm not sure, I wondered that too.'

In mid afternoon two days later on 20 November they took the turn-off for Leicester instead of heading into Braunston Tunnel, and just before Crick Tunnel they moored up near Buckby. For almost a mile, Polly and Verity followed the directions a lock-keeper had given them the day before, heading for Spring Cottage, walking at a fast pace, with Dog on her rope, trotting at their heels. Finally they knocked on the door of Spring Cottage, on the outskirts of the village. As they waited Verity whispered, 'I couldn't live in a place where a murder had been committed, could you?'

'Be quiet,' hissed Polly, who had been thinking the same thing.

The door was opened by a woman of about Bet's age. One who wore trousers and sweaters and had the tan of a boater. Her voice told them she wasn't. 'Hello, can I help?'

Polly said, 'We're Bet's trainees, and just wondered how she was.'

Bet's voice called from deep within the house. 'Good grief, can't a woman get any peace? Let 'em in, Fran.'

Fran looked at their boots. 'I have to put up with Bet's, but three of you is just too much – and tie up the dog, if you will.'

The two girls left their boots in the lobby, and Dog too, who sat looking stoic. Polly rubbed her ears, and told her, 'We won't be long. Be good.' Dog cocked her head; her ears were long and flopped, her coat was short. They'd tried working out the mixture in her but given up. They followed Fran along the tiled floor, horribly conscious of their sweaty socks leaving equally sweaty footprints. Polly said, 'I expect we smell as well.'

Fran marched ahead. 'Of course you do, but I can open a window when you've gone. I just draw the line at boots since I have no intention of mopping the floor. I have quite enough to do looking after this wretch without any extra work.'

'Have you come far to nurse the wretch?' Verity asked.

Fran barked a laugh. 'Not at all, this is my home too.'

She opened a door and ushered them into a room with a huge inglenook fireplace. A rich red rug filled the space between the fire and a bed, and a sofa had been pushed back against the rear wall, leaving two armchairs either side of the fireplace.

Fran said, 'Sit down, do, the seats are leather so your ghastly filthy trousers won't make too much of a mess, and it can be wiped down anyway. Don't excite the wretch, and don't stay long. She thought she was leaving hospital and the crosspatch sister for a smoother ride. That was her first mistake.'

She left the room. In the bed, elevated by piles of

pillows, lay Bet, almost as white as the linen. She said, her voice weak, 'Well, she likes you.'

Polly nudged Verity, who leaned sideways into her. Both laughed. Verity said, 'Crikey, and what if she doesn't?'

'You don't step over the threshold.'

There it was, vintage Bet, Polly thought, however weak the voice, and however sunken the eyes. She beckoned them across, and her hand seemed to have lost all its tan, and strength. Worry tore at Polly, and at Verity too, judging by the way she gripped Polly's hand, fleetingly. Bet murmured, 'Stand close to the bed, if you will, I haven't the voice to shout. I need to thank you for sweet-talking Sid and getting his help to cart me to the hospital. I had excellent care, a rather splendid little room, and I imagine it took a fair whack of money to make that possible.'

Polly said, 'It was Verity's doing.'

Bet gestured to Verity to come closer still, and Polly to take the other side of the bed. She took their hands, and squeezed them. Her skin was hot and papery, her voice thin and tired. 'I'm more than grateful, and the Porters will be too.'

Verity shook her head. 'Money is nothing if you have a lot, and you are important to us.'

Bet smiled weakly. 'When I left, the nurse said that Jimmy would be back on the boat when Steerer Porter brought *Hillcrest* to the depot at the end of the run. They'll not want Dog until then, if at all. Depends if the animal is happy with you. They'll want to give something to you. It could be Dog. So think if that would suit you.'

Polly knew it would, and Verity was nodding. They smiled at one another, and then Polly said, 'You're looking so much better.'

'No, I'm not, but now I'm home it won't be too long before I'm sort of on my feet, but in the meantime, how goes it?'

Verity launched into a catalogue of grumbles concerning Miss Sylvia Simpson, and was almost panting when she finished.

Bet looked at Polly, who nodded in agreement. Bet closed her eyes for a moment, then said, 'You look as though you're standing to attention. Do sit on the bed, for goodness' sake. Fran doesn't bite.'

Polly snatched a look over her shoulder, then said, 'Are you quite sure?'

'Well, she takes a gulp from time to time, but only if the month has an R in it.'

They laughed, and sat down. Bet looked at the grandfather clock to the right of the inglenook. 'I'm sending you on your way in five minutes, because I'm tired and you have quite a way to go. One o'clock means you should be lock-wheeling, or cleaning, or—'

Polly put up her hand. 'The range is perfect and one cannot be accused of causing self-inflicted damage, Miss Bet Burrows.'

Bet laughed again. 'Look, she needs time to shake down, and you might just have to help her do that. Firm but fair, I'd normally say, but I happen to know she comes with a reputation. She is not a team person, apparently, but I think if anyone can sort her out, you two can, or so I told the office. Give her a chance if she starts softening, but if she doesn't, try to sort her out. She won't want another failure on her record, so mutiny if you need. It might just turn her, or "wind" her, if you think in terms of the cut, get her going another way. Or if worst comes to the worst, you can refuse to work with her and wait for another, but will she be any better?'

'What do you mean, wait for another?' Verity's voice was sharp.

'I was your trainer and would have had to pass you on once you were trained at the end of your current trip anyway. Then you would have teamed up with a third waterway woman and your own motor and butty, but the question is, will I be up to finishing your training after this beastly illness? So I have told the office that I think you are quite capable of going it alone, you two and Sylvia, as a team. If you make this run work, you will receive your Inland Waterways badge on your return to the depot. You will, you see, have been perceived as passing the course. There's a war on, remember. We must continue, come what may. Now, I'm sure you didn't come just to share your troubles?'

The girls shook their heads. 'We needed to know you were all right. We miss you – *you* not the training.'

'I needed to be here, in Buckby which is a boater village, with Fran. What could be better than to be with my best friend, the one who introduced me to the boating life, and who loves the cut as I do, eh? Fran Williams taught with me, but is now a naturalist, and a writer. She reads her work to me at the end of the day, and doesn't listen to any criticism.' Bet pulled a face. 'Now off you go. You have work to do.'

The girls almost tiptoed to the door. It opened and there was Fran, reaching for the handle. 'Off, are you? Jolly good, can't have the old bag worn out.' She ushered them into the hall, and to the front door. As they tied their laces, Fran lowered her voice. 'She's so proud of you. You are such a team, such a joy, and to save a child's life – which of course we heard about, and for you, Verity, to pay for Bet's care . . . She has had a beastly time, one way and another, and the cut kept her going, and you two girls warmed her heart, so thank you.'

She started to shut the front door and Polly pushed against it. Dog barked. Fran peered out.

Polly said, 'Give her our love, because we mean it. Please look after her, she's really important to us.'

Fran stared at her, then roared with laughter. 'And to me, so worry not. Off you go, and may the wind be at your backs, you dreadful duo. That's what she called you, you know. Her darling dreadful duo, but now there's a third, isn't there. The dog, I mean. Try and make it a fourth, the girl. She sounds impossible, but who knows, she can grow. And yes, I do listen at doors; a teacher learns to eavesdrop.'

'One last thing.' Polly had her foot in the door.

'Now you mention your role, I need to teach a child how to read, but how?'

The door opened wider again. 'Ah, the Hopkins boy. Yes, don't look so surprised, I get to hear about most things. I find the best way for older children is the tried and tested: CAT SAT on the MAT. Start with words that can be illustrated. Bet said the boy was visually adept, like his uncle, so he'll be interested in shapes.' The door was closing, then stopped. Fran peered out again. 'If his uncle is as good at drawing as Bet says, get him to do the illustrations.' The door shut.

Verity was standing in the lane, hunched against the wind. 'Do come on, Polly. Time's a wasting, and I'm freezing.' They rushed back along the lanes as Polly explained the conversation with Fran. Verity nodded. 'Good idea, and Saul can learn to read at the same time – if he wants to, that is. That way his pride is in place, because everyone will think it is the boy who's learning. He'll have a lot of pride, our Saul, if he's like the other boaters, and let's face it, he is.'

Chapter 27

20 November – Saul and Granfer

Saul ran from the copse and caught up with the *Seagull* and butty as they headed towards Braunston Tunnel. 'Joe,' he yelled. Joe waved, the tiller of the butty under his control. Saul gestured that he'd leap on board the butty in the tunnel, and trotted alongside as the motor towed it in. Once aboard, he bundled the rabbits and pheasants into the crate behind the cabin. 'That'll keep 'em fresh,' he said, dusting off his hands before leaping on to the roof and off on to the counter, taking the tiller from Joe.

Joe said, 'Granfer's 'ad no more trouble from the engine since yer dragged us off the main cut oop the turn past Blisworth Tunnel for yer pal Mikey to work on it at 'is mooring. He's got a good workshop, ain't 'e? Granfer and I winded the boats nice, we did when it were finished, after you set off for yer traps. It's been a mite slow this trip, eh, Uncle Saul, and I reckon I saw 'em women's boats tied up the turn-off for Leicester, Granfer said it was probably Buckby. What they doin' there, I wonders? We've lost a day or so, Uncle Saul.'

'A day or so's not so bad, lad.' It was dusk, the lad looked chilled.

'When you was trapping the birds, did 'em follow the trail of corn, Uncle Saul?' Joe asked. 'Them must be stupid to keep being tricked the same every time.'

'How do they know, it weren't them who were caught before? Them others didn't leave no notes to warn 'em. That's how we learn, in't it, being taught by others. Like yer being taught it's bad to thieve.'

Joe shrugged and headed into the cabin. 'I needs to polish up Grandma's pierced plates, or so Granfer says. Idle 'ands, 'e says.'

'Idle mind, an' all,' Saul called after him. 'Right glad yer hopped back 'ere at Tring, when Jimmy's cousin's come to 'elp him, but you must be fed up with tracing them letters and not knowing their meanin'.'

The boy yelled, 'If yer could read, yer could 'elp me. Mam was trying to. Dad didn't like it, 'it her, he did. But 'e 'it her whether she were tryin' or not. I's going to do the plate.' He slammed down the table.

Ahead Granfer was whipping the knots on the roof to warn others he was coming through. Saul looked up to the top of the bridge. They'd been gobbed on twice today, but they went into the tunnel with no mishap.

Saul shook his head, keeping the tiller straight in the darkness, thinking of Joe, knowing the lad spoke true, knowing that he, his high and mighty Uncle Saul, stood here, at the tiller, hour after hour, day after day, loving it, hating it, cos he didn't have the words to do something else. On and on they pattered, in the darkness, until the light at the end of the tunnel grew.

They came out, into the dusk. Frost was heavy on the trees, his breath beat out in clouds. He pulled his kerchief around his neck. How could that lass, Polly, feel as him did? He were a boater, without letters, but their eyes had looked deep, words been said, and he'd keep her safe if it killed him. Did she know that? Did she know that something grabbed his heart when he thought of her, or saw her, or heard her? Would he have the words to tell her if'n he had the chance?

Taking the motor and butty to Mikey up the cut to have the engine looked at had held him back, keeping him closer to her, nearer to her, and some of that was to keep her safe. But only some. He'd just like to be breathing the air closer to her.

As he held the tiller with his elbow he saw her, clear as day, them eyes, that hair, that smile. He stared at the ripples that ran along the hull, and suddenly heard Joe's words again. Did the lad think he didn't know that Leon hit Maudie whether she were good or not, whether she were trying or not? He looked again at the ripples, and allowed in the thought that haunted his dreams. Were she down there? Were his Maudie in that cold dark water, weed covered, white, lost? He shook himself. He couldn't believe it, mustn't. She was alive, she'd just run off, that's what she'd done. To believe anything else could make it true, could make her a lost soul like Steerer Porter's little 'uns who done drowned, and he couldn't have that, not his Maudie.

He looked ahead to the motor and called, 'Didn't the school teach you no letters? That letters can open the world to yer?'

Joe's reply was quiet. 'They put me at back o' class with the other boaters, and took no notice. I tries but it's too quick. We all tries but . . .'

Saul knew what the 'but' meant. Scum, that's what the boaters was. He checked that he'd wiped off all the spittle on the roof from the bridges.

They tied up on the bank past the Oxford turn-off, brewed tea, ate rabbit that had been simmering all day, and then he drew the metal plate from beneath the cross-bed. 'See 'ere, our Joe. Let's be getting yer to paint the flowers. I got the black background done.'

Joe grinned as he took the brush, and settled at the cupboard flap which was their table. Granfer threw over the bit of tarpaulin they had cut to size before he began. 'No mess, mind.'

Saul sat on the side-bed and lit his pipe, wafting the smoke up through the open slide hatch. He watched the boy; his steady hands working the paint, slick as a whistle, spinning them flowers. Oh yes, flowers. He liked the spring, and then the summer. Them could work for longer, earn more money, and the countryside was like the flowers he drew, and now his boy was drawing. He stopped himself. No, weren't his boy, but were his in his heart. Maudie would come home, and he'd keep them safe, always.

And that Leon could take himself to another cut, head to Oxford, he could, and leave them be.

Joe looked up at him. 'Does we ever paint apples, Uncle Saul?'

'Not 'specially, but you can. D'yer remember apples from t'summer?'

'Course I do.'

Saul watched him paint an apple tucked in beside a red flower, just dead on how they were; so big and round, but the lad hadn't put the stalk at bottom, but to the side. 'Why'd yer put a stalk there?' he asked.

'Cos I like that shape, it's like them letters in t'book. Round with a tail.'

Granfer nudged Saul. 'There, bright as a button, like yer 'e is. Paints a good picture like yer, too, Saul.'

There were other boats mooring up, now. Saul could hear the women chatting as they washed clothes on the bank. He sighed, and took himself to the back-end where the bricks and metal grill were stacked.

He set up the wash-fire while the steerers sloped off to the pub and the wives washed, cooked, cleaned and chased after the children, who ran wild on the land. Why wouldn't they, cooped up all day, like some of them pheasants, while the keepers stuffed them with grain for the shooters?

Mrs Ambrose who was tied up in front called, 'Need 'elp, our Saul?'

'Can manage, it's our lad's clothes. He roars on to wheel the locks and gets up on t'all sorts on the way and gets right dirty. Curious, 'e be.'

'That's the way of it, Saul. I's remember you were the same, when yer ma would send you up the cut. I miss 'er, lad. Bloody 'itler, and his bloody bombs.'

Saul nodded. 'I do too. And I miss Maudie. I just don't knows what to do, 'alf the time. Still, good Jimmy is doing well and he'll be back with 'em when they hit the depot, so the news is.'

'It is, so they say. But that Leon? You seen 'ide or 'air of him?'

Mrs Ambrose was wringing out a towel as though it were a chicken's neck, or p'haps she were thinking it were Leon's?

He stirred his own washing with a branch. 'Time he went on the Oxford cut, or so's we think.'

Joe called from the *Seagull* counter, 'Granfer says 'e's for bed, and so 'tis I, or so he says.'

Saul nodded. 'Then off you go.'

Mrs Ambrose was carting her clothes on to her butty and stringing them on the line they had rigged behind the cabin.

He did the same, then doused her fire, and his. All along the bank they were doing the same. A warden or some such had come along once to tell 'em to put out the fires, but it were a mere glimmer, and no bombs 'ad dropped for a good time. Mrs Ambrose 'ad sent Warden on 'is way, saying they'd put 'em out sharp as a penny, when the bombs started coming again.

Saul grinned at the memory. They'd all checked that the boilers hid the fires so there must 'ave been only a small light. He left the bricks to cool, and the grill, and smoked a cigarette, staring down into the cut. He did love it so, but it weren't enough, not for him, but there was naught else he could do, without the learning.

He saw Polly in his mind, down in the water with that Verity who'd come good, she had. Diving and diving so he'd been told, and them'd found that Jimmy Porter, they had. It'd made his heart so full, everything about her made it full, and fuller. Yes, he'd keep her safe, though it'd only be to send her off back to her own life, but at least he'd do that for her. He'd heard she were just a bit behind now and he'd fixed his engine to fail past Blisworth Tunnel, not that anyone would know that. Now he'd be close if Leon got near her on his way back to Limehouse, and near Joe.

He tossed his cigarette into the cut, tested the grill. It were cold, so too the bricks. He thought once more of Polly, her neck like a swan, her shoulders so set, her walk so stubborn. She deserved a good life, and she'd have it. She'd get the book back an' all.

Chapter 28

22 November – close to arrival at Tyseley Wharf, Birmingham

The Hatton flight of locks, on from Leamington, hadn't been as tiring as it might have been, but only because Polly and Verity had refused to go on unless Sylvia agreed to join in with the lock-wheeling. She had, but only after she had written out a chit recording the 'revolt'. Verity had reached out for it, and her face said it would be filed in the cut, but Sylvia stuffed it in her pocket, dragged the bike from the roof on to the towpath and set off for the first lock.

Not a word had been said between the three of them since, and now, having moored up abreast beyond the Shrewley Tunnel just a bit on from the Hatton locks, in silence three girls ate the remains of the pheasants in an omelette, with mashed potato and leeks, and immediately Sylvia finished she disappeared into the butty cabin. Verity murmured, 'I think we have been sent to Coventry.'

'Don't mention Coventry. We'll be facing the Bottom Road to it soon enough. Her silence is trivial in comparison,' said Polly. They laughed quietly.

'Good to see many more prisoners, German and Italian,' Verity said, as they wrapped up and stepped up on to the counter to smoke a cigarette. They leaned against the cabin. It was so cold that frost was thick on the grass of the towpath and the fields, which glinted beneath the moon.

'Probably picking vegetables, I suppose.' Polly thought of Dog, who had barked and threatened to jump into the cut to get at the prisoners until Polly had cycled back along the towpath and yelled at her. They had also seen more army lorries grinding over the canal bridges in convoy. The troops often jumped out of the back of the lorries and crowded against the parapets, waving and whistling, as the girls waved back.

She said, her teeth chattering, 'I'm too cold and too tired, let's go to bed.' Other boats were moored up but there was no one they recognised. Well, there was no *Seagull* is what she meant. Back in the cabin Polly washed the dishes, handing them to Verity to dry. 'Sylvia'll have to speak to issue her next volley of orders or explain what her next chit is about,' she said.

The girls smiled at one another, too weary to care. They put away the dishes, washed themselves and fell into their beds, waking at 5.30, before the alarm, as had become the habit. With their eyes closed they reached for their trousers, dragging them on, and all three sweaters that were taken off as one, and replaced as one. Then the muffler, next two pairs of socks, and hats. Dog was let out on to the counter.

She would make her own way to the towpath, happy to mill about on her own, and she always returned.

Verity murmured, 'The pom-pom is looking threadbare.'

'I can make another.'

'Please promise me you won't.'

'I'll show you how to make one. It could just be the icing on your finishing-school education.'

'Ha bloody ha.' Verity threw her pillow. Polly laughed and threw it back.

There was a knock on the cabin door. The girls froze. Sylvia said, 'I've made porridge. It's so dreadfully cold, I thought it might be just the thing. See you in a minute.'

Verity stared at Polly. 'Has she poisoned it?'

'Come on, perhaps she's thawing, or perhaps she can't stand your lumpy muck any more. Let's take it for the kind offer it could be. Think of Bet, though we did go off course with the strike, but let's hope we don't have to again.'

Before they left the cabin, they laid more kindling on the warmth of the ashes in the grate, and waited a moment for it to catch. 'We'll bring more into the cabin to dry out as we pick up branches and twigs along the way,' Verity declared, adding coal to the kindling.

They joined Sylvia in her cabin, knocking, of course. They had not been invited in before now, and it seemed strange to see Bet's china, horse brasses and crocheted curtains just as before. What's more, they gleamed as much as, if not more than, when she had been in residence.

Sylvia handed them bowls of steaming porridge. Verity said, 'Bet will be so pleased at how you are looking after her things. We'll write, and tell her.'

Sylvia sat on the side-bed, having directed them to Bet's cross-bed. 'I didn't like to use her bed,' she told them. 'It's bad enough for you to have a team replacement without me moving in completely. I'm aware I'm so much less than Bet is.'

Polly spooned her porridge. She hadn't thought of it like that; neither, clearly, had Verity, who said, 'But no one expects you to be Bet. You are – Sylvia.'

Indeed you are, thought Polly, but maybe . . .

'Will we be at Tyseley by early afternoon, do you think?' Sylvia asked.

Asked? Good heavens, she isn't telling us, Polly thought, looking into her porridge and saying, 'Yes, we could easily be, if the remaining locks are with us.'

The porridge finished, Sylvia looked at her watch. 'Perhaps we should get going. The sooner we're there, the sooner we can leave, and pick up coal from Coventry. Would you like me to be the first to take the bicycle today?'

She reached for their bowls. Verity shook her head, as though to clear it. 'Perhaps that would be a nice idea but we have the long pound first, so we can all just relax.'

They climbed back on to the counter of the motor. Polly whispered, 'She's trying.'

Verity said, 'Indeed she is, very.'

'Did you see she'd picked up some mail from the office by the lock yesterday? I saw the envelope on her shelf. It was from Bet.'

'Ah,' they both said. Bet hadn't mentioned that she'd already dropped Sylvia a note.

Within fifteen minutes they were heading off along the two-and-a-half-hour pound to the next locks, through frost-speckled countryside, with the odd call of a pheasant. Had Saul caught any more? Polly wondered. The two they'd plucked, drawn and eaten had been manna from heaven.

'Perhaps Sylvia sees us as pantry providers,' she muttered to herself as she steered and drove the motor, while Verity sat in the cabin and wrote a letter to Bet, on behalf of the two of them, keeping her abreast of proceedings and chatting, as well, about the increase in the number of prisoners they'd passed, troops they'd seen on the move, the pheasant and other little bits and pieces. They'd post it from Birmingham.

As they drew to the end of the pound Polly called Verity out. 'Come on, I'm pulling us in, you can take Sylvia's place on the butty tiller and let her do her worst on the Knowle locks.'

Once Sylvia was wincing along the towpath bouncing on the impossible saddle, Polly closed her eyes in exasperation at herself. For goodness' sake, she still had the letter she had written to Reggie. She *must* post it when they arrived. She stooped, and could see it tucked between books on the shelf. What would he think of her? Then she realised that he'd think probably nothing because, after all, it was only a matter of days. It just seemed timeless on the cut.

She watched Sylvia managing the first of the locks, and she did well and even smiled as they brought the two boats in. They passed under bridges and as they approached they searched for the gobbers, ducking to avoid clods of manure hurled down as they entered a bridge hole. At the next they waved at the troops, and laughed as usual when the Tommies leapt out of the back of the lorry and blew them kisses. They were a sight for sore eyes, and counteracted the gobbers.

Sylvia tossed the bike on to *Marigold*'s roof, and without pause was washing the cabin floor as though her life depended on it, flapping Dog out of the way. Dog came to sit next to Polly on the counter, then jumped on to the roof. Polly stroked her. The range had warmed her on one side. 'You are a spoilt princess, little Dog. How will you cope, living outside when you go back to Jimmy Porter? He's getting much, much better, you know, and you're the one who found him, you clever girl. Yes, you did.' Dog licked her hand. She was such a gentle dog.

Polly peered back down into the cabin. 'Have a break, Sylvia, while you can. Make some tea, perhaps.' She steered for the centre of a bridge hole, saying, 'You'll wear yourself out.'

'I like to keep busy.'

As they entered, a gob of spittle landed on Polly's hand. She looked up and received a face full of manure. The boys and girl on the bridge cheered, and yelled, 'Boater scum, shirkers, you should be fighting the bloody war.'

It was finally too much. 'You little devils, I'll come up there and you can say it to my face. Sylvia, stop your scrubbing and take the tiller.'

Sylvia appeared from the cabin, startled. 'Polly, no, you can't.'

'Take the tiller while I get up there and sort them out,' Polly roared. Dog barked. 'Why should boaters put up with this? Stay, Dog,' she roared again, then leapt for the side and off up the slope to the road, coming out as the children ran past. She caught two by their jumpers. With a wrench, one pulled free, but she held on to the other. His friends screamed and ran on. The lad, red-haired and freckled, whined, 'My dad'll get you, you see if he don't.'

'Then I'll talk to him too and tell him that you gob us, and the boaters, and that you throw manure. How dare you, when we're carting supplies to win this war, just as the boaters are doing? What would you think if I spat at you right now?'

The boy fought against her, kicking out. 'Don't you bloody dare.'

'Exactly,' shouted Polly. 'It's disgusting, the behaviour of a toe-rag, and that means you when you behave like this.'

At that moment a man came along on his bicycle

and stopped, then flung his bike on the road. His bicycle clips ruined any image of toughness. 'Hey, what's going on? What've you been up to, Henry Arbiter?'

'He's been spitting, and chucking manure on boaters, and if I catch him doing it again, I'll ... Well, I'll tan his backside. He's got no idea how hard the boaters work. Look at my hands, Henry, and let me see yours.'

She thrust out her hand. It was scarred, blistered, calloused. The man, a vicar, she could see now, stood alongside, legs apart and arms akimbo. 'I'll help you tan his backside, young lady, if he should ever do it again. Give him to me, I'll take him home and his mum'll wash his mouth out with soap and be glad she knows what he's been up to. On you go now, or you'll miss your motor.'

He grabbed the boy by the arm, returned to his bike, and together they walked on over the bridge. Panting, Polly shot over the road and down to the towpath, missing the motor, but catching the butty as it came through on a long snubber. She stood on the roof as they exited, and while Verity sounded the horn to get Sylvia's attention, she waved and gestured that she'd come aboard at the next bridge hole.

She timed it to perfection, leaping off the fore-end, running like hell down the towpath and jumping on to the stern counter of the motor before it left the narrow stretch. Sylvia looked worried. 'Did you really catch them? But what if they'd turned on you, what if—'

'Sylvia, go and put the kettle on. If they had turned, I've feet as well, and hands that can smack.'

Sylvia gasped. 'You wouldn't?'

'I rather think I would. I object to anyone thinking they can gob on me, drop manure, or bricks.'

'Bricks?'

'Yes, young Joe, but it's all sorted now. Sylvia, we must stand up for ourselves. How dare they treat boaters as they do?'

Sylvia was clinging to the tiller, her knuckles white. 'I don't want to be involved in this. I want you to write down what happened and make it clear I had nothing to do with it in case the parents complain. We're not really boaters, we shouldn't be fighting their battles, we're better than them.'

'Sylvia, we couldn't hope to be as good, as accomplished, as brave, and as stoic as these people, no matter how long we lived. Now go and make the bloody tea, and listen, a vicar came along and said the mother would be pleased to know about her son's behaviour. Washing his mouth out with soap was mentioned.'

Sylvia ducked into the cabin and Polly sighed. She shouldn't have sworn. She could still feel the spittle on her hand. She swept off her hat. Manure had caught in her bobble. Imagine Joe being spat on – imagine Saul? Her mum and dad? Dog barked, sitting on the roof looking at her. 'Or you, silly mutt.'

Sylvia called from the cabin, 'But you could have been hurt.'

She knew Will would have done exactly as she had. She stared ahead. 'We can't live like that, Sylvia. If our lives mean anything, we have to try to stop that sort of thing when we see it. I won't put up with people telling me it's unkind to the little darlings.'

There was silence.

Sylvia popped up the steps, pushing Polly back and slamming a mug of tea on the roof. Polly looked after her as she disappeared back into her warren, then she laughed, long and hard. Wait until it happened to her, and then see how she felt. It simply had to be stopped, but nonetheless she was glad the vicar had come along and would deal with it.

At Tyseley at the end of the afternoon they tied up at D wharf and dragged Sylvia with them to the public baths, not listening to any objections, and not before they'd seen Steerer Brown on *Golightly*, who had said the men were unloading like the wind today. Granfer and Saul had been in and out on the same day. Must be a day ahead already. 'Best be back early in the morning,' he said. 'Likely you'll be loaded by lunch.'

Mrs Green was at the baths again, and Polly hugged her after she'd handed out the towels, then asked, 'How is Mr Green after the accident on the wharf?'

'Oh, Miss Holmes, he's much better. Things settle,

don't they, when they can't be changed. The past is the past, and he feels he's paid his penance.'

'Do you have any spare rooms tonight? We're not loading until the morning,' Verity asked.

'For you, of course.'

'We'll make sure we each have a good bath, today. We'll pay for two each, and the rooms, of course,' Polly said.

Mrs Green looked relieved. It's what Polly and Verity had decided as they walked along today, because Mrs Green couldn't be expected to give the favour twice.

'What penance?' Sylvia wanted to know once Mrs Green had left. They said they'd tell her later.

As last time, Polly sank into the bath, letting the filth soak from her, listening to Verity singing, 'White Christmas' until Sylvia called, 'Stop it, the last thing we need is snow, even if it comes with Bing Crosby.'

Polly looked up at the vaulted ceiling. Good heavens, Sylvia had made a joke. Later Sylvia joined in with 'Don't sit under the apple tree with anyone else but me'. She had a glorious voice and soon they were all singing. When they finished, Polly said, 'I wonder if I showed Joe an apple, would he think the shape was like an "a"?'

Verity, taking her second bath, answered as she splashed. 'You could try it, but also don't forget cat, sat, mat as Fran said. Perhaps he thinks in patterns as well as shapes, and the "a" will be tucked between other shapes, forming a pattern. Now I'm going under the water and washing the worst of the muck from my hair, imagining I am sitting in the sun, doing very little, so I don't wish to hear anything more from either of you until we've finished.'

At last they were out in the cold air, cleansed, hungry and happy to head for Mrs Green's. They called into the corner pub, the Bull and Bush, first, where the publican recognised them and called, 'Put away your darts, boys, here are the money-grabbers.'

They explained to Sylvia as they ordered fish and chips to eat. Fish was off ration, and sometimes available, sometimes not, and who could blame the trawlermen, who not only had the weather to contend with, but the enemy?

Fish was 'on', and they ate sitting by the fire. Steadily Sylvia's damped-down curls bounced back again, but they still weren't dry until they reached the guest house. Verity found the key under the gnome with the red hat, as per Mrs Green's instruction. It was past nine o'clock and not the same without Bet.

'Time for all good girls to be in bed,' Polly murmured.

'And for all bad girls too,' Verity added. Polly laughed along with her, but Sylvia did not. Instead she followed them upstairs in silence. She had refused to drink beer, choosing tap water instead, and as the evening had worn on, and Verity and Polly beat the two-man team at darts, she had become quieter still.

At room number three, she said, 'Goodnight. You won't go without me?'

Polly shook her head. 'We'll never leave you behind, Sylvia. You're one of us.'

Sylvia hesitated. 'Why was Mr Green doing penance?'

Verity glanced at Polly, who shrugged. 'He accidentally killed a woman. His crane chains on the wharf let go a sack of grain and that was that.'

Sylvia opened her door and entered. 'I'm glad he has left it behind,' she said. Then she shut the door in their faces.

Polly scrambled into bed and pulled the covers around her. Lying in the warm flickering firelight she smiled at the thought of the money they'd won. They had put it in the 'winnings kitty' though what they'd do with the money she and Verity weren't sure. She tossed and turned, missing the warmth of Dog on her feet.

Dog was staying on Mrs Smears's motor just along from them on the wharf, tucked up in the warm cabin with her two older children. 'She should be missing Jimmy, but she ain't,' Mrs Smears had said. 'She's 'appy with you. I reckon they'll want you to keep 'er. A sort of thank-yer.'

Polly stared at the fire, which was dying down. It was what Bet had said, and she hoped both women were right, but only if Jimmy was happy with it. She lay down, and remembered Reggie's letter. It was in her trouser pocket. She *must* remember to post it tomorrow on the way to the wharf.

She turned over. Would Saul be roaring along, or were they still just that one day ahead? Maybe they'd slow up a bit, maybe they'd meet at a mooring, maybe ... She wondered how Reggie was, and hoped they'd always be friends, and that one day he'd meet someone who made his heart beat faster, as hers did when she was with Saul. But more than that, she hoped Reggie lived for many years in which to feel such love.

Chapter 29

23 November – heading to Coventry for a cargo of coal

The butty, *Horizon*, looked as bedraggled as Polly felt as she hauled her through the Brum Bum on the way to Coventry just after sunrise. Soon she would be able to make the journey with her eyes closed, and judge where she was just by the taste of the filth she kicked up from the towpath.

She had tied her tow-line to the butty mast, and Verity had hitched one to the fore-end stub to share the load and try for a better speed through the cut from hell. It had been worth giving it a go, and it did seem to make the load lighter.

They took it in turns to throw their lines back on to the butty and rush ahead to the lock, to open and close it, to wind up and drop the paddles so it was ready when *Horizon* reached its gates. The only downside was Verity's commentary as they set off in pursuit of Sylvia, who was taking the motor through ahead of them. With each step Polly heard Verity furiously shouting, 'What's the point of a lovely bath when this is the result? What is the point?'

It wasn't just the dirt, the dust, the slog and the futility of a bath that was getting to Verity, it was Sylvia and the ease with which she had returned to setting their teeth on edge. Polly laughed quietly to herself. The girl was like the wretched niggling coal dust they were grinding between their teeth.

But it wasn't really anything she had done that was dreadful, it was just that when they seemed to be getting on better, she went all quiet on them; today she had even smirked. Polly gritted her teeth at the thought, then wished she hadn't as she tasted the dust even more. Yes, it was the smirk when she won the toss as to who would drive the *Marigold* through the Bottom Road which had so totally grated.

Polly sighed, knowing she and Verity were being childish, but ... but ...

It was colder and smellier in this strip because buildings towered on either side, trapping the stink and excluding the sun. Polly shivered, and pushed against the tow-line, keeping the butty going. Yes, it was the smirk, the tossed head, not to mention the bouncing red curls that annoyed Polly. Did they ever do anything but bounce, when hers, thick with grime, looked dull and heavy?

Yes, the smirk, and then Sylvia had said, 'Never mind, could be you next time, or not. And I'm usually as lucky with raffles as I am with a toss.'

Verity had said, 'If you win twice, surely you refuse, and put the ticket back and let them draw again to give someone else a chance?'

'No, why should I if I've won fair and square?'

Polly found Sylvia's selfishness strange; it was different to how Verity had been, because there had been a reason for Verity's. She paused; perhaps there was with Sylvia's? She must try harder with the girl. She shouted to Verity, as the noise of a saw and a jackhammer ricocheted off the walls, 'Do stop moaning, just for a moment, you'll get a raw throat in all this dust.'

'But it's not just the dirt, it's her. She's so . . . so . . .'

'We need to think of Bet.'

'What, tucked up in bed in front of a belting inglenook? You are a cruel and horrid girl.'

'No, idiot, think of what she said.'

The buildings acted as a wind tunnel, and it was getting colder and colder. This morning Mrs Ambrose had said, as the *Marigold* left the wharf, 'Could be ice soon. That's bad for boaters. Locks us in, stops deliveries. Don't 'elp 'gainst Mr 'itler, neither.'

A crosswind cutting through between two factories ruffled the water and caught the butty, knocking it away from the side. Hadn't this happened before? Polly couldn't remember as she put one foot in front of the other. The girls groaned and leaned into the tow. In spite of the gloves she had bought in Birmingham, Polly's hands were numb, which was as well, because blisters were forming between her fingers, of all places. Why on earth was that? She adjusted her hands on the tow-line. That was better.

Verity called, 'I do think of Bet, and all she said to

us, and I know I am being childish but honestly, darling.' She coughed. 'Is it my imagination or did she improve, perhaps after Bet wrote to her? But the thing is, I just can't make her out, and never know where I am with her. Sad to say, darling, I just don't feel I will ever trust her, or like her.'

'Ah, we'll make something of her. Look at you, quite human now.'

'All I have to say to that, Miss Perfect, is this.' Verity threw up a rude sign, laughed and, dropping her tow-line, ran ahead to the lock, so that the butty could get on without too much waiting around. Some girls at a factory window cheered. Verity swung round, bowed, and ran on.

Polly felt ashamed as she tugged and tugged at *Horizon*, aware that they were actually a three-girl team, and she and Verity were ganging up. They must try harder. She reached the lock, which Verity had already made ready.

They trudged on through the Brum Bum, not thinking of the other locks they had to wheel through in order to get to the bottom of the flight, and Polly realised that though she had posted the letter to Reggie and her parents at the postbox outside the wharf, she had completely forgotten to read those she had picked up from the office, along with the orders. There had also been two for Sylvia, and one for Verity which she had delivered. Verity had said, 'Dear Aunt Beatrix, she always likes to keep in touch. I'll read it some time.'

They had cast off. She would read hers this

evening, when they picked up the coal. On they plodded, passing a horse-boat rushing along at speed, or so it seemed, towards Birmingham.

''Ow do,' the steerer called. 'Is it ready?'

'Yes.'

'Good,' he said, and was gone.

As they were almost through the flight Polly looked ahead as Verity shouted, 'Keep her in, for goodness' sake. Look who's coming along – but what's he doing here?'

It was *Brighton*, Leon's motor. Close behind his butty was being pulled by two of his men; both boats were heavily loaded. The speed the men achieved kept the butty so close to the motor that Polly and Verity exchanged a look. It was no wonder men with such strength had been able to kick and punch Saul to the ground, but were they the same ones? It was difficult to tell.

They kept their eyes on the ground and pulled. Leon drew alongside. Had he steered into the centre deliberately, and what was he doing on the filthy Bottom Road anyway, when he was supposed to use the route they all used?

He didn't reduce speed but almost nudged them. Dog barked. Polly screamed, 'Stay.'

Leon shouted, 'Yer best watch the dog, the wash'll rock yer, see if it don't. I want me boy back, you tell your fancy man. I ain't see him forrard of yer to tell 'im meself.'

She ignored him, but while Verity continued to

tow, Polly threw off the tow-line and leapt on to the butty, scooping Dog off the roof. While the dog struggled in Polly's arms and Leon laughed she leapt back on to the towpath, and let Dog go. She then ran alongside the butty, looking for the tow-line, which had fallen into the cut. She knelt down in the filth and rescued it, wrapping it around her shoulder and waist again, smelling it, and feeling the wet seeping through her sweaters as she ran along to her towing position. Verity was pulling her tow-line tight, and *Horizon* was riding the wash, as Polly pulled hers shorter and shorter, feeling the suck and tug of the wash fighting her. The butty was rocking wildly, Dog was barking and leaping up at her.

The factory girls were throwing offcuts of wood at Leon. Some reached his motor, several hit him, and he sheltered his head with his arm as Polly yelled after him, 'You're a disgrace to the boaters, a bloody disgrace, and it's time someone stopped you.'

Verity shrieked, 'You should be ashamed, you could have bucked Dog off into the water. You're a damned murderer, that's what you are, trying to kill our Dog.'

Leon's motor was gone, and the wash was easing the strain on the tow-lines. His butty drew alongside, now towed by the two men, and it was bucking too, but Leon's men kept walking, pulling their butty to heel as though it was a dog. Their bulging thighs and shoulders made light work of the tow, in spite of the load.

Polly yelled, 'You should think of working for someone else. He's not a boss to be proud of, he really isn't, so there. So very there.' One of them snatched a look, and for a moment he seemed familiar, but then he bowed his head and powered on.

Verity turned and looked at her, then roared with laughter. 'So very there? That'll frighten them, I don't think.'

The girls up in the factory window were cheering, calling after Leon, 'You'll get what you deserve, see if you don't.'

Polly shouted, 'He's got to be stopped.' Dog was running between Verity and Polly, loving the freedom.

Verity was bending into the tow again. 'But how?'

At the end of the Brum Bum the *Marigold* was waiting for them. Verity and Polly tied on the towrope while Sylvia watched from the counter, her arms crossed. Polly and Verity stood on the towpath by the *Marigold*'s counter. 'Shall we take over the motor now?'

Dog had already decided and jumped on board, skirting Sylvia and jumping up on to the roof.

'A horrid man passed, going much too fast, and he had a message for you, Polly. He said to tell you he'd get you, and he was to have his boy back,' Sylvia said.

Polly explained that Joe was Leon's son but had been taken away by Saul, Joe's uncle, and Granfer because Leon had not only caused Joe's mum to run away because of his cruelty, but had beaten Joe. She also told Sylvia that Leon and his men had attacked someone one night outside a pub and Polly had hit Leon with a stool. She'd hoped he wouldn't know it was her, but so be it.

Sylvia eased herself from the counter on to the towpath, heading for the butty, then she turned, shouting, 'How could you be so stupid as to involve yourself in these people's problems? They're all hooligans, gypsies, whatever you want to call them, and it's not just you who suffers. What about us? It's time you grew up, and quite honestly, your cabin is a pigsty.'

She swept to the butty. Verity started after her, but Polly grabbed her arm. 'Leave her, let's see if she calms down – again. I need a cup of tea, and put into it some of that brandy Sid gave us, for goodness' sake.'

They climbed back on to the motor. Verity, seething with anger, said, 'Shall I offer some to Miss Bouncing Curls?'

Polly laughed as though she'd never stop, then spluttered, 'Best not; she'd probably rather go without than taste anything produced in our pigsty.' She checked behind: Sylvia was in place. Polly hooted and pulled away as Verity disappeared into the cabin. She came straight back out again. 'It's no worse than it ever is, and Bet never said anything about it. Perhaps we need some more plates, and crocheted curtains to make it more homely, but there's never time.'

Polly was heading towards the narrow neck of water with the office beside it. The man who marked their card last time marked it again, asking how she was, linking his arm through hers. 'You all right, me duck?' he said. They bought some leeks from him, and assured him that they had left their trip cards in the boxes provided along the way. Verity muttered, 'Liar.'

'Shh,' Polly whispered. They decided they'd tie up at a pub tonight, and if Sylvia wanted to stay on the butty, that was fine but they needed some fun, a drink, and to win some money for the kitty.

Chapter 30

The evening of 24 November – heading for Coventry

At the Black Dog, near Griff, *Seagull* and *Swansong* were moored towards the head of the queue. Polly looked around her but saw no sign of life. They walked down the path and as they neared the pub the girls heard a cheery hubbub coming from within.

Inside the pub an accordion was playing, the bar was full, and there were some boaters' wives there too. It was a celebration of Jimmy Porter's recovery, or so Steerer Ambrose said, while buying Polly, Verity and Sylvia a pint of beer. Sylvia pulled a face when she sipped it. 'I usually drink a sweet sherry, if I must drink at all.'

Polly whispered, 'I doubt very much they have sweet sherry on the premises and besides, you have been bought a beer and to ignore it would be the height of rudeness, so tonight a beer will suit you very well.'

Sylvia's lips tightened, and she sat down at the table with three spare seats around it by the fireplace. Verity said, 'It's so strange that one fireside table always seems to remain free.'

Mrs Ambrose was sitting the other side of the fireplace, just for once, and she leaned forward, whispering to Sylvia, 'The thank-yer will last for ever. So there'll always be one empty for yer. If others are sitting, them will rise.'

'Thank you for what?' asked Sylvia.

'Nothing much,' said Polly, embarrassed.

There was a bit of dancing at the end of the room as the accordion player was joined by a steerer who sang about the time and tides of life on the cut. He had a wonderful voice. They drank up, wondering if there was to be a darts match for them tonight, but then the room fell silent, and Steerer Ambrose cleared his throat. The crowd parted as though it was the Red Sea, leaving a path from the table by the fireplace to the small stage area. Polly saw then that Saul had been standing with the accordion player, and her heart leapt. She stared, then realised that it must have been him singing.

Steerer Ambrose stood with Saul and raised his glass to the girls. 'We 'as news. Jimmy is definitely waitin' for oos at the depot. 'E's fit as a fiddle, so we lift our glasses to them women.' He pointed to Polly and Verity. 'We 'ope, too, that Bet be well an' all.'

There was silence as the glasses were lifted towards them. Polly and Verity were speechless, then wondered if they should say something, but the accordion began again, the passage closed, and they relaxed. Sylvia muttered, 'So what was that all about?'

Verity grinned. 'Nothing, really. We just hoiked a dripping child out of the cut and Polly pumped him dry.'

Sylvia looked into her glass of beer. 'One wonders why they didn't keep an eye on him?'

Verity and Polly looked at one another. Polly itched to pour her beer all over Sylvia's curls. Then let's see if they bounce back, she thought.

Saul was singing again; this time it was 'Don't Fence Me In'. Sylvia brightened and said, 'I love this song.' With that she was up. Winding her way through the scrum, she stood beside Saul and began to sing, her glorious voice melding with his. Verity kicked Polly. 'Damn, we knew she was good, but she is seriously good.'

As they stood to watch, an ache swept over Polly to see them together. Saul was smiling, and he took Sylvia's hand and twirled her as the song came to an end. Those in the bar clapped. Verity and Polly made themselves put their hands together too, though Polly actually wanted to strangle the girl.

As Sylvia led Saul down to the far end where people were dancing Verity sidled up to Polly and said, 'Come on, let's have a game of darts. The least we can do is to make some money tonight and wash away the taste of little Miss Successful.'

Polly slipped her arm through Verity's. 'I think

probably we're being horrid about her, but honestly, I don't damn well care.'

Two young boaters were by the dartboard, waving their darts at them. 'Come on, give us a game.'

'A bob to the winner?' Verity offered, quick as a wink.

The girls won, but too easily. They gave back the money. 'You let us win, and that's not fair.'

They played for real next time, and still won. As the money exchanged hands Granfer came to stand near them. ''Ow's Bet then?' he asked.

'Getting better, we hope, but she's not sure she'll ever be back.'

'Yer lass's been telling our Saul that Leon made trouble again. She says that some 'ooligan's been fighting with 'im and you were dragged in. Saul told 'er the 'ooligan were 'im. Shut her up, no trouble.' He cackled.

As he spoke, Saul and Sylvia were making their way through the crowd to the dartboard, Sylvia leading, her face set in a sulk. Saul's face was expressionless.

They stopped when they reached the girls. Saul took Sylvia's hand and bowed over it. Then looked at Polly. 'Yer like to dance, our Polly?'

She would, very much. The accordionist slipped into a slow number. She followed Saul back to the dance area. He took her in his arms. She knew she was filthy, and her hair was thick with oil and sweat, and the rest of her too. Saul didn't smell, or perhaps they both did, so that's why it seemed neither . . . Shut up, Polly, she told herself. He stared over her head. Will had said she'd need a short-arse if someone was ever to gaze into her eyes, as she was just five foot four. Otherwise, he'd said, he'd be looking at her parting.

Saul was leading her in the dance, and it was as though she floated. She forgot the filth of herself, the smell, but just danced. It seemed she was wearing sparkling pumps, not boots. He was light on his feet, and the kerchief at his neck was clean; the bobble hat stuffed in her pocket was not. He swung her round, looked down at her and smiled. 'Right sorry, I am, that Leon bothered you again.'

There was something different about him. She said, 'He didn't bother us. He's just a pig, and one day he will get his cards marked.'

Saul looked confused. She said, 'One day he'll get what he deserves.'

It was then she realised he had said you, not yer. Why? She had come to like yer.

They danced for the next half hour, but then she saw Verity waving from the bar and pointing at her watch, and then at Sylvia. She held up five fingers. Polly nodded.

Saul had seen too. 'I will walk you out,' he said, taking her arm, though the music still played. He led her through to the front door, and outside. The sky was clear, the stars bright. In the distance search-lights waved, probing for the enemy. Saul stood next to her, watching as she was. She asked, 'Where's Joe?'

'Safe, with Missus in the kitchen.'

'Surely Leon won't hurt his own son, not really?'

''E'll take 'im, if he can. He would 'ave taken him that night if you 'adn't whacked him.'

He took her hand, and kissed it. 'He's like me own boy,' he said. She lifted her head wanting his lips on her. He looked deep into her eyes, bent and kissed her mouth, so gently.

The door opened, and shut; footsteps sounded. Sylvia's voice tore through the darkness. 'I doubt that your boyfriend Reggie would understand this, Polly.'

Saul jerked up, looked at Polly, his eyes dark. 'Oh, I's sorry. I didn't know.' He spun on his heel and walked back past Verity and Sylvia.

Polly watched him go, still feeling his lips. She walked ahead to the *Marigold*. Behind her she heard 'ouch'. She turned. Sylvia was face down in the mud. For a moment she lay there, then raised herself. 'You tripped me,' she accused Verity.

'Yes. One day you will learn to grow up, be kind, and mind your own bloody business.' Verity walked past the girl, leaving her in the mud, and linked arms with Polly. 'Come on, don't worry. It's not the end. There's something there, with you and Saul, and you said the other evening to me that Reggie was a friend. It won't rest here, I promise. Saul's not a weakling.'

Chapter 31

28 November – at Bull's Bridge depot lay-by

At the depot, Saul stood on the counter of *Seagull*, looking across at the trees, their branches free of leaves as they shut down for the long winter. Is that what was the matter with him, was he shutting down? Whatever it was, something were wrong. They'd arrived late last night, on the heels of the girls, herding them in, but finding a mooring well past them and he'd thought once here, he'd feel he'd want to eat something; p'haps some toast. But he couldn't. Couldn't sleep neither. Granfer had said, as they cleared the hold of coal dust after they'd moored up here, that it were worry about the boy, cos Leon hadn't given up.

Saul nodded but it weren't that, cos he could fight for his own, but 'ow could he fight for 'er. Not if she wanted someone else – this Reggie. She'da been laughing at him, he supposed, and why not, he were a bloody fool, just a boater, not a landsman, a banker. He were a boater who 'ad tried to talk proper at the pub, tried to remember his 'h', his 'you', not 'yer'.

He peered into the cabin. Joe was pulling out

Polly's book from beneath the cross-bed mattress. Saul said, 'Yer lookin' at the pictures again?'

Joe shook his head. 'I's givin it back. It's the right time.'

Saul looked at him. ''Tis, is it?'

'Jimmy Porter's back. She been good to 'im, she and Verity. Time I was good back.'

Saul nodded.

Joe said, 'But yer got to come with me. I can't do it on me own.'

Saul shook his head. It would be too hard, hurt too much, and he'd had enough of hurt. Mum, Da, Maudie . . . He still looked, wherever they were, but nothing.

Joe said, 'Yer must, or I isn't taking it back. Is yer shamed of me, is that why? Is yer?'

'Course I ain't. Never that.'

The *Marigold* had arrived late at the lay-by the evening before in the dark, its headlight at the fore-end shrouded. Sylvia maintained all the way that her arm hurt though she wouldn't let either of them examine it. Instead she had dripped about just managing to eat heartily, and to steer the butty tiller; though nothing more. She was insistent that she needed a Southall doctor, and that he would probably sign her off on the sick.

Each evening they had broken the blackout as they kept going past dusk, but there were no ARP wardens to shout at them while on the cut, and still

Saul and Granfer followed, shepherding them in. Once they'd arrived, Polly and Verity had thrown themselves into bed, after rushing to the lavatory, followed by Sylvia who had fashioned a sling for her arm as they approached the depot.

This morning she was at the doctor's, still blaming Verity, who had apologised once, but then said that people tripped if they kept putting their feet in their mouths. For a moment it had cheered Polly.

Verity had set up a fire on the bank, once Sylvia had trotted off to the doc, and was washing clothes, while Polly had drawn the short straw and was cleaning the hold. Coughing, she walked along the bottom boards, trying to see it through Bet's eyes. Finally satisfied, she pulled herself up and out. She had collected up the remnants of coal in a couple of buckets and hauled them up earlier. These would keep them going for a few days.

She deposited the coal in the box beneath the bottom step of both boats. Then she shot off to the lavatory and washed as best she could. It probably got right up the boss's nose, but who cared. He'd not say anything as long as they cleaned up after themselves. Back at the *Marigold* she changed into a couple of Will's sweaters, those she kept for best, and her one pair of relatively clean trousers.

On the bank, Verity was poking the Brum Bum trousers which were so clogged with coal they'd need several goes in the boiler. Her hair was streaked with sweat, or perhaps it was steam? Polly dumped her load of sweaters with the others at the side of the boiler, for a cooler wash. Verity muttered, 'Give us a hand wringing these little devils, Polly. I think I've shrunk one of Sylvia's sweaters, it sneaked into this wash.'

'Call me when you're ready.'

'I wonder how she's getting on at the doc? I can't believe he'll sign her off, though perhaps Bet would then come back,' Verity said, prodding as the trousers bubbled free of the water.

Polly shook her head. 'Bet's not well enough, but it won't happen. I caught her cutting some bread with that hand when I nipped down into the cabin yesterday.'

She took herself for a walk along the lay-by, encouraging Dog to come and stretch her legs, wondering once again if Sylvia was cruel or stupid or just a believer in what she perceived as the truth? Well, she must take care what she told her in the future. She threw a stick for Dog, who roared along, snatched it up, tore back but wouldn't give it to her. 'Silly girl, how can I throw it again if you hang on to it,' she muttered, wanting to go and see Saul, and explain about Reggie, but why would he believe her?

Women were washing as always, and some clothes and bedding flapped on lines. Smells of cooking wafted from cabins, and she saw a familiar figure: Mrs Ambrose, sitting on a stool on her counter, crocheting. When she saw Polly she brought her crochet down to the towpath, working as she talked.

'Have you seen Jimmy, 'e's a way down there? Him and his mam is wanting to see yer.'

'I'll walk on then.' She hoped they didn't want Dog back, not yet. Just a bit longer. She stroked her as she sat at her feet.

''Ow's that lass, the one that fell?'

'At the doctor. We'll see.'

'If'n she says she's bad, though she looked right perky to me, likely young Joe'll be yer runabout on yer next run.'

Polly hadn't thought that far ahead, and surely Sylvia would be fine. Anyway, how could she ask Saul? It would be too hard to ask a favour, too difficult to make him trust her. She touched her mouth. She could still feel the warmth and gentleness of his lips every time she shut her eyes, and see the hurt in his dark eyes, his sense of foolishness. She walked on, and saw Jimmy ahead, playing on the towpath, bouncing a ball. Dog stayed by her side. She said, 'You'll have to go back to him if he wants you, Dog. He's your owner.'

As she approached, Jimmy's mother, Mrs Porter, was washing, her sleeves rolled up in spite of the bitter cold. Polly was sure there had been ice on the edge of the cut this morning and the last of the leaves seemed to have gone from the trees almost over-night. 'How do,' Polly called. Dog barked and ran up. The woman stroked him, but then he ran back to Polly. 'Jimmy,' the woman called. 'Come 'ere, an' say 'ello to Missus Polly. She and 'er friend did 'ook you out, and pummel yer till yer breathed.'

Jimmy nodded, looking confused, and went back to bouncing and catching his ball. Dog virtually clung to Polly, who said into the pause that had fallen, 'I am happy to have Dog. That's what we call her, but I understand if you would like her back.'

Mrs Porter dried her hands on a tea towel, then said, 'I wanted to see yer special like. You saved more'n our boy. I reckon yer saved oos. We'd a gone mad if we'd lost 'im on top of t'others, so anything I can do, I will for yer, and t'other lass.'

'I do want some help, Mrs Porter. It's young Joe, I want to teach him to read, because he seems keen on books, but I don't want it to be charity.'

The woman nodded, throwing the tea towel into the boiler. 'He's keen on letters but not school. None is. We's always movin', yer see, an they stuffs 'em at back, and mocks. What I's think is that yer give me summat yer'd like to give young Joe, to 'elp with 'is letters, and our Jimmy'll tell 'im yer teaching 'im a bit. He'll come along then. 'Ow's that?'

'That is perfect.'

Polly strolled on a bit further. She had mail to pick up, and perhaps, just perhaps, she would wangle yet another windlass from the blacksmith, so she'd turn back soon. These lost ones were using up the kitty money, though they'd not yet broken into the 'winnings kitty'.

She drew abreast *Seagull* and Joe called from the counter of their motor, ''Ow do, Missus Polly. I needs a talk to yer.'

She waited while the lad joined her on the bank, his hands behind his back. As he did so, Saul clambered out of the hold, dirty from clearing it of coal. He jumped from the hold gunwale to the bank, lithe and light on his feet. There was coal dust all over him, including his face, and his hair stood stiff with it. He came to her and stood with his hand on Joe's shoulder. He nodded. "Ow do, Miss Polly.'

She nodded in return. "Ow do, Steerer Hopkins.' She grinned. His face didn't move. Dog whined at her side, and moved closer to her.

Joe took the book from behind his back. 'It's right you 'ave it back now,' he said. Saul nudged him. Joe braced himself, and looked her full in the face. 'I thanks yer for letting me 'old it. I likes the pictures. I like the letter shapes. One looks like an apple, so it do, don't it, Uncle Saul?'

Saul nodded. Polly squatted and took the book from Joe. 'Will you let me show you what that apple shape means, and how it sounds?'

Joe shook his head. 'I don't need it. I's a boater, in't I, Uncle Saul?'

Polly stood, and looked at Saul, who said, "E do need it, Missus, but he don't want it.'

Polly looked down at Joe. 'An apple shape is the shape of the letter "a". The cat sat on the mat, wearing a hat, eating an apple. I will be helping Jimmy with his letters, maybe . . .'

Joe yelled, 'I's don't need yer giving. I don't, you sees if I don't.' He ran past her, heading towards

Jimmy's boat. Would Mrs Porter talk to him? Polly wondered.

Saul started to move back to the motor; she reached out, and gripped his rolled-up sleeve. He pulled away. She blocked his path, caught hold of both his arms. 'Please, Saul. Reggie is a friend, and for that he's important to me. He knew my brother, and me, when we were all children.'

Saul nodded, then looked at the hands that held his arms. 'What is I?' he said. 'Is I a friend?'

She shook her head. 'No, well – yes, but no, I mean you are more, and you are here in this world, where I am now.'

He was looking down at her, right into her eyes, his forehead furrowed, soot deep in the lines.

'For 'ow long you be 'ere?'

'How long is the war?' She could see their breath mingling in the chill.

'There be life after the war.' His eyes were still fixed on hers.

'Yes.'

'So which be yer world then?'

She shook her head, gripping his hand now. 'All I know is that I am here, now, and you are too. I don't want to let you go, Saul.' They looked at their entwined hands, his so brown, dirty and calloused, and hers so brown, not quite so dirty at this precise moment, and calloused. When she was with him she felt as though she was returning to life.

There was silence between them, and then she felt

him tighten his grip, more and more, and now his eyes were drinking in her face, just as hers were sweeping over his. Still silent, they were in an oasis amongst the banging and shouting of the depot, the chatter and laughter of the children, the pat-patter of passing motors. As she moved closer a cry broke through the moment.

'Polly Holmes, what on earth are you doing? We've come all this way to see you, surely you received our letter?'

She peered past Saul, and closed her eyes, then opened them again. It was her mum, standing on the towpath midway between Polly and *Marigold* with Verity, who was on tiptoe behind her, pulling a face which quite clearly said, *Oh crikey, get over here*. Her dad waited alongside her mother, shaking his head surreptitiously. She smiled up at Saul. 'I must go.'

He held on to her hands, and she didn't want to go either. He smiled that smile and released his grip. She left but called back, 'I really want to help Joe read. Can I leave some pictures I have drawn on your counter, to help him understand, and some books that might help? Perhaps you'd copy my pictures, so they are proper drawings.'

He shook his head. 'Leave 'em a bit further away, then 'e'll think 'e's found 'em, and that'll be better. Then I'll copy 'em.'

With Dog at her heels she hurried along the towpath, past the boilers, skirting around the children who were playing jacks, and two girls dressing dolls. One woman was wearing the hat that Polly had knitted and called, 'Bob gave me this you done for me. It suits a treat.'

She arrived with Dog at her heels. Her mum asked, 'Did you read our letter? Surely you did.'

Polly lied, 'Mum, of course I did. I had forgotten, what with everything else.' She moved to hug her mother, who pulled back and said, 'Polly, you're filthy, and who was that man you were talking to? Were you holding hands? It won't do, it simply won't. These people—' Her mother pointed along the bank. 'Well, look at them. It's not what I thought. Not at all.'

'Hello, Dad,' Polly said. They all walked back to *Marigold* where Verity picked up the bucket in which they boiled the clothes. The handle was scorching hot, and wrapped in a towel. She tossed the sludgy water into the cut. 'Just a minute, Mum,' Polly muttered. She sank the dipper into the cut, and refilled the boiler, which Verity placed back on the grill. Polly looked at her parents now. 'Come on board, see what it means to be a wartime trainee.'

She emphasised 'wartime'. Her dad winked, and followed, gesturing to his wife. 'Come along, you insisted on visiting your daughter, the one who chose something safe at our behest.'

Polly flicked a look at Verity, who was looking with great fondness at her dad. Polly realised that Verity never mentioned her own, only her mother, in *that* voice. As she thought that, she also realised that Sylvia never mentioned either of her parents.

Her mum and dad stood on the tiny counter, staring around as though on another planet. Polly said, 'This is our palace. We stand here twelve hours a day at the tiller, or dashing along on the bike to work the lock, or perhaps we're cleaning the hold, or the cabin.' She pointed up to the roof, where the bike with the split saddle lay, next to the water can. 'You see those flowers painted on there. That man I was talking to, Mum, is an artist. He paints these as well as running his boat and butty with his grand-father because his mother and father were killed in a bombing raid.' Was her voice as icy as the wind? She rather thought it was.

She opened the cabin doors and said, 'Do go in.' Her mum, her mouth pursed, stared, then ducked down the steps. The range was on, thank the Lord, and never had Polly been so pleased to have it lit. There was the smell of rabbit simmering in the oven. 'Sit down, do.' Polly gestured to the side-bed. 'This is where I sleep.'

Her mother stared. 'Sleep?'

'Yes, this is our home. We eat, sleep and read here. We charge the batteries for the electric light in the engine house, or if it is low, we use the hurricane lamp. We use a Primus or the range for food, hot water, heat.'

'And the bathroom?'

Her dad closed his eyes, sensing the answer. Polly

did not spare her mum. 'A bucket, in the back-end. We wash in here, using that bowl. If we're very dirty we sluice off in cut water, which is where we empty the bucket, too. We collect clean water from taps as we go along, or from kind pub owners, but we are safe.'

'Pubs? Women in pubs?' Her mother was clinging to her handbag as though to a life raft.

Her dad said, 'We wrote and said we'd take you to lunch.'

Polly's gaze drifted to the bookshelf. Their letter was unopened, stuck in *The Water Babies*, with Reggie's.

Her mum had followed Polly's gaze.

'Are those our letters?' she asked.

Polly nodded. 'We're just so busy.'

Her mum shook her head. 'No one is that busy.'

Polly put *Winnie-the-Pooh* back on the shelf and insisted, 'Come with me.'

They followed her out of the cabin, and back on to the bank. Verity called, 'Polly, just help me here, for a moment. Get the other end.'

She had rinsed the corduroys and hauled one pair out with tongs. Together the girls twisted the water out. Her mum tutted. 'You need a mangle.'

Her dad muttered, 'Don't be absurd, Joyce.'

Polly walked them to the butty, which lay along-side, stern to the kerb as always. 'These boats are over seventy feet long. This morning I have been cleaning the hold of both to get rid of the remains of our coal delivery. Therefore I am filthy, but this filth is after a wash. Look at my hands, Mum.' She held them out, and showed the cuts, the broken nails, the callouses, then she rolled up her sweaters, revealing the blisters around her middle from the towing rope, and the cuts, and bruises. Her mum gasped. Her dad nodded. 'We have to pull this butty by hand,' she explained, 'through the locks and short pounds of the Bottom Road, the one we call the Brum Bum running from Birmingham to Coventry. We're the equivalent of horses, but we are safe.'

Her mum's face wore that 'I am not amused' expression.

Polly said, 'Listen, Mum.' She gestured at the depot, where the workers were hammering, the tannoy was playing its tinny music, and every few moments calling 'Steerer someone or other' to the office.

'We're waiting for orders, and also for one of the team to return from the doctor, as she has hurt her arm. If she can't work, we will borrow a ten-year-old off another boat; he's called a runabout. So, today, with you, we will eat in the depot canteen, because we could have to leave at any moment to collect a load from Limehouse Basin, also known as Regent's Canal Dock. It will be a load which is essential to the war effort, and we will deliver it to Birmingham. We will then collect a load from there, or Coventry, and deliver it somewhere along the way to support the war effort.' She drew breath. 'And yes, in the evenings we will tie up and sometimes go for a drink, or sometimes we boil our clothes on the bank, or wipe down the cabin, inside and out and scrub out the bucket. It's what we do, and above all it is safe.'

Verity came to stand alongside Polly, nodding. 'Yes, it is what we do, and proud we are too, because we're becoming better at it, but never will we be as brave and stoic as these boaters; they're wonderful people, Mr and Mrs Holmes.'

She waved her arm up and down the lay-by. 'Now I suggest we go for lunch while the boiler is cooling, and before we are given our orders.'

Mrs Holmes allowed her husband to take her arm, and they walked with Polly and Verity along the lay-by as people called, "Ow do' to the girls. Dog stuck at Polly's heels as she explained that after they had helped some boaters, Dog had adopted them.

In the canteen it was warm; there was still the smell of boiled cabbage and the hum of talk, the layer of smoke from cigarettes and pipes. Mrs Holmes's lips tightened, but Polly led her to the canteen counter as the women in their white caps and overalls slapped liver and bacon on their plates. One woman, their friend, grinned at Polly and Verity and asked, 'So, how much you won on this trip, girls?'

'Won?' her mother whispered faintly.

'Dab 'ands they are at darts, and beats a good many of 'em. I've warned me old bugger off 'em.' The canteen women roared with laughter. Polly said, 'Come on, Mum, we're holding up the line.'

They chose a table with a few free places, and sat down, listening all the while for their names to be called. Polly whispered to Verity, 'I haven't had the chance to actually ask Saul about letting us have Joe, if Sylvia goes off sick.'

Verity whispered back, 'I reckon, from the look of the hand-holding, he'd give you the skin off his own back, so don't worry about that.'

They smiled at one another as her mother poked at the liver and complained, 'It's overdone.'

Polly's dad said, 'Eat it and be grateful we're here with our girls.' He winked at Polly and Verity. Verity leaned over and clasped his hands. 'I like to be called one of your girls; it's comforting. Thank you both for coming.'

'Yes,' Polly agreed. 'It is lovely, and you both look well. Much better, actually.'

The feather in her mother's felt hat was wobbling as she chewed. Opposite her a man said, 'Come to keep them girls on the straight and narrow, then? Well, no need for that; the cut is pretty much straight and narrow, Missus.'

The men laughed, including her father. Her mother's smile didn't reach her eyes. She ate the spotted dick with more relish than the liver. The girls hoovered up both, because a meal they hadn't made was a meal in paradise.

They drank tea out of thick white cups, and stirred it with the teaspoon chained to the serving counter. Verity held out a packet of cigarettes to Mrs Holmes, who sat back as though she'd been burned. Without thinking, Polly took one, and her father did too. Her mother stared at Polly and said, 'A lady doesn't smoke in public.'

Verity smiled, and patted Mrs Holmes's arm. 'This Lady does, Mrs Holmes; it keeps her going. Don't be tough on Polly when she's working so hard, as are we all.'

The man across from Mrs Holmes tipped his tea into his saucer to cool it, then back into his cup, slurping it. 'They do an' all, work 'ard, you know, Missus.'

Mrs Holmes's feather danced wildly as she looked from side to side. All through the meal the tannoy made announcements, and now they heard, 'Steerer Clement to the office. Steerer Clement.'

Verity shot up, gathered her own and Mrs Holmes's plates, her cigarette wedged in the corner of her mouth. 'I'll take these, you take your dad's. So nice to see you but we have to go.' She hurried out, dumping the dishes on the trolley. Polly was gathering up the plates, and standing. 'So sorry, we have to make ready the boat and butty.' Her mind was saying, thank heavens, thank heavens. Nothing had been said about Saul yet and now there was no time.

She hurried them out into the yard. Verity was queuing outside the office, talking to Sylvia, who was gesticulating with one hand. Her other was in a sling. Verity, moving to the doorway, waved to Polly. Polly said to her parents, 'So lovely to see you, thank you so much for making the effort, but we have to go, really we do.'

She pointed to the gate, and kissed her dad, and her mum, though Mrs Holmes couldn't bring herself to hug her. Instead she said, 'That man, that boater, you were holding his hands, and ... you smoke. It's ... Well, none of it is respectable, and it must stop. And darts, betting on darts ...'

Polly shook her head. 'Mum, Will taught me to do that. Will. If he was doing it I expect that would be all right?'

Her mother dragged out a handkerchief and held it to her mouth. 'Reggie? Poor Reggie, where does he fit into your life? That lovely boy, risking his life in a bomber, while this ... well, this boater is here, safe. It must stop. You have no future here, what will you do, live in a cabin?'

At that moment Sylvia came up, shouting at Polly, 'Look what you've both done. I have a chipped bone, or so they think, because I'm in such pain. That's what comes of a toffee-nosed Lady Wotnot tripping me up, and it's all because of you, canoodling with that Saul. You've no loyalty to your Reggie. Well, I'm going to complain, and what's more I've been laid off sick, so there. Now what are you going to do?'

Her dad stepped between Sylvia and Polly. 'I won't have you talking to my daughter like that. Now, be off with you and take to your bed, if you're going off sick. I dare say there's *something* you could do if you stayed; a chipped bone shouldn't stop you from working, for heaven's sake. There's a war on, you know. Best not complain, I always say. It can come back and bite you.'

Mrs Holmes's mouth had dropped open, just as Sylvia's had. Mrs Holmes said, 'Really . . .' Polly's dad said, 'We've heard quite enough from you for one day too, Mother. All I can say is I'm bloody glad I'm not the one sitting on a bucket doing my business, and I dare say that wouldn't suit you either. Now we're off home.'

As Sylvia still stood, open-mouthed, Verity came rushing out of the office, waving her order. 'Come on, Polly. We've got to make ready. Go and grab Joe.'

Polly looked from her mum to her dad. 'I've got to go.'

Her dad held her fast, saying quietly into her ear, 'I don't like to say so but your mum's right, you know. This isn't respectable, not as she or I know it. It's not your world, and the war will end. What then?'

Polly hugged him. 'I love you, Dad. And you, Mum. But it is my world, right this minute, and how many minutes more have we got? I've got to go.'

Chapter 32

28 November – leaving the depot for Limehouse

The *Marigold* was ordered to Limehouse to pick up wood destined for Birmingham. There was peace on the *Marigold* and *Horizon* without Sylvia, though Joe was no ray of sunshine. They tied up overnight at Paddington, but he barely spoke, resentment in every gesture. He minded the tiller the next day, the 29th', while Polly lock-wheeled. He ate what they cooked, and ignored *The Water Babies* left out for him.

Saul had given him some drawings of apples, but he wouldn't look at those either. Polly left others, of a cat sitting on a mat. Verity looked at them, and said she wasn't surprised he showed no interest. Polly made a rude sign.

When Verity had moved into the butty cabin in order to leave room for Joe with Polly, as Granfer suggested, she found, and brought across, a mouth organ for Joe. Polly had grimaced, and was heartily pleased when he seemed less than interested. Her memories of Will sucking and blowing into one for what seemed like an unconscionable time still resonated. It was only when his lips tingled too much that he grew weary of the thing, and chucked it into next door's garden. It wasn't until later in the day that Polly realised it had been a 'pure' memory, one that had made her smile, and not withdraw into misery.

They headed on to Limehouse and once loaded, and on their way back, they met Saul and Granfer heading towards them. Saul and Polly waved at one another, looking, looking until they were well past, while Joe sat on the roof and stared ahead. She wondered how anyone ever got to really know someone they loved on the cut, because they so often merely crossed when going in opposite directions.

They finally passed the lay-by and set off for Birmingham on 1 December with Polly steering the motor, and Verity on the quiet of the butty. Joe ran ahead to lock-wheel, but Polly took over at midday. Joe stood on the box Saul had brought when he delivered the lad, and steered, looking over the cabin and the tarpaulin-covered cargo. Polly pedalled on the bike, delighted to see a motor approaching as they climbed through the locks heading for Watford.

She stopped, yelling across the cut, "Ow do, is it ready?'

The boater tipped his hat. "Ow do. Yes, next five is. Traffic's 'eavy heading south.'

She waved and rode on, as Joe, with Dog sitting on the roof, steered on, and into the cut, as though he was born to it. Well, of course, he was. Verity glided the butty alongside. Its fender bumped gently against the gate. 'Perfect,' Polly called down, as she shut the gates then opened the paddles while Joe and Verity ran up the narrow steps and tied up at the mooring studs. As the boats rose with the water they tightened the mooring straps, Joe so quick and sure.

He called to Verity, 'Yer need a better hitch. Watch me.' She looked across the lock as he hitched. She copied. He nodded. Dog was barking on the roof as the boat rose, but knew better than to launch herself into the water.

Polly pushed on the beams, and Joe took the motor through, and hauled the butty. Polly took off on the bike again waving at a boat and butty approaching from the north. Too late she saw it was Leon. He revved past her, rocking the motor and butty, and pointed his hand in a gun shape, his face grim. Each time they'd passed he had threatened. She believed in the promise – but when, and how? She thought of Joe, and how Leon would now see that she had him, that he was without Saul to protect him. She cycled back but it was too late; Leon was passing the motor, and as he did so he spun round, watching his son taking the *Marigold* on towards Birmingham.

He called to one of his men, who took the tiller. Again, as she had on the Brum Bum, Polly thought she recognised the man, but then it was gone. As the *Brighton* motored on, Leon ran across the cabin roof and the top planks. Once at the fore-end he stared after the *Marigold*, every fibre of his being full of rage. 'I'll get yer,' he roared. 'I'll get yer and take 'im back, and don't think you'll 'ave a boat when it's over, or a life.'

Polly cycled alongside, keeping pace with the *Marigold*, calling across, 'You're safe, Joe. I promise you're safe. The whole cut is protecting you.' Joe stared ahead and didn't even glance her way, though he had turned pale. The only thing she could do was to carry on lock-wheeling. But then, on a long pound, she took her place back on the motor, steering while Joe stood gazing behind him. She said, 'What about looking at the book and letting me help you understand it?'

'Why don't yer bugger off. Yer no 'elp to man nor beast.'

She shook her head. 'You can say what you like, but I'm not leaving your side for one single moment, and we have Dog. She'll look after us.'

Polly continued to steer along the cut past Kings Langley, pointing out the shadowed slope still festooned in frost, though it was early afternoon and the sun had been shining, thin and weak. She pointed out the starlings flocking, late. She talked of Christmas, and a tree with baubles. The roast chicken before the war, with such lovely parsnips, but said that she now preferred pheasant. She heard the pheasants' call, and pointed out some in clumsy flight, and later, some geese. 'Has your uncle shown you how he catches them? I reckon he lays a trail of corn, then Bob's your uncle.'

Joe looked at her. ''E's not. Saul's me uncle.'

Polly nodded. 'Yes, silly of me.'

They were passing sheep that were scratching at the frost-spiked grass. 'They'll be hungry,' Polly said, checking behind. She knew that Verity would be doing the same. Had Leon winded the *Brighton*, turning it around to come after them? Her stomach churned. *Bang*, his lips had mouthed as he clicked the imaginary trigger. This boy was his son, stolen from him, in his own mind. But there was no way he'd get him back while she was in charge and had Verity in her gang. They were 'invincible'. Somehow they'd stop him; still, she made a note to find a thick stick when she was next on the towpath. They were heading for a bridge hole. She snatched up the knotted rope and beat at the cabin top, then glanced at the parapet. So many dangers, so many nuisances. Had she said to her parents it was safe? The parapet was clear, they entered the hole.

She said, 'I thought there might be an echo, which happens when the sound comes back at you, like another person repeating your words. I sometimes do it.' She continued slapping.

'Braunston might,' he said. They'd come out into the daylight, and the cold wind froze her nose. Was Joe thawing? He reached out to stroke Dog, saying, 'She's good. She didn't bother about yer slapping the knots.'

Polly nodded. 'I hope Dog doesn't have to go back to Jimmy one day. I will miss her so much. I really love her.'

He looked at her for a moment, then at Dog.

He turned his back again, and stared out at another field where there were sheep nibbling. Polly noted that some ice had floated free from the edge of the cut. Then Joe screamed, and Polly swung round, shocked. 'Look, look, a sheep, it be stuck. Look. Caught, it is. It'll freeze, 'e'll die. I gotta go.' Dog jumped down to the counter, barking and leaping up at the boy. Polly scanned the field and saw it, on her side of the cut, halfway up caught against the wire fence on the left.

She shouted, 'No, not you, I'm bigger and stronger. Take over the tiller as we go under the upcoming bridge. I'll jump off, then I'll catch up. If another pair approach, remember to steer to the inside but not too close.' *Oh be quiet, Polly*, she told herself, he knows this.

She shot down into the cabin, found a sharp knife and leapt up on to the counter as Joe steered under the bridge, his hand ready to slam *Marigold* into reverse.

'No, do not, I repeat, do not, slam her into reverse, or you'll have the butty up your rear. You should know that. I said I'd catch you up.'

He looked at her, his face screwed up between anguish and hatred, but he did as she said. She hooted, then blew Bet's horn.

Had Verity understood the warning that things were afoot? She leapt off, on to the towpath, yelling, 'Remember, I'll catch up, and, Dog, you stay.'

She heard Joe: 'Don't yer kill 'im. Don't yer bloody do that, with that damned knife.'

Polly took no notice and ran back along the towpath, waving a hand at Verity, who shouted, 'What the hell are you up to?'

'A sheep in trouble.'

'Bloody hell, catch us up, for heaven's sake; I'm not fit to be in charge of a child, and—'

The rest was lost to Polly as, panting, she reached the field and followed the barbed wire along the edge of the towpath, clambering over near a post she could hang on to. The barbs hooked her, she tore free, ripping her trousers and slicing her thigh. Damn and blast. She ran on over the slippery grass, slid, fell, the knife spun from her hand, the sheep were scattering, baaing as though she was flaying the lot of them. It was tempting, but even more so was the urge to just walk away. She struggled to her feet, found the knife, and with freezing hands continued her run towards the fence.

The sheep were gathering on the crest of the slope, bellyaching, and grizzling. A rook cawed and she shouted at them all, 'If I had mint sauce or a shotgun I'd deal with the lot of you.'

As she ran she was torn between laughing and breathing. Finally she reached the animal, and while it kicked and butted she saw that it was indeed snagged on the barbs and there could be no untangling. She hacked at the fleece. She knew it contained lanolin so perhaps it would help heal the latest of the broken blisters. She was clumsy because her hands were numb, and her nose ran as she bowed over the animal, but finally she sawed through the fleece.

The sheep fell, then struggled to its feet, and scampered after the others, baaing with never a thank-you. But after all, it was an animal from the cut, so how could there be?

She wiped her nose on her sleeve. Her mum would tut. She sighed. She must write to her, but what could she say? Nothing her mum would want to hear. It would likely be, mind your own business, Mum, for heaven's sake, so best to say nothing, do nothing. She wiped her nose again, regaining her breath. She had written to Reggie, though, her usual friendly letter. Why not? It was comfortable.

She snatched some of the wool off the fence and stuffed it in her pockets and was heading back to the towpath when she heard, 'Stand still or be shot.'

Leon? She remembered the sign of a gun he'd made. She stood, barely daring to breathe, but then heard, 'What the hell did you do to my sheep?'

Of course it wasn't Leon. She turned in the direction of the voice, to see a man storming down from the crest just as Dog appeared, running and barking towards the sheep. The farmer raised his gun. She yelled, 'No, please don't. Dog, Dog.'

Dog wheeled, and charged towards her, leaping into her arms as the farmer lowered his shotgun, and now the man's sheepdog appeared over the crest and almost crept on its belly to its master. Another was circling the sheep, gathering them into a whirling mass. As he approached, the farmer yanked his cap from his head, slapped it against his corduroy trousers, and put it back, shouting as he broke his shotgun, letting the barrels hang harm-lessly, 'You've no right to be on my land, and if I see you on it again, I'll shoot. I'm not having you lot poaching my sheep. Don't mind my pheasants but my sheep are out of bounds, d'you hear? Not out of bounds just to the boaters, they're out of bounds to everyone so don't feel hard done by. I'm a reasonable man.'

'Well, I don't think you are, shouting at me like that, when I've done you a favour. My lad saw one of your sheep caught on the barbs. I cut it free. You owe him a vote of thanks. And me.'

The farmer was close. He stopped a few feet away. He was middle-aged, florid, and his breath billowed, much as that of one of his bulls might, or so she thought. 'You're one of the women canal trainees, aren't you? You're doing a good job.'

At that, Polly lowered Dog to the ground. 'Sit,' she commanded. Dog obeyed. Polly pulled out the wool from her pocket, gesturing back to the wire fence. 'This is what I took after I'd cut him from that barbed wire.'

'A her, actually.' He settled his cap yet again, then smiled. 'She'd have frozen stuck there, because there's going to be a sharp ice-up tonight. Early for it, but it happens here. Get yourselves tied up near a pub. You can always warm the cockles over a beer. Keep the wool, rub it on your hands. Might rescue them.'

He slung the gun over his shoulder, then dug in his pockets and brought out a shilling. 'Give this to the lad, and take half yourself.'

She shook her head and thought for a moment. 'No need for that, but if your children have early-reading books – you know, for beginners – would you leave them on the fence, on the opposite side of the cut? We'll pick them up on our way back. Got to get our lad – this runabout we've borrowed – to learn to read.'

She looked down the cut, to the end of the butty which stuck out from the bridge hole. They hadn't moved on, then? They'd lose time.

She started to walk away, and the farmer called, 'Right you are. Time your runabout learned to read, as there's not going to be much for them when this bloody mess is over. Shame, it is. A right shame.'

He nodded, and headed back up the hill, which is when she noticed his limp. Perhaps he'd been in the war? Dog barked after him, and Polly gripped her collar and kept her close until they were the other side of the wire fence.

She still carried the knife, her pocket bulged with wool, her trouser leg flapped where it had torn. What a sight she must make.

She let Dog go once they were on the towpath

and they ran together towards the bridge. From the butty counter Verity called, 'Mint sauce needed?'

'Oh, do shut up. You are watching for Leon, aren't you?'

'Of course, Skipper. He pretended to shoot at me and yelled something about the boat going down too, so I'm watching for him, all the time.'

Polly nodded. 'And me, but I've just met a man with a much bigger gun, and all I had was a knife, and Dog. Dog's our secret weapon, you know; she'll rip out Leon's throat, I reckon.'

She ran on towards the motor, hearing Verity calling after her, 'You sounded as though you enjoyed that thought. Shameless, you are.'

Dog arrived first. Joe had held the engine in neutral, mooring *Marigold* up, and to give credit to him, he hadn't left the motor for a single moment, as far as she knew anyway. 'The sheep is all right, Joe. The farmer was pleased. I'm going on to wheel the next lock.' She dragged the bike down. 'Verity is watching for Leon. You are safe. Put the knife back for me, then pull away. You should really have kept going, you know. Let's try and catch up on time. Hoot three times if you need me.'

She held up three fingers, and counted out three. Joe nodded. 'I knows some of me numbers.'

But this time he didn't shout, or glower.

She pedalled off, and the motor pulled away and headed for the centre. The tow tightened and the butty headed past her too. Dog was with her, and

433

as she kept pace with the *Marigold* Joe called, 'I thought yer would 'urt the beast.'

'Then you don't know me, Joe Hopkins.'

'Me name ain't 'Opkins, but I wish it were. It's Arnson, like me da.'

'I'm sorry, Joe Arnson.' Her hands were frozen on the handlebars.

Joe called again, 'Mayhap we could go over them letters tonight, and you could show me the cat on the mat.'

She grinned. 'Maybe we could, Joe.'

She cycled on and as she did so Verity hooted. The wind was in her direction so she had heard too.

Every evening Saul pored over the lessons Polly had left with Mrs Porter, and which she had given him for Joe. He had copied them, and passed them on to Polly when she asked to borrow a runabout. Granfer sat with him, of an evening, and so they learned their letters together. Saul wanted nothing more than to walk past Verity and Polly one day, with the newspaper beneath his arm, having read it. He'd offer it to Verity, that he would.

Chapter 33

15 December – the *Marigold*'s return trip to the depot

They were north of Kings Langley, days later than they had thought, because not only had they had to wait two days to be loaded, but the engine had yet again needed work near Braunston Tunnel. They had called in at Saul's friend, Mikey, for a new gasket for the exhaust manifold. Once all was well they headed south, with a few vowels tucked under Joe's belt. As they drew near the spot where Polly had released the ewe, she and Joe saw a tarpaulin bag strung on the fence. The farmer had fixed it halfway up the field, out of the way of passing boaters. 'Let me off at the next bridge hole, Joe,' Polly said.

Joe grinned as they headed for the upcoming bridge. She smiled back. Things between them weren't perfect but they had reached a level.

They didn't have to go as far as the bridge, because Joe recognised a tie-up just before it, which would leave the hole clear for any boats coming through. 'Can I go, Polly?' he asked.

Polly nodded. 'Why not, you can stretch your legs while you're doing it.'

He didn't understand. She had to explain it was just a saying. She watched as he tore along the towpath into the field. He was up the field like a ferret up a drainpipe while she hung on to Dog's collar, because the animal was desperate to follow. She saw Joe snatch the bag off the barb on which it was hanging, and look inside. He turned, waved, and headed back as though the bag weighed a ton.

He half ran along the towpath, waving to Verity who hooted at him, and leapt on to *Marigold*'s counter, clutching the bag and toppling over into Polly's arms. As she steadied him, he didn't pull back as she expected but looked up. ''E's put in some lamb, he 'as, Polly. Lots, and eggs. 'Ope they 'aven't broke. And me books are there an' all.'

She hugged Joe, and though he let her, he didn't hug her back.

She said, 'He was pleased you wanted to read, you see. It's sort of a reward.' Dog sat by Polly's side, sniffing the bag.

Joe pulled free now, and took off along the gunwale. 'I'll take the lamb and eggs and 'ang 'em at the back-end. He's put 'em in a gauze bag.' He headed off, and hung the bounty on the outside hook, slinging the tarpaulin bag over his shoulder, and returned the way he had come, jumping on to the counter as Polly hooted to Verity and pulled away. Joe was down on his knees close to Polly poring over the books. One was called *Lassie*. 'What's it about, Polly?'

'A dog called Lassie. We'll bring Dog into the cabin and work on it this evening with Verity, shall we? Then one day you can write a book of your own, about Dog's adventures. There are enough of them.'

He looked up at her and laughed, really laughed, then called, 'Yer 'ear that, Dog. I's to write about yer. Me, Polly and Verity will.'

On 16 December they reported to the office for orders, having telephoned in about their slow progress, and they had also passed messages on through the other steerers to Granfer and Saul, who were on their way back from another run. The office manager said, 'You girls can take leave, if you like. It's almost Christmas and you haven't had a break for a while.'

They chatted in the yard, huddled round the side of the office, having a cigarette. 'Mum invited us both but I've just replied and said we would be on a run. You weren't very keen, and neither am I,' Polly reminded Verity.

Verity shook her head. 'Well, I certainly don't want to go to mine either, so we might as well just deliver another load.'

Later that day Verity collected the letters and brought them back to the motor cabin – Polly's mum's letter was brief. '*I would appreciate a reply to our invitation. It could be that Reggie will be home on leave, and then that will bring you to your senses.'*

Polly showed it to Verity, who grimaced. 'You really did reply, didn't you?'

'They must have crossed. She would have received it by now. I slipped a ten-bob note in, so that she could buy herself and Dad something. I expect she will think it's our illicit darts-match winnings, and might send it back.'

Joe, who was writing his exercise while he ate his Spam sandwich, looked up. 'Well, it were some of your winnings, weren't it?'

Verity roared with laughter and ruffled his hair. 'Wasn't it, get it right, young man, and yes it was. But she could still buy something nice.'

Joe grinned as Polly opened a Christmas card from Reggie. *'Thank you for your letters and yes, I'm glad we're friends too. I agree, anything else will be too complicated and then we'd lose one another. I'm still safe, I hope you are too? War's a funny thing, it takes us to places we would never usually be, and changes us. It's whether we can move on and find ourselves again? Who the hell knows.'*

She showed it to Verity, who said, 'You can't have too many friends. He's a good man, you know, and you're so lucky you have two good men, and true. It would just be better if you and Saul could meet up a bit more often, rather than waving to one another as you pass. Tell you what, let's take a couple of days' leave and then we can wait for him and

Granfer, and you can meet up at the pubs if you're both going the same way at the same time.'

Joe looked at Verity. 'Ain't yer got a good man, Verity?'

Verity looked at the floor, crossing her arms. After a moment she said, with a brittle laugh, 'One day, young man. One day.'

Polly squeezed her shoulder. Verity shrugged her off. 'What do I need with a man,' she whispered, and there was a warning for Polly in her voice. There always was, if the conversation veered close to Tom.

The other letter was from Elisabeth Burrows, or so the name on the back of the envelope said. 'Who's Elisabeth Burrows, for goodness' sake,' Polly mused aloud.

Verity, who was sitting next to Joe and helping him work out the word 'Monday', nudged the boy. 'Joe, what's the matter with this Polly, for goodness' sake. Polly, Elisabeth is Bet, you idiot.'

Polly tore open the letter and read it quickly. 'Bet's asking us for Christmas, telling us to take a break overnight with them, if we have a load to deliver, or even if we haven't – for Christmas Day and the night. Oh, Verity, let's.'

'But what about Joe?'

Joe was looking from one to the other. Polly asked, 'How about it, Joe, would you like to spend a day and night on the land, like a banker, as that's what you call us land people?'

Joe grinned, and finished writing *I sat on the bed*

then fed the cat between the lines that Polly had ruled on the back of the roll of wallpaper she'd found shoved between two metal filing cabinets in the Enquiries office. She had coerced Alf into letting her buy it.

Joe looked up and sucked his pencil. 'If'n Uncle Saul is doing a run, I could stay with 'im till yer's back. I know yer needs me still.'

Verity muttered, as she sprawled next to him on the cross-bed seat reading the newspaper, 'Saul's a day behind us, apparently. The office think we're going on leave, so we won't be called for a trip until the *Seagull* gets here. Tomorrow, when he ties up, we'll ask Polly to put herself out and toddle down the towpath to find him, shall we?'

'She likes goin', she does, silly.'

Polly grinned at them both. So far she and Saul had managed to tie up at the same pub, and even danced or sat holding hands in the pub twice. Mrs Ambrose just smiled when she saw her and said, 'Enjoy life while you can, me ducks.'

There was a call from the bank. 'Polly, I 'ave yer books to give back.'

Joe jumped up. 'It be Mrs Porter. I'll go. Shall I give her yer new drawings and letters, or should Uncle Saul make 'em good?'

Polly nodded, and pointed to the pile. He leapt up the steps, and Polly followed, joining Mrs Porter on the bank. 'How's Jimmy doing?'

'Getting the 'ang o' it. So's your Saul.'

Polly looked at her. 'Saul?'

''E's tryin' too. 'E knows the cut ain't goin' to be worked for ever. 'E knows he'll 'ave to do summat else, some day. Granfer's at it an' all.'

Joe stuck his hands in his pockets and frowned. ''E didn't want 'er to know. 'Twas to be a surprise.'

Polly put her hand on his shoulder. 'Then it will be. Don't you worry, you know what my memory's like.'

Chapter 34

17 December – *Marigold* and *Horizon* head to Buckby

The office had given them orders at Polly and Verity's insistence, and on the afternoon of 17 December they'd set off to Limehouse with Joe, pushing on into the darkness, determined to be at Buckby for Christmas. Saul and Granfer had arrived back at the depot sooner than expected and received orders which allowed them to follow close on their heels. The girls pushed even harder after loading with Spitfire parts. They skirted London, pulling in late at Alperton on the 21st where they found Steerer Ambrose and the family, and the Porters. They spent the evening in the pub, she and Saul sitting close by the fire.

Polly had said nothing about Saul's reading and neither had he. They had just been content to be together, while Joe stayed in the kitchen. Granfer, Joe and Verity left a few minutes before Polly and Saul, who pulled their mufflers around their necks as they stepped out into the cold. They kissed and clung together in the darkness of the porch. 'I'll be close,' he had said against her mouth.

'I know,' she replied against his.

They pulled apart, then kissed again. Joe called, 'Come on, Uncle Saul, it's late.' They laughed; Saul kissed the top of her head.

Once Joe had been tucked into the side-bed, Verity and Polly dragged on their mufflers again, and their macs and hats, to huddle on *Marigold*'s counter, leaning up against the cabin, smoking. Verity said, 'I'm so pleased to see you happy, Polly.' She exhaled, looking up at the stars.

Polly waited, wishing for a similar happiness for her friend. She said, feeling she should – and must – mention Tom, no matter how Verity pushed her away, 'And what about you? How do you feel about Tom now?'

Verity spun round. 'Out of bounds, darling.'

'No, it can't go on like this. You loved him, he hurt you and I suppose I want you to heal and be as happy as I am, and find someone else.'

Verity inhaled, exhaled, then leaned against Polly, and sighed. 'Darling Polly, that would be so divine.' Her voice was brittle with the effort to brush it aside as Polly had half expected, but she wasn't going to play Verity's game any more, and stayed silent.

Finally, Verity stood straight, staring at her cigarette, holding it up. 'The thing is, dearest Polly, I don't think I ever will. He was everything to me, and still is, and I just can't really believe that he would . . . Well, any of it. I would have trusted him with my life, not just my love. I feel somehow that these two are the same. How can I have life without his love? And I thank God I have you, and our dear little boats, and that runabout, young Joe.'

Polly hugged her friend. 'Oh, Verity, of course you can have a life and love.'

Verity laughed slightly. 'Tell me how?'

'Time. He's only one among many,' Polly muttered helplessly, wondering why on earth she'd felt she must interfere and knowing how weak she sounded.

'Ah, that's where you are wrong, my little Polly. He was quite heads above every man I have ever met.'

They headed up towards Birmingham, the *Swansong* and *Seagull* following close; Steerer Ambrose and the Porters were also in convoy. Christmas was special, different; the cut friends kept together. This year, as they travelled north, it was the same. They worked the locks hard and long to head through Berkhamsted, Tring, Leighton Buzzard and Fenny Stratford over the next two days. Their lay-overs were relaxed and at last Polly was with Saul for each evening. While there was still a vestige of light, they walked Dog along the towpath then joined their friends in front of the pub fire. Later Polly and Verity returned to the *Marigold* with Joe, to read and write, while Saul and Granfer walked back to their moorings, perhaps to do the same.

On from Fenny Stratford on Christmas Eve,

passing Wolverton, Cosgrove and Stoke Bruerne and through the Blisworth Tunnel.

'Not far now,' Verity shouted to Polly, having run along the top planks of *Horizon* to the fore-end. 'Just the last few steps up the staircase to Norton Junction, and then the Buckby turn-off. I'm so excited, I could dance.'

'Please don't,' begged Polly on *Marigold*'s counter, laughing, but feeling exactly the same.

On they pushed, on and on, and even when dusk was far behind them, they lock-wheeled through the flight leading up to the Buckby turn-off.

As they turned off at last Polly gazed up at the sky. The moon and stars were threatening to be worthy of a child born in a manger. It was past ten o'clock as they eased along the cut leading to Leicester, but there was sufficient moonlight to see the frost on the trees and ground glistening, and to hear the ice cracking along the edges of the cut as the boats rippled the water. The excitement in Polly and Verity was rising until Joe laughed, and yanked Polly's hat further down to completely cover her ears, and eyes. She pulled it up by the bobble, and told him she'd knit him one with just as big a bobble if he didn't behave.

'I'd like a red 'at, Polly, but no bobble. Red was Ma's colour.' His speech was changing as his reading improved; not a lot, but it was more distinct. She wasn't sure it was a good thing, but he was hungry to learn. She looked behind. *Seagull* and *Swansong* were there, in the distance.

They were all to moor up at the Buckby frontage and they kept going as the cold deepened, their hands numb, their feet too. Verity hooted from *Horizon*. Polly hooted back. Yes, they were almost there. Within ten minutes she edged the motor in to the side, and Verity did the same. They moored up and Polly asked Joe to wait for her in the cabin, just for a moment. Puzzled, he did. Polly knew he'd be straight into one of his books. She beckoned to Verity, who was running along the towpath towards them. She leapt on board, a parcel in her arms.

Together, in the cabin, they gave Joe his present, calling it a Christmas Eve gift, nicely wrapped in newspaper. Verity grinned. 'The best we could do, but see, it has ribbon.'

Joe was staring at the parcel, and then at them.

'Go on, open it, it won't bite,' Polly said, sitting beside him on the side-bed.

When he saw the painting set, and the notebook with 'Joe's Stories' written on the jacket, and the ink, and the fountain pen, he fell silent. 'I ain't got nothing for yer,' he muttered.

'You have given us your time, so we are obliged, and all children can have gifts at Christmas.'

He looked from Polly to Verity. He stood, and spat on his hand, and offered it. Solemnly they both shook it and Polly grinned as Verity surreptitiously wiped her hand on the back of her thigh.

There was another hoot, and Polly made her way to the towpath, Dog too. It was *Seagull* and *Swansong*.

Saul came to the *Marigold*, and handed over a hessian sack. 'Pheasant?' Polly asked, while Verity packed a few things on the butty to take to Bet and Fran's.

'It is,' Saul said, speaking carefully as he was prone to do now, catching the 'h'. 'For Bet. I 'as another for you which I'll keep cool on the motor roof. Happy Christmas, our Polly.'

'Happy Christmas to you, our Saul.'

They stood close together, smiling at one another. He removed his hat, tightened his kerchief, bobbed his head, and kissed her lips. 'I miss you,' he murmured against her mouth.

'I miss you,' she said. His arms came around her and held her close, and she was complete. Joe leapt on to the towpath. 'Look, Uncle Saul, for me stories, and me painting.'

Verity yelled from the butty cabin, 'Time for something to eat, and bed. We're off to Bet's early in the morning.'

Saul broke away. 'I'll look after you always, Polly.' He ducked off the motor, trotting easily back to the *Seagull*. She looked after him, watched as he sprang in one easy leap on to *Seagull*'s counter. He waved, she smiled and he disappeared into the cabin.

Steerer Ambrose was pulling up behind, as were the Porters on *Hillcrest* and their butty, *Leicester*.

In a way, Polly wished she was staying.

'Come on,' Verity called from the motor counter the next morning. Polly was tired, but it was a good tired, because as they had looked at their Spam sandwiches once Saul had returned to the *Seagull*, they'd heard a knock. Granfer had brought pheasant stew in a special china bowl, and vegetables in another. Both were steaming, and he and Saul crammed in, and all five of them ate though only the adults drank the beer Saul had brought. Along at *Hillcrest*, the Ambroses and Porters were doing the same.

Polly smiled to herself now. It had been the most perfect Christmas Eve for her and even for Verity, who said she hadn't relaxed so much for a long while. Granfer and Saul had taken Joe back with them, and as he left the cabin Joe had taken her hand, and squeezed it.

When everyone had gone she had thought of her mum and dad who would not understand her happiness, but never would they hurt her as Verity's mother had hurt her. She had thought of Will, and though the sadness had been there, she knew that she had absorbed his loss. She had thought of Verity and hoped that somehow she would find love. Finally she thought of Reggie, and hoped her friend would live, stay safe, and that his trembling would stop.

Verity called again, 'Fran's here. With our carriage, which awaits.' She was laughing fit to burst.

Polly picked up Saul's hessian bag containing the pheasant for Bet, and her own kitbag, and in another bag were the bottles Sid the Alperton publican had sold her, plus a free beer from him for Bet. Polly patted the range, and addressed the cabin. 'You behave yourself. Our friends will look after you.' She left with Dog because she had been invited too, and they locked the doors on both boats, just in case, meaning Leon might somehow find them.

She joined Verity on the towpath and before they headed off towards Fran who sat on a large tricycle, they looked both ways out of habit. There was not a sight of Leon. It seemed, or so someone had said, that he'd been ordered to the Oxford Canal to take over from a steerer who had been crushed in a lock. Would he come back?

How they hoped not.

They reached Fran, who was ringing her bell. 'You two, get a move on and hop in.'

'Hop in where?' Verity asked.

'The cart, silly.'

They moved to the back of her, to a wooden cart in which lay two cushions. 'Put your derrières on those and hang on tight. It's on a downhill slope so we'll get a good lift-off. Dog can run alongside.'

Polly sighed, and murmured, 'I'm rather afraid we really will get a lift-off – right over the side.'

Verity nodded. 'You fly out first and I'll land on you.'

Fran pedalled the tricycle round and set off, and even Polly's teeth jolted as they rattled over stones and into potholes while Dog ran alongside. Verity clung to the side of the cart, her knuckles white. The beer bottles clashed together, and Polly hauled the bag on to her lap. There was no way she would allow them to break. After what seemed forever but was actually only fifteen or so minutes, they were at the gate she remembered from their previous visit.

'Out you hop.' Fran leapt from the trike.

Verity sort of slid over the side, saying, 'My legs have gone. Never have they been so jolted in their life.'

Fran laughed. Polly handed the hessian sack and the bottle bag to Verity, and slid over the side too, fearful that her legs wouldn't carry her and that her spine would never recover. They followed Fran down the path, at the side of which grew lavender. Further over, at the edge of the garden, were two beehives. Ah, thought Polly, smiling. So the honey from the friend that Bet brought to the boat was her own and Fran's. Now Fran was calling over her shoulder, 'You might remember from your last visit that the road is on the other side, and this is the back garden. Bet would really like it to be on the bank but, who knows, one day we might move. Bring Dog in, I know you come as a package.'

They traipsed behind her into the old farmhouse kitchen. Bet sat at the table peeling potatoes. The room was hot from the range, and the smell of goose lingered. 'We have coffee, don't ask how,' Bet said, putting down her knife and holding up her arms. 'Come and give your old boss a hug.'

They did, in turn. Bet said, 'You've brought the smell of the cut, and the cold of the outside. Perfect.'

The two girls relaxed, and so did Dog, curling up

by the range and getting in the way of Fran, who didn't seem to mind, giving her a sly stroke from time to time. The girls joined in the preparation of the meal, sipping coffee laced with brandy. They were to eat at five, which would give them a chance to linger, before going to bed early, to rise at five in order to return to the cut. Polly sat back in the Windsor chair, the potatoes and onions finished, the sprouts too. There was some celery and they had made stuffing out of herbs and the awful British loaf. The goose would cook for hours on a low oven, and provide goose fat for weeks to come.

Sitting around the kitchen table they talked of the war and Italy's unconditional surrender, of the U-boats withdrawing from the Atlantic as a result of the Royal Navy's efforts. They talked of the cut, to Bet's unmitigated delight, of Sylvia who Bet had heard might be giving it another go because the arm seemed to have healed, or so the office had reported. Polly and Verity tried to smile. Bet nodded. 'She probably won't stay the course, I fear she hasn't a strong enough core, but she insists on a third try. They will allow it, as the absence can be put down to an injury. If nothing else, it means young Joe can go home. From what I hear, he's been a boon?'

Polly agreed, saying, 'He has, bless him. He's so quick, so knowing. We love him, don't we, Verity? Verity is teaching him his numbers, I'm sticking with the reading and writing. How do you know all this, anyway?'

Bet settled herself more comfortably in her Windsor chair. Fran hurried to her, and wrapped a shawl around her shoulders, telling her, 'You're to lie down when you're tired. No heroics, if you don't mind.'

Bet patted the hand that Fran placed on her shoulder. 'Fran's a first-class nurse, if a tad bossy. Now, there is a school where some of the boaters send their children. I'm not sure if it costs money, but it might be an idea for Joe. It's boarding, of course.'

'I don't think he'll go until he knows what's happened to Maudie, or she comes home,' Polly said quietly, the heat making her sleepy.

Bet shook her head. 'Still no news, then?'

'Nothing, but I don't know what that means. Was she the sort of woman who'd go off and leave her child?'

Fran was standing by the range, smoking a cigarette. 'I suppose she might, if she was in fear for her life, as she was with that oaf, from what Bet tells me. After all, as you very well know, Polly, Saul is a reliable uncle, someone she would trust to protect her son. And no need to blush. The whole cut knows that there's a bit of a spark between you two.'

Polly *had* blushed, and expected a lecture about this not being her world, but all Bet said was, 'It's a hard life, and won't carry on too much longer, but I dare say the boaters will find other work near the cut, and some on it, still. Could be that there will be a call for holiday boats. That's the way Fran and

I are thinking, aren't we, love? I couldn't leave the cut for good – or not move far from it, anyway.'

Bet put her hand to her forehead, and paled, quite suddenly. Fran gripped her hand as Bet murmured, 'But for now I will have to go and have a lie-down, or I won't make the meal. Why don't you girls enjoy the bath, and hot water, and I know, Polly, you will head straight for the lavatory, if I remember rightly.'

Fran helped her to her feet and Bet said, 'By the way, to answer your question, Fran is my conduit for news. She picks up a lot from the boaters who head past Buckby en route for Leicester and beyond. We moor our boat, *Blossom,* on the cut, so Fran's always checking on her.'

The day drew on, and after their baths they moved into the sitting room, which was still doubling as Bet's bedroom. The inglenook fireplace held a roaring fire, and with Bet asleep Polly and Verity stretched their legs out in front of it, leaned back, and they too slept until called to eat. The goose meat fell off the carcass, the stuffing was sublime, the Christmas pudding had been made months before and steeped in hoarded brandy. They talked, laughed, and after all the food was finished, they sipped more than one brandy each.

When the clock struck nine they followed Fran up the stairs and into the beamed bedroom they were to share. The beds were high, the mattresses thick, the blankets and eiderdown light. They smiled at one another before Verity said, 'I can't believe there is a world apart from the cut and this cottage. Yes, the cut is harder than I ever thought possible, and sometimes I even forget about Tom, but not really. Sorry, I'm going on. I've had too much to drink and am too comfortable.' For a moment there was silence. 'Does one ever forget someone you love, even when they've gone?'

Polly saw Saul as he had been in the cabin, laughing, his thick black hair washed, his eyes so dark and kind. Would she forget him if she moved on? She knew she could not. And Will? Well, he was her twin, they were part of each other, so he would never, ever be forgotten. So perhaps one didn't forget but it just became easier. She started to say this but saw that Verity was asleep, so reached across and turned out the light. It was strange to be still, not to feel the boat shifting as the wind caught it, or a passing pat-patter set up a gentle wash. She missed it, was her last thought before she slept.

Chapter 35

Mid January 1944 – on the cut

Polly and Verity were slogging along the Bottom Road, on their second trip since Christmas, and shouting about the message the office had passed on, regarding Sylvia. She'd be waiting at Braunston Tunnel, southern end.

Verity yelled, 'What a surprise, it's you and me hauling the butty while little Joe takes the motor through because Little Miss Snotty Nose prefers that the hard work is done before she gets her toes dirty.'

Polly shook her head. When Joe had heard he'd said, 'She won't last. She's not like yer two and Bet, and them other toughies. She's a lightweight, my Uncle Saul says, like a boat that won't carry a load.'

There had also been a letter from Polly's mum in the office, and a letter for Verity, from hers. Verity had read hers this time because *Urgent* had been written on the back of the envelope. Her horse had been shot, because her mother had ridden it to hounds and it had fallen at the second fence. Verity was still white with rage.

Polly repeated, as they continued to haul the butty along the Brum Bum, 'It was an accident, she wouldn't have done it deliberately.'

Verity shook her head. 'As I told you when you brought it up earlier, my mother can't ride well enough to handle Star. Only my father can and he forbade her from taking him out, so he must not have been at home. Why the hell did she tell me?'

'Perhaps she felt you should know, and that she wasn't hurt.'

'So, now I know and a fat lot of good it's done me.' Verity stamped along ahead of Polly, and remained silent for the rest of the day, but when they finally reached a tie-up, her tears had smeared her coal-dusted face. Polly held her, soothing her, and knew the tears were for more than Star. 'Don't worry,' she whispered. 'Somehow things will work out.'

'It's all right for you. Everything is bloody fine, for you.'

Almost immediately Verity put her hand over her mouth, shaking her head. 'I didn't mean that. I really didn't.'

Polly hugged her again. 'Yes, you did, for that minute, and you have every right. Life's bad for you at the moment but I'll do everything I can to make it better.'

She felt so fierce that she was shaking Verity, who looked up and laughed. 'Or kill me in the process. Stop shaking me.'

They continued hauling the butty, laughing from

time to time, but at least, Polly noticed, Verity had some colour in her cheeks.

After picking up the coal they continued on to Braunston Tunnel, pat-pattering through, the shaded headlight on the fore-end stand cutting through the darkness. As the light at the end of the tunnel way ahead of them grew she saw that the *Seagull* and *Swansong* were tied up as she had hoped. Polly smiled at Joe, who was at the tiller. 'Your Uncle Saul got our message, then.'

He shouted, 'Hello, Uncle Saul.' The echo came back. He and Polly laughed.

When they finally emerged into the daylight they saw that Sylvia was standing near *Seagull*'s wash boiler, talking to Saul and Granfer. Her wave was enthusiastic, her arm seemed quite better, and her smile was a pleasant surprise. She waved at Verity too, as *Horizon* exited. Her hair was the same, with curls bouncing.

Verity called, 'You look better, nice and clean – that is more than can be said for us, after slogging along the Brum Bum.'

Polly winced, but it bounced off Sylvia. Ah, perhaps she was toughening. Joe called to Saul, 'The fly-boat gave yer the message? Tim Hores said he would, didn't he, Polly, so I can come home now?'

Polly felt a pang. She would miss him, and so would Dog. She called to Saul as they slowed and glided into the side, 'You made it. We'll pull up behind you.'

He walked towards them. Joe threw him the

mooring strap, then leapt down into the cabin, bringing all his books, his lessons and clothes in the hessian bag that Polly had rescued from Bet.

Polly followed him ashore, and stood close to Saul; so close that his right side was pressed against her left. He gripped her hand and she wanted to stay like this for hours. He said, 'We'll be glad to have our lad back.' Joe, who'd been hugging Granfer, ran to Saul, who let go her hand and swung his lad up into the air. 'You've grown.'

'Have you heard from Ma?'

Saul sighed and put the lad down, but held him by the shoulders. 'I'd have told you if I had.'

Joe looked seriously at his uncle. 'You said you, not yer, and you said your "h".'

Saul laughed, turning him around. 'Go and help Granfer wring out the clothes.'

Verity had joined Saul and Polly and she said quietly, 'We'd best get on, Polly. It won't be quite such plain sailing now.'

Sylvia was telling Granfer how to wring clothes properly. Granfer ignored her. Polly called, 'Come on, Sylvia, lovely to have you back but the cut waits for no man – or woman.'

Sylvia clambered up on to the butty, and straight to Bet's cabin. 'Oh, you haven't moved your clothes back to the motor cabin, Verity. Never mind, I'll put them in a pile, and polish the brasses.'

Saul turned Polly towards him, and put his finger under her chin. 'I'll not be far ahead, and will see you at the pub, one or t'other. Till then, if you need me, use the fly-boats. They just shout it as them dash past. Remember, Leon's not here no more, he's said to be on the Oxford run still.'

Polly nodded, took his hand and kissed it, before walking back with Verity who said, 'Is it my imagination or is he talking differently? Just a bit, but it's there.'

'I think learning to read shows him how it should be, but I hope he's not doing it for me. I love him as he is.'

Verity turned. 'Ah, love, eh?'

Polly said, 'I'm sorry, I shouldn't have said that.'

Verity pulled Polly's hair, a curl came loose. 'Look, if one of us can be happy then I'm glad.'

Polly clambered on to the motor and headed to the engine room along the gunwale. She tinkered with the engine, which caught and died. She gave it more choke and tried again. This time it caught and held. She hurried along the gunwale as Dog jumped from the cabin roof on to the bank, ran towards Joe and leapt up at him.

From the counter, Polly called to Saul, 'If she wants to stay, is that all right with you?'

At her voice, Dog tore back and leapt on board. Saul called, 'She just wanted to say goodbye. Nothing's goin' to drag her away from you.'

He held her gaze and smiled. She nodded. She thought he meant that nothing would drag him away from her, either.

Behind, Sylvia sounded the horn. She was ready. In the cabin Verity sighed as she swept the floor, and called up, 'Well, let's see how it goes, eh?'

The three of them shared the lock-wheeling, and while Sylvia cycled her stately passage along the towpath, arriving late to open the lock after Blisworth Tunnel, at Stoke Bruerne, Verity and Polly steered the boats, slapping their arms, trying to keep their circulation going in the bitter cold. The last two mornings had seen thick ice at the edge of the cut, but at least it hadn't iced it all over. Apparently, some winters iced in the boats, which was no help to anyone, and cut back the money. Once through the locks, they tied up, tried to wash a little of the grime of the Brum Bum from them, then called in at the pub near Cosgrove. Sylvia didn't drink but neither did she behave like a granny. Perhaps she really was trying?

They took up their place by the pub fire, and found Steerer Ambrose there, with Mrs Ambrose and the Porters. All called, ''Ow do.' Sylvia called back, 'Hello, I'm back.'

Polly sat down, watching the clock. At nine in walked Saul and Granfer, with Joe who went through to the kitchen, his book in his hand. 'Is he reading now?' Sylvia asked, as she played with her cup of tea.

'Rather well, actually, and he's learning his sums,' Verity said, her eyes on the dartboard, waiting for the present game to finish.

'It's amazing what can be done if these people spend time with those who are educated,' Sylvia said, putting another log on the fire. Polly and Verity exchanged glances. Of course, she hadn't changed. But they said nothing. At nine-thirty Saul came to talk to them. He squatted beside Polly, telling them that Joe had missed them but was glad to be back too. He said that tonight would be colder and they should keep the slide hatch shut, and the range ticking over. 'You too, Miss Sylvia, in your butty cabin.'

'Why, thank you, Saul. Shall we sing a few tunes tonight?'

He shook his head. 'Not tonight, the accordion isn't coming. He's gone further on.'

The dartboard was free, and two men were gesturing Polly and Verity over. They went, and thrashed them, with Saul, amongst the onlookers, smiling at Polly.

They walked back to the boats, all six of them, through spiked and frosted grass, the cold so sharp it dug into their throats. Saul said, 'I met them Tommies guarding the POWs. A couple scarpered way back in November. They thought we knew, but no one told the boaters. Now they want us to keep eyes out for 'em. Daft buggers, they should have done a runner in the summer. Bit cold for 'em now. As I says, keep that slide shut round 'ere and the doors locked.'

Verity said, 'At least Leon's still on the Oxford.'

Saul shrugged, his face tense. 'Just heard he's maybe back, but we ain't seen 'im. Keep an eye out for 'im too, eh.'

Sylvia looked at Verity as Saul headed for the *Seagull*, walking behind Granfer and Joe. 'I wonder, Verity, if you'd rather have your cabin back. It seems a bit rude to take it from you and I can bunk in with Polly.'

Verity stepped on to the motor counter. 'No, I don't want it back. Lock your door, Sylvia, and you can always keep Dog with you. She'll fight off anyone but she'll want to sleep on your bed.'

Polly took pity on the girl and said, 'I'll come and check your cabin with you, Sylvia. Then you must just lock it from the inside. Or do you want Dog to stay in your cabin with you, too?'

'No, it's most unhygienic. I'll lock it, and Dog will bark if she hears anyone near, won't she?' It was a real question.

'I'm sure she will.' Polly wasn't, at all, but she didn't want to be standing here all night. She walked along with the girl, saw her into her cabin, and headed back to the motor. Saul was smoking on *Seagull*'s counter. He waved in the starlit night. She waved back. There was no need for words. They just . . . were. Just like all the other boaters had to be.

Polly took the bicycle once they were past Fenny Stratford heading for the rising locks to Cowroast Summit near Tring and in spite of herself she looked to left and right, just in case there were two strangers lurking behind trees or bushes. Though what they would want with her, she couldn't imagine. They'd hardly make good their escape on her bike, and besides, they'd be over the hills and far away by now, if they had any sense. Probably they'd head for a port. What with Leon and prisoners of war, there was never a dull moment. She laughed quietly.

Ahead was a bridge, with soldiers marching. They waved. Polly called 'Hello', and returned the waves. She was so busy looking at them that she skidded on ice; feeling an idiot, she steadied the bike, concentrating until she was much closer to the bridge. There were lorries going over now, and one of them skidded too, then stalled. Men scrambled out of the rear while a sergeant shouted directions, standing with his back to the cut, waving his hands. The wind, in the other direction, snatched his words so it was hard to hear. She stopped and watched as the troops got their shoulders behind the lorry and heaved. Slowly the lorry moved up and over the humped bridge, then slid down the other side, leaving the soldiers cheering.

One saw her watching, and waved just as the *Marigold* came along with Verity eating steaming porridge from a bowl on the cabin roof and reading a book. Dog was barking at the mayhem, because now most of the men were leaning over, shouting and waving. Verity ignored them. She and Polly had acquired the boaters' habit of doing several things at once; in Verity's case it was reading, eating, steering. The only time Verity would look up was when she needed to judge the centre line through the bridge hole. At that point, she would leave Daphne du Maurier's *Rebecca* for as long as it took.

Polly cycled under the bridge, speeding to get

ahead and to the lock first. She put her head down and pedalled harder out into the daylight. Again she skidded, and slowed, breathing hard just as the motor came through. She continued cautiously. Then she heard, 'Verity, it's me, Tom. Verity, I know it's you. Turn round and tell me why you gave your mother money to pay me off. Why? I've written but you wouldn't answer. Why?'

She spun round, and stared at the bridge. A young soldier was shouting, his hands cupped round his mouth. He called again, 'Verity.'

Verity couldn't hear above the engine noise as she left the tunnel behind. Polly waved frantically at Tom, shouting as loud as she could, 'She can't hear. I'll tell her but she didn't do that. It was her mum, not her. Her mum.'

But that sergeant was dragging him away as Verity pat-pattered on, oblivious. Polly shouted again, 'I'll tell her but it wasn't like that. Where are you going?'

Tom was clambering into the lorry, looking back along the cut to the *Marigold*. He hadn't heard Polly. She threw the bike down and scrambled, slipping and sliding, up the horseway to the top of the bridge, but the lorry had disappeared. She ran along to the bend, but it was too far away, and hopeless.

She rushed back, sliding down the slope, leaping on to the bike, pedalling hard until she passed the butty. Sylvia was reading too. Polly put her head down and kept her eyes on the towpath, determined not to skid again, but equally determined to catch up with the motor. The breath was heaving in her chest as she came alongside and shrieked to Verity, 'It was him, it was Tom.'

Verity couldn't hear, just shouted, 'I know you're late, stop flirting with the troops and get on and open it.'

The lock was ready, so as the motor slowed, and edged in, with the butty slinging itself up alongside, Polly shut the gates, yelling at Verity, 'It was Tom, on the bridge. Tom.'

Verity could hear now. She froze, the mooring strap in her hand, and then she threw it to Polly, saying, 'Tom? Don't be stupid, you don't know what he looks like.'

'I do now. Brown hair, straight nose, tall. He was yelling, and yelling, asking why you had asked your mum to pay him off, saying he'd written to you but you'd never replied.'

Once out of the lock it was Verity who tore back along the towpath on the bike, but the soldiers and their lorries were long gone. She returned, telling Polly there was no sign. Shaking, and weeping, she grabbed Polly. 'That's what he said? You're sure that's what he said.'

'Yes, and I told him I'd tell you, but I don't know if he heard.'

'We've got to find him.'

Polly nodded. 'Your parents must have his address. They employed him, after all.'

Chapter 36

20 January – at the depot

Polly and Verity took two days' leave when they returned to the depot. Sylvia wasn't due any, but was given it, because there was a limit to what she could do on her own. The girls didn't ask her to join them. She said she had plans, anyway. Those plans, she assured them, did not include cleaning both holds on her own, so they could not leave early as they had hoped. Instead they all had to pitch in. It meant they didn't leave until 21 January for Dorset, with finger-nails and hair that as usual resisted soap and water.

'What will you say?' Polly asked in a carriage filled with women and children, and was so nervous at the thought of what was to come that she rather wished she hadn't offered to accompany Verity. She suspected the others in the carriage wished neither of them had, either, judging from the rolling eyes, and handkerchiefs held to the noses.

'Darling, I have no idea.'

Polly thought, however, that her friend probably had a very good idea, judging by the light of battle in her eyes, and the thinness of her lips.

The corridors were, as always, lined with soldiers, sailors and airmen, most sitting on kitbags, smoking and thinking, as though they had seen the light of battle rather too often.

As the train steamed into Sherborne, Verity nodded. 'Come on, boater. Out we get.'

They walked to a bus stop but Verity ignored it. Instead she started to thumb a lift. Polly was appalled. 'It's not safe, it's not what we should do, it's not respec—'

Verity laughed, tipping her head back. 'Respectable? Come on, you're in love with a boater, I with a chauffeur who didn't seem to actually want money instead of me, and both of us are filthy, wearing corduroy trousers, and several sweaters belonging to your lovely brother, and just look at these boots. Sweet girl, don't be absurd, do you really think that we are respectable in any way, shape or form?'

They continued walking. They had brought a small bag each with overnight clothes, just in case the visit to Howard House went well. If it didn't, Verity knew a pub where she and Tom used to play darts and spend precious moments together.

A Morris Minor pulled up. A GI opened the door and said, 'Hey, gorgeous girls, thought you were two lads in need of a lift, but now we see it's not. But you need a lift anyway. Where to, ladies?'

They dropped the girls at the bottom of a long drive, having taken a turning as directed by Verity. 'Thanks, fellows. If you carry on you will get back on to the

London Road. Have a great time, and leave what buildings we have "entire" while you let off steam.'

The GIs laughed, and said, 'How about getting a wash, ladies.' They opened the car windows, waved, and roared off. The girls were mortified.

'Where are we?' Polly asked, looking around. There were fields, and a barrier of evergreen trees to the left. Verity linked arms with her, and led her to the huge wrought-iron gates. 'Beyond the gates and leylandii is my dear little home, Howard House. Come on, let's take our stink to meet the parents.'

She pushed open the gates and they crunched up the gravel drive for what seemed to Polly like miles, but was only a quarter of a mile, Verity assured her. Weeds sprouted through the gravel. Verity tutted. 'This would not have been allowed before the war. Mother would have had the gardener's boy's guts for garters. He must have been called up.'

Polly said quietly, 'As for Tom, has it occurred to you that she might have been thinking she was protecting you?'

Verity snapped back, 'Like your mum? Oh, come on, Polly, I think mine's left yours in the blocks for interference, don't you?'

The trouble was that Polly agreed with Verity.

They continued, arm in arm, as the drive swept round a left-hand bend, and there it was, the dear little home. Only it wasn't. It was a massive manor, or mansion, or stately home, Polly wasn't sure which. Either way, it was splendid. Verity led them up the portico steps to the wide double doors. Polly wondered if they should approach through the back, as their boots were so grubby. Verity shook her head. 'We enter from the front because we are doing good, honest work, Polly, and don't you forget it. But let's keep to the tiles and wood and not besmirch the somewhat priceless rugs.'

Verity opened the door into a foyer resembling that of the luxurious hotel Polly had visited for a relative's wedding reception. How on earth, Polly wondered, had Verity coped with the cabin?

She followed her friend round the silk rug. The grandfather clock chimed four. Verity said, in a voice laced with irony, 'My word, we're in time to take tea.'

The sitting-room door opened, and a glacial and elegant woman stood there.

'Verity?'

'Yes, Mother.'

'I thought I saw someone like you passing the window. But I wasn't sure, and looking at you, I'm still not. Neither was I expecting . . . I've written many times . . . You have not replied. Whatever do you look like?'

Verity stood quite still, staring at her mother. 'I look like a boater. It's what I do. This is my dear friend, Polly. She is also a boater. We are wearing her brother's jumpers, three each. We find they keep out the cold, if not the wet, but that doesn't bother us now. May we take tea with you?'

Lady Pamela Clement's gaze swept her daughter,

and then Polly, clearly searching for words that wouldn't come. She stood to one side, and ushered them past.

'For heaven's sake, darling, you smell, and you really are filthy. You should have come in through the dogs' room.'

Verity walked around the rug before the massive fireplace in which a fire blazed, pulling Polly with her. They stood with their backs to the blaze while Lady Pamela sat, ramrod straight on the sofa set at right angles to hearth. She rose briefly to pull a silken rope, and then sat again. 'I will instruct Rogers to bring a blanket, then you may both sit.'

Verity half laughed. 'Oh, Mother, it's so reassuring that you don't disappoint. I'm here because I know what you said to Tom.'

The shock was writ clear on Lady Pamela's face. Not in the least like Verity, she was dark-haired, dark-eyed, with thin lips. She said, 'What he said to me, you mean.'

Verity shook her head. 'No, he saw me on the boat, I know what you did.'

Her mother flushed, as a man came through the door. Lady Pamela waved him away. 'Not now, Rogers.'

He bowed and backed from the room.

Cleverly done, Verity, thought Polly. You heard from me, but have not left that loophole for your mother to drive a horse and cart through it, or sure as eggs is eggs she'd blame me for concocting a story. She moved away from the harsh heat of the fire to stand behind the sofa. Verity followed, resting her hands on the back of the sofa.

Her mother shook her head. 'Your nails are disgusting, how can you appear in society as you are?'

Verity sighed dramatically. 'The mind boggles at the conundrum. It's coal, for the war effort, or have you managed to obtain some which should in fact have gone to the armaments furnaces?' She pointed to the fireplace. 'We had to clear out the hold before we left, you see, so it's worse than usual. We take a trip to the public baths in Birmingham, then mess it all up when we haul the butty like a couple of horses through the short pounds and locks of the Birmingham Road, up to our elbows in soot, sludge, dogs' poo and heaven knows what.'

There was a heavy silence during which a maid entered the room carrying the tea tray. A welcome distraction. Polly didn't dare move, but stayed by Verity's side as Lady Pamela poured herself tea in a porcelain cup, and only then added milk. Polly preferred her milk in first. Verity didn't mind either way, now.

Verity said, 'I want to know why you lied to me, and broke my heart. I found it hard to believe Tom would ask you for money, so why on earth did I believe your story? Ah yes, because you are my mother. But you must tell me why you lied. Do you hate him that much, or is it me you hate?'

Lady Pamela sipped her tea, then replaced her

cup, brushing a non-existent 'something' from her cream silk afternoon dress. 'I don't hate him, or you, but you don't know your own mind, and I won't have you bringing embarrassment on to the doorstep of Howard House. You and Tom would never have worked, and the ridiculous relationship would have blown itself out and we'd have been left with a disgusting mess. I was merely protecting you.'

'But you weren't. You've just admitted you were protecting yourself, and Father, and the doorstep.'

Her mother flashed, 'Don't show off, Verity. Flippancy is not for those of our standing.'

Verity gripped the sofa more tightly. 'So lying is for those of our standing, and so too riding out on Star when you know you can't control her. You had her shot. You've taken two people I love most dreadfully away from me.'

Her mother stood. 'A horse isn't a person, and Tom was a chauffeur and not one of us, or at least, not one who can be measured against your father and me.'

Polly thought she had never been in the presence of such a dreadful person, but Verity was talking again, keeping her voice ice-cold, and dignified. 'We're going, but not before I have Tom's address.' She paused, as though thinking. At last she said, very slowly, 'But let's go back just a bit, Mother. What do you mean, Tom is not one of us, or you and Father, anyway? Why am I different?'

A voice from the doorway said, 'Pamela, I advise you to think of your answer very carefully.'

A distinguished-looking man in a tweed suit entered. He stood erect, his shoulders back, but he rested on two walking sticks. Verity said, 'Father.'

He walked round the sofa slowly, put both sticks in one hand and held her close. 'Dearest Verity, won't you both stay for tea, or for dinner and the night? I'm sure one of your evening dresses will fit your friend.'

Verity laid her head on his shoulder, just for a moment. 'I have to return. We have a job to do, and actually I'd rather not stay.'

Her grey-haired father, his face drawn with pain but his steely blue eyes steady, so like Verity's, smiled. 'Don't give up on us, darling. Go and see Rogers before you leave.'

He released Verity and reached out a hand to Polly, who shook it. 'This is an awkward meeting for you, my dear. I do hope we do it again, when this mess is resolved.' She didn't know if he meant the family impasse or the world war, but nodded.

Verity didn't speak to her mother as she left the room. Polly stayed close behind her. For a moment, in the foyer, Verity paused, but there was no call of 'Goodbye' from her mother. She shrugged, linked arms with Polly, and said, 'Come on, we need to see Mrs B and Rogers, bless them. They'll be fed up if I go without speaking properly to them.' They headed to the green baize door off the hall, leading to the staff quarters, and all the time Polly was aware of portraits of ancestors looming over her. She looked behind her. There was mud on the floor, and she grimaced.

They clumped down stone stairs and along a stone corridor into a huge kitchen. Rogers was sitting drinking tea with a similarly aged woman of about fifty. They both stood, and the woman held out her arms to Verity, who ran into them, asking, 'Mrs B, do you know where Tom is?'

Rogers came to her side, and she hugged him too. 'We have an address for you,' he told Verity. 'I heard a little of what was said, and we went through Annie's housekeeping records of employees.' He beckoned to Mrs B. 'That's right, isn't it, Annie. Or where he was, anyway. You keep going until you find him again. He's no fly-by-night, not that boy. We thought it beyond belief that he would do as Lady Pamela described. You could do far worse, young Verity. He'll be true, for the whole of your life, but don't you go playing with his heart. He don't deserve such a thing. But it's a big step, won't be what you're used to, not here anyway.'

Verity looked from him to Mrs B and asked, 'What do you mean?'

Rogers coloured. 'Well, your new life, of course. Look at you.' They all laughed. 'Hardly ready to be presented to the King like that, are you, but I reckon it's all for the good. You won't be the princess you could have been.'

Verity laughed, and it was a good sound, full of hope.

Chapter 37

16 February – approaching Tyseley Wharf

It was mid February as they approached Tyseley Wharf. Polly had thought January was cold, but this was grey with an unremitting freezing wind, and frost which lasted throughout the day and night. If Verity wasn't writing to the Red Cross and the army, the churches, the Salvation Army and anyone else she could think of, she and Polly were using their leave to track Tom from rented house to rented house.

On their last trip back from Tyseley Wharf to the depot at Bull's Bridge, Southall, they had left Sylvia in charge of the coaling at Coventry, and found out from the ARP warden that Tom's Coventry address had been bombed; the whole street had gone, with most of the people still in their houses. As they approached Tyseley Wharf this time, Verity had thought of the local authorities, and the hospitals, and included return postage on the envelopes this time. There might just be a relative of Tom's who had been through their hands and could point them in the right direction. Verity vaguely remembered Tom mentioning a sister, but not a mother.

She, Verity and Sylvia posted the letters outside the wharf on arrival, but there was no time to make their way to the public baths, or to Mrs Green's, because they were to be unloaded immediately; after which they towed the butty back through the Brum Bum to Coventry where they took on coal in the motor, and wood in the butty. As they continued down the cut, Polly decided to write to her parents, because her mother might have spoken her mind, but hadn't lied to Saul, or approached him, and, Polly felt, never would.

Three days later they were through the Braunston Tunnel. It had been slow because of a broken-down motor in front of them, which had jammed a lock, and there was no time to see Bet, because Verity was in a rush to check at the depot for replies to her letters. They tied up past Stoke Bruerne, and there moored further ahead were the *Seagull* and *Swansong*. Polly smiled to herself, as they double-checked the tarpaulin which had come adrift over the wood in the butty, because soon she would see Saul, and it had been two weeks since they had coincided.

As they finished, the pat-patter of a motor passing disturbed her and the butty rocked in the wake of the speeding boat. There was no ''Ow do'. She turned, as she hitched the last of the ties, and there was Leon, standing at the tiller of his motor, with his men on the butty. He was back: his Oxford run had finished.

She felt fear grip her as they passed on their way to Tyseley, but then she remembered *Seagull* and *Swansong* moored up at the same kerb, so they were safe. Besides, Leon was heading in the opposite direction. She turned her back on Leon's *Brighton*, and called Sylvia to help wring out the clothes that Verity was washing on the bank, after which all three girls walked to the pub because there was the promise of chips tonight, and they were too tired to cook.

They sat at the table by the fire, and waited. Soon Saul and Granfer arrived, having left Joe playing with Jimmy on his motor under Mrs Porter's eagle eye while she washed clothes. Polly said, 'But Leon's not long passed, so is it safe?' Granfer nodded. ''E'd not mess with all the boaters 'ere, and Dog be at the boats, too. She won't let no one near our boy.'

Saul sat next to Polly, and Granfer took the chair between Verity and Sylvia. They played dominoes, and all five of them ate crisp chips with their fingers. Sometimes Polly's hand nudged Saul's and they exchanged a look. There was no need for anything else, no need for special words. It was enough for Polly just to be with him, to see his strong fingers handling the dominoes, to hear his soft singing as the radio played dance tunes.

Over to the right, in the alcove, a darts match was in progress, and Saul nudged her foot with his, saying, 'Aren't you playing?'

Verity grinned. 'Why not, come on, Polly, let's find some people willing to take us on.' Sylvia shook her head and said, 'Honestly, you two don't improve. Well, it's not for me, as you know, so I'm off to bed. I'll lock from the inside tonight, I think.' She left, weaving her way between the boaters who crowded the bar.

Polly and Verity knocked back their drinks, then winked at one another. Verity nodded. They stood and one of the darts players called, 'Uh-oh, batten down them 'atches.' The laughter was friendly and loud, but not too loud for above it they all heard the scream, 'Fire, fire.'

The room fell silent for a split second, then there was a scramble for the door, with chairs being knocked over, and drinks too. 'Wood, we've wood on the butty,' yelled Verity. Instantly there were other voices. 'Oos too.' 'Yes, oos'n all.'

They all tore along the path to the bank, looking to left and right, and there it was, a blaze suddenly shooting sparks and flames high into the sky and the noise of hissing, crackling and spitting on the cut. Whose boat was it? Whose? Where were all the children? In bed? In the blaze? No, no. Polly ran towards the flames. There were no screams, just shouts: 'Call the brigade', 'Get some buckets', 'Whose is it?' 'It's wood, yer can smell it', 'We is all carrying wood.'

Was it their butty? Sylvia was running towards them, dragging a struggling Joe and shouting, 'It was him, he set it, a man caught him, hung on to him, and told me when I saw them, and all the while

478

that damned Dog was yapping at him. Joe broke free and tried to run away, but I caught him. Look at him, his hair's singed and he stinks of smoke.'

Joe was wriggling. 'It weren't me, course it weren't. It were 'im, the man, not me.'

Sylvia shouted, 'It was him. The bloke saw him, and look what else I found. He had it clenched in his hand, and some are gone.' She held out a small book of matches. Polly stared at the matches, at Joe's singed hair, while all the time boaters ran past, knocking them as they went. Verity had run on, and now came back. 'Polly, for pity's sake, it's *Horizon*. It's our load. Just ours.'

Polly stared from Sylvia to Joe, who stood there, his lips pressed shut. No, not Joe. She looked again at the matches in Sylvia's hand. 'Oh, get him to the pub, keep him there safe from the flames. We've got to get the motor moved. Go on, and don't say a bloody word to anyone, Sylvia. Just keep your mouth tight shut for bloody once. Of course it's not him, ask where he found them. Now let us get on.'

Polly ran after Verity, who was running faster than she'd ever seen her run before. Granfer and Saul had gone to the left, and were beating out sparks that had reached *Swansong*'s tarpaulins, beneath which wood was stacked. She saw that the tarpaulin of the Porters' butty was smouldering, and they were beating at the flames, while another boater used the dipper to throw water on to his load.

The *Marigold*'s coal tarpaulin was smouldering

too, but that could just be the heat from the butty which was roaring now, the sparks soaring into the air and being carried all over the place by the wind; there was crackling, and the cut was alive with the fire's reflection. It was much too late for the butty, but while Verity wrenched off her top jumpers and beat out the sparks on the *Marigold*'s hold, Polly released the mooring straps, started the engine, and took the *Marigold* out into the cut. She moved past other boaters also starting their engines while their wives attached a short tow-rope to the butty. The boaters followed the *Marigold*. Polly tied up at least a hundred yards along the cut; others stopped before and behind.

Polly ran back to the butty. Verity stood, staring at it, as Polly reached her. They clung to one another, stepping back from the blistering heat, hearing the bells of the fire engine, and more shouts. Saul was taking his load out, with Granfer on the butty. Polly shouted at Verity over the noise, 'Sylvia said it was Joe. A bloke caught him . . .'

Verity shook Polly, staring into her face. 'She's mad. Joe wouldn't.'

Polly nodded. Her voice breaking, her eyes and throat sore from the heat and the soot, she said, 'I know, but he had matches. I told Sylvia to take him into the pub, and to shut up. Why didn't I just send him to his butty away from here? I wanted him safe, you see. I wanted him on land.'

The fire crew were rolling out the hoses and

pumping water from the cut. They directed the hoses on to the butty and water shot like cannons on to the fire. A fireman grabbed the girls by the arm, shouting, 'You're too close. Get back, but stay where we can talk to you.'

They backed away, but didn't go into the pub. Instead they stood holding hands, watching, and all the time Polly could have screamed, knowing she should have told Saul to take the lad far away, because what the hell would Sylvia say? Within half an hour the fire was out, leaving *Horizon* a stinking, hissing mess, with the fore-end low in the cut, as though sinking.

Saul came to her, pulling her round, his grip hard, 'Them's taken Joe. That damn girl, she says he set it. Course he didn't. Them taken him, cos a man done told 'er 'e 'ad. Or so she said.' Verity turned. 'What?' she exclaimed.

Polly shook her head. 'Hush, Verity. Who's taken him? Leon?'

Saul's wild and desperate face grew calm. He said, 'Not Leon. The police, but not Leon, so 'e's safe. That Sylvia told 'em he stole your book, Polly, and the kitty, and dropped the damned brick on yer. Told 'em he had matches. That Sylvia told 'em that, and that some bloke told her he were running from it. Course he were running, to tell us. They asked 'er who the bloke was. She said she didn't know, but 'e weren't Leon . . .'

Verity muttered, 'I'll bloody swing for her.' She

was off, running into the pub. Polly followed. Sylvia was standing at the bar shaking her head at Granfer. Verity ran through the bar, knocking aside the tables and chairs, grabbing Sylvia and swinging her round.

'You had no right, what have you done? To our boy? To us? Of course he wouldn't, he was our friend. How could you have said all that about him?'

Polly was close behind, and now she said, 'I told you to say nothing. I told you.' Polly was still berating herself for not sending Joe to the motor. What the hell was she thinking of when she should have known the firefighters would get the police to follow them?

In front of them Sylvia was red-faced, with trembling lips. 'They asked, I answered. They said, was he a troublemaker? Had he ever caused mischief? I had to tell the truth. And I had to give them the matches and tell them he smelt of smoke, and his hair was singed, and a man had caught him at it. It was the honest thing to do. They said they'd take him in case the boaters took matters into their own hands.'

Polly slapped her then, hard, across the face. 'The stealing was at the start, he's a good boy now, you can tell he is, and back then he was missing his mother. Well, he probably still is, but a boater would never set the fire, never put us, or Dog, in danger, and neither would they ever take matters into their own hands where a child was concerned.'

Verity grabbed Polly's arm. 'Dog? Where is she?'

Polly turned to Sylvia. 'You find out where they've

taken Joe and we'll go and sort it, but first we have to find Dog – and stop your damned snivelling.'

They tore out of the pub, Polly shouting, 'Saul, stay there, make sure she finds out where they've taken him. Don't leave that idiot girl for a second. Dog, Dog.'

Polly thought she couldn't bear it. First Joe taken, then Dog missing. Please no, not in that heat, those flames. Saul rushed after her, calling, 'Granfer'll stay, let's find Dog or that'll wound our boy too.'

Steerer Ambrose caught hold of her as she and Verity ran along the bank one way, while Saul ran the other. Ambrose said, 'I saw a bloke with a dog. Had her tight under his arm. He were going on over the bridge. The dog were barking, and I think gave him a bloody nip. I'd forgotten, what with the fire . . .'

But the girls were running now, panting and racing for the bridge, up the slope that the horses would have taken. They reached the road, and Saul was with them now, before rushing ahead of them, calling, 'Dog, Dog, where you be, lass?'

They found her at the middle of the bridge, lying on her side, her rear haunch bloody and ripped open. Polly sank to her knees, weeping, gathering her up. Saul pulled her away. 'Let me.'

He probed Dog by the light of the moon with gentle hands before picking up the animal. She yelped. Verity clutched Polly's hand and said, 'Our darling's alive. She is. Oh thank God.'

Saul laughed softly. 'She's a boater's dog, so o'

course she's alive. Bet she gave the bastard a bit of a gnaw too.' He carried Dog down the slope to the towpath, past a few boats which had been moored near the bridge out of the way of the fire. Wives were preparing children and themselves for bed. Every one of them called softly as they passed, 'So sorry for your trouble, all on yer.'

They each nodded, and carried on to the *Seagull*, which had been run well past the original mooring. Saul stepped on to the counter without pause. Polly opened the cabin door, and waited for him to pass down the steps, then Verity, and finally she followed. 'You light the lamp, my lass,' said Saul. 'Missus Verity, bring down the cupboard table.'

They did as asked, Polly using the Swan matches. The lamp cast a soft glow over all the woodwork, the painted cupboards, the plates, as Verity closed the doors and the slide hatch. 'We'll look after her,' Polly insisted. 'You need to find out about Joe.'

Saul laid Dog on the cupboard table, leaned round and kissed Polly's forehead. 'Granfer will be about that. Let's see to Dog, and then we'll sort it. "E's with the police, so he's safe.'

Saul bumped up the range to boost the simmering kettle, and snatched out the bowl from beneath the side-bed. 'You lay your hands on Dog to let 'er knows yer there, cos I'm going to 'ave to hurt her, but she knows it's for her own good.'

Within a minute he had poured boiling water over the needle and gut he had taken from the top shelf of the cupboard. Verity sat on the side-bed to keep out of the way but never took her eyes off Dog. Polly watched Saul's preparations, a question in her eyes. He nodded. 'We need the gut sometimes, so best to have it. You should an' all. You hold your Dog, at her head, Polly. You, Verity, slide along the side-bed. Hold t'other end.'

They did, while he poured antiseptic in the wound. Dog did not flinch, though she lay with her eyes open, fixed on Polly. Saul sewed. Dog whimpered, but held still.

At the end, Polly leaned down and kissed Dog. 'Who would do this to you?'

Saul put the catgut away, poured boiling water over the needle. 'I been thinking. You know, course you do, Leon, or his men. That's who the bloke was, trying to catch our lad, I'll bet my life on it. But we needs to find them buggers and get 'em to the police, cos 'e's not going to any borstal, my boy ain't.'

Chapter 38

Later that night – at the mooring

They seemed to be wearing a path to the pub, but as they entered Delphie Higgins was coming out of the kitchen with tea. Sylvia trotted along behind her with a plate of biscuits, and the publican, Frank, hurried just behind the pair of them. 'Baked this morning,' Delphie said. 'We has rooms up top for guests, and they likes a biscuit.'

Sylvia came straight up to Saul. 'I've apologised to Granfer, and now I apologise to you. I only said what I felt was the truth, but I expect you're all correct about the boy, but, then, well, it is a bit odd, having those matches, isn't it? Why did he have them, if he hadn't used them? Then that man told me it was him.'

Verity was standing at the fireplace shaking her head as though she was about to explode. She shouted as Sylvia finished, 'You almost pulled off that apology, Sylvia, but you never know when to stop. So a word of advice, just don't start.'

Sylvia looked affronted, but had the sense to stay quiet. Frank said soothingly, 'Let's all have a cup of tea and decide what we should do. Is that a plan, my lovelies?'

Saul was sitting at the bar next to Granfer, their heads together as they talked. Polly made her way over. Frank put thick china mugs of tea in front of them as Saul slipped his arm around Polly and pulled her to him. 'We was just saying, we leave our Swan matches by the range, and only have the one box. So we need to see the ones our boy had. Was they Swan, or what? If they was Swan, we saw them in the cabin just now, didn't we, Polly and Verity? – and you can come too, Sylvia, to check I ain't cheatin'. So was they Swan or what?' He was calling this last to Sylvia, who tossed her curls, shook her head and said, 'I can't remember, but they were not a box, they were one of those little books you get in clubs, or perhaps cafes.'

Polly's mind was ticking. 'Yes that's right.'

Sylvia nodded.

'Do the police have it?'

Frank who was leaning on the bar said, 'They took everything the lad had, and the matches were about all, except his handkerchief. They was kind, you mark my words, but they took everything from his pockets. I think they was concerned because he said he wanted his mam but she had gone missing. I knows the sergeant and he treated him right. Has kids 'isself, but they'll be looking to put him in a 'ome, I reckon, or even back to his dad. They'll be fretting at his history of stealing, and throwin' the brick. They think 'e's running wild, p'raps.'

Granfer shook his head, and muttered, 'Yon Leon deals in the dirty end of things. I reckon he might supply to clubs. We needs a look at that book, that we do, and then to find where the place is, and get 'em to say it weren't our boy who were given the matches, then we need to get 'im back. No way he's going to Leon. Did the bloke thrust the matches at 'im?'

Frank said quietly, 'You got to have a solicitor, you have, to talk the beak's language, and the constabulary. Everyone's twitchy about sabotage. There's a ruddy war on, let's face it.'

There was a heavy silence but then Polly pulled herself together. She leaned forward. 'Can I use your telephone please, Frank. My dad's an ARP warden and he's on shift with a solicitor, my old boss. But I think Mr Burton will charge.'

Verity nodded. 'I'll get the winnings kitty. That can go towards it. Mother's stopped my allowance so I can't help at the moment, and Uncle Freddy's Trust has been blocked by some nonsense she's cooked up. We have our pay, Polly. Sylvia, you can damn well cough up.'

Saul said, 'We 'as money, tucked away, so we might have enough, and we'll pay back every penny.'

Polly made her way to Frank's back office, and placed a telephone call to her mum because her dad would be on shift. She checked the clock. It was midnight, and to hear the telephone ring would frighten her mum, but needs must. Perhaps her mum would get a message to Mr Burton and he could make a call to the police?

She braced herself as it rang and rang but there was no reply. Disappointed, she replaced the receiver and then, wondering if it was worth trying again, dialled the operator once more, who put her through. This time it was picked up immediately. 'Hello, hello.'

'Hello Dad, why are you at home?'

'Oh, Polly, are you all right? What's wrong? Are you hurt? Are you all right?' he repeated.

In the background she could hear her mum's voice, and the receiver was snatched from her dad. 'Polly, we received your letter. We love you too, yes we do. It was all so silly and I shouldn't interfere and you shouldn't get so upset because it's only that I love—'

Her father snatched the receiver back. 'Are you all right?' he asked again.

She replied, 'Yes, and I'm sorry to telephone so late but I need your help, Dad. Well, Mr Burton's help. We need a solicitor.' She explained the circumstances, but Verity had entered the office now, mouthing, 'We have six pounds ten shillings, and the boaters have come in with money they've just raised. You know how word spreads. So we have eight pounds ten shillings, or thereabouts. Sylvia is claiming she has no money.'

Polly nodded, and told her dad, 'We have eight pounds and ten shillings. And I repeat, why are you home? You should be on ARP shift, shouldn't you?'

Her dad laughed. 'We do get a night off to catch up on sleep, but that's not of use, is it, when you have a daughter waking you in the small hours. Where are you telephoning from?'

She gave him the number and explained about the pub, the King's Head, and where it was. He said, 'I'll telephone you back as soon as I hear. Will that be possible your end?'

She ran into the bar to check. Delphie said, as she washed the glasses, 'Of course it is. Stay here as long as you like. If you have a drink, put the money in the box. We'll head on up to bed because we need our sleep. Just keep the noise down.'

Saul called, 'Will yer friend come?'

'Dad's going to telephone him now, and perhaps Mr Burton can make a call to the police tonight.'

They waited in the bar for her father's return call; even Sylvia, who was dozing on a settle in the corner, but who woke suddenly, sitting bolt upright and exclaimed, 'Oh, heavens, I've just remembered. That man who said he saw Joe . . .' She stopped and looked around. 'Well,' snapped Verity. 'Go on, we're not mind readers.'

'You see, he had a scar on his face, just here, and an accent.' She pointed to her own face. Polly swung round to look at Verity. 'Remember that POW, the one who was at the end of the column when the lock gate was stuck? You said he probably boasted that it was a duelling scar. We heard a while ago that two POWs had escaped, so was he one of them? Did he think he was sabotaging the war effort and poor Joe caught him in the act? Or, if he was one of Leon's men, he'd be happy to do it, course he would. When you think about it, where better to hide out than on a boat, where everyone is lumped together, as a ruddy boater and they're on the Oxford cut anyway. Something niggled at me when I saw him on the Brum Bum ages ago, and then later. Bet he didn't expect to have to come back here?'

Saul and Granfer were looking from Sylvia to Polly and Verity. Saul said, 'A scar? One o' Leon's new men had a scar, don't you remember, Granfer, when they went past just now.'

Polly was thinking, trying to sort it out, but wasn't it all just one coincidence too many? If it *was* the German . . . 'Hang on,' she said. 'If it was the German who set the fire . . .'

Verity chimed in. 'But even if he is Leon's man, Leon wouldn't get his own son into trouble deliberately, surely?'

Saul leaned forward. 'He wanted his boy. He wanted 'im, and the way to keep 'im when he got young Joe was to scare the living daylights out of 'im by saying 'e had to stay on the *Brighton* or he'd be put in clink. D'you know what I reckon . . . Dog went for the German bugger, who let go our Joe, told yon Sylvia the lad was the fire setter, then Dog tried to chase 'im off, 'e carted her off, then knifed her.'

He sat back, clenching and unclenching his fists.

He looked at those as he asked Verity, 'What were it you said about swinging for 'er?' He nodded towards Sylvia, who looked shocked.

Verity flushed, and said, 'Well, you are enormously irritating.'

Saul stood, then paced. 'Well, I could swing for 'im, that Leon, I could, you know. I's glad the boy's with them police, for now, cos Leon can't reach him there.'

Verity left them to check on Dog who was with the Porters and Jimmy again, further down the towpath.

Still Polly's parents didn't telephone. One o'clock went by. Then, as Verity returned from the Porters', bringing the latest news on Dog, 1.30 chimed. At two in the morning, the telephone still hadn't rung, but instead there was a knocking at the door, hesitant at first, but then louder. Polly jerked from her doze. Saul was on his feet, saying, 'The police 'ave brought him back.'

He drew back the bolts and opened the door, but it wasn't the police. Polly and Verity recognised her mother's voice. 'Hello, young man, we've brought Mr Burton. We can't have children being carted about the country, and put into big old orphanages or borstals or whatever the police do with them these days, indeed we can't, and a personal appearance is far better than a call. After all, the law doesn't know if Mr Burton is really a solicitor if he telephones them; could be the milkman.'

She hurried into the bar. 'Ah, here you all are, but no drinks before you, which is quite the surprise.' Polly and Verity sprang to their feet, their hair a mess, their hands filthy, a fact that was, they were sure, about to be drawn to their attention.

Her mother bustled over with her dad and Mr Burton in her wake. Mrs Holmes spread her arms wide, her handbag swinging on her arm. 'Come along then, a kiss for your mum, Polly, and I'll have one from you too, Verity Clement, and you can tell Mr Burton all about the pickle you're in.'

They obeyed, confused. Her mum waved her husband and Mr Burton to the seats vacated by Saul and Granfer. She sat on Polly's chair, flattening her gloves on the small round table, then looked up. 'We have work to do, a child to bring home. Mr Burton needs all the details, *all* do you hear, young man, *and* you two girls, no fudging now.' Polly looked at her dad. He smiled. 'This is the woman I married. I think you might recognise her?'

Verity laughed. 'Well, I certainly do. Polly, meet the one in whose image you are made.'

Sylvia said, from the settle, 'You'll need me too. I'm one of the girls, and I saw the most.'

Polly heard Verity's sigh and it was difficult not to join in.

Her dad squashed as many as possible into his car: Polly, with her mum on her lap, Saul with Verity on his, and Granfer with Sylvia, after Mr Burton had looked worried and mentioned that his respectability might be brought into question, should his trousers be creased by having someone sitting on his knee.

At the police station, they all somehow fell out of the car and followed Mr Burton into the police house, because that's what it was, just a house.

They banged the counter bell. The room was cold as the fireplace held only the embers of the daytime fire, and it was now almost 3 a.m.

A policeman finally arrived, his shirt buttoned up wrongly and his hair unbrushed. 'Morning all,' he said. 'Where's the fire?'

Mr Burton took over, explaining that the fire had been earlier in the evening, and that a young boy had been brought in, as the possible perpetrator. 'He's gone,' said the policeman.

Saul and Polly pressed closer. Mr Burton waved them back. 'Might I ask to where?'

'Castlewood Children's Home, the special division. Well, it's a couple of rooms, really. It's where we keep 'em if a crime might have been committed, but more serious really is that there might be summat a bit tricky about his 'ome circumstances, and a report was taken from a Miss Sylvia Simpson that there was a history of brick throwing, occasioning injury, and theft.'

Mrs Holmes sucked in her breath, and pulled up her gloves around her fingers even tighter. She poked Mr Burton in the back. Mr Burton asked the policeman if there was somewhere they could talk in peace.

Mrs Holmes's expression showed her opinion of *that* remark. Mr Burton was beckoned even further forward. The policeman leaned over the counter, listening. Finally he nodded, walked along to the counter hatch, lifted it, and gestured Mr Burton through. They disappeared into the back room.

The others looked at one another. Sylvia whined, 'It wasn't my fault.'

'Be quiet, Sylvia,' said Verity and Polly together. But this time there was a third voice, as they were joined by Mrs Holmes. Sylvia sat on one of the chairs that lined the room. The wall tiles were dark green, like the lavatory at the depot, and at the thought Polly remembered the butty, and that they had not told the depot. Well, it must wait its turn.

The three girls, Saul and Granfer walked back to the pub. It took an hour in the gloom but nobody complained. Instead they were quietly happy and none more so than Polly, because her mum was better. Yes, her mum's son was dead, but she was recovering. This would escalate as her parents had offered to keep Joe with them until a decision was made about his future, and that lad would be enough of a handful to keep her mum occupied. Mr Burton was standing as the equivalent of guarantor, but he doubted it would come to court, if only they could sort out the match book, and the foreigner.

As they walked to the pub Granfer strode along at Polly's side. 'Fine woman, yer mum is, to take on our boy until it's all sorted. Reckon they'll let 'er in that Castlewood Home to get 'im out?'

Verity tapped him on the shoulder. 'Would you stand in her way? Mark you, she will have Mr Burton and Mr Holmes with her, and I reckon those three could cut through enemy lines and take a bunch of prisoners before they'd had their boiled egg for breakfast, don't you, Polly?'

Polly laughed. 'With their accumulated arms tied behind their backs.'

Sylvia muttered, 'We need to trace the book of matches soon. Have you all memorised the name of the club? We need to gather up as much information as we can get for the police, because they're calling it sabotage, or at the very least, hooliganism. Someone's got to go and ask questions.'

Saul squeezed Polly's hand. 'I reckon our Mr Burton's got a trick or two oop 'is sleeve, but you're right, Sylvia. We need to know if Leon goes to t'Blind Weasel in Wellington Street, t'name on the match book, or so Constable Reed done told us. When we get back to the depot, I 'ave work to do.'

'But what if the manager at the club writes out a statement or something. *You* can't read, Saul, and won't know if it's gobbledygook,' Sylvia objected.

Verity's sigh was loud in the night. 'What have I told you about keeping your mouth firmly shut.'

Saul said, slowly and clearly, 'I can read so they won't fox us with gobbledygook.'

Granfer said, 'And so's can me, but slower. We

been teaching ourselves from Polly and Verity's drawin' lessons. 'Mazing what you can do of a night-time, after a 'ard day's work. Does you know what an 'ard day's work is, Missus?' He was looking at Sylvia.

Sylvia strode on ahead, her curls bouncing. Polly said quietly, as an owl hooted in the cold air, 'She might just turn herself around.'

Verity slipped her arm through Polly's while Saul held her other hand. Verity said, 'Mr Burton did say Constable Reed was going to double-check the description of the escaped POW now that we've told him of the scar we noticed on the man on Leon's boat, and then the one at the fire. He'll also circulate an additional description – a burn or even a dog bite, should they ever find the bugger.'

'Indeed. And no fee required; as yet, anyway. Depends how much he has to do along the line.'

Saul began softly singing, 'I'll be seeing him, in all the old familiar places . . .'

Soon they were all joining in, singing him, instead of you, because he, the German, if that is who he was, would be found. Saul whispered quietly to Polly, 'The German will involve Leon in it, I bet you, and I will then be seeing Leon. It's all got to stop.'

She felt a shaft of fear. 'Don't do anything stupid. Joe needs you.'

'Only Joe?' he asked while the others sang on.

'You know the answer to that.'

They didn't speak of love, but it was there, as solid

as a rock. Saul murmured, 'The police said they'd put Missing posters round to try and find our Maudie, but that was all. She coulda just walked off, so they says, but I'm not sure any more. I feared 'e hurt her bad, for a while, and when I find Leon, I need to ask him what 'appened, but I needs to ask 'im in a way he has to answer, for I have fears . . .'

It took a while for Polly to realise what he meant. 'Oh no,' she whispered. They had reached the cut, and she looked down into the cold turgid water. So much lay on the bottom of this canal, but surely not Maudie. No, things like that didn't happen in real life, only in films.

Saul's arm slipped around her shoulder. She stared again at the water, but then at the fields across from the pub. No, Maudie would be working some-where, building up money to take care of her Joe . . . but now the thought of an alternative was in her mind, she knew it would not disappear.

Chapter 39

21 February – the *Marigold* heads back to the depot

Saul and Granfer were off by six the next morning, heading south for the depot, in a hurry. Polly crossed her arms, standing on the bank watching as they grew smaller. 'Please don't do anything that will make you swing for him, Saul. Please,' she whispered.

She had said this when they kissed goodnight. He'd said, 'Don't you fret, Polly. I got a lot to live for, but I got things that 'ave to be sorted.'

She understood.

She lifted her hand to the *Seagull* and *Swansong* as they disappeared into the freezing mist. There was a hoar frost today, and it felt as cold as it looked. Verity called as she walked on to the towpath from the direction of the pub, 'I telephoned the depot. They say to get on back and they'll deal with it once we tell them everything. They're bloody furious – not with us, but with whoever did it. Alf told me on the quiet that they don't think it's our Joe, not for a minute. Once they might have, but not now.'

Sylvia was cleaning the butty's cabin roof. The

hoses had saved the cabin itself, and, unable to sleep anyway, they had removed all Bet's pierced plates last night by the light of the hurricane lamp. The fore-end had sunk in the water, but still floated. Would the depot be able to tow it?

Delphie had said that they could wash Bet's possessions before they went, and between the two of them they lugged the bucket of pierced plates, brasses and crocheted curtains into the pub's kitchen. Frank was in the cellar, and Delphie was preparing breakfast for her guests. It smelt wonderful.

They finished washing Bet's stuff as Delphie packed up cooked bacon and eggs in an aluminium tin. 'There you are, dearies. That'll help you along, and make sure you get some sleep tonight.'

They stashed Bet's belongings into the back-end behind the engine room, taking a quick look at the cargo of coal. Verity raised an eyebrow at Polly, who nodded. They clambered on top of the load, filling the bucket they had collected from the back-end with lumps of coal. Polly lugged it down the path to the pub coal bunker. She lifted the lid, and tipped the coal in.

Delphie called from the kitchen, 'That's right nice.'

'You've been so kind. I'll bring another couple of buckets, and that's our thank-you.'

Delphie said, 'Use that old bucket of ours by the bunker, and bless you, Polly.' She closed the door. Polly half ran down the path, the buckets banging into her legs. She threw one up to Verity, who caught it. It swung against the coal as Polly clambered up with her buckets. Sylvia bobbed out of the cabin, stepped on to the gunwale, stood on tiptoe and took in the scene.

She opened her mouth. Polly said, 'Shut that mouth immediately.'

Sylvia did, and bobbed back into the cabin. Verity murmured as she threw coal into her bucket, 'She'll split on us at the depot, see if she doesn't.'

'She must know that everyone takes just a little bit from time to time. Tell you what, if we see any along the towpath we can suggest she picks it up and puts it on top of this lot, if she feels so strongly.'

Verity laughed. 'You are, under that sweet-as-pie look, an absolute horror.'

By eight they were off, and without the butty it was not only crowded, but fast. They tied up at Leighton Buzzard, before the flight of locks, and Verity and Polly crammed themselves into the cross-bed, with Dog on the floor. They let Sylvia have the side-bed though she moaned twice about the narrowness. The third time, Polly threw her boot and yelled, 'Be glad you haven't Verity snoring in your ear, and her elbow and knees sticking into you. Now go to sleep.'

Sylvia did, and at last Polly slept, but dreamed of Joe, covered in soot, being chased by Leon who had a scar on his cheek. He caught Joe, who then became Polly and he shook her until her teeth rattled, and shouted, 'Wake up, wake up, for heaven's sake.'

It was Verity. Polly stared at her. 'What—?'

Sylvia threw the boot back at her. 'Now you're the one shouting.'

The girls gave up trying to sleep at 5.30, made porridge and set off, taking turns at lock-wheeling. Verity and Polly watched Sylvia heaving on the gate beams without complaint. They moored early at Berkhamsted, but this time Polly made up a bed out of their coats and clothes on the narrow floor space and stretched out with Dog at her feet. They kept the slide hatch shut because there had been a slight smattering of snow, as well as a driving, freezing wind. But a draught still crept through the doors. She was so tired, she slept, and this time no one had to throw boots.

Once on their way again the locks came thick and fast. They met boats coming up heavily laden so most of the locks were ready. It was like a knife sliding through butter, Polly said as they pat-pattered along in between the locks, but the other two groaned. Sylvia ripped off her gloves and brandished her blistered hands, and Verity's lips were so dry and chapped they had split. But all the time the girls looked to the front and behind, watching out for Leon, and wondering what the depot would say, and what would happen to Joe.

At last they were back amongst the houses, and saw red London buses and heard *Music While You Work* from factory windows that were only open a slit in this weather. The *Marigold* was unloaded at a paper factory, and they had to listen to interminable grumbling from the foreman because he'd been expecting wood as well, and wanted to know why the depot hadn't told him sooner they weren't bringing any.

In the end, as the coal was almost unloaded, Verity stepped forward and stared up into the foreman's face. 'You silly little man, we could have been burned to a crisp because our butty was sabotaged, and set on fire, but here we are, slogging along to you with your bloody coal, and I suggest you stuff some of it where the sun doesn't shine.'

For a moment he was speechless, then shouted against the sound of coal unloading, and other boats arriving, 'I'll have you sacked.'

Polly stepped up, Dog at her heels, stitched up but perky. 'They need us too much, or would you rather do our job? I think you'd prefer to stand here, though, like Herr bloody Hitler, insulting everyone in sight.'

He backed up a step. Sylvia stepped forward. 'So very there,' she said.

The other two girls looked at her, and burst out laughing. The foreman shouted, 'Get out of my sight. I'll be reporting you. You're a disgrace, all three of you, not one decent woman amongst you.'

He strutted off, after which a much older man brought the girls a mug of tea while they waited for the last of the coal to be offloaded. Coal dust floated on the tea and crunched between their teeth but it was hot and wet. 'Sorry about Albert,' he said. 'He gets in a fret because he's on ARP several nights a week, and he's too damned tired, but I expect you are too.'

Verity finished her tea and handed her mug back. 'I feel bad now. We're not as old so we can cope rather better, I expect.'

The other two drank theirs, thanked him, and waited until the unloading was finished before cleaning out the bilges, scraping away at the black silt, then washing the buckets overboard. They replaced the floorboards, then brushed out the hold. They'd give it another going-over at the depot, but they'd decided to do what some of the boaters did, just to see if it made cleaning the hold any more efficient.

Finished at last, they looked at one another. 'We should apologise,' Verity muttered. 'To Albert?' asked Sylvia.

'Of course,' said Polly and Verity together. They all jumped on to the wharf and followed Albert's voice, because he was shouting at someone else now. They found him bossing his men around and sorting out the unloading of another narrowboat. Verity touched his arm. 'Excuse me, Albert.'

He spun round. 'Now what?'

'I was rude,' Verity said.

'So was I,' Polly said.

'Me too,' Sylvia added.

Albert scratched at his forehead, looked from them

to the narrowboat. He yelled, 'Get a move on, Harry, we haven't got all day.'

They stood there. He finally turned to them. 'You know what you girls have got to do?'

They waited, resigned but knowing they were going to be told, and it wouldn't be pleasant. He said, adjusting his spectacles, which had slipped down his nose, 'What you've got to do is to stand together like you are now until the end, against old codgers like me and those bastards who fire your boats or try to hurt you. It's the only way you're going to get through. I reckon that Herr 'itler ain't done with his bombs and things, and you need to keep strong.' He laughed now. 'I'd like my girls to be like you, tough, holding together, fighting your corner. Now 'op off, I've work to do, and you take care now. See you on your next trip, eh? No smoking around any wood cargo, and get that there dog of yours to bark its head off if some toe-rag comes near with a match. Got it?'

Verity reached forward and kissed his cheek. She left soot on his face and reached up to rub it off. He gripped her hand, hard. 'You hear me, you three. You stay strong, and look after one another.' He walked away, and Polly called after him, 'My dad's in the ARP. A grand bunch you are.'

He waved, and they turned back to the *Marigold*, and Dog who sat on the roof, her ears pricked up, waiting. They fired up the engine, and motored on. Polly blew the hunting horn when they passed the foreman. He jumped. They cheered. He shook his fist and laughed. On and on they pat-pattered, until at last the lay-by came into sight. Verity shafted at the fore-end and Sylvia at the stern as Polly reversed in. They turned around the tiller, and headed off to the office.

They had not seen the *Seagull* as they approached, so, having clocked in and written their report, they were told to go on leave for a couple of days until a new butty could be found. The office manager had a thick envelope on his desk, and as they turned to leave he called them back. 'Your post,' he said.

The three of them walked out into the freezing wind. The puddles were still solid ice. They walked along the lay-by and Sylvia headed for the cabin, to pack her few things while Verity and Polly found the *Seagull*. Granfer was there, but not Saul. He said to Polly, 'You know where 'e gone?'

She nodded. 'To find the club and get them to tell him they gave the matches to Leon or the POW. He will get them to write it down. Then he'll find Leon, and take him to the police.'

Granfer nodded. Verity asked, 'So what about you, Granfer? How will you manage your loads?'

'Steerer Ambrose has a coupla runabouts I can have, his brother's boys. We'll manage.'

'We're going to see Joe at Mum's. I'll bring back news. Or would you like to come?'

Granfer shook his head. 'I'd like that fine, but I needs to take the load.'

They picked up their kitbags, and as they disembarked Verity slapped her pocket. 'Hang on, the post.'

She handed out a letter from Reggie and another from Polly's parents, and two to Sylvia, who put them unopened into her pocket. There was one for Verity, who put down her kitbag and ripped it open. She read it, her face alive, her colour building. She held it out to Polly, who took it.

Dear Verity,

I have your letter. I couldn't believe it when I saw you driving the narrowboat. Your hair is shorter and I like it. I don't know what to say to you. In your letter you said that it was your mother who told you I had taken money to leave you alone. I took no money, because it broke my heart. It has taken a while but I am making a different life now. I was called up, I am in signals. I am not anyone's servant. I am respected. We should meet on my next leave and talk about things. Shouldn't we?

Kind regards
Tom

Sylvia walked with them to the station, but instead of a train, she took a bus. 'I am going to stay with my aunt until I decide what I should do: stay or go.'

Verity nodded, and held out her hand. Sylvia shook it. Polly kissed her. 'You did well this trip but you need to make up your own mind. If you stay, let's try and make a strong team, for Albert's sake, as well as ours.'

Once home, the two girls walked to Polly's house. They had telephoned but no one had answered. They walked down the front path, and knocked. Again no answer. Polly lifted the flowerpot, and the front door key was there. Should she use it, or would it annoy her mother?

She pushed the key into the Yale lock, and opened the door. There was no newspaper on the floor. Verity and Polly exchanged a look. Polly called, 'Mum?'

Her mother appeared in the front-room doorway. 'Good, you let yourselves in. Come along, we have the fire on.'

As Polly and Verity started to undo their boots Mrs Holmes flapped her hand. 'Oh, just wipe them on the doorstep. Come along now.' In the front room the fire was blazing, and, to Polly's amazement, Joe was working at the dining-room table, on his sums. This room had been a mausoleum for so long.

He looked up, and bounded round to them, hugging them both. He looked taller, somehow, and the furrowed brow was clear. 'Auntie Joyce said I could stay off school today to see as much of you as possible.' Polly hugged him again, and then her mum. 'I love you, Mum.'

Later, when the clock chimed eight in the evening, and all five of them had eaten supper in the back room, with its photographs of Will back in their rightful place, Joe took himself up to bed. In half an hour he called down for his bedtime story. Mrs Holmes looked up from her knitting, which was a jumper for Joe. 'Off you go, you two. It's you he wants.'

As they climbed the stairs Verity said, 'I'm not so sure about that. I rather think Auntie Joyce has worked some magic.'

'Perhaps Joe has too.' Polly led the way to the box room, but it was dark and empty. She heard Joe call, from Will's bedroom. Slowly she opened the door, and there he was, in Will's bed. There was a new bedside lamp, and photos of Will and Polly on top of the chest of drawers.

Joe sat up in bed. He held up Will's copy of *Swallows and Amazons*, with its torn jacket. 'I can read it myself, but Auntie Joyce says it's nice just to rest before sleep. So she reads a bit every night. She said she did this for you and Will. She says you have *The Water Babies* on the *Marigold* and p'raps I can read that too, one day, and *Winnie-the-Pooh*, properlike.'

Verity sat one side of the bed, and Polly the other. 'We will read one page each three times. So how many is that?' asked Verity.

'Oh, don't be daft, Polly. It's six. That's easy.' The two girls laughed.

Downstairs again her mum and dad told them that a police inspector had told Mr Burton that if they could get to the bottom of the book of matches, and the man who claimed he had caught Joe in the act, Joe would be as free as air. Until then, he could remain with Mr and Mrs Holmes as long as he attended school and Mr Burton continued to act as surety. After that, they would have to see.

At last it was their turn to sleep, but they lay in the twin beds, talking quietly about Tom.

'I won't stop until I find him.'

'You won't need to, he wants you to meet, idiot.'

Verity rolled on to her side. 'I know, but he said kind regards. Not love, but regards.'

Polly raised herself on her elbow. 'He's been hurt but you should have heard his voice when he called you from the bridge. It was that of a man who loves you. Trust me, just as much as you would if I was backing in the *Marigold* . . .'

Verity burst out laughing. 'Has it come to this, that we measure everything by the cut and the boats?'

They slept until Joe woke them in the morning, late, just as he was going to school. 'Uncle Saul has telephoned. He has found the German POW at the same club where the matches came from. Uncle Saul wrote everything down that he said, and made him put his name on the bottom. The German told the police where Da was when Uncle Saul took him to the police station in London. He told him, too, that Da didn't know where my mum was. Uncle Saul says we must hope she comes back one day. Auntie Joyce told him she would tell Mr Burton and he will help to sort it all out. She told Uncle Saul he had to come to lunch too, because you were here. Auntie Joyce says I must come home from school for me lunch, to see him.'

Polly lay on her back. In her bag was her letter from Reggie. It was that of a friend, one that had a nice sweetheart now, though he said if she ever needed him, he would be there for her, as Will would have been.

She felt a pang at the thought, but then she smiled. Steerer Saul was coming, here, to her home, at her mum's invitation. That was something that meant the world. She thought of Will, and whispered, 'All is well, now, my lovely Will. Everything is all right but we will always miss you.'

THE END

Hello Everyone,

So, how did I arrive at *The Waterway Girls*?

Train journeys are wonderful gossip factories, or is it simply that I impose myself on others. Perhaps I am a nuisance, which is not a thought on which I care to dwell as it doesn't fit in with my perception of myself. Though no doubt my kids would enthusiastically agree with the concept.

Anyway, let's get back to where I was, namely gossiping. I was chatting to an elderly woman on a train whose relative had known a woman who had worked on the canals in the war. I was fascinated. These waterway girls were the equivalent of land girls, but far less well known. Apparently the Ministry of War Transport started a scheme in co-operation with the Grand Union Canal Carrying Company to train women to join the existing boaters on the Inland Waterways, delivering much-needed wartime cargo.

Would it make a novel? As is so often the case in the life of an author, something else happened to make me think it would. I was chatting about this to a friend, Wynne, who mentioned that she had taught 'boaters' (traditional families who ran the narrowboats) children and told me more about it. I found I was absorbed by the tales she told of the lives and culture of these traditional boaters. It made me wonder how on earth the 'incomers' and 'boaters' co-existed.

I researched, visited canal museums, read literature, walked the canal towpaths, took trips on the canal, tried to understand locks; the opening and closing of the rascals. I found *The Amateur Boatwomen* by Eily Gayford, a trainer, and *Idle Women* by Susan Woolfitt (Idle Women was a nickname given to the girls once they had completed their training. Why? The initials of the badge they were awarded were I.W. – Inland Waterways, or Idle Women. Though they were anything but). I also read *Maidens' Trip* by Emma Smith, amongst many others.

The women lived extraordinary lives: hard, cold, filthy and somehow separate from the rest of the world. I wanted to focus also on the boaters, and Sheila Stewart's *Ramlin Rose* was a joy.

I really have to thank Ealing Local History Centre's archivist, Dr Oates, who talked me through the route from Southall Station to the depot. Everything, everywhere has changed so much over the years so the help he gave me was crucial. Any imaginings are mine.

With all bases covered, I created a world. I hope it shows the spirit and heart of everyone involved in that real world, though the characters and happenings are totally Milly Adams. Apologies for any errors and my heartfelt admiration for all those involved.

I have to say that when the weather is cold, wet and appalling I do think of life on the canal. Not just for the girls, but the 'boaters'. How stoic, how gruelling, how admirable – and let's not even glance at the bucket. Bravo, the lot of them.

I do hope you enjoy *The Waterway Girls* series.

Warmest wishes,
Milly

ALSO BY MILLY ADAMS

Milly Adams
At Long Last Love

Can she make
peace with
her past?

'Would anyone ever think of her with real love?'

It's July 1942, and twenty-three year old nightclub singer Kate Watson has made a home for herself in bombed-blitzed London. A motley crew of friends has replaced the family she's not spoken to in years. That is until the evening Kate's sister Sarah walks back into her life.

Sarah has a favour to ask: she needs Kate to return home to Dorset for one month to look after her daughter, Lizzie. Reluctantly Kate agrees, even though it means facing the troubled past she hoped she'd escaped.

Kate is confronted once again by the prejudice and scrutiny of the townsfolk, including the new village vicar. As the war continues, Kate must fight her own battles and find not only the courage to forge a future but perhaps, at long last, love.

arrow books

May 1940, England

Bryony and Hannah are sisters, but they couldn't be more different. And the war has created a rift between them.

Hannah is young and headstrong. No one will stop her from doing what she wants, and she wants to stay in Jersey. But Bryony is happiest amongst her family and loved ones, and at Combe Lodge everyone is pitching in. The family home has filled with evacuees and Bryony has joined the ATA, helping to ferry planes across the country, whatever the risk.

When Jersey is occupied by the enemy, Bryony knows she needs to reach out to save her sister. But is she too late?

arrow books

June 1940, Waterloo Station

On one of the hottest days of the year, newly-qualified teacher Phyllie Saunders is evacuated with her school to Dorset.

As she struggles to control the crowd of tearful children, she sees Sammy. Her oldest and dearest friend is on the way to join his submarine, and as he kisses her goodbye, everything changes for them.

But now that war is tearing them apart, is it too late?

Phyllie throws herself into village life, determined to protect and nurture the children in her care. But war leaves no one untouched, and Phyllie will need all the support of the community to help her through the next few years, as she waits and prays for Sammy's safe return . . .

arrow books